MESSIAH

AND THE PRINCE WHO SHALL COME

REVELATIONS
BOOK THREE

TERRY JAMES

Messiah
Terry James

CKN Christian Publishing
An Imprint of Wolfpack Publishing
9850 S. Maryland Parkway, Suite A-5 #323
Las Vegas, Nevada 89183

cknchristianpublishing.com

Paperback ISBN: 978-1-63977-795-2
eBook ISBN: 978-1-63977-108-0
Library of Congress Control Number: 2022945012

MESSIAH

PROLOGUE

He was chosen to speak by the council of one hundred as the most influential person in global politics. The old man was assisted in approaching the podium where he stood, gripping the lectern's top with shaking hands caused by the Parkinson's disease he suffered.

This coming-together of the secretive council was the first to be broadcast for the world's media to disseminate among all their venues. Usually, the men and women of the body maintained a low profile, most preferring to remain unknown despite the great wealth and influence each represented.

The 92-year-old speaker, although frail, spoke clearly and in a strong voice, in English, accented by his German ethnicity.

"We consider at this crucial hour a pandemic that grows more virulent, more wide-spread by the hour," he said. "Economic collapse and the starvation of millions appear to be a certainty if not dealt within new, creative ways…and it must be done soon. There is little time.

"Nation-states with nuclear weaponry are facing off in potential war-making that will be catastrophic for all mankind if allowed to come to fruition. Climate change due to man's perversion of use of resources such as fossil fuels make earth's future bleak indeed, without universal compliance to a singularly directed, global-governing body.

"The world faces today profound crises. In whatever direction one looks upon humanity's horizon, threats exist. Almost certain calamitous events impose dire eventualities upon man's ability and means to control our beleaguered planet.

"It seems that all mankind seeks deliverance from conditions beyond the apparent governance abilities of human agency. This is the purpose at the heart of the Great Reset to which our collective attention must turn.

"We have set in motion such a reset. We have assembled the infrastructure that will give the governing instrumentality he needs to begin the task before us."

Dr. Randolph Faust, leaning slightly forward in the wheelchair, looking at the monitor, hit several keys with his fingertips, causing the words the speaker had just spoken to replay. The German-accented words sounded again as the old man spoke them with firmness.

"We have set in motion such a reset. We have assembled the infrastructure that will give the governing instrumentality he needs to begin the task before us."

Faust's eyes widened with realization. The speaker, known as the person perhaps most central to the globalist elites' determination to develop a one-world government, had apparently let it slip. The word "he" was used instead of "we." Or was it a slip? Either way, the fact that this man who had helped run presidential administrations for decades and had influenced, even dominated, international affairs for years, had let it be known that there was a "he" who was at the apex of the cabal determined to bring in world government.

This fact had not been divulged, and its being released now must almost certainly have profound meaning.

∽

HE MOVED UPWARD ALMOST as if drawn by an unseen force, rather than by stepping on each of the rough-hewn planks that made up the narrow stairwell. Light was scant in the dark shaft, but the sliver of illumination provided by the slightly opened door while he looked upward urged him forward.

Reaching the top step, he peered through the slit, seeing the room lit with candlelight that made discernable a number of men sitting or reclining around a lowly constructed table. The men were dressed in clothing unlike people of modernity. They looked to be actors playing out a scene from ancient times.

They were passing around a bowl-like vessel. Each man was handed what looked to be a torn piece of bread by the man who dipped the morsel into the liquid and handed it to each. He tried to make out the faces of the recipients of the wet pieces of bread, but he was prohibited by the meager light given off by the candles.

When the man handing out the torn pieces of bread dipped it, then handed it to one man in particular, the one handing him the bread piece bent near the recipient's ear and whispered something.

The one sitting cross-legged, his knees beneath the table's edge, took and ate the piece he had just been handed. He then scooted from under the table, rose to his feet, and began walking toward the door to exit the room.

From the observer's vantage point just outside the door, the man came to within a foot of his own face and opened the door wide. He thought they would collide because of his blocking the doorway and the stairwell being too narrow to let two men pass.

But the man walked, as if right through him, never noticing him. His bearded face was a mask of determination, his black eyes glistening beneath dark eyebrows. On his forehead, just above the left eyebrow, was a small, star-shaped scar. It stood out whitely against the dark, olive-hued skin. His black hair seemed to stream from the forehead backward, as if a strong wind was blowing in his face while he rushed past Tyce Greyson. It was a face etched deeply in his every waking moment since the fifth time he had partaken of the same scene within the past five nights.

≈

SAN ANTONIO, TEXAS

"I don't think so. It's against hospital rules."

The doctor peered into the room, seeing the old man in the bed with tubes attached to his body in various places.

"He's dying, Dr. Masters. Can't we grant him this final wish?" The young nurse, too, looked into the room, while she wiped a tear from her cheek with a tissue.

"Well," the doctor said. "He is lucid, and we don't know how long that will last. He has a will of iron, that old guy. Why not? Go ahead and do what needs to be done to get it accomplished." Masters then quietly pulled the door to the private room shut.

Marlaina Joske's pretty face transformed from an expression of distress to a bright smile. She reached to hug the doctor, who returned the gesture and patted her shoulder.

"What good is it to be the doctor in charge if you can't break the rules now and again?" he said, then turned to walk toward the room of the next patient on his rounds.

Fifteen minutes later, Marlaina walked into the room with an intern who carried a laptop.

"We're going to grant you your TV program, Dr. Faust," she said, moving aside the cart with the tubes.

Randolph Faust smiled, feeling strength return that he had not known since before entering the hospital three days earlier.

"Is he on the line yet?" Faust said weakly.

"He will be by the time we get you all set up to do the Zoom call, Dr. Faust."

The nurse straightened the pillow after raising the angle of the bed's incline. She carefully made sure of the old man's comfort before placing a tray over his body, then nodding to the assistant to put the laptop on the tray.

"Thanks so much, sweetheart, for doing this for me," Faust said, looking at the girl.

"No problem at all, Dr. Faust. We are going to see to it that it's the best hospital-bed TV presentation ever."

Faust laughed weakly, bringing on coughing that caused the nurse to silently vow not to incite him to laugh again. She held a cup of water while he sipped, then slumped back on the pillow.

"Well, I've been in my share of TV programs," he said,

"but this is definitely a first for me." He wanted, through the attempted levity, to help assuage any guilty feelings she might have.

The intern, his technical expertise having completed its work, nodded to Marlaina.

"Your friend will be on the line from Jerusalem any second," she said, watching the monitor along with her patient.

In Jerusalem, Tyce Greyson reached to click the button that would complete the Zoom connection.

"Dr. Faust," he said, seeing his ill friend's face appear. It took a moment for Faust to focus on the younger man's image.

"Tyce. Is that you?"

"Yes, sir. It's me."

Faust seemed to struggle to sit more upright but settled back on the pillow.

"Tyce...there's little time. I've got to let you know—"

The old man was obviously distressed as he choked out the words. Randolph Faust wanted to skip the courtesy phase, to get straight to the reason he had requested the video meeting.

"Yes, Dr. Faust. I'm here, sir. I'm listening. What do I need to know?"

Faust's eyes seemed to bulge as he spoke, widening as he forced the words. "I've been told to inform you...to instruct you—" The old man seemed to lose concentration, then sank more deeply into the pillow.

"Just take it easy, Randolph," Tyce said. "Just relax. I'm here. I want to hear what you have to say."

Faust then began, expelling the words with labored bursts of breath. "Israel...Israel is searching...is looking for its Messiah. It is nearing the time of...the great delusion..."

The older man looked to be losing consciousness, his eyes closing and his countenance relaxing into one of sleep. Tyce had the sinking momentary impression his friend might have died in mid thought.

"Sir—Dr. Faust, Randy," he said, searching the video image, seeing a hand reach in and touch the patient's face.

The nurse said, "Dr. Faust, it's okay," patting his cheek lightly. "Dr. Faust, it's your friend, Tyce, from Jerusalem. You need to talk to him."

The old man revived, his eyes blinking, again seeing Tyce's image on the screen.

"You are to...to pursue truth about that which seeks to bring about the evil one, Tyce."

Faust seemed to again struggle to raise himself up, the words coming in barely audible bursts with each breath.

"I have been told to say to you...to tell you that you must...you must follow your...your vision. It is a vision from the Lord. You must—"

Faust fell back, his eyes shut.

"Nurse!" Tyce shouted at the monitor.

Momentarily, Marlaina turned the laptop camera toward her own face. "He's okay for now, Mr. Greyson. He just needs to rest now."

～

ONE DAY LATER

"Your history is of such unusual...experience. Frankly, Tyce, while I can't embrace some supernatural...reality, I must acknowledge strange, indeed very strange, elements in all these...dreams, visions, or whatever."

Dr. Victor Mandell, speaking in English with an Israeli accent, shifted as if he was growing uncomfortable in the chair beside the psychiatrist's couch, crossing one knee over the other and placing the notepad and clipboard atop the top knee.

"Your…history, with the abilities you have been documented to have demonstrated through the Remote Viewing, the episodes resulting in somehow foreseeing things before they happen—I must say it's inexplicable from the vantage of the discipline of psychiatry."

Tyce Greyson, lying on his back, glanced toward the ceiling, rubbing the bridge of his nose with his right index finger and thumb. He faced away from the doctor, who sat just to the rear of Greyson's head while making notes.

"Yeah. Well I more than *embrace* the visions, or whatever they are, Doc. They are driving me bonkers. What I'm seeing now in these…inexplicable dreams, visions, or whatever, as you call them, comes at me at all hours, day and night. It's getting so I have trouble telling these apart from my conscious reality."

Mandell made notes while his patient talked, before offering a question: "And you believe this is all about something to do with prophecy?"

"*Bible* prophecy. Yes. It's all about Bible prophecy. It has been about Bible prophecy since that snake bite in that cave…"

"The Patmos experience?" Mandell asked.

"It wasn't just an experience, Dr. Mandell. It was an event that changed my life beyond anything I can describe. Since that snake latched onto my hand, my life has gotten so mixed with this, this craziness, that I'm not sure what is real and what is…prophecy, or something else driving me toward insanity."

The psychiatrist studied his patient's words before asking, "And this latest episode? You say it involves you being present in the Christian New Testament story of the Upper Room? You are, in this…episode…in that ancient setting, observing Jesus and His disciples while they partake of what is called the Last Supper? Is that your dream or vision experience?"

Greyson lifted his head and turned as far as possible to try to see the questioning Mandell, but couldn't, so returned the back of his head to the pillow and again stared at the ceiling.

"I tell you, it is no dream. I'm there. It is as real as this moment when you and I are talking. I know it's not possible. But I also know what it's like. It's unforgettably vivid, and I remember everything, especially…"

Tyce let the thought die, his remembrance bothering him to the point that he wanted to let it drop.

"And it's this part that troubles you most—the part about Jesus telling this disciple to do something?"

Tyce let the question linger while recalling the way the moments in the ancient setting always ended.

"It's not so much the disciple being given instructions, Doc. It's the face of the man…the disciple. I see clearly every feature of that face. It is before me constantly. His features are etched on my brain. He passes right by me, not a foot from my own face. I can close my eyes now, and I see that face."

The psychiatrist again paused to make a note. "And what do you think it means?" he asked. "Constantly having this man's face in your thoughts?"

"I believe the guy is Judas Iscariot. It has something to do with Jesus telling him to go do what he must do—you know. Go betray Jesus to the Jewish authorities and to the Roman government. But, it keeps coming to mind.

Why, when I'm seeing such a scene in vivid detail, don't I want to concentrate only on Jesus, Himself? Why not? He is probably the greatest person—the most famous—in all of history. Why is my concentration solely on seeing the face of this betrayer? I couldn't describe Jesus or any of the others in the room, but I can draw a picture of this one man I believe is Judas."

"And do you have any thoughts on why this is? Why, do you think, can't you concentrate on the others—on Jesus?"

"Dr. Faust says he believes it's because God wants me to remember the man's face...for some heavenly purpose."

"Dr. Faust? This is your religious friend?"

"Yeah. Dr. Randolph Faust, the guy I told you about who helped me through some of the things in DC and in Israel—the government things I got drawn into."

"And what do you think?" the doctor pressed. "Do you think this might be the case—that you are being given these...experiences...for some purpose directed by Heaven?"

"Look, Doc, you've got my complete history, including that detailed, secret information the Israelis let you see. You know something weird is going on, about me going through all that...*experience*...as you call it. The one who led me through it—"

"—Michael?" Mandell interrupted.

"Yeah. Michael. Dr. Faust convinced me he was...is... the angel assigned to defend Israel in the last days."

Mandell was silent for several seconds before issuing the next question: "And why are you convinced...that this Michael is an angel?"

"He protected Israel in a special way," Tyce said. "I can't divulge details. Michael, let's just say, used my...*experience*...to defend some of Israel's most vital interests."

"And do you believe that Dr. Faust is right, that these are the last days?"

"I don't know." Tyce's intonation was one of frustration. "Whatever is the truth, Michael was—*is*—real. He is a supernatural being. He defended Israel at a critical juncture. He must be fulfilling his role, according to the scripture Daniel the prophet wrote. So, yes, I guess these must be the last days."

Ten minutes later, after his patient exited his office, Mandell finished scribbling some notes, closed his journal, and put it aside on the desk. He picked up the phone near the journal and punched the numbers.

"Kocah," the voice answered.

"Yansika, Victor," Mandell said, then spoke in Hebrew. "My patient of interest was just here. He related an experience very similar to yours and the others. Eerily similar."

"This...Tyce—Tyce Greyson?" Rabbi Yansika Kocah said in whispered amazement.

"It seems there is much about these...visions...that call for deeper investigation," Mandell said.

There was silence on the line for longer than Mandell could wait. "Yansika, what do you think?" the psychiatrist said.

"This man...Greyson. We have studied his history, as you know, Victor. A number of us view his...unusual abilities...as something of profound importance—of extraordinary significance, with regard to Israel's future. His experience in this matter runs almost precisely parallel to that of Jarbin, Weisman, and the others. We must encourage this man, Greyson, to carry out whatsoever divine exigency as has been assigned."

"And how can I assist in this...this *encouragement?*" Mandell said after a moment of silence on the line.

"Through his wife, I should think, rather through his wife's father," Rabbi Yansika Kocah said.

"What do you think about hypnotherapy?" Mandell said.

"Whatever works, Victor. We must do whatever it takes. Israel's destiny almost certainly hangs in the balance."

CHAPTER 1

"The insane leadership of Hamas' al-Qassam Brigades has no affection for Al-Aqsa. They want only to keep all of Islam stirred against us."

Geromme Rafke spoke in Hebrew about the plot just uncovered by Maglan operatives to destroy the Al-Aqsa Mosque atop Mount Moriah.

"What you think, then? You think we've never seen this degree of scorched earth…against their own?"

Morticai Kant glanced from the monitor at the skirmish taking place at the foot of the Temple Mount to look into the intensive blue eyes affixed to his own gaze.

"What I *know*," Rafke said from his standing position to Kant's left, "is that these devils want the entire Muslim world to turn against us by destroying their own religious center." The Israeli colonel added, "They would destroy Mecca if it suited their plans to bring all-out vengeance against Israel."

Kant listened, then shifted his attention back to the large screen. His unspoken thoughts turned to the matters involved that his colonel was not privileged to know—facts much more troubling. The new American regime dominated the cerebral storm that swept through his always-alert mind, ever scanning Israel's precarious position among world powers.

Finally, he spoke.

"Well we did uncover the plot to destroy Mecca, as a matter of fact. You weren't with us then, but I know learning of it was part of your preparation for joining Maglan."

"Yes, sir. It was a brilliant counteraction. I studied it," Rafke said, sorry he had spoken before thinking through the matter.

"What has your group come up with?" the Maglan chief asked after sipping from the steaming coffee in front of his monitor.

"I don't think you will like it," Kant's adjutant said.

"That violent, is it?"

"Well, it seems it is they who have already thrown petrol on the fire," Rafke, said making a hand gesture toward the screen.

"So give me the bottom line."

"The Brigade—the entirety of the Brigade—must be eliminated. Cut off completely, the head—or the heads—of this serpent," Rafke said. "This will disrupt their plotting both now and for the foreseeable future."

Morticai Kant sipped again from the coffee while watching the intense expression on Rafke's face, then turned back to his younger adjutant.

"You believe this can be done?"

"Yes, sir. In one action."

"Not through a hunt-down-and-assassinate operation?" Kant said, surprise in his voice.

Colonel Rafke leaned forward with the heels of his hands on the edge of the computer desk and peered, unblinkingly, into his chief's eyes. "It can be done when they gather in two weeks in the Gaza compound they use."

Kant diverted his attention to the door to his office when it opened and a Maglan operative made the announcement: "Sir, your daughter is here."

Kant looked again to Rafke. "We will discuss this later today, Geromme. Thank you."

The Maglan chief stood while the officer left through the doorway. He spoke when he saw the young woman, who reached to embrace his own outstretched arms.

"And how are the newlyweds?" he said in English. He kissed Essie's offered cheek and gave her an extra hug.

"All is well, Papa," she said, returning the affection. "Well...Tyce continues to experience these...troubling episodes."

"And what is the latest?"

"He keeps seeing the same face that he obsesses on. It's the face of the man he sees in his recurring vision that he says isn't a dream. It is a vision as clearly experienced as in real-life situations, he says."

"The so-called Upper Room matter?" her father said.

"The same. It is identical...exactly the same time after time."

Her father spoke after assessing her words for several seconds. "This Tyce of yours is quite steeped in mystery, daughter."

"That's because you are...so steeped, Abba. I have always wanted to figure you out. It has been a goal not reached."

"So the daughter seeks a man like her father? Is that the expression?" Morticai Kant said with a muffled laugh.

"That is the way my Aunt Gussie always put it," Essie said, nodding agreement.

"Yes, well, your mother's sister is always right, so we can do nothing less than agree with her."

Kant took Essie's hand and led her to a chair near his desk.

"Sit, daughter. It is this vision matter involving Tyce that I want to discuss. It's the reason I asked you to stop by today."

Essie said nothing, studying his face while he sat in a chair across from her, hearing in his voice the same mysterious tone she had heard many times just before he divulged something from the deepest strata of Maglan business.

He started by speaking hesitatingly, his eyes shifting while looking at the space on the floor between them, searching for the best way to begin.

"You know my...my skepticism...with regard to reli-gion." He looked then into her understanding expression.

"I am skeptical about religion itself. But I am not skeptical about my close friends of many years who hold wholeheartedly to their religious belief system."

"Yes, Abba. I know your closeness with the rabbis who are your long-time friends, and your respect for them," Essie said.

"And we know the strange circumstances involved in the matters with Tyce and his...his interaction with...the visions, the involvement with the one he named Michael."

Her father's look was quizzical while he waited for her response.

"Yes, 'strange circumstances' is putting it mildly," she

said, remembering her own brush with death at the hand of her deep-state captors.

The Maglan chief again studied the floor between them as he searched for how to begin to explain.

"Yansika Kocah, Amir Lubeka—all that group—say they are…seeing the same things that Tyce is reporting to Mandell." He looked at Essie, whose expression was one of raised eyebrows.

"All that group of Orthodox rabbis in Yansika's group say they have dreams exactly the same as your husband's. They watch as the man at the table is handed something to dip in a bowl. He does so, then gets up and exits the room after having something whispered to him by the one who hands him the piece of bread—"

"And these visions, they are not one-time experiences? They are recurring with each of them?" Essie interrupted.

"Many recurrences. The visions plague them… disrupt their nightly sleep," her father said, his eyes cutting toward the office door to see a uniformed man enter.

"Sir, your phone call is ready," the man said.

"Excuse me, sweetheart. It's about Tyce. I shouldn't be long," the Maglan chief said and exited the room while the soldier held the door open.

Essie's phone chimed after two minutes had elapsed.

"Tyce?" she responded, seeing his name come up.

"Hey, Ess. How's the meeting going?"

"Actually, I'm still in the middle of it."

"Oh, sorry. We'll talk later."

"No, Papa is talking to someone in another room. He said it's about you."

"Me? What about me?"

"Don't know. I guess he will tell me when he's finished."

"It's about these…episodes. Dr. Mandell, no doubt, is involved," Tyce said, a bit glumly.

"It does have something to do with your episodes, I think. Abba was just getting ready to tell me more when the phone call, previously arranged, I presume, came."

"Then we will just have to wait to find out what it's about. They've asked me to come to their kibbutz. I got a message just a few minutes ago."

"Who? What kibbutz?" Essie said, her eyes wide with surprise as she looked to see her father reenter the room.

"Their parapsychology group, I take it. They want to discuss my participation in something."

"Abba just came in. Maybe he will have more."

They said goodbyes as the Maglan chief sat again in front of his daughter.

"Who was that?" Kant said.

"Tyce. He said he's been summoned to a parapsychology group of some sort. Is this something of your making?"

"Well we certainly are going to have to get our security minds in order around this place," Kant said with irritation in his voice.

"I still have clearance, Morticai," Essie said with equal irritation.

"Not for this, Essie. Not yet, at least. They should have advised your husband to say nothing about any of this. All will be made clear shortly—to him and to you. But we must clamp down on this. That's my job, and I will handle it." He looked at her then, his features softening. "I know I can count on you, baby," he said in Hebrew.

Essie smiled, hearing his pet name for her. He was apologizing through the affectionate designation.

"Very well, Papa," she said in English.

YANSIKA KOCAH MOVED about the semi-darkened room, placing small dishes before each of the rabbis around the circular table. He then filled each of their small, silver goblets with wine. The dark-bearded men dressed in rabbinic garb partook of the meager, ritual fare, their faces illumined by a mini menorah at the table's center.

Rabbi Amir Lubeka spoke in Hebrew from his position directly across the table from Kocah, who had just taken his seat.

"We agree that we are joined in some inexplicable movement into the time of Mashiach. We have been anointed by Hashem to carry out Mashiach's introduction to the House of Israel and to the world."

All eyes were on the eldest of the group's priestly leadership. He looked around the table at each while speaking again in a low, sing-song chant.

"Now we lift in unison our voices."

All within the group spoke slowly as one in Hebrew while Amir Lubeka led in the ritual mantra by saying:

"I believe with perfect faith that Hashem the Creator, shall His Name be blessed, is the Creator and Leader of every created thing; and he himself made, does make, and will make everything.

"I believe with perfect faith that the Creator, shall His Name be blessed, is the only One, and there is no unity in any way like His, and He alone is our God, who was, is, and will always be.

"I believe with perfect faith that the Creator, shall His Name be blessed, is no body, and all properties of matter do not apply to him, and there can be no physical comparison to Him at all.

"I believe with perfect faith that the Creator, shall His Name be blessed, was the first and will remain the last.

"I trust with full trust that the Creator, shall His Name be blessed, only to Him there is right to pray, and there is no point in praying to any being besides Him.

"I believe with perfect faith that all words of the Nevi'im [prophets] are true.

"I believe with perfect faith that the prophecy of our rabbi, Moses, may he rest in peace, was true, and he was the father of the Nevi'im [prophets], both those who came before him and those after him.

"I believe with perfect faith that the entire Torah that we have in our possession is the same that was given to our rabbi, Moses.

"I believe with perfect faith that our Torah won't be exchanged, and there will never be any other Torah from Hashem, shall His Name be blessed.

"I believe with perfect faith that the Creator, shall His Name be blessed, knows all actions of human beings, their thoughts, as it is written (Psalm 33:15), 'Who fashioned the hearts of them all, Who comprehends all their actions.'

"I believe with perfect faith that the Creator, shall His Name be blessed, gives rewards for those who keep His mitzvos [commandments] and punishes those who transgress them.

"I believe with perfect faith in the coming Messiah; and although he may tarry, even though I wait every day for his coming.

"I believe with perfect faith that there will be a revival of the dead at the time when it shall please Hashem, shall his

*name be blessed, and his mention shall be elevated forever
and ever."*

The rabbis said then in unison, *"Selah."*

Amir Lubeka arose from his sitting position at the table and read in Hebrew from a small book he held open. Each rabbi around the table listened intently to the elder man's slow, methodical reading.

"As it is written, *oh-LAHM hah-BAH* surely will visit this generation. All signs and wonders appointed are in view. Now Mashiach makes known the presence of Hashem among our circle."

The seated rabbis nodded and, in a prayerful, chant-like tempo, said three times in unison, *"Tehillah Hashem."*

Lubeka looked to the young rabbi sitting beside Yansika Kocah and addressed him, saying, "Rabbi Jerham Levitosh, we will hear the vision sent by Hashem."

The small, thin man stood and, with hands clasped beneath the black-robe sleeves, he began to speak.

"I have seen Mashiach," he began. "Like each of you who are member of the Council of *oh-LAHM hah-BAH*, I have now seen the face of Israel's Warrior King."

All eyes were upon the young man while he described a recurring vision he had experienced the past seven nights. When he had completed his statement, he sat down and Lubeka again stood to speak.

"Each in this council has confided privately to me and to Rabbi Kocah the vision you have had for a period of seven days or nights. You have been silent to tell any other than the two of us about what comes to you each time in the vision-state."

Lubeka looked around the table at each face. All eyes were on him, the time of the council's need for secrecy foremost in each man's thoughts.

"Rabbi Levitosh is the last of you in this council to have seven full visions. Each of you have reported, without comparing notes, the same vision experience over each day for seven days. There is no other conclusion to be reached."

The old rabbi paused to glance quickly at each face around the table, then said in a firm voice, "Hashem is preparing to introduce Mashiach Ben David to this world of evil."

CHAPTER 2

Rabbi Amir Lubeka's new bride moved toward him with her hands outstretched. Her beauty was all he had anticipated, the sheer fabric of her wedding night gown flowing with her graceful movement toward his extended hands. But his Shekkah was now gone. She passed to the land reserved for the righteous dead a month ago. Yet his love reached to him now, not at age 80, but young, beautiful...on their wedding night.

But while she reached to receive his offered embrace, she transformed before his eyes. Her beauty again became his wife in old age. Still lovely, still the woman he had loved more with each passing of their sixty-two years together. When they touched, her eyes pierced to the core of his transfixed innermost being. She spoke to him as in an echo chamber that reverberated throughout the ages.

"The Holy one speaks to you this night," the echoing, cavernous, though familiar voice of his beloved wife said. "Mashiach moves soon to make His presence known among men. Seek truth concerning His coming through the one you will be directed to choose to undertake the mission of revelation."

The rabbi awakened, instantly fully alert. He wanted to speak, to carry the impressions caroming within his astonished realization to their deepest level of meaning. But there was nothing else to be said or understood. He knew, without question or unresolved expectation, what he was being told. He must pursue the prophesied Mashiach at the direct command of Hashem.

Esur Solomon, escorted into the Oval Office by a Secret Service agent, surveyed the room, seeing several men in business suits standing between the large sofas facing each other. Each turned to meet him with handshakes. Their expressions were solemn as the greetings were made.

After two minutes of polite chatter, a door opened to the left of the big desk, and a man and woman entered.

The President of the United States, followed closely by his wife, reached to take Solomon's extended hand.

The Israeli foreign ministry envoy looked to the elderly first lady. Seeing no desire on her part to shake hands, he let his own hand drop to his side. Neither the president nor the first lady had smiled; no others in the room had, either.

"Have you kept this meeting from the prime minister?" The president's words were issued harshly, like he was speaking to an underling.

Solomon, taken aback by the bluntness and tone, hesitated, then slightly shook his head. "Yes. Only the select group is aware," he said.

"Let's make sure we keep it that way," the president said, then looked to the tallest of the other three men.

The Israeli noticed a puzzled look on the chief executive's face. The man spoke, then, as if reminding the president. "Sir, it is necessary to preempt the Israeli subversion entity in their move against the mosque matter."

The president nodded understanding, then turned to his wife. She whispered something into his left ear, and he again nodded and turned to look at Solomon.

"I have to see after a deal with—"

The first lady interrupted the president's words. "We are scheduled for a meeting, but Hans, here," she said, touching the coat sleeve of the taller of the men, "Hans is fully authorized to follow through on the president's behalf."

When the president and his wife left the room, the man the first lady had indicated spoke.

"Esur, what is the latest on your Maglan chief's plans to stop our friends in the Moriah matter?"

"Mossad has numerous people embedded within those who will destroy Al-Asqa," Solomon said in slightly accented English. "I have a list of those individuals, along with photographs and other vital information."

"That's excellent," Hans Ingram said. "We have things set up at State to begin the process of removing those people. We will coordinate with the Palestine leaders who will carry out the excision."

WHEN THE MEETING BROKE UP, Hans Ingram made his way from the West Wing into the bowels of the basement complex. He placed the brief bag he carried at the side of the desk and picked up the phone after being seated in the desk chair.

He spoke when his party was on the other end. "It's done. We have them. There are four embeds with Hamas."

He listened while the voice on the other end spoke: "Give them to me and the excision will be accomplished."

Ingram lifted a briefcase from beneath the desk and opened it after sitting it atop the desk. He took a sheet of paper from the bag and typed the names into the encryption device.

"On the way," he said, after completing the task.

"Got 'em," the voice on the other end said.

THE GATHERING of al-Qassam Brigade's leadership in the Gaza compound settled when an Arab in a burnoose called for order. He spoke while letting his dark eyes scan the group that sat in rapt attention.

"Al-Aqsa is our target, as we know."

He directed a pointer toward the graphic on the large screen. The Mosque of Omar glinted brightly in the Jerusalem sunlight, the live shot framing it while all eyes took in the scene.

"With this single action, we will bring all of Islam down upon the throats of the Jewish dogs," he said, his black eyes glistening while the room erupted with sounds of elation over the prospect.

"As we gather, Allah's mighty hand is upon us," he began, eliciting from all in the room *"Allah be praised"* in Arabic.

"Our purpose will be accomplished…Allah's will be done."

Again, all in the room shouted in unison, *"Allah be praised!"*

"Our mission was endangered, for there are among our numbers traitors. These have conspired with the infidels to interfere with our bringing the Jewish dogs to destruction."

The men looked around their ranks, mumbling their amazement at the revelation.

At that moment, the doors in the back of the room burst open and a contingent of heavily armed men in Hamas military gear rushed in. They quickly captured the four men of their search, roughly jerking them to their feet and hustling them from among the gathering.

The speaker smiled a grin of satisfaction and said with a lilt in his declaration, "Now, our ranks are again pure. Allah has found out the traitors.

"Our mission is now unimpeded."

He turned his attention again to the large screen that displayed Mount Moriah and the contentious groups surrounding the area near the Al-Aqsa Mosque.

"We shall assault with numerous drones. The Al-Aqsa will be no more. The Jews will be blamed, and the international order will be inflamed against the blasphemous Israelis."

Thirty minutes further into the lecture, the doors to the rear again opened in a violent burst. Again, a contingent of military-garbed men stormed into the room. They searched the large group of Arabs, all of whom who were stunned as the weapons-wielding men shoved and jerked at their robes.

"Where are they?" one of the military men shouted to the speaker, who stood dumbfounded.

"Where are the traitors?" the man again shouted angrily.

"They were taken from us already!" the speaker near the screen yelled back.

"That's impossible—we are here to take them," the man in charge of the contingent screamed.

Suddenly, the room erupted in flame, with violent concussion that instantly blew apart flesh and the building's structure. Several explosions followed until only the roaring of flame, fanned by the desert winds, presented evidence that the Hamas plotters had existed.

CHAPTER 3

The Israeli prime minister was perplexed. He cocked his head as he questioned the Maglan chief.

"What the hell is this about, Morticai," he said, his tone tinged with anger. "You've arrested Solomon?"

Morticai Kant gave a tolerant smile. "That's why I have the job, Napie," he said, stepping several feet from the door to be seated in a side chair beside the Israeli's big desk. "He is a traitor."

"I presume you have that all documented and tied down," the prime minister said, his face taking on the pallor of one in shock.

Kant's language changed from English to Hebrew. "Napie, you know me. You know Maglan. I do nothing for which I haven't the documentation prepared. The man is a traitor. He was in collusion with your friend, the president of the United States, and all of that cabal."

The prime minister sat silent, then broke into a slight smile, wanting to tone down the direction the hostility was taking them.

"Yes, yes—I know your ways and the ways of Maglan," he said finally, then stood from behind the desk and moved to nervously straighten photos of his family on the nearby credenza. He turned back to see the subdued smile on the Israeli Maglan chief's face.

"Then I guess all to be said, Morti, is 'well done.' I wish I had been told, however."

"'Need to know,' Napie. You know our agreement. You know the rules. The fewer who know in these critical matters, the better. The Knesset Privy Council were quite wise to make it that way, don't you think?"

The Israeli prime minister switched again to English.

"Yes, of course. It is the only way to carry out such crucial missions, I agree."

He paused to cast a frowning expression toward his Maglan chief. "But I resent you calling this president of the United States my friend. He is no friend to any of us."

"Preaching to this choir member—Amen, Mr. Prime Minister," Kant agreed.

"I understood there was something afoot with regard to Al-Asqa, but didn't understand we had an operative within our ranks who was aiding and abetting Hamas directly in planning to bring the world down around our necks with such a blatant move."

"The problem is solved. That group of Hamas won't be a problem ever again," Kant said, rising from the chair and walking to the door of the prime minister's office, turning and smiling.

"Now I have some truly internecine matters to which to attend."

Rabbi Amir Lubeka stood looking out the floor-to-ceiling window, awaiting the arrival of Morticai Kant and the others. As head of the *oh-LAHM hah* Council, there was much on his mind, the dream-vision of the nights haunting his every waking moment. His precious Shekkah, reaching from the other side to reaffirm what he must do. Hashem spoke directly through his beloved wife from the other side. The Mashiach was at the point of movement into Israel's latter-days history. This was the time all of Israel throughout the millennia had been awaiting.

A knock at the massive door and its opening disrupted the troubling thoughts he couldn't shake.

"The others are here, rabbi," the young woman said from the doorway.

"Yes, Meka, send them in please."

The seven members of the council entered, greeted by only a slight expression of recognition from Lubeka.

"Mr. Kant should be here any moment," Lubeka said, gesturing for the men to be seated. Almost at the moment he spoke, the Maglan chief strode through the door opening.

"Haven't missed anything, have I?" he said lightly in Hebrew.

"No. we were just seated," Lubeka said, bidding Kant to take a chair near the front of the gathering.

The *oh-LAHM hah* Council head wasted no time getting to the reason for the hastily arranged meeting. "Matters are moving beyond anything we could have fathomed, my brothers," he said, his face a somber mask of intensity. "You have been given all the details, so there is no need to repeat them here, at this time."

He paused to pace in front of the group before speaking his gathering thoughts.

"Hashem is all but speaking directly as when He spoke to the prophets of old. The Mashiach is among us. But it is up to us to find him, to bring him to Israel's direction—to our defense—in these prophetic times. It has been deemed so by Hashem. We are not to accomplish this in our own way. We must seek Mashiach, I am convinced, through this Tyce Greyson. Morticai, are you prepared to assist in this holy directive by Hashem?"

One of the men arose from his chair. "Rabbi, will Hashem so bless an effort led by one who is skeptic?"

The others nodded agreement with the question, casting glances at Kant.

"Did not Hashem use those other than from the holy councils to accomplish His will? Are we not blessed to have one of such placement to assist in this most profound mission—perhaps the greatest mission of all? To find our Mashiach and bring peace and safety to our people forever?"

Lubeka's words were firm, unrelenting. It seemed to satisfy the question posed.

"We will hear from you, Morticai." With that, the head of *oh-LAHM hah* Council took his seat.

Kant stood in front of the eight men, his penetrating blue eyes seeming to invade those of each of the robed council members.

"First, let me say, I did not request this assignment, nor was I appointed to it by anyone. So, perhaps my skepticism is not so locked in stone as you might think."

He paused to give effect that he had thoroughly prepared before addressing the religious council.

"My primary wish, my only wish, is the safety and security of Israel. This is why I occupy the position of Maglan chief. If it is Hashem who has destined that I take this mission in order to preserve and bring peace to our beloved Israel, then I'm on Hashem's side."

He again hesitated for effect before continuing. "Over these past months, I have seen miraculous things in my own life, and particularly in the lives of my daughter, Essie, and the man who is now her husband, the man who is the subject of this gathering. Tyce Greyson has been at the center of some truly profound occurrences. I cannot deny this truth. Tyce is, as you all know, experiencing the same images—the visions and dreams—as some of you in this council. I do not scoff or deny facts when I encounter them, my friends. There is something happening beyond what I or anyone else can explain."

He paced now, his thoughts coming quickly.

"I have passed all this by my daughter and have inquired as to her and her husband's thoughts on helping us in this…this…finding Israel's Mashiach, if this is what you believe the mission to be, given you by Hashem.

"Greyson has not agreed as yet. He says that he must first consult with his American friend, Dr. Randolph Faust. Tyce is in touch with the old gentleman, who is very ill. He is flying to America tomorrow to meet with Dr. Faust."

THE GULFSTREAM BEGAN LETTING down from thirty-five thousand feet as it crossed the Atlantic while nearing the US coastline. Tyce Greyson felt the familiar popping of the ears during the descent toward Hartsfield-Jackson Atlanta International Airport.

"Abba had to pull some strings to get us use of this plane," Essie said. "It sure beats having to wear the masks."

"Sure beats going through all those lines. I'm sure your father was just thinking of his little girl in convincing the IAF for its use in this trip," Tyce said, taking his wife's offered hand and squeezing it gently.

"He said to consider it his contribution to the honeymoon we haven't had time to take," she said, grasping his hand with both of hers. "He wants this matter to move forward as quickly as possible. Private transportation takes care of that priority. That's the reason, the real reason, for Papa's generosity. Israel comes first always with him."

"Be sure they are fastened," came the voice from the cockpit, followed by the thumping of the landing gear opening and the slight shivering of the G-650. "We will be on the ground in Atlanta in five minutes."

When the aircraft rolled to a stop at the direction of the ground crew, the pilot came on the intercom again.

"There's something going on here, Mr. Greyson. Seems we have a greeting party of some sort," the Israeli pilot said. "I'm told we are not to move forward to refuel."

"We were supposed to be here only an hour then head to San Antonio," Tyce said, straining to see the activity just outside the plane. "Looks like we're about to be visited."

Essie strained to look past her husband, seeing several men dressed in business suits standing beside a dark sedan.

"They look official," she said. "What do you suppose it's about?"

"Knowing this government these days, there's no telling," Tyce said, watching the men walking toward the jet's now-open door at the left front.

"We are here on our honeymoon, and to visit friends

in Texas," he reminded Essie. "That's all we need to divulge."

The first of the men entered the plane and spoke to those in the cockpit doorway. He and another of the men in business suits then came to them.

"Sir, are you Tyce Greyson?" the larger one spoke, glancing first at Tyce then at Essie.

"Yes. I'm Greyson. This is my wife."

"Sir, we are instructed to bring you to FBI headquarters in Atlanta. We will make this as convenient as possible. You should be on your way within a couple of hours."

"What is this about?" Tyce said.

"Sir, I am just told that we are to bring you to headquarters in downtown Atlanta. You will have an explanation there, I'm sure."

"What about my wife?"

"She is to stay here." The agent looked into Essie's concerned gaze. "We will get him back just as soon as possible, ma'am."

Tyce stood and patted Essie's arm, then reached down to embrace her briefly. "I'll go with them, Ess. It'll be okay."

"May I see your credentials?" he said, then, prompting the agent to reach into his coat pocket.

Tyce studied the card. "Okay, Agent Lester. Take care of her," he instructed the pilot, who stood nearby observing things.

"Yes, sir. We certainly will," the pilot said.

Essie watched through worried thoughts while the black sedan with her husband left the parking ramp heading in the direction of downtown Atlanta.

She stood and faced the pilot and copilot when the sedan was out of sight.

"Contact Morticai. See what he knows about this matter," she said.

THE IAF PILOT made it through to Maglan offices after fifteen minutes of trying. The female officer spoke in answer to the pilot's request to get in touch with the chief. "Mr. Kant has left for his home," she said.

"His daughter wants to speak with him," the pilot said.

The Israeli Maglan officer gave him the number she was instructed to give should his daughter or her husband call.

Within two minutes Kant was on the phone. The pilot turned the phone over to Essie.

"Abba, the American FBI has taken Tyce from the plane. What is this about?"

There was silence on the line while Kant summoned an adjutant silently with an indication of his index finger.

"I have no idea, sweetheart. But we shall get to the bottom of it."

Essie spent the next two minutes explaining the situation. Kant said, "Very well, Essie. I'm putting our people on it at this very moment. We will get it resolved. Just be assured that I have it under control."

TYCE WALKED between two of the agents while they entered Atlanta's federal building. His trepidation was somewhat assuaged. This was indeed a federal headquarters. He was not being kidnapped by unknowns. Was it better, though, to be brought into custody by this organization, which, over the past decade, had earned the reputation of one akin in some respects to the old KGB?

He was issued into a large office complex, then to an inner office.

"Be seated, Mr. Greyson," one of the agents said, directing him to a chair not far from a desk. The men then left the room, leaving him looking around at the oak-paneled walls. Just over ten minutes later, an office door swung open and a woman stepped in.

She placed several items on the large desk before turning to face Tyce. She was dressed in smart business attire, her look one like news anchors he had worked with over the years.

"Mr. Greyson, I'm Cheryl Madison, director of the Bureau here in Atlanta."

The announcement took him aback. She was a woman...she was...too anchor-like...

"What's this about, Ms. Madison?" was all he could think to say.

"It's about you being back in country after such a long absence," she said, both her tone and facial expression serious to the point of being threatening.

"My citizenship hasn't changed. My wife's papers are in order. I repeat, Ms. Madison, what's this about?"

She raised an eyebrow, cocking her head in an inquisitive manner, before speaking in a more soothing tone. "Your...involvement...with the Israeli government, with your wife and her father, the head of Israel's most-secretive clandestine ops, has stirred our curiosity. Our agency must maintain domestic tranquility, Mr. Greyson. My job is to see that this is done when foreign interests become...domestic in nature."

"My wife and I are making this part of a honeymoon

trip we have yet to complete. She's agreed to visit a very sick friend in Texas, in San Antonio."

"Dr. Randolph Faust? This is your sick friend?"

"You already know the answer."

"Kathryn, please bring us some coffee," the director said, pushing an intercom button and speaking into the instrument.

"How do you like yours?"

Tyce said nothing, causing her to make the order anyway. "Make it black, Kathryn."

"Our dossier on your involvement with the previous administration makes our curiosity somewhat necessary, Mr. Greyson—Tyce."

He sat silent, determined to let the woman divulge her purpose.

"Your 'talents,' shall we call them, make you a particular person of interest, as you know. Your involvement with the AI technologies…the remote viewing…many of the esoteric things you were involved in with the previous American and Israeli administrations is the reason for this…interview."

The office door opened; a young woman came and placed a cup and saucer beside Tyce's chair, then did the same for the director at her desk.

"So, Mr. Greyson, what is your purpose for coming to see Dr. Faust? He was equally involved in matters those previous national administrations were engaged in. My duty is to assure that there is not a repeat of damage done in those previous operations."

She sipped from the cup, looking over its rim at the journalist.

"I just want to visit my friend," Tyce said. "They have said he might be dying. And any damage done in those times was aimed at that previous administration—at both administrations, of the US and Israel. There were rogue operatives working to subvert what the president and the prime minister were trying to accomplish. They were trying to preserve both nations."

Greyson sipped from the coffee, finally, looking to see the woman's response. She smiled calmly, straightening a bit in the high-back executive chair.

"Yes, well, the voting public of both times seems to have disagreed significantly about who was subverting whom. They voted both regimes out."

"The subversion was manifest in that both elections were stolen."

The director looked long and hard at him, a wistful expression crossing her perfectly made-up face. "It's all a matter of perception, I suppose. Now things are back in order, and we are determined to keep them moving in the right direction. So, we must and will preempt any efforts to take national and world order down tracks counterproductive to stability."

"I have no problem with those objectives. My wife and I are just here to visit a sick friend," Greyson said, sipping again on the coffee, struggling to maintain a calm façade.

"Yes. Well you are sent to see that sick friend in a G-650 by Israel's most clandestine service. Your wife's father is the head of that service. This hardly smacks of a visit that is without significance."

Tyce felt a strange sensation. He clumsily tried to place the half empty coffee cup on the saucer. His senses darkened, the woman across the desk from him seeming to weave in undulant fashion while she gazed at him.

His next conscious realization was of having constrictive straps placed upon his head and body, his head drawn backward and held firmly against a hard surface. A deep, burning sensation, followed by a complete disconnect from reality, took him into a realm remembered in that time of the past when his spiritual essence seemed to invade regions occupied by the enemy.

But it was now his own thoughts were being probed, invaded by whatever force would have the innermost secrets exposed for their own nefarious use. Secrets that somehow, without any effort of his own he could manage, remained out of their reach. The technology, painfully probing and trying to elicit from him truth of his mission, unsuccessful at breaking through the cerebral defense positioned as vanguard against intrusion.

Somehow he knew, even in this seemingly helpless moment at their mercy. They could not rip from him the deepest thoughts, bolstered by some force he couldn't identify. They could not penetrate that supernatural force that guarded against the evil that was at the heart of the black cabal that constituted this new-world-order principality in high places.

And yet, at the same time, he looked across the desk at the undulating director in her perfectly modeled femininity and saw her again come into focus. All remembrance of the experience faded to nothingness, while he again came to full consciousness.

"Are you okay, Tyce?" The woman was now directly in front of him, patting his cheek with the cool, slender fingertips of perfectly manicured crimson nails.

"MORTICAI SENT somebody to look into their taking you. He was livid. The prime minister spoke directly to the FBI director in DC."

Essie embraced her husband, looking him over for any harm she could perceive having been done to him. "What did they do? What was their purpose?"

"They consider me some sort of threat to their deep-state activities, based on those things that happened when I did the work for the president—the remote-viewing work while undergoing those things under the AI devices."

"You seem out of sorts, Tyce. Are you okay?" Essie noticed an apparent strangeness in her husband's eyes.

"They slipped me something," he said. "After about a half cup of coffee, I started getting woozy. Everything went out of focus."

"What happened then?"

"I don't know. I can almost recall something, but it's just all gone. Things came into focus again, and the woman, the FBI person in charge, was touching my face and asking if I was okay."

The Gulfstream began its take-off roll and climbed quickly after the aircraft rotated from the runway with nose pointed upward.

"It's a little less than two hours to San Antonio," the first officer's voice announced over the intercom after the bird had climbed for two minutes. "ETA is 4:30 p.m. Central Time."

"What were they up to, do you think?"

Essie held his arm tightly next to her on the armrest that separated them. She firmly gripped his forearm with her other hand, still fearful of how his absence could have ended badly. Might have separated them forever.

"Director Madison—Cheryl Madison—didn't say, exactly. But her whole problem with me being here seemed to be that your father obviously thought the trip was important, because he sent us in a government jet."

"What do you think they plan to do?"

"She talked about the time I was involved with the last administration and with Israeli black ops that I took part in."

"Why did they give you the drug?"

"I guess because I wasn't forthcoming with the information about being here. They must think it involves things that will interfere with their administrative state plans again. I don't know how long I was out, or whatever. But, somehow, they must have tried to get me to divulge any deeper reasons for our trip."

Essie spoke in an irritated tone. "And are there plans you haven't told me about? I mean, things other than a visit to Dr. Faust?"

This woman was not one to be easily parried with by verbal fencing. He said, after a moment to consider her question, "The *oh-LAHM hah* Council chose me to look into these dreams. Rabbi Lubeka asked your father to enlist me in trying to find out who this Mashiach, as they call him, is. Dr. Faust and Morticai have talked, and they didn't want to risk any electronic eavesdropping. They say it must be a face-to-face meeting with Dr. Faust."

"What does Dr. Faust have to do with these matters?" Essie said.

"Something about Mashiach being of profound importance to the safety and security of Israel. That's why Morticai is so determined to follow through and go along with Rabbi Lubeka's supposedly spiritually motivated plan to find this Mashiach."

They both were silent while reflecting on Tyce's words. Then Essie spoke.

"The Mashiach," she said, "is the one who will be sent from Hashem to deliver Israel at the end of days. He will be a great military champion, like King David of old. He will also be at the spiritual heart of bringing Israel to the center of Hashem's holy will for the nation."

"Well, Dr. Faust has things to tell me about all that, apparently. That's all I know about this trip we're making to San Antonio."

"And this dream that recurs, the council, Rabbi Lubeka believe that the scene everyone is having has something to do with the Mashiach?"

"They believe the one I and the others see in these visions might be the one who will be the Mashiach."

"But, as I understand, this vision is of the Last Supper —the time when Jesus and His disciples gathered to eat just before He was crucified. Jews who are not Messianic and converted to Christianity don't have any regard for that tradition. Jesus, to them, was an imposter of the one who will be the Mashiach. Why would they have this dream?"

"I guess we will know more about all that as we look into it."

"There is, everybody seems to think, something supernatural about it, so I guess heavenly influences are at work."

CHAPTER 4

Hans Ingram sat on the edge of the bed and punched the button to answer the call. He cursed under his breath, seeing the number calling in. The young woman reached across the bed to tug at his arm, her face displaying her own displeasure about his answering the phone.

"Are you having fun with your little whore, Hans?" said the German-accented English speaker on the other end of the call. The familiar, growly, voice of the old man was harsh, mocking.

Ingram said nothing, and the voice spoke again. "We hope you are doing much better with her than you did with your last assignment, Hans."

"Sir, I—"

"Your last effort was a disaster, Hans. The Israeli matter, the failure, was absolutely beyond acceptable. Do you understand why?"

Before Hans could answer, the voice spoke. "You did

44

not secure that the plan to bring the ire of the Muslim world and all others down on the Jewish dogs was kept secret. Do you realize what a monumental failure it is that Israel preempted the actions of Hamas?

"Was your mind on the little whore there with you now? Were you thinking with your glands rather than with your brain?" the voice continued in mocking tone.

"Sir, I assure you we took every precaution," Hans said. "Everything was checked out many times over—"

"Obviously," the voice interrupted. "That's why the Israeli dogs were able to completely destroy the heart of Hamas operations in a single blow."

The girl in his bed moved to press against Hans, impatiently pulling him toward her while he listened. He moved her hand from its grip and stood.

"You were placed in this administration by the council to accomplish our purposes," the reproach continued. "You have let us down. You placed dalliance with your bimbos above the good of global peace and security. We are most displeased that our purpose to bring things into compliance is nothing to you. What do you think we should do about this fact, Hans?"

Ingram's normally tanned face became a mask of pallor. "I've always fulfilled my assignments, sir," he said, his voice unsure in its declaration.

"Yes. But not this time, the most important assignment you have been given. 'What have you done for us lately?' I think is the American expression."

Silence ensued, the desired effect causing Ingram to search for words to answer.

"Sir—"

"You will meet with us at the Grove next time at the usual hour, if you can tear yourself away from your concupiscence for an evening."

"Yes, sir. I'll be there."

"HE IS IMPROVED CONSIDERABLY, MR. GREYSON," Marlaina Joske said, leading Tyce toward the private suite. "The area will give you and Dr. Faust privacy."

Randolph Faust's demeanor brightened when Tyce walked into the large room. The old man had aged considerably since the two had last been together. Tyce, making an effort to not show the shock at seeing his friend in his declining state, bent to embrace Faust, feeling the frail frame of age, a condition that he knew had been accelerated by illness.

"Tyce, where is your beautiful Essie?" Faust's voice was still strong. He looked past Tyce and his nurse for Essie.

"We didn't know if you'd be up for more than one visitor at a time, Randy," Tyce said, looking to Marlaina for her thoughts.

"Please get her, Marlaina," Faust said. "My goodness, I must see her immediately!"

The nurse smiled. "Then she will be ushered in immediately!" she said with enthusiasm equal to his.

"What's this about being accosted in Atlanta?" The old man's question was offered with a twinkle in his eyes, knowing Tyce would be surprised that he knew of the incident.

"You know about that?" Greyson said with the inflection the old man wanted to hear.

"Yep. I have my sources, you know."

Tyce laughed, realizing the man he knew well was still the same mentally, if not physically.

"Yes, I know. Don't guess you want to divulge your… sources," he said lightly.

"No secrets among friends," Faust said. "Morticai and I talked about an hour ago. He told me all about the FBI picking you up when you landed in Atlanta."

Tyce said nothing, and Faust, after looking for his friend for response and hearing none, said, "And what about the Mickey they slipped you? What is that about?"

When Tyce started to answer, Essie walked quickly into the room and to Faust's bedside. She took his feebly offered hand and held it in both of hers.

"And how is our Randy?" Her question was offered lightheartedly, but Faust could see in her eyes her pain of seeing him in his condition.

"I'm still topside of terra-firma," he said with a chuckle. "They tell me I should get past this bout. Question is: Do I really want to get past it?"

"Don't talk like that," Essie scolded brightly. "Of course you want to get better and quickly. You are needed!"

"Well, to be with the Lord is better, but you are right. We are supposed to be among the living until the Lord says otherwise." He turned his gaze to Tyce when Essie had released her grip and taken a seat beside the bed.

"Tyce, you were about to tell me what you think the drugging was about."

"I don't know. I took several sips of the coffee a girl brought in, and the next thing I knew, I was feeling the director's hand patting my cheek, trying to wake me up, pull me out of it."

"Do you have any thoughts about the…the taking you from the plane in…on the drugging, etc.?"

Tyce stood from the chair and paced while he talked.

"It must have something to do with getting me to

reveal some secretive reasons for Morticai sending me over here in the Mossad's Gulfstream. That was on the director's mind when we first talked. She said there must be some very important business because of the fact that he sent Essie and me in that expensive private jet as opposed to a commercial flight."

"Yes. I can see it was heavy on her mind. She— whomever—insisted on taking you from an Israeli military aircraft. That would require special permission from the Defense Department, maybe even higher."

"Yeah, well, all regulations and protocols seem out the window with this administration," Tyce said, returning to his chair.

"Do you suppose they got anything—any information —from you in that drugged state?" Essie said.

"I don't think so," Faust said. "He wasn't told anything of significance before departing Tel Aviv—were you, Tyce?"

"No, sir. Only that Morticai wanted me to be in your physical presence when you and I talk. That's about all I know."

"And that is why we arranged this get-together," Faust said. "We have a lot to talk about, but not in this hospital setting. I'm going home tomorrow, and there are safeguards that the Maglan folks have set up. We can talk then."

TEL AVIV, 2:15 AM

Jerham Levitosh heard the voice but couldn't determine its source or even the direction it emanated was coming from.

"Hashem calls," the echoing words said with authority, causing the rabbi to sit up in bed and look around the dark bedroom.

"Who—" Levitosh started to say when the voice interrupted.

"Come. You must know your mission," the voice instructed in Hebrew.

The rabbi's eyes widened, seeing the large orb of diffused light, like an effulgent mist of luminescence within the large circle.

He seemed to move without effort, being conveyed through the darkness of the room to within the sphere.

He said nothing, muted into stunned silence by the profoundly unknown thing that now had his entire body encompassed so that he could make out nothing because of the brightness of the radiance that engulfed him.

When next the orb began to dissipate, he stood upon a hard surface. The vista began to take shape, it becoming obvious that he stood upon a mountainous area, his vantage overlooking a vast landscape below.

"Behold a New Earth, Jerham," the cavernous voice said.

A dazzling scene of a beautiful landscape beyond any he had seen or even imagined suddenly appeared across the entire, curved horizon before him.

"Do you understand, Jerham?" the voice said.

"No, I do not understand," the rabbi answered in Hebrew.

The scene before him changed to the lights of thousands of skyscrapers in glowing brightness across the vast expanse. The display filled his senses with powerful cerebral pulses of realization. This was the world to come. Hashem was making him know the future of a glorious Planet Earth.

"Behold, Jerham Levitosh." The voice spoke, and the horizon above the earth took on the form and shape of a human figure. The form grew until it stood high above the cities that were the New Earth.

"Behold your Mashiach," the voice said. "Mashiach is come."

Levitosh was finally able to say, "But…but what am I to do?"

The figure against the horizon suddenly grew gigantic, becoming a glowing human form so bright that it blinded Levitosh to the magnificence of the New Earth that had been before him.

"Israel must find its Mashiach. Hashem charges you and your council with this mission on Heaven's behalf. To do this in a timely manner is to assure Earth's peace and safety. Go and find your savior."

Jerham Levitosh continued to sit upright in bed. He looked around at the darkness. His eyes could not yet make out anything in the room. The light of the vision still pulsated within his retinas, like after walking from the bright sunlight into a darkened theater, blinding him to the reality he found himself surrounded in.

"Come stand before Hashem's emissary," the deep, cavernous, voice said in Hebrew from somewhere in the darkness of the room.

Levitosh glanced down at his wife, sleeping soundly, unaffected by the voice.

Had it been a dream that disrupted his sleep?

"Come. Stand before Hashem's emissary," the voice said again.

"What strange thing is this," Levitosh said almost under his breath, looking into the darkness but seeing nothing.

He seemed to instinctively know he must go into the

adjoining room. He did so, and was met by a shimmering light that appeared to lay down a pathway of illumination to the home's rearmost area.

When he stepped through the back patio French doors, the area he knew as the garden his wife attended so faithfully now was glowing with light. The light was coagulant, fog like, preventing him from distinguishing any feature that might be present within its blinding radiance.

He squinted to try to make out what he thought was a shape forming in the painful brightness. He fought to tamp down the fear rising within while he walked slowly toward what he could see now was a human-shaped figure. It was indistinguishable as to specific features. The voice again spoke: "Take your sandals off your feet, for the ground upon which you stand is holy ground."

Levitosh recognized the words; they were the ones given to Moses while he had been on the mountain of the Commandments.

He did as instructed, awestruck by the figure of brilliant light facing him.

"The time of Mashiach has come," the cavernous voice began while Levitosh gawked in amazement. "Israel's savior and king awaits his moment of revelation," the voice continued in Hebrew. "Say thus to the kibbutz *oh-LAHM hah* Council. Your council is charged with finding Mashiach, of then gathering with Israel's future warrior king for purposes that will be forthcoming from Hashem when all is come to fruition."

TEL AVIV, THE NEXT MORNING

"Rabbi Lubeka was most exercised."

Col. Geromme Rafke spoke in Hebrew the moment Morticai Kant entered his Maglan office complex. "He wouldn't confide in me," Rafke said with an amused hint of false irritation in his gruff voice. "Just wanted to speak directly with Maglan's chief the moment he arrives, was his order."

Kant said nothing, knowing his number-one adjutant's enjoyment over perceived intrigues that required top security that precluded his own involvement in any such discussion. There was nothing the Maglan head withheld from his top lieutenant.

"The prime minister also wants to talk," Rafke said, "but I've bumped the rabbi to the top."

"Curiosity getting the better of you, eh?" Kant looked at Rafke with a serious expression, one eyebrow slightly cocked upward.

"Sounded positively apocalyptic," Rafke said. "If as serious as the tone, it must take priority."

"Very well, then," his chief said, continuing the subtle levity while reaching to press the button on the intercom on his desk.

"Gundra, please get me Rabbi Lubeka," he said in English.

"He is on line 3," the secretary said after about thirty seconds.

"Morticai," the head of the *oh-LAHM hah* Council said excitedly, ignoring greeting protocols. "There has been a development...in the matter of these things involving the Mashiach. It is critical to Israel's immediate future."

"What development, Amir?" Kant said in Hebrew,

looking into the eyes of his adjutant, his own eyes widening a bit.

The rabbi's breathing was labored with excitement, and he launched into an explanation.

"Rabbi Levitosh has heard directly from Hashem's emissary. The time of Mashiach's arrival is at hand. The council has been commanded by Hashem to search out Mashiach, who is already among us."

When Lubeka continued the explanation without pausing, Kant broke in.

"You are going too fast, Amir. Am I to understand that your Rabbi Levitosh had a dream?"

"No! No! It was not a dream, but a vision," Lubeka said breathlessly. "He had a visitation from the emissary sent by Hashem on high—from the very God of Israel."

Kant was silent for several seconds, thinking on the revelation.

"Are you there, Morticai?" Lubeka's question was issued in a panicked voice.

"Yes, Amir. I am here. What should we make of this... visit from...on high?"

"It is obvious, Morticai! This means the time of the Mashiach is at hand. The Kingdom is about to come to be at a time that is very near!"

"The directive from on high is to search for the Mashiach? And what is your request from me?"

"You are the most capable investigative agency in existence. We must have your assistance in this search. Hashem, I believe, wants your people to search for our savior. Do you understand this?"

Again Kant was silent for several seconds before speaking. "Yes. I do understand what you are telling me. I have not received any message directly from Hashem, however."

"My appeal is proof to you that Hashem wants you to accomplish his blessed will. The council is depending on you and Maglan, Morticai. Can't you see this?"

"We serve at the will of the Knesset, Amir, at the behest of Israel's government. Seeking out the Mashiach's identity is something they would never assign to Maglan. However, as I told you and the council, I have experienced many seeming miraculous things. This greatly intrigues me—strangely so. I have sent Tyce Greyson, who wants to consult with a man, a spiritual man Greyson reveres as being very close to God. I await the result of that meeting."

"Morticai, if you don't do this, I fear what might take place on us—on you, personally."

"Are you trying to frighten the chief of Maglan?" Kant's voice had a humorous lilt. "Haven't you been made aware that we are among the fearless, the most formidable force within Mossad?"

The rabbi was silent on the other end.

"Come, come, Amir. I take your exhortation seriously. It's just that you must not twist my arm in such a school-yard way."

"I am sorry, Morticai. I just—"

"—I'm aware of why you are so passionate, my friend," Kant interrupted. "Let me think on it for a short time. I will get back when I have heard from my son-in-law."

"You think on it, Morticai. I shall be praying on it," the *oh-LAHM hah* Council head said.

RANDOLPH FAUST LOOKED around at the walls of his San Marcos, Texas, great room. The trips to the hospital for days at a time always made him appreciate the things of home. He wondered silently why the Lord didn't call him home. That would be the ultimate homecoming. The older he got, the more he looked for that trip home.

"Are you feeling up to talking with Mr. Greyson and his wife?" The nurse's cheerfully delivered words drew him from his thoughts of the afterlife.

"Yeah, Ellie, send them in."

Momentarily, Tyce and Essie stepped through the doorway, happy to see their old friend sitting in the wheelchair, the early morning light streaming from the window to his right, bathing him in warmth.

"It's wonderful having you two here," Faust said, motioning for them to be seated in the overstuffed chairs.

"Glad to be home, I bet," Tyce said, while Essie went to hug Faust before taking her chair.

After a minute or two of greetings, Faust's demeanor became more serious.

"Tell me, Tyce, what is your thinking on this matter of the visions you've experienced?"

"Well, they are, I would say, dreams, not visions."

"Yes, but they are very real, you've said. Is that correct?"

"Yes, sir. They are as vivid as if I'm awake and talking to you right now."

"Then I would say they are visions—dream-visions, I suppose," Faust said.

When the old man was silent for several seconds, Tyce said, "They are in my mind constantly...every day. I can't get away from seeing that same scene, that same face, while I watch the man, whom I believe to be Judas Iscariot, walk as if right through me."

Faust's brow wrinkled in thought, his eyes' slits betraying maximum concentration.

"Judas Iscariot because the scene looks like your preconceived idea of what the Last Supper looked like?"

"I suppose so, yes. What I remember seeing in the painting of the Last Supper. I guess that has some influence on the…dream-vision."

"It's much, much deeper than that. I just talked with your father, Essie. Morticai told me that one of the *oh-LAHM hah* Council's rabbis has, the rabbi believes, had a visit from an emissary from Heaven…from God."

"From God!" Tyce's raised voice made Faust smile.

"Yes. The council rabbi said the emissary instructed him to tell the council they are to search out the Mashiach…the Messiah. The Mashiach, he was told, is here, now, and Israel's redemption depends upon his being discovered."

"What is Abba to do? Why did they come to him?"

"Well, Essie, as Maglan is one of the world's top investigative bodies, Lubeka, the council's head, wants to enlist Morticai to find this Mashiach."

"Why does Israel have to search out their Messiah? Makes no sense," Tyce said. "If God is in it, why is there a problem with finding this Mashiach?"

Randolph Faust's expression changed a knowing smile preceding his words.

"Now that is an interesting question, my young friend. We must look into all that your question entails more deeply."

CHAPTER 5

JUST AFTER SUNSET, SOMEWHERE IN
MARYLAND

The black stretch limousines rolled one after
another into the spaces between the huge trees.
The ground between the massive trunks were well-
worn, the result of many such usages for parking among
the thick grove.

The big Cadillac, maneuvered by its dark-suited
driver, pulled into the spot reserved for the meeting's
oldest and highest-ranking member. The driver quickly
stepped from the limo and went to the rear door. When
he opened it, he reached to assist the elderly man, who
slowly and with effort, struggled from the seat and
stood. He used a cane while he shuffled toward several
dark-suited men, the driver assisting him by holding his
other arm.

When the two men joined the others awaiting them,
they all turned and walked farther into the now almost
totally darkened woods.

A glow of red hue appeared and cast a strange luminosity upon the men while they approached a stone façade, atop which sat a pyramid structure thirty feet high at its apex.

The large double doors of dark, weathered wood with metal rivets covering their surfaces swung slowly open when the group drew near. Hans Ingram stood just inside when the group, led by the elderly man and his driver/assistant, walked into the semi-darkened foyer.

"Good to see you made it," the old man said, speaking in the direction of Ingram in German-accented English. "We hope your…lady friend…can bear to be without you for an evening," he added in a chiding tone.

Ingram said nothing, looking around sheepishly with an uncomfortable, tight-lipped smile at the others. He walked with the group toward the innermost bowels of the semi-darkened edifice.

They arrived at a large chamber configured within walls that were in a circular arrangement. The area was illuminated by lighting that caused everything to glow with a crimson iridescence. There was blood-red, plush, theater-like seating in rows of complete circles surrounding a raised tabletop made of stone. The stone itself was also blood-red, framed by grooved stone conduits shaped like roof drains.

All took seats that encircled the table. Soft thumping, like a heartbeat, sounded once all had settled in. Ten minutes later, all eyes turned to the parting of curtains at one point along the wall. A stooped figure, accompanied by the limousine driver, emerged.

Hans Ingram watched the old man, draped in dark red velvet from his hooded head to his feet, as he shuffled to a raised platform at one end of the stone table.

With assistance of the man at his side, he sat in a large, high-backed chair—also of blood-red velvet.

One of the group stood in front of the man seated on the platform and turned to face outward from him. He held a book that required both hands to hold because of its width, and began reading from the volume: "All present have placed lives and spirits in the hand of destiny's child. Do all affirm?"

The group responded in unison, "All have pledged life and spirit to destiny's child. May it forever be."

The old man, with obvious effort, reached to take the book from the man holding it. He then raised the opened volume to just above his own head.

The heartbeat, thumping sound raised in volume while he spoke.

"Nothing of value to the world to come is of true value without sacrifice to the power and authority that is bringing it to fruition."

The gathered assembly replied in unison: "So must it be done."

All eyes looked to the left on the one side of the stone table, and to the right on the other side. A large, heavy velvet veil against the wall parted at the center. Two men, dressed in the red velour robes and partial hood like that worn by the old man holding the book pushed a draped cart they wheeled to the stone table.

A human figure, covered by similar cloth, lay on the cart's top. The men who wheeled the cart into the chamber carefully lifted the figure to the top of the stone tabletop. One of the men unveiled the human figure by removing the cloth, revealing the nude body of a young girl.

The old man lowered the spread book and read from it. "Blood of the youth gives life and power to the body that inherits the order he is building. Let the sacrifice be done. May the sacrifice be pleasing unto he whom we pledge to serve."

The gathered assembly replied: "So may it be."

Another figure, dressed like the ones who wheeled the cart, entered through the drape's opening. He carried a flat, wooden box in his outstretched hands. He came to a stop beside the stone table.

One of the men who had pushed the cart took the box from the man. The man opened the box and withdrew a large knife, its blade glinting red from the light illuminating the chamber.

The elderly head of the conclave closed his eyes and lifted his face toward the ceiling. He said, "We dedicate this sacrifice to you, our father, and to your son who now dwells among us. May his conquest be swift and forever."

TYCE TURNED from embracing his wife when the phone on the nightstand rang. He groaned with irritation while reaching to pick it up. He swung his feet to the carpeted floor when he heard Morticai Kant's voice.

"Sorry to call so early. I just realized that it is much earlier there," the Maglan chief said.

"Yeah, it's early," Tyce said. "What's up?"

"Did Dr. Faust tell you of the vision our Rabbi Levitosh has experienced?"

"Yes, sir. He said that the rabbi was instructed by God, Himself, to search out Israel's Messiah."

"Yes. That is the gist of the vision," Kant said.

There was silence on the line for several seconds

before Greyson spoke. "What do you think? Did he *really* hear from God?"

"That's a question for your Dr. Faust," Kant said. "'Beyond my pay grade,' as they say."

"You're bound to have had some thoughts."

"Strange things are moving through our times, like your own visions...like US authorities knowing you landed in Atlanta and subsequently taking you to FBI headquarters. Like doing whatever was done with the drugging. Times are indeed strange. We must be cautious as we move forward, but move forward we must."

"Well, I suppose this call is to let me know how we must...move forward."

"You are very perceptive," Kant said. "There will be further...contact...to instruct how we will proceed."

"When, who?"

"Not for this conversation, Tyce. You will know soon. Now, may I speak to my daughter?"

"Your dad wants to speak to you," Tyce said, handing Essie the phone.

"Yes, Abba?"

Her tone had a curious tone as she lay beside her husband.

"Sweetheart, you won't like me telling you this, but you will have to separate from Tyce for a time. We don't know where this...intrigue...will lead. Our people will fly you back here. I must secure your safety."

"And what about my husband? Doesn't he need his security assured as well?"

"You know the ways of Maglan, Essie. We take risks, but they are well-calculated risks."

"Then count me in as part of your calculus, Morticai. I'm staying with my husband."

~

LATER THAT MORNING, Randolph Faust didn't look as well as he did when they had arrived the day before, and Tyson and Essie had to fight with their emotions to keep from letting the old man know. But he wasn't fooled, and smiled weakly as he spoke.

"Don't worry. When you are this age, you have good days and you have bad days," he joked, trying to assuage their worry. "I don't think the Lord has my mansion ready just yet!"

"Thank you, Ellie," he said, taking pills given him by his caregiver. "But I wish He did have it ready at times," he continued after swallowing the medicine.

"Don't talk like that," Essie said, standing beside him and stooping to give him a hug.

"I don't know how much time is left to this old, earthen vessel, my young friends," he said patting Essie's hand. "But you two have been chosen to do some important things, and you must make the most of it."

When they didn't reply, the old man's expression changed from a smile to a frown of concentration.

"Tyce, I have always been one who is critical of those who gratuitously tell of dreams and visions, of words of knowledge, and such things. These stories too often have rung hollow in my spiritual ears."

Faust paused, his face taking on an even graver expression.

"But I, without a doubt, know God has spoken to me in the night. The dreams have been seared into my very soul. I don't know all there is in regard to their meaning or their ultimate purpose. But I do know they are to instruct you."

Faust shifted in the wheelchair, first eyeing Essie, then fixing his gaze upon her husband.

"I have always been against any sort of mind alteration. I believe it to be unbiblical—from the dark side. But I have been told in my spirit...in these night visions...that you, Tyce, must undergo a heavenly hypnosis. That is the very term that is, as I say, burned into my every lucid moment. You are, somehow, to use the human agency of hypnosis to get heavenly understanding."

Faust paused to study their faces, seeing they were hanging on his every word. "I have spoken to no one about my messages from above. These words are for you," he said to Tyce, then turned to Essie. "And to you, Essie, I must, I'm convicted, leave it to the Holy Spirit to provide understanding to you as you move forward in our Lord's service."

The old man's demeanor took on one of resolve, and he straightened a bit in the wheelchair.

"You are commissioned from above. You must not fail. The Lord will lead you, show you the next step."

CHAPTER 6

J et lag had taken its toll. Both Tyce and Essie felt the tug of sleep, but the final leg of the return to Israel from Rome, they were told, must be made without layover. Morticai Kant had insisted they get back to Tel Aviv as soon as possible.

As always with the Maglan chief, the message was couched in terms that could be fully understood only when Maglan deemed that understanding be given. Maglan, Morticai Kant determined, required a face-to-face explanation in this case.

When the G-650 sat down at the prescribed Maglan secretive location, three men sent to pick them up hurriedly placed the luggage in the gray SUV and drove swiftly into the darkening evening.

"Must this be done now, Papa?" Essie said into the phone while they rode toward Morticai's location. "Can we not do this after a night's rest?"

Tyce watched her blink and nod while she listened to her father on the other end.

"Very well. We'll see you shortly," she said finally, before turning to her husband.

"He said it cannot wait. The *oh-LAHM hah* Council wants to meet with you tomorrow. Morticai must talk with us tonight."

They were kept waiting for fifteen minutes after arrival at the secretive Maglan operations base. Kant emerged when the door opened.

"The prime minister called. Sorry to keep you waiting, sweetheart." He hugged Essie tightly, kissing her cheek, then grasped Tyce's hand and shook it vigorously.

"And the flight? Did you have a good trip?"

"Good as any," Tyce said, his fatigue causing shortness of patience.

"I am sorry for the urgency of this, but want to speak to you myself, rather than leave it to someone else. I must leave tonight for Washington."

He urged Essie to move to a chair by nudging her by her arm. Just before he was seated in front of them, Geromme Rafke stepped through the doorway. "Sorry, sir. The president is on the phone."

Kant started toward the door but stopped.

"Tell him I will return his call within the hour," he said to his adjutant, who left the room.

"I always think, when I hear such an announcement, that it was the previous president. This one…" With a wave of his hand and in a tone of irrelevance, he let the thought drop.

"What is this about, Papa?" Essie's tone betrayed her own fatigue.

"Rabbi Lubeka wants Tyce to meet with Dr. Mandell, at 9 o'clock tomorrow morning. He will arrange the session." Kant turned to speak directly to Tyce.

"Lubeka wants Mandell to probe a bit into your

recurring dreams or visions. Also, to, somehow I don't understand, give hypnotic suggestion for helping in your quest to know more about this Mashiach they believe you are commissioned by God to find."

Tyce said, again with impatience, "Like I told Randolph, or maybe told you, I don't understand. If this...this Mashiach...is sent by God, why must He be found through a human search?"

"It is because of your...unusual...personal history. That history is, as you must admit, strange indeed. And, the consensus—and that includes myself—seems to be, that you are the one to explore the matter, to find this person whom the council believes will be Israel's savior from great trouble predicted in the Hebrew Bible."

"But you have never been into the religion of the Jews," Essie said. "Are you now a believer in these...prophecies?"

"Something is changing in my thinking, daughter. Let's just leave it at that for now."

A MAGLAN LIEUTENANT negotiated the congested parking lot, threading the big Lincoln Navigator between rows of vehicles. The massive building shimmered in the early-morning sunlight, its mostly glass windowed façade almost blinding to look at as they approached its base.

He wasn't told why the burly driver was assigned to him. But his father-in-law wasn't prone to divulge reasons for doing what was done. The man was his chaperone...for how long? For as long as Morticai Kant prescribed.

"You can let me off..."

"No," the driver said emphatically. "I will escort you to Dr. Mandell's office, sir," he said, equally emphatic.

Several minutes later, the agent did just that, opening the door to the psychiatrist's office on the sixteenth floor. He allowed Tyce to precede him into the reception area.

"Good morning, Mr. Greyson." The young woman behind the tall receptionist barrier came to stand at the table.

"You don't need to fill out any paperwork," she said. "Dr. Mandell is expecting you."

Mandell stood straightening books against one wall when the two men entered the room.

"Mr. Greyson," he said, offering his hand.

"Theodore," he said, nodding in the direction of the agent.

"Is it set up?" the big Israeli said.

"Yes. The technicians spent several hours making sure all is in readiness," Mandell said.

"What has been…set up?" Tyce asked, looking around the room and seeing only a psychiatrist's office walls.

"The hypnosis will be conducted in conjunction with special technology to assist in unlocking things that inhibit subliminal possibilities," the psychiatrist said.

"And exactly what does that mean?"

"Agent Gesin here will set things up. You will see," Mandell answered.

The agent bent to retrieve the large attaché case he had taken from the SUV before going into the building. The psychiatrist opened a door, and the agent, carrying the case, walked in first.

"This is an area used for this technology, Tyce," the psychiatrist said.

The agent set the case near one wall while Mandell

walked to where the case had been placed and pushed a series of print plates attached there, causing the wall to come apart, unveiling yet another room.

The agent again preceded them and sat in a swivel chair in front of a control console that was alive with pinpoints of lights of different colors.

He reached for the attaché case and thumbed the lock mechanism until the proper number code had been reached. He popped open the case and from it removed a device of straps. Tyce quickly recognized it.

"A Stimulator," he said, his tone one of amazement.

"We knew you would recognize the instrumentality, Tyce," Mandell said. "Sorry to keep you in the dark."

"Am I to go through the Stimulator process like before?"

"This device is much different," Mandell said. "Although it looks quite similar, its capabilities for the user are far beyond the Stimulators' capabilities several years ago. We call it the SEER—an acronym, of course, that stands for 'senses-enhancing energy rush.'"

Memories of that time ran swiftly through his thoughts. The Stimulator device that caused his mind to move as if bodily into the meetings of the deep state's plotting to bring to fruition the one world order they were desperate to establish. The times that Michael, Heaven's agent, interacted in all of that intrigue, bringing about the result Heaven wanted. How could a device go beyond the Stimulator?

"Our purpose in this session is to attempt to unlock any...experience...your conscience cannot bring to the surface. The SEER will prompt you to reveal...that forgotten experience."

"Is that the only thing this...this thing can do? Seems

the Stimulator went far beyond that," Tyce said, looking over the control console.

The psychiatrist nodded understanding.

"Indeed, the Stimulator went far beyond the capability of helping someone recall their experience. The SEER also provides—for lack of a better word—video, as well as audio."

Tyce's look of puzzlement brought a slight laugh from Mandell, who pushed a console button, causing a large screen to emerge from the cabinet top.

"The SEER actually presents a picture...a video presentation, more or less, of what the subconscious thoughts are emitting. That is, we can see on screens such as this one what one is thinking."

"You're joking," Greyson said, unable to suppress his amazement.

"No. It isn't a joke, Tyce. With this device we can get visual representations of what one is thinking subconsciously. It is one of the most secretive of Israeli technologies. You are among the first, outside of Maglan, who have been given the knowledge of SEER technology."

"Why me?"

"Ah, my friend. Think for a moment. We are talking about the very substance of Jewish hope throughout the millennia. We are talking about Israel's Messiah!"

"I always thought that scientists didn't believe in things...things of a spiritual nature," Tyce said.

The psychiatrist studied Greyson's expression for several seconds before speaking. "Oh, my friend, we who are of the scientist community in Israel have learned much about...spiritual matters. And this instrument has been a catalyst for that learning."

"And I'm part of providing further...learning?"

"It is your demonstrated background in the extradimensional planes of existence that we seek to explore. We expect to know more about these dreams, these visions, you are experiencing.

"These experiences, and the others of similar nature that those within the *oh-LAHM hah* Council are experiencing, promise to yield quite interesting results when probed by the SEER."

"So that's all that's involved—just me wearing this SEER device?"

"Oh, no. I will first put you in a deep hypnotic state. There will be much preparation of the subconscious mind before we even apply the device."

The psychiatrist saw the look of concern. "I assure, Tyce. It will all be done safely. You will suffer no ill effects whatsoever."

"Can't be any worse than the snake bite on Patmos," Greyson said just under his breath.

"What?"

"Nothing," Tyce said, waving off Mandell's question. "Let's give it a try," he said, looking over again the lights and gizmos on the control board.

"Now, we will adjust the SEER. It will take a minute or so," the psychiatrist said, fidgeting with the straps of the instrument until it seemed to fit properly.

"Is that comfortable?"

"Yeah. It's comfortable. Is it turned on yet?"

"No, we first have to do the hypnosis. Then the SEER will take over, once you are…under."

"You will lie down here," the psychiatrist said, motioning for Tyce toward the pillow at the head of the padded board that looked to be his mental picture of the typical arrangement when he thought of the psychiatrist's couch.

Tyce stared at the tiled ceiling, the fear factor rising a bit as Mandell began the hypnotizing technique.

"You are tense. Just relax, Tyce. It is painless, and the session will be over before it's barely begun," Mandell said, completing the device's arrangement on his subject's head.

The psychiatrist's soft, mesmerizing tone began its work and Tyce soon felt the drowsiness give way to an altered state.

∼

"Now. That was not a terrible experience," the psychiatrist said lightly while removing the SEER.

"I don't remember any of it," Tyce said, swinging his legs to sit on the side of the couch. "Just a little woozy," he added, kneading his eyes and nose with his thumb and index finger.

"That's a common sensation," Mandell said. "It will quickly resolve."

"What next? What's my next part in all this? I have no memory of any of it."

"We will assess all that the SEER has extracted, analyze it, then bring you back to input information from our findings that will provide all needed to pursue your...commission."

"To find this...this Mashiach that the council and Maglan wants found?"

"Yes, this will greatly enhance your cognitive processes and your intuitive perspective," Mandell said.

"That doesn't sound very scientific," Tyce said.

"I assure that you will find the input by the SEER to be of significant enhancement."

"When will this second session take place?"

"The SEER is even now analyzing everything, putting all it learned into proper assignment. We should be ready for the next procedure within an hour, I should say," the psychiatrist said, helping Tyce to his feet by holding his forearm.

"There, your head will clear momentarily," he said, patting Tyce on the shoulder.

"What do you hope to learn from this?"

The psychiatrist paused several long seconds to consider Greyson's question. "To be honest," he said hesitatingly, "you are a special case, Tyce."

"Special? You mean kind of a weird, mental-patient case?"

Mandell laughed. "No, no. You are special because you have all of the...the history of the very unusual, the strange, experiences. The time on Patmos and after, the alternate world you experienced. We just don't know how all this history will play within the SEER's analysis, then input. You are unlike any of the previous subjects we have taken through the process."

Forty-seven minutes later, Theodore Gesin, monitoring the console, called to Mandell who sat talking with Tyce.

"The data is in," he said, prompting the psychiatrist to walk to the console where the agent sat. Tyce followed him, seeing a row of lights flashing in various colors.

"What about it?" he said. "What is the...data?"

"Nothing that is definitive in terms of what we can understand simply by listening or looking at the screen. Not at this point, at any rate," the psychiatrist said, looking at the coded marks and numbers spread across the big screen and moving across the bottom in a rapid scrawl.

"We will have all this data translated after it has been

input through the SEER...and run through your thought process," Mandell said.

"And there's nothing harmful...that will adversely affect...my brain function?"

"The technology has been tested for quite some time," the psychiatrist said, glancing up to see the look of concern on his subject's face. "We are confident that there are no adverse impositions to the subject's brain function. There's no need to worry."

"Then let's do it," Tyce said.

With the SEER device again in place, he lay his head back onto the pillow, and the psychiatrist began a slow count as part of the hypnotic process.

CHAPTER 7

"Okay, Tyce. The session is over and our work here is done for the moment."

The psychiatrist's voice began the process of unscrambling Tyce's thoughts, while Tyce struggled to sit on the side of the couch.

"How long—?" He couldn't complete the question.

"You were under for about an hour," Mandell said, helping him to sit straight on the couch. "Your mind will clear momentarily."

He sat still, staring quietly into nothingness for thirty seconds before speaking.

"Did you get the stuff you need?"

"We will again have to await information gathered by the SEER. But the things we need to evaluate all matters necessary are undoubtedly there, in the SEER Cloud. We will extract it and study it, and, of course, bring you in again to go over everything with us."

Twenty minutes later, Gesin herded the SUV toward the hotel at the center of Tel Aviv. He glanced at Tyce sitting next to him.

"How was that?" he said in Israeli-tinged English.

"I remember absolutely nothing," Tyce said, his head still a bit fuzzy. "The experience was nothing more than going to sleep, sleeping really deeply, then waking up with a hangover." The agent said nothing, watching the heavy traffic of mid-city.

"How did you get involved in the SEER project?"

Tyce's question caused the burly agent to again glance toward the journalist, then straighten his gaze again toward the traffic.

"It's interesting, my involvement." His smile broke into a chuckle. "I was perhaps the least likely of the candidates to be assigned."

"Oh? Why?"

Gesin was silent for several seconds before speaking. "I am a Christian."

"I thought you were Jewish," Tyce said.

"I'm still Jewish," the agent laughed. "Just not a congregant of Judaism any longer. I am a Messianic Jew —a believer in Jesus Christ."

Tyce was surprised and had to gather his now-reassembling thought process to grasp the revelation. The agent preempted Greyson's further conversation.

"We—we who are as I am, believers in Jesus as Messiah, are still few. But we are growing in numbers."

"And what is your thinking? Do you believe the Messiah is about to be discovered, or revealed?"

"And, may I ask before answering, what do you believe?" Gesin said. "You are in this project, as I understand, because of dreams, visions, and so forth. Dreams and visions that involve Israel's Messiah."

"That's what I'm searching out. There is something to the Messiah being among...in the world. But there still seems something not right."

"Something not kosher?" Gesin put in with a subdued laugh.

"Yes, something not kosher," Tyce agreed. "That is why I've agreed to become part of this search. I'm a journalist, and one with a rather strange background, most will agree. I'm more than curious. Compulsively so."

"Yes. I've heard about your part in the project involving the SEER...your background...your experiences in the—"

"Some say in madness," Tyce interrupted.

"No. I think not," the agent said. "In your *supernatural experiences*, I would say."

"You're kind. I've been accused of being a bit looney," Tyce said, sensing his and the agent's relationship warming.

Both sat quiet for several seconds, watching ahead the traffic become increasingly thick the farther they proceeded toward the city's center.

"So, how do you view this Messiah thing? I mean, why does He have to be sought out? If God wants Him to be the king of Israel and whatever else, why am I getting all these dreams and visions? Why am I searching for him? Shouldn't He make Himself known without human help?"

"The Mashiach will make Himself known, my friend. He will need no help. But I guess it's your...mission to..."

Tyce, watching the traffic surrounding them, listened intently but looked to the agent behind the wheel when Gesin stopped mid-sentence. Theodore Gesin was no longer there.

The SUV was moving slowly, as was the heavy traffic. It began to veer left into vehicles moving alongside. Tyce grabbed the steering wheel and struggled to throw his foot across the console and onto the brake. He managed to stop the SUV an instant before slamming into both the car on the left and the vehicle ahead, which had slowed because of traffic volume.

The sound of horns honking increased as all traffic seemed stopped on one of Tel Aviv's most heavily traveled thoroughfares.

Tyce looked again at the driver's side, seeing clothing rumpled on the seat behind the steering wheel. He reached to pick up the cloth. It was the clothes the agent had been wearing, the necktie still looped and knotted beneath the collar of the shirt—the shirt still within the suitcoat Gesin had been wearing. He tried to remove his foot from the brake and back across the console. His own shoe caught beneath and flipped the still-laced shoes that the agent had been wearing.

He opened the door and got out, looking up and down the congested street. All traffic was stopped, with other people milling outside their own vehicles.

Theodore Gesin had disappeared! The thought kept pounding at his now-throbbing brain. The Israeli agent was gone! Only his clothing remained!

Some sort of attack on Israel! Their enemies had assaulted with some unknown weapon! The agent had vanished! But he, himself, was untouched, unharmed. The attack had not affected him.

Whatever had happened, the effects were evident. Others standing outside their vehicles, like himself, seem stunned. Had others disappeared, too? Was that the reason for their obvious panicked reactions?

He reached back into the SUV and retrieved his phone. He started to call the number Maglan had provided. He thought then of Essie. Had the attack affected Essie? She would be with Israeli agents, her father protecting her. But, did the impact of the weaponry, or whatever caused the effects on the human body, cause them to—

He checked the newsfeeds on his phone but saw nothing about what was had just happened. He then fumbled with the device, trying to call the Maglan people. It wouldn't accept any number he tried. He then worked to find other information. Still nothing.

Sirens sounded in every direction—the low, eerie, moaning sounds of those not of the high-pitched police or emergency vehicles forewarning possible attack from Israel's many surrounding enemies.

MAGLAN HEADQUARTERS WAS in tumult when he finally arrived. The ride from several blocks over from the thoroughfare street where he left the SUV, too, was wild. He never would have been able to get the SUV from the blocked roadway. The fifty dollars he offered the emotionally upset man in American currency was too tempting for the driver to resist.

When he had the near-panicked driver let him out in front of the heavily guarded Mossad compound, he was met at the iron gates with a number of armed, uniformed troops. They were IDF regulars, whereas the gates were normally stationed with plainclothes men and women manning small guardhouses that were little more than booth-like structures for no more than two or three people who wielded only light firearms.

He had quickly produced identification provided long ago by his father-in-law and was permitted into the compound. But he wasn't allowed to walk the sidewalks to the Maglan building unaccompanied. Two IDF soldiers, one on either side of him, walked with him to the entrance of the building, leaving only when the door had been electronically unlocked and Tyce had been vouched for by those inside.

"Where's my wife?" Tyce's question made one of the otherwise job-focused people look up from her preoccupation.

"My wife?" Tyce repeated. "Essie Greyson—Essie Jorba. She is Director Kant's daughter."

"I will check," the woman said, picking up a phone. After a minute of conversation, she turned to Tyce. "She is in the building. I will take you to that area."

When they arrived, Essie ran to embrace her husband. "You are safe," she said, tears streaming from her eyes. "Thank God," she said in Hebrew.

"What's happened? Does your father know anything?"

"I really don't know, Tyce. I haven't talked with him except to learn that you were missing from the SUV and something happened to the agent assigned to you," Essie said.

"Yeah. Something happened okay. One second I was talking with him, the next second he was no longer there. He just...vanished, disappeared. All I found on the seat were the clothes he had been wearing."

"There are reports of many things like that," she said. "Papa said a number within Maglan have had this happen to them."

A man approached the pair as they stood talking. "Director Kant wants you to join him, Mrs. Greyson," the man said.

"Tyce is here now," Essie said. "He is coming with me."

"Very well. I presume you have credentials," the operative said, looking at Tyce suspiciously.

"He is my husband—Tyce Greyson," Essie said impatiently, starting to walk in the direction of the Maglan chief's office.

Activity inside the Maglan complex was as frenzied as that in all parts of the headquarters of the Israeli Defense force. Morticai Kant was busily engaged with several other men, their attention focused on a tabletop with lighted maps. One of the men told the Maglan chief that his daughter was there; Kant looked up to see them and came to them, taking Essie and Tyce by their elbows, leading them into his office.

"There is total chaos everywhere in Israel," Kant said, getting right to the point. His distress was obvious, and Essie saw it for the first time ever in her father's demeanor.

"Papa," she said with alarm. Then, in Hebrew, she asked, "Are you okay?"

"I don't think any of us are okay," he said, moving quickly to his desk to answer his ringing office line.

"Yes, Shemir," he said into the receiver in Hebrew, his voice continuing to reflect the distress that so disturbed his daughter. "I know about the children. This the most troubling matter. It has all of our nation in upheaval."

Essie and Tyce continued to watch the Maglan chief talk into the phone as he worked his way around the desk to sit in the chair.

"What's he saying?" Tyce's question to Essie received a delayed response.

"All of Israel is in turmoil. The children are all missing," she said, her own voice as pitched with anguish as her father's.

"Missing? The children are gone?"

"They have vanished in this...whatever has

happened," she said, continuing to listen to her father's words while he spoke to the caller.

Several minutes later, he slowly placed the receiver onto its base. He sat in silence, staring at the desktop. He then looked up at his daughter and Tyce.

"People across Israel are in panic." He now spoke in a calm, bewildered tone. "Women—mothers in particular —are in absolute panic. Their children have just…just disappeared."

One of the doors to Kant's office opened quickly. Geromme Rafke stepped through the opening and stood holding the doorknob without coming all the way into the room.

"Sir, we are getting signals that all nations of the Arab coalition are gathering in and around Damascus. Word is they have placed missiles near the city's interior. They are nuclear, as we have gathered recently, as you know."

The Israeli colonel spoke in Hebrew. The only word Tyce knew he heard for sure was the "nuclear."

At that moment, another phone line lit up on Kant's desk. It was red and glowing—the direct line between Kant and the Israeli prime minister.

"Yes, sir," Kant said after giving a hand gesture for his adjutant to stay in place while he took the prime minister's call.

"Understood, sir," the Maglan chief said in Hebrew. "We will provide precise coordinates. We have them ready at all times. The offensive placements are on the perimeter of Damascus."

Kant looked at his daughter, to Tyce, then to Rafke, who continued to stand stiffly, holding the door open.

"Yes, sir. It is my absolute opinion that Consuming Fire is the only option. We must strike within minutes to prevent the ordnance from launching."

He again let his eyes meet those of his daughter. Kant's eyes were almost ablaze, like she had seen on other occasions her father was determined to protect Israel.

"Yes, sir. It is time to strike," Kant said.

He listened, his expression portraying grim surprise while the prime minister spoke.

"I see. Yes. This is most troubling." He slowly placed the receiver on its base without saying "goodbye" to the Israeli prime minister.

He looked to the three others in the room. "You are witnessing history in the making," he said, his voice calm, but as determined as his countenance.

He said then in English, his brows raised, forehead wrinkling. "Children are missing throughout the world, not just in Israel. Even children not yet born are missing."

CHAPTER 8

Sirens screamed nearby and in the distance while Tyce and Essie made their way into the underground bunker beneath the huge Maglan annex a hundred meters from the headquarters building housing Maglan offices. The big IDF soldier with an AR-16 strapped to the back of his shoulder held the door open while Essie hurried through.

"Proceed to the stairs over there," he said in Hebrew, pointing quickly at an opening beneath a painted yellow and black shelter emblem.

A series of large rooms came into view as they descended to the lowest level of the stairwell.

"Come," another officer, an IDF colonel, said, motioning to Essie, followed by Tyce. "Here you will observe best," he said in broken English.

They entered, seeing the walls lined on every side by monitor screens, each alive with video.

"These are all intelligence video from drone reconnaissance," the colonel said with a proud tone in his voice. You will be able to see Israel dealing with her enemies during this strike."

The screens were alive with bird's-eye views of territory in all significant areas surrounding the Syrian city of Damascus. The videos honed in on the tops of buildings with large, flat roofs in particular.

"These," the colonel said, pointing to a couple of the screens, "are the buildings our intelligence tells us are holding areas for nuclear-capable ordnance. You will see shortly from these monitors, here," he pointed to other, larger screens, "our fighter bombers that will deal with these buildings."

Momentarily, the screens displayed the videos taken by the IDF Air Force jets while they unleashed a number of missiles that themselves had video cameras while they rocketed into the roofs. Other video then showed the destruction, the explosions continuing while drone coverage of the attack took over from the jet fighters' cameras.

"Chief Kant wanted to keep you fully abreast of these strikes. The objective is to…actually…avoid the nuclear option. We shall do all possible to avoid using our tactical nuclear capability."

Tyce watched the carnage erupting on every monitor. "Why are we allowed to see all this?" he asked.

"Morticai has always kept me informed in major actions," Essie said. "He has always placed me in safe shelters such as this and allowed me to watch on the monitors. Of course, there has never been such technology as all this," she waved her hand at the many monitors. "That's why I have the clearances," she said.

"But about me? I haven't got the clearances."

"You were put into the systems when we married.

You really didn't have the option of agreeing," she said lightly.

"That's good…I guess," he said, amazed at the tremendous level of destruction taking place on the screens.

Suddenly, a row of large, circular lights above several of the monitors flashed bright red, causing the officer to rush to a console against one wall and begin pushing buttons. He picked up a receiver and placed against his ear.

"Then Consuming Fire is now being implemented? Very well. All manned assets are on their way out of ground zero?"

The colonel got the answer he wanted, then turned to all but three of the largest monitors, which showed video from more than twenty miles distant from Damascus. All other monitors went black.

"Watch these," he said gesturing toward the large screens showing three different angles of the city. All screens suddenly were filled with brilliant light so bright that Tyce had to close his eyes for a moment.

The screens then began to lessen in brightness, and the scene in the distance became clear. A mushroom pillar of fire, glowing red, orange, and yellow began rising from what seconds before had been Damascus.

TYCE'S journalistic instincts were in overdrive. The reports of all that was going on in Israel, the United States, Europe, and particularly Russia more than fascinated him. His gut told him that things were at the tipping point upon which continuation of life itself on the fulcrum of balance had been altered.

He thought on these things while stuffing clothing, toiletries, and other items into the suitcases.

The Europeans were in full global-governance mode. The leadership of France, Italy, Spain, and others had condemned Israel's unleashing of the first nuclear detonation in military action since Hiroshima and Nagasaki in 1945. The US government was quiet on one side of the geopolitical spectrum, and in a rage on the other.

The right still supported the Jewish state while the left insanely ranted about how Israel must be condemned in the strongest terms.

Israel's support within the US was greatly diminished, the facts showed. Many who had been on their side in the American government and other crucial support areas had vanished in the inexplicable disappearance of millions across the planet.

And the children...all disappeared.

"Did you get Dr. Faust on the phone?" Essie's question pulled Tyce from his thoughts.

"No," he replied. "There's no answer. I've tried a number of times."

"What about his friends you know that have homes nearby?"

"I tried several. Most don't answer. Others just sound stunned because of what happened. They haven't checked on Randy. They have their own issues to contend with, I guess."

Essie remained silent, and Tyce could feel her eyes on him while he got back to the packing. He stopped and turned to her.

"What is it, Ess. What's wrong?"

"Nothing," she said, looking away.

"Come on, babe. I know something is on your mind,"

he said, pulling her into an embrace. "What's the matter?"

"There's something about this trip, Tyce. I…I can't explain. There's something—"

"It's about this disappearance," Tyce cut her off. "All the small children, the babies, and even unborn babies are missing. It's got everyone in the world in a panic."

"Yes, I know," Essie said. "But it's more than that. You being sent on a mission to Europe based on information, upon these strange recommendations taken from that SEER session. The way the Americans, the FBI did what they did, and you can't remember any of it. It puts you in danger, and Papa won't be able to see that you are protected once you leave Israel."

Tyce brushed his wife's lips with a kiss, then lifted her face with a finger beneath her chin.

"There's something to these visions, Ess. The rabbis say their own dreams and visions are…sent from the Almighty. They have been shown, they say, that I'm chosen to find out who Israel's Messiah is, that He is here now, and His presence is the key to Israel's future. They say that their dreams and visions somehow must be investigated because the location of Mashiach is key to peace and safety for the world."

"Do you believe that to be true?" Essie countered. "Do you think that finding Israel's Mashiach can save Israel… can save the world?"

"I don't for a minute believe that God has chosen me, of all people, to…to save the world…or Israel, for that matter. But I am having these visions…and they are driving me nuts. These rabbis are having the same kinds of dreams, or whatever they are. I've got to search all of this out."

"Exactly what are you supposed to do? What can you accomplish in Brussels?"

Tyce turned to continue placing things in the suitcase. "The results of the SEER analysis indicated that somewhere in my brain, my mind, I've been given an indication that the one who will be Israel's Messiah is among the Europeans gathering in Brussels."

"Did your mind divulge the name?"

"No. They told me... Dr. Mandell said that they had the image of the guy, but no name."

"How will you know? Did they present an image you could see?"

"No. For some reason, his face was obscured."

Tyce straightened from his packing chore and faced Essie, his expression one of confusion.

"It's really funny. The guy's image, his facial features, were the only thing blurred, so that I couldn't really see how he looked."

"Then how will you know him?"

"The one I have seen maybe twenty-five times in my —dreams, or nightmares, or visions, or whatever—are vivid in my memory. If it's him, I'll know him."

Essie studied her husband's face before asking, "Why doesn't that face of the visions you've had show when they do whatever the SEER does? Can't they get that image?"

"Again, no. Only certain things are recorded. That image of his face doesn't record."

There was silence for a moment while he resumed packing. Finally, Essie spoke, her voice tinged with a tremble worry.

"Tyce...do you think this thing, the disappearing, might be something to do with Bible prophecy?

Randolph talked about things he said would happen that would involve some sort of vanishing."

"The Rapture, yes. Randy believes a Rapture will take place before Christ's Second Coming. He said it will involve millions of people around the world."

Again there was silence, both reflecting upon what they remembered Randolph Faust telling him about his belief in how things would play out in God's prophetic plan.

"He said only...believers...would disappear, didn't he?"

Essie's hesitating question brought a slight ripple of chill up the back of Tyce's neck.

"Yeah, that's what he said," Tyce said, his own voice issuing the words in deliberate, detached nuance.

The apothegm, "That's just whistling past the grave-yard," quickly traversed his brain. This disappearing almost certainly was the prophetic event his biblically astute friend had been predicting for as long as he had known him. To dismiss it with false bravado was foolish at best and dangerous at worst.

Randolph Faust always had answers that were true; rather, the Bible and Randy's view of what it had to say was always proven true. The old man believed with all his heart that the scriptures were the very word of God. One thing sure: He and Essie were still here. They didn't disappear. The Bible had answers about what would come next. The assignment, with the government-granted cover of being a reporter for the Israel News Service would be valuable in his search. Tyce vowed he would put all his reportorial ability into searching out what that book had to say about things that would next come to pass.

～

"I'M GOING WITH HIM, MORTICAI."

His daughter's words were issued with a steely-eyed glare Morticai Kant was all too familiar with. It was the same as her mother's expression when she had reached the point that there was no room for debate. In spite of the tender feelings of remembrance, he maintained his own combative demeanor.

"You can't be with him on this trip, daughter. This is a time unlike any other. Do you realize the scope of what is happening?"

The tone of his lecture, issued in Hebrew, was stern. "We are literally at the point of nuclear war. The destruction of Damascus has the Russians preparing. Even I, the chief of Maglan, can't say for certain what will happen next.

"The whole world is in chaos. Every young child in the world has...has been taken by this event. Not even the pregnancies have survived. People around the globe are going crazy. It isn't safe."

Kant's tone became gentler as he went on. "I can't let you go, sweetheart," he said. "What kind of father would I be—considering especially that I am in charge of all of Israel's safety—to let the one I love most depart on such a dangerous and unknown mission?"

He saw Essie's eyes soften. Again, it was the same look her mother dissolved to when tactics were about to be changed. He dreaded the look. It meant he had lost control of the argument and was about to be defeated.

She spoke in English so her tenor and tone would make an even more profound impact, and he knew the victory was already hers. Her words were soft, imploring rather than demanding. "Daddy, I know how much you love me. And that is why you must let me go with my husband. I am to be with him. Remember, you gave me to him at the ceremony."

Ten hours later, the G-650 began the descent into the big Brussels airport, special permission having been granted for the flight.

All air traffic in the direction of Europe had been strictly curtailed. An eerie quiet had settled over the Mediterranean and beyond. The world of governmental officials—the diplomats who worked—were all wondering what came next.

Tyce let these and other things move swiftly through his mind while sitting beside Essie, who disrupted his introspection. "What are you thinking about? You've hardly spoken since we left Tel Aviv."

"I was thinking that no one, not even your father, has a clue of what's going on," Tyce said. "That is, nobody in governmental circles of the world. Probably nobody on earth much knows what's going on."

"What do you mean?" she asked.

"I mean that every believer in Christ...if Randy is right...is no longer here. No one knows what has happened that many of those who've now left the planet could have explained."

"There's no one who understood?"

"There are some who have a head knowledge of what the Bible says, but it's all religious postulation to them."

"Then who can explain to them? If there's nobody left here to explain, how will they know how to confront... deal with the crisis?"

"With thousands of crises, Ess. This is unlike anything that's ever happened. It must be explained to a world of...of unbelievers. And that's what I intend to do. I can sense that's what I'm here to do. To explore what's involved, then explain where all these people who left the planet have gone. To Christ, I suppose. At least I want to find out for myself."

"Are you a believer? If so, why are you still here?" Her questions were in a puzzling tone. "How can you understand the true meaning of all this, these unbelievable things that are taking place?"

"I've become a believer, Essie, at least a believer that what Randolph Faust's God has said in His word is coming to pass. I sense it's the reason I've been placed here by providence...at this time and place. I'm supposed to find out the truth of what's involved in all this, this prophetic...fulfillment...of Bible prophecy."

THEY WERE MET by a number of the Lokale Polizei when they walked down the expansive hallway. The German police force in charge of the Brussels airport blocked them from proceeding.

"You speak English?" one of the black-uniformed men asked gruffly.

"Yes, we both speak English," Tyce said.

"There is trouble ahead. You must wait for all to clear," the policeman said while his fellow officers blocked the way, explaining to other just-arriving people.

"What kind of trouble?" Tyce's reporter's cognitive process kicked in while he tried to get a better look at the melee taking place farther down the concourse.

"A person with a weapon kill many people," the policeman said. "All must stay until things have cleared."

While awaiting the police action to clear the scene, Tyce checked his phone for news. Every site he checked had only stories of the disappearances and the tremendous upheaval to societies around the world the occurrence had inflicted.

He saw it then, his brain at first unable to absorb the visual image it processed.

The man...it was the image of the man who had burned into his mind's eye over the months. It was the man with the black, flowing, swept-back hair. The olive-toned skin. The whitish, star-shaped, tattoo-like skin imperfection just above the left eyebrow.

There was no audio for the clip. He couldn't get audio! He cursed under his breath. He had to find out... had to know where, who, what... It was maddening for that moment, then the scene cut away and the image on his phone's screen changed to show crowds of rioters destroying and burning in a European city. He looked again, his mouth trying to verbalize his amazement.

"What's wrong, Tyce?" his wife said. She saw a look on his face she hadn't seen before. His countenance was completely changed—a mixture of amazement and fear.

"What's wrong?" she repeated, more insistent.

Tyce finally looked at her when the image he had seen changed yet again, this time to one of riots somewhere in Chicago. He was pale, as if he had seen a terrifying specter.

"It was him, Ess. It was the guy—"

"What guy?"

"The one I've had the visions of, the same guy."

"What was he doing?"

"Being interviewed. I couldn't hear what it was about, just saw he was being interviewed by a panel of journalists, or something."

"Are you sure?" Essie asked after several seconds of watching Tyce's expression return to normal.

"Oh, yes, I'm certain," he said, looking around, impatient to get out of the airport and on to whatever providence obviously had for him to accomplish.

~

IT WAS THE SAME EVERYWHERE. People were filled with rage. Mass shootings were no longer limited to large, lawless groups within big cities. No longer confined to rare mass killings from lone gunmen with mental issues or perverted ideas or radical political ideologies.

Arguments in neighborhoods in suburbs had exploded into killings virtually everywhere across the world. It was as if the entire world had lost its mind.

While he tried to somehow gather all the reports he had collected from the Internet and other sources, Tyce again tried to reach Randolph Faust in Texas.

The phone finally came alive when someone answered Faust's number.

"Hello," was the one-word answer, not the "Dr. Randolph Faust's residence" that his assistant had always responded when answering.

The voice was unfamiliar.

"I'm Dr. Faust's friend, calling from Brussels, Belgium. My name is Tyce Greyson. I'm trying to get in touch with Dr. Faust," Tyce said.

"I'm sorry, sir. I'm a deputy sheriff. I just happen to be here because I'm checking houses in the area to see who's missing. I'm afraid Dr. Faust is one of 'em."

"And there's no sign that he has been there?"

It was a stupid question, especially of a journalist of such experience and talent as his, he thought with an inward smirk.

"Well, sir, it's the strangest thing," the deputy said.

"It's like a lot of these houses we've been checking. There are some clothes we've found. It's just like…the clothes just dropped off them."

"What do you mean, 'just dropped off' them?"

"Well, sir… It's just as if they are in a pile right where the people were standing or sitting, or whatever. There are the outer clothes—you know, the shirts, pants, and so on. Then there are the inner clothes…the underwear and so forth. Even shoes still have socks in them."

Tyce took seconds to assess the deputy's description before asking, "What about Dr. Faust? What did you find in his home?"

"We found clothes in a pile like that in a wheelchair. Some more were piled nearby, like they just fell off somebody. Same situation as we've found all over the county," the deputy said.

When Tyce was silent, the deputy said, "It's the same here as the national news is reporting. All the kids…the small kids, and all babies are just…they are just gone."

The deputy's words came wrapped in stifled emotion. "It's the same with my grandkids," he said. "My grand-kids are missing."

Thirty-five minutes after the call with the deputy in Randolph Faust's home, Tyce watched the strange mixture of limousines and military vehicles marked with NATO insignias move smoothly and lumber heavily along the boulevard. There was hectic activity in every direction he looked while he tried to negotiate his way between parked and moving vehicles.

He stopped when he found enough space so that he would be out of the way of the foot traffic, set the attaché case on the concrete walkway, and checked his suitcoat inner pocket to retrieve the leather wallet.

Satisfied it was the credentials he had brought with

him from Tel Aviv, he placed the wallet inside the coat and walked again toward the entrance of the European Union Building a hundred meters ahead.

A sudden roar disrupted the noises of vehicular traffic as three NATO military jets soared above the twenty-story building, headed for their base somewhere in the distance.

He thought how this place dedicated to the establishment of peace, presumably, was pulsing with activity that seemed to have nothing less than war-making in its prospects. The diplomatic powers that be who resided within this edifice that sought a new world order full of peace and safety seemed to offer anything but peace and safety at this strange time since the disappearing of millions.

Tyce handed the credentials he had pulled from the wallet to the uniformed guard. The man looked it over carefully, then checked Tyce's face against the photo.

"Come here, please," the guard said, directing him to stand beneath a device that moved to a position just in front of his face.

"Very well, sir," he said with a British clip to his accent. "Here are your credentials."

The guard pointed to a set of escalators. "You may proceed to the next level. You will find elevators and the media chamber on floor ten."

Stepping off the elevator on the designated floor, he was met by several NATO troops in battle-ready uniforms, not the dress uniforms he had anticipated. They were there as part of the alert Brussels and the rest of the world now endured.

"Okay, Mr. Greyson," the soldier said, checking Tyce's stamped verification of the facial scan that had validated his right to be there. "You may proceed," the trooper said, standing aside and gesturing in the direction from which a speaker's voice was emanating.

For some reason, Tyce's thoughts went to Essie. The Israeli ambassador's wife had taken her instantly under her wing when they had gone to the Israeli Embassy. The wife of Ambassador Yadi Kershan assured him his "beautiful wife," as Kreisa Kershan had said, "will be very safe with me."

Still, there was a hint of something dark — a thought that troubled. No doubt the foreboding moment came as a result of the event the speaker was even now addressing while Tyce excused himself as he passed by the knees of those who sat listening.

He pulled a tiny earbud from the small console that separated his chair from the person seated to his left. He pressed a button marked with the word "English." The translation from German, the speaker's language, to English through the console's linguistic technology was clear and precise.

"Although the things we have witnessed over the past forty-eight hours have been, some might say, terrifying, let us create from it something world changing. Let us bring at last—using this crisis—an unprecedented world filled with peace, safety, and freedom for every citizen of a new earth that is not only possible, but absolutely accomplished."

Tyce scanned the vast chamber while he listened to the speaker eloquently describe the creation of the new world the disappearing of millions made possible. Was the face he had seen—the face of his dream-visions—somewhere in this room? If the man was to be Israel's Mashiach, he would be within this forum. At least, that was the opinion of the Kibbutz *oh-LAHM hah* Council, the reason they had sent him here under cover of acting as a reporter for Israel News Service.

If Israel's God had given him and the members of the council direct visions from the Almighty—as it seemed—the opportunity would, it was reasoned, be presented by the Deity to…to what? Why did Tyce Greyson have to find such an eternally powerful as Israel's Messiah? What could he do to influence the corridors of destiny by interacting with the one who would be Israel's Savior?

Yet the dreams were profoundly present in his every sleeping and waking moment—in the sleep and waking moments of the Kibbutz *oh-LAHM hah* Council…

"Soon will be the time for unveiling of a new world order!"

The German stood, a bit haughtily, Tyce thought, his jaw jutting. The look reminded him of the old black-and-white film of Benito Mussolini during World War II. Like El Deuchae of that long-ago time, the speaker stood silent, his chin lifted, while the applause arose to fill the chamber with a deafening roar. He stood in the pose until all cheering had settled to a muted rumble.

"And when it is thus unveiled, we will stand in awe of the creation we have ourselves constructed. The blueprint is even now being brought into the light of this new sunrise of humankind! And there is one ready to bring to fruition man's most glorious hour. Let us applaud his coming into the light, although this must yet be for a future moment of revelation!"

CHAPTER 9

"China has just attacked Taiwan. We are being threatened by the Islamic states. North Korea is said to be about to send nuclear missiles into Seoul. Pakistan is said to be set to release a nuclear strike upon India, and vice versa. The Americans seem helplessly in a state of collapse of some sort. Their military is denuded, as is much of their population in key places. This has apparently given these antagonists around the world the...the insane bravado or whatever to do things they were afraid to do before this...this disappearing. The United States policeman is no longer on the beat, and the evil nuclear-armed leaders of the world know it."

When the Maglan chief finished his assessment, the Israeli prime minister said after a long moment of thought. "We can't control the rest of the world, but we must control Israel's integrity. I shall immediately make sure our and the world's media know that any attack upon Israel will be met by the destruction of Mecca and Medina to begin with, if coming from an Islamic state.

Otherwise, we will directly attack the capital city of whatsoever nation-state attacks us."

Morticai Kant, looking up at several monitors displaying military actions from around various capital cities, said, "Very well, Mr. Prime Minister, Maglan will keep you apprised in every instance of every possible scenario."

When he shut off the top-secret transmission line, Kant swiveled in the chair to look at Geromme Rafke.

"See to it that every general is immediately in full Code Joel Red," he said, standing and walking toward the door leading to the War Room.

Essie jumped to consciousness when Tyce suddenly sat up in the bed beside her. The scant light coming from the window to Tyce's right framed his face in barely visible illumination. His eyes were wide, his mouth open as if awestruck by what he was seeing.

"Tyce! What's wrong?"

Her question didn't bring a response.

Essie grabbed his arm and shook him lightly. "Tyce? What is wrong with you?"

Her words made him blink, and his facial expression became normal again. He turned to look at her, his eyes still wide, but blinking.

"What is wrong, Tyce?"

"I really don't know, Ess. It was another vision…"

"The man with the scar?"

"No…no. It was of your father. He was talking to the prime minister. He was assessing the world's various nation-states. He was going over the tensions between many of the nuclear nation-states. China and Taiwan, Pakistan and India, North and South Korea, others…"

"A dream? Was it a dream? Just a nightmare or something?" Essie sat up, leaning to rub his shoulders and neck while he stared into the darkness, explaining.

"No, it was a vision. It was as if I was there in the room with them."

"With who besides Abba?"

"His chief of staff."

"Geromme Rafke?"

"Yeah, Colonel Rafke. He and your father were watching monitors, and Morticai was checking the monitors that were all filled with a lot of activity...military and things of that sort."

They sat with Essie continuing to massage Tyce's neck and shoulders. Then she broke the silent reflection both were processing. "What does it mean?"

"I guess it means that World War III is inevitable. I really don't know."

"Can you call Papa, ask him if the...the vision you had, has any...any basis in fact? Were he and Rafke really in that place doing those things?"

Both drifted into sleep, with Tyce agreeing to call the next day. When Tyce awoke again, he checked the clock on the bedside nightstand: 2:50 a.m. He stood from the bedside and looked at his sleeping wife before turning toward the French doors to the hotel balcony.

An urge he couldn't resist nudged him to open the doors and step to the 16th-floor patio.

The Brussels night was ablaze with the city's many points of light. But they all began to blur, then fade, until Tyce looked into darkness that seemed to move him more deeply into its thickness. His senses became oblivious to all but the warmth produced by the diffused light that expanded and brightened the darkness to merge with him and embrace him.

In front of him there came into view an object that

grew within the light until he could see that it was a book. The book grew until it was gigantic and he watched it slowly open. The thin pages began rippling in a strong breeze that blew into a stiff wind.

The pages blew apart and began turning until the wind stopped and the pages settled to display the book being opened to expose its pages. The open book again grew in size until it almost completely filled the vista directly in front of him.

It was a Bible—a gigantic Bible, Tyce's mesmerized brain analyzed.

His eyes were drawn to the page, as if forced to read the specific lines that stood out in relief he couldn't miss. A cavernous voice read the words in echoing reverberation:

"And I saw when the Lamb opened one of the seals, and I heard, as it were the noise of thunder, one of the four beasts saying, Come and see. And I saw, and behold a white horse: and he that sat on him had a bow; and a crown was given unto him: and he went forth conquering, and to conquer. And when he had opened the second seal, I heard the second beast say, Come and see. And there went out another horse that was red: and power was given to him that sat thereon to take peace from the earth, and that they should kill one another: and there was given unto him a great sword."

Tyce could do nothing but stand with his eyes affixed upon the words. The words resounded over and over within his reeling senses. Then, as the voice grew louder, the vision before him changed to that of a galloping white horse that looked as if it would leap out of the diffused light.

But the advancing horse and its rider remained within the radiance. The rider's face obscured as he seemed to urge the steed onward with powerful thighs that slammed into the horse's sides.

The horse and its rider then simply dissipated within the orb of scattered light, and a second horse and rider galloped closer and closer. The horse was a flaming red color, its nostrils flaring and collapsing with each powerful stride. The rider, like the previous, urged the crimson steed forward.

The scene changed yet again, the red body of a gigantic image of a flaming red horse morphing into a boiling mushroom-shaped cloud of reds and yellows that climbed rapidly and spread until it filled the entire sphere of the vision's expanse.

"I'M SORRY, Mr. Greyson. Chief Kant is in a meeting."

The accented answer from Morticai Kant's secretary caused Tyce to look at his wife. He knew the woman was instructed to *handle* any caller who wasn't a priority entity, thereby preserving the Maglan chief from being bogged down by unnecessary phone conversations throughout the busy days.

"She says he's in a meeting," Tyce said.

Essie took the phone from him.

"Sheera, this is Essie. If Morticai is available, please put him on the phone."

"One moment, Essie. I'll get him for you," the woman said.

Shortly, Kant spoke. "Daughter, are you okay?" he said in Hebrew.

"Yes, Abba. We are both doing fine. Tyce must speak to you. Here he is."

Tyce took the phone.

"Morticai, I've had a…another vision, and it involves you and a series of…nuclear-armed nations. You were talking with the prime minister. Then you gave the order to Colonel Rafke to implement Code Joel Red. That was what I saw and heard."

There was brief silence before Morticai spoke. "This code is an IDF secret of the most profound sort, Tyce. How did you learn of it?"

"I just told you. I had a vision. I saw and heard you give it to Rafke following a conversation you had with the prime minister."

Again, silence.

"I've had no such conversation," the Maglan chief said, finally. "It is true that there are numerous hot spots with nuclear-armed nations. But the prime minister and I have not yet spoken with regard to the…possibilities this portends."

"It was as real as you and I talking now, Morticai. What do you think it means?"

"I can't discuss these matters any further, but I will consider this some sort of forewarning from…from Providence. I will do so because of your knowledge of our code. This is a most highly guarded matter. And now it must be altered."

"Sorry. But I thought I should fill you in. You sent me here, upon the council's request. I thought it important enough to let you know."

"Yes. You did well to…fill me in. No harm done. We appreciate your action, Tyce. Now, please put my daughter on the phone."

"Yes, Papa," Essie said after being handed the receiver.

"Essie, things are looking very dark. Tyce's vision just adds to our assessment—my assessment—of things. His vision, his premonition might indeed be legitimate. I want you to be safe—as safe as possible under these growingly problematic circumstances."

"What do you want of me, Papa?"

"I want you to stay near the Brussels headquarters. I know there are absolutely secure underground facilities there to protect you. Do not stray far from those shelters. Now, please put your husband back on the line."

She returned the phone to Tyce. "Tyce here, sir."

"Tyce, take care of my little girl. I'm counting on you. Now, was there anything else that you wished to speak to me about?"

"Before I saw the things going on about the nuclear-armed countries and the code, and so forth, I saw a gigantic Bible being opened."

"A Bible? A Christian Bible?"

"Yes. It grew in size, and wind blew its pages open to a specific page. It was in the book of Revelation."

"What prophecy?"

"About the riders on the horses—the first verses of chapter 6 of Revelation."

"What is the prophecy?"

"The first rider came riding onto the scene…"

"The scene? Did you see it happening?"

"Yes, I read the words. And after that, I heard a voice that sounded like thunder. As it spoke, the scene appeared as in a large orb of light—diffused light, like a fog that has a bright light in the middle. The riders came riding. First the rider on the white horse, then the second horse, the red horse. They just galloped toward me and then each just…disappeared from the sphere of light."

"And the vision of the riders—what do you think it means?"

"I'm not sure. I know that the rider on the first horse,

the white horse, is thought by some to be Antichrist. The second rider on the red horse is supposed to represent world war—"

"And what about the third and fourth riders?" Kant interrupted.

"They didn't appear. Only the first two."

"Let me know if you have further visions. Meantime, take care of my daughter."

TYCE STRAINED to remember the prophetic scriptures, the ones Randolph Faust had tried to explain all those times when they were together.

They wouldn't come easily.

He knew the ultimate outcome. *Armageddon*. But getting there—that was the course he sought to extract from within his troubled thoughts. What would come next. What to expect next.

They were there, somewhere in the neuron-to-neuron synapses, but they couldn't be pulled to the front of his remembrance. The scriptures held the answers to what it all meant, to where it was all headed.

He watched the television screen while he researched. It was the same message—or generally the same. The corporate media, whether broadcast or through cyberspace of the world, no matter the language, called the catastrophe some kind of cosmic disturbance. A growing number claimed it was an alien invasion that had stolen all children and even the millions of adults for some sinister experimentation. Others thought the disappearances involved people being taken to reeducate them—to inculcate them in the way they should act and react as good citizens of the planet, thus to improve peace among the peoples of the universe.

Tyce longed to talk with his friend. Randolph Faust would have the answers. He wished he had paid more attention when they had talked, had taken more to heart what his friend had said about a coming time when believers would be called into...into the clouds.

Maybe he could find the verses—the specific mention in the Bible of clouds and people being removed from earth to the clouds. A Google search brought him to a scriptural reference he jumped to via a link to an online Bible.

He silently read the scripture he found:

1 Thessalonians 4:16 For the Lord himself shall descend from heaven with a shout, with the voice of the archangel, and with the trump of God: and the dead in Christ shall rise first: 4:17 Then we which are alive and remain shall be caught up together with them in the clouds, to meet the Lord in the air: and so shall we ever be with the Lord.

Tyce sat back in the desk chair, his thoughts going back to his time spent with his friend. He recalled the passage Randolph had gone over while they talked about things involving Bible prophecy that might be wrapped within his visions of the scene that was, in their minds, the Last Supper.

But there was more. More about this disappearing catastrophe. Other verses. Maybe he could find other references via Google. He looked again at where he had found the clouds reference. Yes. Other references were mentioned about the Rapture, and he quickly jumped to one of the links.

He again read silently:

> *1 Corinthians 15:5 Behold, I shew you a mystery; We shall not all sleep, but we shall all be changed, 15:52 In a moment, in the twinkling of an eye, at the last trump: for the trumpet shall sound, and the dead shall be raised incorruptible, and we shall be changed.*

He remembered going through this and other passages with Randy. He had paid so little attention! But he did remember...it was crystal clear that the scriptures indicated that only believers would be involved in this "change" in the "twinkling of an eye." All others would be left behind to face—what? The worst time in human history, Randy had said. From the lips of the Lord Jesus Christ. He remembered the old man saying that then, following the Rapture, the disappearing, it would be a time of horror on planet earth liking nothing that had ever had been, or would ever again be. This Jesus himself had prophesied.

The catastrophe from the world's perspective would be a glorious time of going Heavenward for believers. Yes. That was what he and his friend had talked about during those times when Tyce had tried to make sense of the dreams.

He typed in the search box the words "Jesus saying the time will be the worst that ever was or ever will be again," and found the following:

> *Matthew 24:21 For then shall be great tribulation, such as was not since the beginning of the world to this time, no, nor ever shall be.*

It was then as if he could hear the voice of his friend. He remembered the words he heard often when talking with Randy about the Bible: "Always, always, when looking at biblical passages, look at context. Context is everything. The context will eventually make clear meaning. Always, it's context."

Tyce again read the prophecy.

Matthew 24:21 For then shall be great tribulation, such as was not since the beginning of the world to this time, no, nor ever shall be.

He scanned the page. What is the context? What is the meaning of this dire warning, issued by Christ, himself?

He read quickly.

24:15 When ye therefore shall see the abomination of desolation, spoken of by Daniel the prophet, stand in the holy place, (whoso readeth, let him understand:) 24:16 Then let them which be in Judaea flee into the mountains: 24:17 Let him which is on the housetop not come down to take any thing out of his house: 24:18 Neither let him which is in the field return back to take his clothes. 24:19 And woe unto them that are with child, and to them that give suck in those days! 24:20 But pray ye that your flight be not in the winter, neither on the sabbath day: 24:21 For then shall be great tribulation, such as was not since the beginning of the world to this time, no, nor ever shall be.

When Tyce read the words "the abomination of desolation," his eyes went to the note along the side of the screen about that verse:

The abomination of desolation is in reference to Antichrist. This is the "prince that shall come" of Daniel 9: 26. He is the one that makes desolate, that brings

God's Wrath like a flood upon all rebels of Daniel's seventieth week.

He remembered Randy's words when they discussed Bible prophecy. "The Antichrist will come as a peacemaker. But he will be a false maker of false peace. Daniel is the book that gives the prophecy."

Tyce couldn't recall the chapter and verse, but he looked again at the note and saw "Daniel 9: 26–27." That is where it could be found.

He quickly clicked that link, scrolling down until he came to the verses:

Daniel 9:26 And after threescore and two weeks shall Messiah be cut off, but not for himself: and the people of the prince that shall come shall destroy the city and the sanctuary; and the end thereof shall be with a flood, and unto the end of the war desolations are determined. 9:27 And he shall confirm the covenant with many for one week: and in the midst of the week he shall cause the sacrifice and the oblation to cease, and for the overspreading of abominations he shall make it desolate, even until the consummation, and that determined shall be poured upon the desolate.

Tyce studied the monitor, his mind racing through recollections of his time with his friend in conversation about these very matters. He again looked at the book of Matthew.

The *abomination of desolation.* This *prince that shall come will confirm a covenant for one week.*

He recalled that Randy said a week is a week of years

in Bible prophecy terms, at least concerning the reference in the book of Daniel.

> This prince that shall come will confirm a covenant for
> seven years.
> He will be the abomination of desolation.

The words ran swiftly through his reeling brain. He read again from a note in the margin of the screen.

> The prince that shall come is the same wicked person as
> the first beast of Revelation the thirteenth chapter.

Tyce continued his research until he found what he was looking for. He read the words in a whisper:

Revelation 13:1 And I stood upon the sand of the sea, and saw a beast rise up out of the sea, having seven heads and ten horns, and upon his horns ten crowns, and upon his heads the name of blasphemy. 13:2 And the beast which I saw was like unto a leopard, and his feet were as the feet of a bear, and his mouth as the mouth of a lion: and the dragon gave him his power, and his seat, and great authority.

His vision suddenly darkened, the overwhelming emotion flooding his brain, his senses taking him back to the Patmos cave, to the snake wrapped around his hand, to the vision of the serpent creature raising from the Mediterranean shore far beneath the cave where John had received the Revelation.

CHAPTER 10

"You were staring at the computer screen, Tyce. I couldn't get your attention no matter how hard I tried."

Essie stood in front of her husband, whose pupils continued to be dilated. Finally, she saw him slowly return to full consciousness.

"What happened? You were in a trance."

"I…I don't know. I was reading from the Bible." He gestured toward the laptop screen.

"The Bible?"

"Yes. I was reading, and the remembrances came flooding back, Ess. I was reliving that time in Patmos."

"The serpent bite and those visions?"

"Yes. I was looking into what the prophets said about what will happen near the time of Christ's return."

Essie studied Tyce's face, reaching to feel his forehead and cheeks for fever.

"Do you believe, then, that what is in that book is true? Do you believe it tells what is to come?"

"Yes. This…vanishing. It was…something supernatural, not some space-alien invasion or cosmic burp like they're trying to feed us."

"And what does this have to do with what we're doing here in Brussels—with von Lucis?"

Tyce looked away, trying to himself grasp and answer the question.

"I don't know, Ess. I honestly don't know."

Neither spoke while they let the question simmer.

Essie said, finally, "The council...do you think it's time to see if they can offer something, some thoughts, on what is happening with these things you're seeing?"

"I know it has something to do with a covenant," Tyce said, standing and walking near the window to peer into the late Brussels afternoon.

"What covenant?" his wife said, walking to his side and embracing him, resting her face against his arm.

"The scripture in that book," he said, pointing to the words on the computer screen.

"Does it say something about a covenant? What kind of a covenant?"

"I don't exactly know. But it has something to do with the worst time in human history. A time that's yet to have happened on the planet. A time that's coming."

Tyce turned to wrap his arms around Essie and hold her to his chest.

"This disappearance, all the children taken...it's set in motion the final fulfillment of what's in that book. This...prince. The Bible calls him 'the prince that shall come.' He is to confirm some sort of covenant. And that will cause seven years of Hell on earth. It will lead to Christ's Second Coming."

Essie strained to look upward into her husband's. "This...prince. Is he Israel's Messiah? Who is he?"

"That's what I'm researching. That's what I was doing

when I read that part of Revelation, where it talks about the beast that comes out of the sea. That's the vision I had on Patmos those years ago, after that snake bit me on the hand. I saw a tremendous, monstrous beast rise out of the Aegean—just like John described in the Revelation."

"This beast," Essie said, "what does it have to do with this prince?"

"They are one and the same, according to what I remember Randy telling me. What I remember from that coma I was in after the snake bite. The beast vision was symbolic of this prince, according to the notes in the Bible."

"Then he can't be good for Israel."

"No, sweetheart. He will definitely not be good for Israel."

IF ONLY RANDOLPH FAUST were available to talk with. There was so much that Tyce needed to know.

He anticipated the speeches he would have to sit through on this dreary day in Brussels. The rain pelted against the window of the van that carried him and others toward the European Union Headquarters Building near the city's airport.

His thoughts drifted from those times with Randy and discussions of things involving Bible prophecy to discussions he had had the night before with Amir Lubeka.

The rabbi and Tyce's own thinking just didn't seem to connect. The Kibbutz *oh-LAHM hah* Council still insisted the man of their mutual vision was the long-awaited Mashiach. Despite Tyce's own misgivings about

114

the vision being about Israel's Savior-King, Lubeka insisted the council's almost total consensus meant the visions were from Hashem.

Whatever was involved with the Last Supper scene he and those in the council were experiencing, no matter the strange submergence into cerebral dissonance involving the Patmos vision upon the Aegean beach and the beast from the deep, the most profound matter at hand was the vanishing of millions across the world.

The immense thing to consider was that this cataclysm completely other prophetic possibilities fade into insignificance. And he didn't have anyone who understood the things at hand. There were no Randolph Fausts with whom to discuss the true nature of the calamity that had just happened.

All who might have understood were gone. Taken. It was not the lies being perpetrated by the globalist press that explained the vanishing, it was the prophetic event he and Randy had talked about. It was the Rapture. It was the removal from earth to...to the clouds of Heaven...to the presence of Jesus Christ.

And now the world was in for what that same Jesus had forewarned would be the worst time in all of human history.

All the world now was panicked. They had witnessed the disappearing of every small child, of every infant, of even the fetuses in the wombs of their mothers. But if they knew—truly knew—the things that the Savior of the world, Jesus Christ, forewarned, there would be panic far beyond what they were enduring at present.

The fear of nuclear exchanges was nothing compared to what Christ forewarned. Maglan, in all its anticipatory intelligence, had not a clue. Tyce, himself, didn't have a clue. But the nagging, gut-wrenching gnawing was there. He knew things to come would soon storm upon the world in a rage never before experienced.

Yet he was here, in Brussels, heading for the EU headquarters. He had a mission, a commission, to—what? He was far from certain.

But, from the moment of the snake bite in that Patmos cave, he knew it was from on high. The commission was real. No matter what, he would follow it through to wherever it led. He had no choice.

The search for Israel's Mashiach—Messiah. This was his commission. Or, at least the scene from the Rembrandt-like depiction of the Last Supper he witnessed over and over again in the almost-debilitating night visions were at the heart of the commission from on high. That was what he had come to believe. The man who left the supper, the one with the white scar that looked like a small star, the one that must have been Judas Iscariot—this was the central character of his Heaven-appointed search.

Yet the rabbinic council, Lubeka and the others, insisted the man was their *Mashiach*.

The rain intensified, the water gushing down the windshield in such profusion the wipers couldn't keep up. The driver of the van assigned to transport him and other journalists from the hotel cursed, slamming the palms of his hands against the steering wheel.

A roadblock somewhere ahead halted all traffic. The frustrated driver looked around to see if he could take the vehicle into the lane beside them.

They heard, then, the siren and saw the flashing red and blue lights of an escort in the lead of a group of stretch limousines. They watched as the procession behind the car with the lights flashing moved slowly past where they sat.

Even the cars being escorted had to stop, as they paused before moving again toward the EU head-quarters.

Tyce looked at the limo that was paused next to his window. His eyes met those of a man whose features were at first obscured by the rain on Tyce's window and on the man's window in the rearmost seat of the stretch limo.

The man had thick, black hair, swept back. His skin was dark. Above his left eyebrow was a whitish, star-shaped scar.

Tyce's senses became electric. It was the man—the man of the visions! It was the same man, without the beard. It was him!

The man turned to look straight ahead, then back at Greyson. A thick, blackened pane of glass began to rise within the limo's door until it completely blacked out the man's features.

The limousine moved ahead behind its escort.

IT TOOK MORE than a half-hour for the van to reach the portico, each vehicle having to pause beneath the shel-tered covering to let their passengers step onto the concrete disembarking area.

Tyce was desperate to see the man. Now he was certain that the person he and the council searched for was part of the meetings held within the European head-quarters.

Tyce checked his phone to make sure the battery power was full. He double-checked to assure there were enough computer bytes to film all he wished to film. He had to get photos of the man. He had to send them to Lubeka and the others.

While he looked at the device, he saw Essie had sent a text message.

"Morticai wants you to call."

He typed in, "Will do when I can find time and place. Very hectic here now."

As he stood in line with a number of other journalists, each having to show credentials and have them stamped, he searched the crowd milling within the large chamber. He wanted to see the object of his search, the man whose features burned in his mind's eye. He knew he would not find him in the mob that moved about within this large room. But he had to find him, get his photo to send to the rabbis.

"Your papers, sir," the voice of the young woman said in English.

Tyce produced a small, leather portfolio. She looked it over, stamped it, and handed it back.

He saw him then, the man he had seen across the rain-drenched expanse. It was the man of his visions and the ones reported by the rabbis.

The man was among several other men who cleared the crowd so he could easily pass.

Tyce raised his phone at arm's length above the heads of those between himself and the subject he wished to photograph.

The distance was too far for a clear picture, but maybe there could be technological work on the photo that could bring things into much better focus.

He checked the image on the device. Yes. It was clear enough that, with work by the Israeli Maglan technologists it might be useful. He would spend his time trying to get better shots. Obviously the man was a participant, a speaker or something.

Tyce was excited. He had seen this subject many times in visions. It all had some obvious prophetic meaning, and now it seemed to be coming to fruition. The commission from on high was a thing that had been born that day on Patmos.

Tyce caused irritation to two who stood speaking in French to his left as he tried to get free of the mob surrounding the pass-validation point.

He ignored their frowns and words of anger, pushing past them and toward the point where the man and his escorts had moved just seconds earlier. He must find the man, get more—better—photos.

He saw the group, then. Passing through a doorway to the left of the main entrance to the chamber where the speaking would take place.

Tyce finally manipulated past the crowd and reached for the door handle; the door was locked.

Frustrated, he slapped the door and looked around the gathering of the many people milling about.

What to do now? Tyce started to turn, his journalist's optimism rising, thinking that he would find other opportunities.

As he pressed against the door to turn, he felt it give way. Someone was opening it, and he looked into the darkness of the area beyond.

There was no one in the opening. The door had somehow opened when he had lightly pushed on it. Light scantly illuminated the area when he entered. The door seemed to close on its own behind him.

He glanced around to get a full understanding of his surroundings. Just a small room with a set of steps, no more than ten, that led to a higher area.

When he reached the top of the steps, he saw an elevator framed within the wall to the right. He started to reach for the "UP" button, but before he could touch it, the doors slid apart.

There was no one within the conveyance. An eerie sensation traversed his spine while he stared into the semi-darkness of the elevator.

His ambivalence about entering wasn't strong enough to prevent his compulsion to enter. It was as if an unseen force suctioned him forward. Once inside, he had the thought to quickly step back out, but before he could, the door slid shut and the carriage began its rapid upward movement.

Surreal ambience swirled about his senses, the strange purple and muted blue and red lights within the enclosure, making him think that he was floating rather than being swept upward by the G-force acting on his body.

The remembrance was deja vu from his time in Patmos; he had experienced similar sensations back then when he was swept upward in elevators. Always there were significant, strangely inflicted repercussions from those times. This feeling was the same, and he braced himself with resolve to find what came next.

Despite the speed of the elevator, it suddenly came to a stop, but without so much as a minor jolt. He looked at the lights above the door and the floor number: "13." In spite of his weird circumstances, seeing that number struck him as funny. The unlucky, iconic, occultic number "13."

He exited the elevator cautiously, looking up and down the hallway; it was completely empty of human traffic. His senses seemed to force him to the left, and he moved as quietly as possible toward…he had no idea toward what.

He stopped at a door along the immensely long hallway. There were sounds coming from beyond the door. As he reached to touch the ornate brass doorknob, his hand lost all sensation. It seemed to pass through the knob.

He tried to feel along the face of the metal door, but like with the knob, his hand passed through. His mind then went into hyperdrive, his normal thought process superseded by something irrational. His only thought was to walk through the door.

The next moment, he found himself inside a room that pulsed with the familiar purple, blue, and red lighting that illuminated the darkened area slightly. His hyper sense of being on a quest, of mission, drove him forward, and he walked through the next door of solid metal, finding himself, finally, standing among a gathering of men in business attire, their attention centered upon an individual—the man whose face he had seen in the limousine window.

They didn't see him. They had no idea he was there, his having just walked through walls.

The man with the dark-hued skin faced the others and him. Yet there was no indication that he recognized that Tyce stood watching.

Was it an effect—a technological rather than a supernatural effect? Was it the SEER device causing the surreality? Was it the SEER's influence upon his mind? Or was he really here, looking at the person who had for so long bedeviled his dreams?

The man spoke to the group, but Tyce couldn't hear the words. There were no sounds coming from the room. It was as if he, himself, was completely deaf.

He had to get photos! He could at least get pictures to show the council, to show Morticai Kant that he had been here, and had found the man that the council believed to be their Messiah.

He focused the camera on the group from behind, then specifically upon the man himself. He adjusted the device to get his face in close-up, framing the left side of his face, making sure the scar above the right eye was captured.

Then, as he was taking various shots of the group and the man in front of them, the men all stood from their chairs. They all then knelt, while the object of their apparent worship stood before them, his face at first stoic, then breaking into a slight smile.

Tyce snapped several shots, and while did so, the scene before him faded. The next instant, he found himself standing before the door—the one he had at first tried to open. He stood blinking, then reached to grasp the doorknob. This time it was solid, and it was locked.

He backed away, stunned at all that had just transpired...or at least he thought it had transpired.

The camera!

He checked the camera for the photos he had shot. He looked several times, before realizing that there were no photos to be found—not even the one taken while he had been in the limousine.

"YOU SAW HIM?"

Rabbi Amir Lubeka was excited while posing the question.

"You took photographs?"

"Yes...I mean no. What I mean is, I took photographs

of the guy...and the group, but they didn't take. When I looked at my phone, there were no photos to be found."

Lubeka silently assessed what Tyce was telling him. "Why do you think the photographs did not take?"

"I can't tell you. The whole thing was...was like I was there, but I wasn't, at the same time."

"Oh? What are you saying? Not there? How could you then take photographs?"

"I mean it was a surreal experience. It was as if it was...supernatural, not something that was natural. I actually...walked through doors. Not through open doorways, but through the doors themselves."

"This was Hashem's permitting you to do so, Tyce. What did you hear? What was said?"

"That's another thing. There was absolute silence. I couldn't hear anything; I could just see everything."

"It was nonetheless a miracle of Hashem. Only he could perform such miracles."

"Yeah, well, whoever got me in there didn't let those pictures come through," Tyce said, his irritation with not getting the photos to show up on his phone still nagging at him.

"But you were there...in the same room with the Mashiach. This is the permissive will of Hashem. This is a most wondrous development."

Tyce was silent for several seconds, the remembrance striking. Then he said, "These men that the Mashiach stood in front of, they got up from their chairs. They got on their knees before him, like they were worshiping him."

"And did you see him, following this miracle? Did you follow up and find him among the delegates?" Lubeka asked, ignoring the remembrance Tyce thought most important.

"No. He didn't show up at any of the sessions today. But I will continue to follow the proceedings. I'll check all of the sessions, but there is no indication on any of the order of sessions they are handing out. There is no indication of anybody I would consider as describing this guy."

"Very well," Lubeka said with patient resolve. "Hashem will reveal Mashiach when he is ready to do so."

When the line between Jerusalem and Brussels was broken, Essie moved next to her husband.

"Tyce… What is this about? Is this something that they have programmed within you? Is it the technology as you have though possible? Or is it from…from like the time of the cave…of the serpent bite…of the visions on that island?"

He held her against his body, feeling her warmth, breathing in her fragrant femininity. Hers was the only presence that felt real with all that was happening.

Essie was his one comfort in this life. If this was indeed the time Randolf Faust had talked about with him --the time that Christ described as the worst in all of human history— it would soon turn out to be a time that would make his life…and the life of this girl he loved so deeply, hell on earth.

HE READ everything he could find online that dealt with Bible prophecy, the Rapture, and things to come following the event he knew beyond any doubt occurred on that strange, catastrophic day—that had happened in one stupefying second of time, just as the Apostle Paul foretold.

He reread it now, one of many times he had reread it, trying to make sense of it all.

He began to read silently in Paul's first letter to the Thessalonians the apostle might have written from a prison during one of his many troubled travels:

1 Thessalonians 15:51 Behold, I shew you a mystery; We shall not all sleep, but we shall all be changed, 15:52 In a moment, in the twinkling of an eye, at the last trump: for the trumpet shall sound, and the dead shall be raised incorruptible, and we shall be changed.

He let the words sink into his thought process, then again silently turned to Paul's first letter to the Corinthians:

1 Corinthians 4:16 For the Lord himself shall descend from heaven with a shout, with the voice of the archangel, and with the trump of God: and the dead in Christ shall rise first: 4:17 Then we which are alive and remain shall be caught up together with them in the clouds, to meet the Lord in the air: and so shall we ever be with the Lord.

Tyce looked again into the darkness of the Brussels night. *The dead...*the thoughts tugged at his memory of when he and Randolph Faust had talked. The times when the old man had told him that the dead would one day be raised to life. Was this what Paul was foretelling? Was it the Rapture? Was it the disappearing event that would also bring resurrection from the dead? Tyce looked at the words again:

...and the dead in Christ shall rise first: 4:17 Then we which are alive and remain shall be caught up together with them in

the clouds, to meet the Lord in the air...

If the dead were to be resurrected when the others disappeared, there would be proof. The proof would be in corpses missing from their coffins, their graves.

The epiphany struck and caused renewed vigor within Tyce's oppression-fatigued mind, instantly bringing him from the depression.

He went to the search engine again and typed in: "Documents on the dead resurrecting at the time of Rapture." Looking through a number of the documents the search pulled up, he clicked on the one that looked most promising for his purpose, scrolled to find specific information, and began reading.

This passage presents the truth of the Rapture of the Church. What lessons can we learn from Paul's writing? They certainly include the following:

1. Spiritual ignorance is not complimented in the Word of God. By paying attention to the sure word of prophecy that God has given us in His Word, we can become knowledgeable, rather than ignorant Christians.
2. Christians who have died are with the Lord, and they will be brought by Christ to the Rapture. Many Christians are concerned about the location and state of mind of departed loved ones even today. The scriptures reassure us that they are "safe in the arms of Jesus" and are tenderly cared for by Him.
3. Christ will descend from Heaven to meet believers in the air. Notice that the Lord Jesus does not return the entire distance to this

world but, rather, awaits that rendezvous in the air and will catch us up to that point of greeting and reunion. We can, therefore, suggest that this moment of tender reunion will not be observed by the people of earth. Indeed, even their observation would profane so holy an occasion.

4. The Rapture will be the occasion of the resurrection of believers. One of the cardinal doctrines of the Christian faith is that of the resurrection of the body. This resurrection for believers will be on the identical occasion of the Rapture, at which time the bodies of Christians, glorified, will be reunited with their spirits that have been in the presence of Jesus Christ.

5. The resurrected dead at this time, like their Lord on His occasion of resurrection following His crucifixion and burial, will explode in powerful resurrection light as Christ calls them from their graves.

Tyce sat back in the hotel desk chair. The revelation provided by the document gave direction to his convoluting thoughts.

The proof that this was indeed the Rapture event he and Randy had discussed was the disappearing event that had turned his world and the rest of the world upside down. The proof was there—in the graves of the believers. If the bodies…had exploded in resurrection light, as the writer said…

But he was in Belgium, not in the United States. Getting to the truth he wanted would have to wait until he returned to America.

CHAPTER 11

"Although there have been a number of threats of nuclear nature, there have not been, since the destruction of Damascus, any nuclear arms unleashed."

The British broadcaster's voice gave the news while Tyce sat awaiting Morticai Kant's phone call. Essie placed a freshly made cup of coffee on the little table beside his chair.

"Thanks," he said, reaching for the chiming cell after using the remote to turn down the TV.

"Tyce," the familiar voice of the Maglan chief said gruffly.

"Yes. It's me."

"My MGO—Maglan Operative—will be by in a few minutes to encrypt our communication. Are you prepared to talk?"

"Yes, sir. I believe so."

"Good. His name is Walik Geersin—one of our top guys in Europe. You don't need to do anything, make any special arrangements. Geersin will do it all with the technology."

"Yes, sir," Tyce said.

"Is Essie okay?"

"Yes, sir. You want to talk to her?"

"No…no time. I've got to get back to business," Kant said. "Tell her I'll speak to her soon."

Tyce glanced over at his wife, whose expression hadn't changed.

"She heard. She's okay with that."

"Love you, sweetheart," Kant said, knowing the phone was on speaker.

"Love you, Abba," she responded.

"Geersin is at your door now. Please open the door."

Tyce walked to open the door as instructed, seeing a short man dressed in an athletic jumpsuit. Geersin glanced at Tyce and, without acknowledging him, walked past him, gave a quick look in Essie's direction, then set the case he was carrying next to Tyce's laptop.

"Let me speak to Walik," the Maglan chief said.

When Tyce handed him the phone, the little man brushed it aside, instead reaching into the case he had brought with him. He retrieved a hand-held device, walked into the bathroom, and closed the door. He emerged in five minutes, the same non-communicative expression on his face while he fidgeted with the case and its contents.

Finally, he spoke. He instructed Tyce on use of the device, careful to make sure he understood what he could do and should not do with it.

He pushed a small lever from right to left on the base of the instrument.

"Now you are encrypted," he said. "You may talk to Chief…"

Tyce spoke into the device, still bemused at the man's instructions and demeanor.

"Okay, Chief, I'm on with you. We are encrypted," he said, causing Essie to stifle a laugh.

"Sorry about all this, Tyce, but these are strange times, as you know."

Tyce said nothing, awaiting Kant's questions.

"Tell me about your look into things. Anything out of the ordinary?"

Tyce told him all that had happened: seeing the man in the limo, following him all the way to the secret area on the thirteenth floor, realizing it was the man in his visions, passing through doors.

He especially relayed how the men who looked to be leaders or officials had knelt before the man the Kibbutz *oh-LAHM hah* Council believed to be their Mashiach, and how he believed the disappearing to be the biblically prophesied Rapture of believers in Christ.

When Tyce was finished, Kant spoke.

"And what do you think? How do you conflate this mysterious man these men seemed to worship with this…disappearance of believers in Jesus?"

"The Rapture is something Randolph talked about," Tyce said. "He said that after the disappearance, the Rapture, many strange things would be happening.

"He said there would be leaders who would bring in a time of Tribulation. In particular, he said, there would be a man who would be the worst dictator of all history. I've read what the Bible says about the time following the Rapture."

"And you think this person of your vision is somehow connected to this evil man predicted to bring this great time of trouble?"

Tyce paused to form his thoughts in a way that wouldn't sound like one wracked by paranoia from all he had been through.

"Morticai, you said we were in strange times…"

He awaited the Maglan chief's acknowledgment.

"Yes. That's what I said."

"Well, there is one way to prove that this…this truly was or was not the Rapture."

"And it is a strange…proof…we will need to validate this…Rapture?"

"No stranger than anything else going on," Tyce said. "Do you want to hear it?"

"Of course."

"The Bible says that when the Rapture takes place, believers will go to Christ, who calls them into the clouds. All who are alive at the time, the implication is, will vanish from the planet. They will just vanish—exactly like has happened."

"Yes. Thus far I understand," Kant said.

"But the Bible also says that all believers who have died since Christ's crucifixion, burial, and resurrection, will also be called into the clouds to be with Christ. These will, like Christ, be resurrected to life to join all who have disappeared. They will all then go to Heaven with Christ."

"And the proof is in the crypts…the graves…the coffins," Kant said.

"You got it," Tyce said.

Again there was silence on Kant's end of the transmission.

Finally, Tyce broke the silence. "What do you think?"

"Trying to think of Christians I know who have died lately," the Maglan chief said, matter-of-factly.

Tyce looked over at Essie, who smiled knowingly of her father's analytical mind. He was genuinely thinking on all that had been discussed. He was trying to think of Christians he knew who died recently.

"We will look into the matter," he said. "Meantime, keep trying to learn of things as the council has requested." The call ended and Geersin packed up and left with the encryption device.

~

THE NEXT MORNING, Tyce stuffed the few things he thought he would need for the day of listening to the EU and other diplomatic types, then kissed Essie at the doorway. She broke away from him to go back into the room to answer her chiming cell, and indicated it was her friend at the Israeli Embassy she had plans with that day. She blew him a kiss with a wave of her fingertips as Tyce left.

The drive was in contrast to the previous day. A bright, blue sky had taken the place of the dark gray clouds of yesterday. Tyce thought of how the day's brightness gave false optimism about hiding the evil pall that hung over the things of the European Union headquarters building several blocks ahead.

The world was figuratively, and in some cases literally, ablaze with rumors of wars and wars that threatened nuclear conflagration if the leaderships in the building couldn't resolve the issues they faced. The call for peace and security rang loudly throughout the chamber during the sessions. But there seemed no peacemakers—at least not to this point.

Tyce watched the crowds walking the expansive sidewalks, many choosing to walk to the building rather than risk getting caught in the thick vehicular traffic that inevitably clogged this main artery. But the roadway ahead looked relatively clear this early morning. He should make the morning session with plenty of time to spare.

He watched as the van in which he and six other men were riding came to the intersection of a wide street that ran east to west. The stoplight turned red and the van halted.

Out of the corner of his eye, Tyce saw a large, black van pull just ahead on his left side. It then turned right, directly in front of the vehicle, blocking his driver's way forward.

The sliding panel on the black van slid open and he saw a tripod, with a mounted gun barrel pointing toward the van's front.

"No...!" Tyce heard the driver scream. He heard the loud chatter of machine gun fire, and the inside of the van seemed to explode with violence. Again and again the machine gun fire raked the front of the van.

Tyce unbuckled his seatbelt and tried to lie flat on the floorboard.

Still the gun chattered. He heard the thumping of the rounds, and he felt the splatter of flesh and blood splash and soak his clothing. He endured the fire for what seemed an eternity, expecting at any moment the searing pain of metal ripping into his body.

At last, he heard the assaulting vehicle's tires screeching as it sped from in front of his own decimated van, and he heard groans coming from a couple of the men. He checked himself. He was totally covered with blood, flesh...brain matter.

But there were no injuries, no wounds he could find.

He moved to try to help those around him. Only one man was still moving. The man took his last breath as Tyce looked into his wide eyes, seeing the mouth of the dying man expel blood with his final breath.

The vehicle sat smoking, and the smoke made him dive from the row of seats for the door, over a dead man to his right. He landed on the sidewalk, his knees and elbow feeling the impact—shooting sharp pains throughout where the flesh had torn from the contact.

Suddenly the van erupted in flames; the full tank of petrol had ignited. Tyce got to his feet and limped farther from the flames, finally collapsing onto the grass at a safe distance.

Several pedestrians on their way to the EU building hurried to him, asking questions in French.

"English," was all he could manage.

"Yes. I was asking what happened," one of them said, bending to look him over.

"I…I really don't know. There was gunfire," Tyce said, continuing to check himself out.

"How many are in the vehicle?"

The question made him look to the blaze shooting high, black smoke curling upward.

"My God," he said, finally realizing what had happened. He had escaped death…but how? All were dead but him.

"I don't know. Six or seven of us, I guess," he said, while the man slightly squeezed one arm, lifting it a few inches to look at his suitcoat that covered his side.

"You don't seem to have any injuries," the man said. "You say there was gunfire?"

"Yes they riddled the van. I…I don't know how I wasn't hit…"

"Well, there's certainly no one alive in there," the man said. "Do you think you're hurt?"

"No, except for the knee and elbow when I jumped from the van onto the sidewalk."

"Then let's get you to a car so they can take you to a

health center," the man said, turning to look toward the crowd that stood at some distance gawking.

"Thanks. But I have people who will come get me. They'll get me to a doctor if needed."

The man helped Tyce to his feet, watching a couple of uniformed men approaching.

They spoke in French. The man helping Tyce informed them that he spoke only English.

"You were in that burning vehicle?" One of the policemen questioned while he looked suspiciously into his eyes.

"Yes. I'm the only one to make it out," Tyce said, now shaking uncontrollably from the trauma.

"We must ask you to accompany us to our headquarters," the officer said. "We must find the reason for this accident."

"It was no accident. It was an attack," Tyce said.

He sat less than a half hour later beside the gray, metal desk at the Brussels Capital Ixelles police headquarters. He awaited the interview while dabbing at his knee with a tissue. His thoughts ran over and over the shooting that had killed all but him.

His remembrance compounded the agonizing sounds, sights, and smells of the van's interior while the machine gun's rounds had ripped into all the men around him.

His agony again called up the time in DC when he had sat at a red light...the car beside him at the stop light...the dark window rolling down and the Uzi pointed directly at him. He remembered seeing the hand and finger pulling the trigger. But nothing happened. There had been no fire...the car had sped away.

This time, the gun fired—seemingly endlessly. All around him were hit. But not a scratch on himself…

His thoughts were interrupted by a woman's voice.

"You are…Tyce Greyson?" The woman said in French-accented English.

"Yes," he nodded, continuing to mop at the knee below his raised pants leg.

"Oh, you are wounded. We must tend to that."

She beckoned to someone behind her. She spoke in French, and a young woman hurried through a doorway as instructed.

"We will take care of this, Mr. Greyson."

"It's just a scrape from when I hit the sidewalk," he said.

"And this was your only injury?"

"Well, that and my elbow." He pulled his shirtsleeve up to show her the gravel-peppered abrasion.

"Yes…we will treat this also."

The young woman soon returned and swabbed both Tyce's knee and elbow, then she bandaged the wounds.

"Thanks much," Tyce said, smiling his gratitude to the girl, who nodded back.

"Now. Please recount for me precisely how this attack occurred," the policewoman instructed.

"We had stopped at an intersection when a dark van pulled beside us. The van then moved forward and cut directly in front of our vehicle before we could move forward.

"The van door slid open, and there was a tripod-mounted machine gun pointed at us. It began firing and kept firing… Until…"

"And you are the lone survivor?"

Tyce shook his head *yes*.

"We have been informed, Mr. Greyson, that you are

here in Brussels on assignment by a Jewish council…the Kibbutz *oh-LAHM hah* Council. Is that correct?"

Tyce's surprise at her knowledge brought an expression that made the woman frown in concentration.

"You seem surprised that we know this. Your… mission for this council isn't a secret, is it?"

"No. I just didn't think anyone would be interested in why I'm here in Brussels."

She hesitated, looking at the sheath of papers in her hands.

"We have quickly gone through the information on all the victims that were in your vehicle. We are trying to understand why there would be an assault on you and your fellow passengers," she said finally. "With this… catastrophe we are facing," she said, placing the pages on the desk, "we are on high alert for any possibilities."

"Possibilities?" Tyce said, letting his pants leg drop over the bandaged knee and sitting back in the chair.

"The disappearance of people from all over the city has our capabilities stretched, as you might imagine. We are expected to investigate."

Tyce thought how the complaints of this Belgian police officer was no different than those of cops in DC or in any other place around the world. She was complaining without outright doing so, trying to express frustration over why people couldn't understand the overwhelming job they faced—the impossibility involved in trying to look into the individual cases of missing people.

Tyce said nothing in response, while the woman shuffled the pages nervously before looking to him.

"So we have to concentrate on the more intense matters…like this mass killing."

"Understood. Any way I can help…?"

She again examined the papers in front of her. "Information from INTERPOL presents rather interesting things about you, Mr. Greyson."

"Oh? Like what?"

"You are married to the daughter of one of the Israeli government's top clandestine services leaders."

"Yes. There's nothing...clandestine...about that," he said lightly, bringing a slight smile to the woman's face.

"Yes, but we see that both you and she have top-secret security clearance for the Israeli Defense Force. That is a rather clandestine matter, wouldn't you say?"

"So you think me having security clearance...might be the reason for this attack?"

"We must investigate everything, Mr. Greyson. And yours is the highest profile of any of the men killed in that attack. Therefore, we must look into your situation very closely."

Again Tyce sat in silence. He would let her lead in trying to find his reasons for being in Brussels.

"So, is your only reason for being here at this time to report on things the EU people plan to do about this global catastrophe?"

"There is no reason I can think of why anyone would want to...take me out," Tyce said.

"But that didn't answer my question, Tyce," the officer said, the use of his first name, he thought, an effort to loosen his reserve against giving full disclosure.

"May I ask your name?" Tyce said.

"Claudine Laroque...Inspector Claudine Laroque ," she said looking at him with a curious expression.

"Well, Claudine, I've been assigned by the council you mention to check into finding a person they believe to be their Mashiach." She stiffened and sat straighter, her face a mask of not understanding.

Tyce waited her out, inwardly amused that she doubtless was searching through her brain to get the meaning of his words.

"Oh? It is some sort of a religious matter, not to just investigate what the EU and the others plan to do about this calamity?"

"No. I'm here to search for their Mashiach," Tyce repeated.

Inspector Laroque was silent, obviously not wanting to be ignorant of matters involved in his revelation.

Tyce said nothing further, still waiting her out.

Finally, she said, "This...Match—"

"Mashiach," he corrected.

"This Mashiach...exactly who or what is this?"

"The Mashiach is the one the council believes to be Israel's prophesied Messiah," Tyce answered matter-of-factly.

"Oh. It is a man, I presume?"

"The Mashiach is or will be...a male. Yes."

"And this is a part of Israel's...prophecy?"

"Yes."

"And, do you believe there is such a man? Here in Brussels?"

"I don't know, Claudine," Tyce said. "That's why I'm here—to look into their belief."

"Their belief?"

"Their belief that Mashiach is present and is a part of the activities of these leaders here in these EU meetings."

Again there was a prolonged silence, the woman's eyes shifting back and forth and shuffling the pages, indicating that she was struggling to form a cogent line of questioning.

"What...what is the importance of discovering this

Mashiach? Is this important to Israel in some way? Does it have something to do with Israel's defense?"

Tyce sensed a note of irony. The woman had, without having any idea, hit the proverbial nail on the head.

"The only thing I'm aware of is that the council, the Jewish religious leaders, want to bring Mashiach to realize that he must act on behalf of Israel in ways to fulfill his role as Messiah."

"So, this is a strange, religious matter—some sort of supernatural matter?"

"Well, I don't know how strange it is, considering the circumstances all around us at this very moment," Tyce said.

"You mean the vanishing of people around the world?"

"Exactly. Can you think of anything more strange? Doesn't it smack of something…supernatural?"

"And, do you believe Mashiach being here at this time has something to do with this disappearance?"

"Well, maybe my investigation will answer your question. I just don't know."

Tyce spoke again when she seemed unable to form a question.

"Let me ask you, Claudine. Can you think of any reason such a supernatural matter, if that's what it is, could induce an attack on me? And if so, why am I the only one who survived the attack?"

She still sat quietly, and he moved to put her at ease.

"All I can say is that there are things in all of this that go beyond explanation. Every child on the planet, apparently, has vanished—even unborn babies. Every infant, every young child, and even older ones. They are all gone. Can you imagine the toll that's taking on the world's psychology? And that doesn't take into account all the other things going on. The almost certainty of nuclear war…"

Tyce saw the woman's eyes fill with tears and spill on to her cheeks.

"Sorry," he said. "Didn't mean to upset you."

"It is okay," she said while dabbing at the tears. "I have sisters, both of whom have lost children. Another friend lost a baby…she was pregnant. The baby just disappeared from within her. She had a terrible time both physically and mentally with the loss. It took a terrible toll on her body. And we have had to prevent suicide on several occasions…"

A uniformed woman came near and spoke in French to Tyce's interviewer, who replied to her, then turned back to him.

"Someone is here for you, Tyce. We are finished. I have your phone number, so you are free to go. Likely we will need to speak with you in getting these things cleared."

Tyce sensed in the woman's demeanor a need for more explanation about all they had discussed, and it made him want to give her a comforting hug. He did not; rather, he said, "I hope things turn out well for you and your family, Claudine."

She nodded a tearful thanks, unable to speak.

"HE MUST HAVE MORE security than this, Morticai," Tyce heard his wife's demand when he walked into the Israeli Embassy office. "It is a miracle he wasn't killed like the others."

He saw the intensity in Essie's green eyes while she spoke with her father.

"Yes, well, please get some people to accompany him, Papa," she said, turning back and forth with one arm tucked tightly beneath the elbow of the arm that held the phone to her ear.

Finally, with the conversation completed, she embraced Tyce. A tear of emotion rolled down her cheek.

"You must never go there alone again," she instructed. "This must never happen again."

She held him tightly and he felt her shudder.

"It's okay, sweetheart. I'm okay," he said, returning the embrace.

A door opened, and Israeli Ambassador Benjamin Knape walked into the room.

"Ah...Tyce!" The tall diplomat reached out his right hand to take that offered by Tyce.

"We are not certain that the assault was specifically directed at you," he said while moving around to the chair behind his desk. "But we are proceeding with the supposition that it was. We will no longer make assumptions. You will have accompaniment at all times while in Brussels."

"Thanks. I'm not so sure it's a bad idea," Tyce said, trying to sound less than overly concerned.

"Thank you, Mr. Ambassador," Essie said, her tone much more appreciative.

"These...murderous rampages are happening within cities around the globe," the ambassador said. "Violence has broken out across the world, is the report we are getting. It's as if people no longer have a governing conscience."

Knape's attention was drawn to one of his office doors when it opened and a woman stood in the doorway.

"Yes?"

"Ambassador," the woman said in Hebrew, "the Israeli office in Tel Aviv is calling for Mr. Greyson."

"It's for you, Tyce," Essie said before the Ambassador could interpret for him.

"The phone is in there?" Tyce pointed to the direction of the opened door.

"Yes," Knape said. "You will have a secure line."

Moments later, Tyce was handed the receiver in a small anteroom. The woman shut the door behind her.

"Tyce," the familiar voice said. "There are things happening that are somewhat out of control. We must take measures…"

"What's happened, Morticai?"

"There is great trouble in the United States. The government is in shambles as a result of this vanishing. Economic problems are apparently overwhelming, in that the system is collapsing, and there's nothing anyone can do."

Tyce was silent, assessing Kant's words.

"The military, too, is completely in disarray. The most powerful military in history, and its vast nuclear arsenal…it's a disaster awaiting…"

"Disaster? What do you mean?"

"There are those who are even now plotting how to… steal America's arsenal in some way. And there seems little chance of Israel being able to influence the situation. We cannot intervene. We have been shut out of proceedings as to how to help reestablish control and to again bring order to things internationally."

Again, Tyce couldn't think to offer thoughts; it was all he could to do try to assess what he was hearing.

"The Western alliance—NATO and all who oppose the forces of Russia, China, the diabolist states—is dependent on the American nuclear umbrella. This has been shredded."

"And Israel? Where do you stand in this…this shredding?" Tyce said, not knowing how else to respond.

"We have significant nuclear deterrent—more than anyone knows. But there might easily be underestimation by the Islamic lunatics that we were depending upon American nuclear forces to deter them. Of course, with the present administration—I should say, the administration that held power before the complete US diminishing—didn't have our interest in mind. That president was as against us, as are most nations of the UN."

"This is all terrifying, Morticai. I'm glad you're being open with me. But, of course, I have to ask *why*. Why me? Why are you divulging this most secretive, apocalyptic matter to me, a lowly journalist?"

"Tyce, it's your…call it *paranormal* abilities. They are demonstrable capabilities. That's why the Kibbutz *oh-LAHM hah* Council chose you to search for their Mashiach. That's why you are in Brussels to investigate things at the European Union meetings."

"What do you want me to do?"

"First, my daughter must be placed under heavy security. I would like her here with me. But she will fight with all that is within her. She will demand to stay by your side. You must tell her no. She is a Hebrew. She will obey her husband, but not her father."

"Why? Why wouldn't she be safe with me under your Maglan guardians?"

"You see how they attacked. It was you they were after, because they know you are searching out Israel's Mashiach. I do not want Essie to be under such constant stress."

"How do you know they were targeting me? It could have been any of the others in that van."

"Suffice it to say, Tyce. Maglan has its way of finding out truth about any situation."

"I'll talk to her, but it won't do any good. Now, what do you want me to do to help deal with this...collapse of my country? Of this danger to your country?"

"Again, you are blessed...or as you feel, perhaps *cursed*, with this gift. I am believing whatsoever—whoso-ever—is behind this...gift...will somehow reveal through you plans, that is, plotting to steal American assets. To take advantage of the United States losing control of economy, of military power, of everything."

"How can I do this, sir? I don't have some magical formula I can use to just...call up these visions. They just happen."

"This is something you must know, Tyce. I would never divulge the matter were it not that the very existence of this Jewish state depends upon it."

There was a long pause, Morticai Kant wanting to give him time to reflect on his preface to what would come next.

"You know of the movie...*The Manchurian Candidate*?"

Again there was a long pause of silence as Tyce assessed the Maglan chief's meaning.

"Are you telling me— Oh, no. Are you saying they—?"

"Now Tyce, the technology is not harmful, organically speaking. You will suffer no ill effects."

After cursing, Tyce regained control. "I want to know everything, Morticai. Don't hold back any detail. Other-wise you will get no cooperation out of me. Or do I have that option—to refuse *SEER* brain-manipulation?"

"We, as a people, have no option, Tyce. You can save

Essie, Israel, perhaps your own nation, and even the world, if we do things right."

"And how's that?"

"We must retrieve each and every piece of information that is spoken of in the secretive cabals of the Europeans. Also, of Russia and their allies. They are planning something big. You can be...most helpful...in getting into their heads, as well."

"Into their heads?"

"The SEER capability is much, much more than you have been told, Tyce. Its technologies, developed by our scientists here, have tapped into areas that are beyond this world of comprehension."

"You mean the paranormal world?"

"Yes, and even beyond that, we believe. Into, perhaps, other dimensions."

"Dimension?"

"Yes. You have knowledge of the CERN supercollider in Geneva?"

"Yes."

"This is far beyond what has been done there. There are portals our scientists have managed beyond anything scientists at CERN have discovered...or opened."

"And I have all that knowledge implanted in my brain?"

"Not all, of course, but a significant amount. It is *artificial intelligence* taken to a quantum level."

"And how...can this...be put to use through my...cooperation?"

"We—that is, our scientists—can control your actions, with your cooperation, by inputting information. You will then be in an altered state in which you will be able to...walk through solid doors and do other things that are—"

"So that was how I could go unnoticed in that meeting where I saw that man they think is their Mashiach."

"And, Tyce, it was why that machine-gun fire killed those other men in the van, but didn't touch you."

Tyce was stunned. The Maglan chief moved to put him at ease.

"This is, if you want to call it such, a God-send. It has been given our scientists by Hashem, they are saying, because we are in the biblically prophesied times for the coming of Mashiach."

Tyce spoke after a period of astonishment-produced silence.

"I just don't know how to take this all in. I'll need time to think on it, to know what to do with it."

"Time is a thing of which we haven't much, Tyce. We must act on these matters now."

"Then what will you have me do?"

"For the moment, continue to go about your journalistic duties within the EU meetings."

"How will that help?"

"As you operate, the SEER technology will help us know your various situations. The operatives can send you into whatsoever interdimensional state is required to accomplish the mission the SEER perceives."

"What then?"

"Once you are finished with your mission at EU, we will need you to interact within other dimensional states. Perhaps in Moscow, and in Washington DC."

"This will all be determined by SEER?"

"Yes. The technology also analyzes algorithms and other factors a million times faster than human operatives. The SEER will be running the show, so to speak."

"And there's no harm…to the brain. To *me*?"

"No. As a matter of fact, the SEER anticipates harm to the body it indwells. For example, it can discern when there might be an attack from your immediate vicinity."

Again, Tyce's emotions and thoughts compelled him to pause. He said, finally, "What about…times of privacy? What about those moments? Like when your Essie and I want time to ourselves?"

This time, the Maglan chief took time to reflect on his son-in-law's question.

"First, you said you would speak to Essie about coming here so we can protect her. But, if she won't relent, I can promise your private time will be your own."

"Well, you weren't very honest with me. I've been implanted. I'm, in effect, a Manchurian candidate. How can I believe you?"

"On my daughter's life, Tyce. I pledge to you this promise. On my Essie's life."

CHAPTER 12

With the move from the hotel to a suite in the Israeli Embassy made the day before, Tyce now poured his concentration into the assignment the Maglan operative had presented him.

"You will now not speak to me because I will not agree to go be with my father?"

Essie's angry words were thrust in his direction while Tyce input thoughts into the laptop.

"This will not make me change my mind. I am not leaving you to go…hide in Israel, or anywhere else, no matter how much silence you give," she said, her accented Israeli-English breaking into tearfulness.

Tyce stood from the desk and came to her. "It's okay, Ess. If you don't want to go, you don't have to. It's okay."

She held her cheek against his chest, then looked up into his eyes.

"There is sufficient security here with the embassy," she said. "Papa has promised increased security for you. I will be protected."

"I don't like it, Ess. But you have a right to make up

your own mind. And, yes. The security will be good to cover our safety, I'm sure. And…I don't really want you to leave."

She sighed, relieved, and touching her tears to remove them. "Then it is agreed. We will find out together all about what is going on."

He released her and sat again in front of the computer.

"What is next? What do they have for you to do? We can talk here, can't we?"

"The embassy is secure. At least that's what they tell me. So, yes. We can talk."

"Does it have something to do with this American matter? The troubles over there?"

He swiveled the desk chair to face her, while she removed their clothing from a suitcase.

"My job is to try to find out the Europeans' thinking…their plans…about how to work with collaborators within the American government, particularly within the American military, to seize America's military assets. Maglan has word that there is a cabal both here within the EU leadership and the American collaborators to secure, in particular, the US nuclear force. The ICBMs specifically."

"And do you think you can do this?"

"Under normal circumstances, I would say that a journalist, no matter how good an investigator, couldn't get to first base in this…"

"First base?" Her question made her husband grin.

"It's a baseball term," he said. "It means you couldn't reach first base… Oh, never mind. It means a journalist like yours truly wouldn't normally have a chance at getting that kind of information. I could never be a part of such intrigue under normal times, normal circumstances."

She looked at him, her puzzled expression melting into one of understanding.

"But now you think you can get to…first base?"

"Yes, sweetheart. I think so. These aren't *normal* times. These aren't *normal* circumstances."

"And what will make the difference? Why will you now be able to get to first base?"

He stood and went to her, hugging her to himself.

"See? This is why I couldn't let you go to Morticai. What would I do without you?"

He kissed her, then forced himself to move away. He had work to do, and this fantastic woman he called wife could easily occupy his total attention for the rest of his evening. He had to get the work done. And the strange abilities with which something—someone, somewhere—had equipped him, clutched his brain now in a vice-like grip, driving him toward…what? He would find out. He had no choice. The impulse to plunge forward, to get to the bottom of what would be the final destination, was unrelenting…too powerful to resist.

NOW THE MORNINGS were almost indistinguishable from the late evenings. The boulevard stretching in the distance while he rode in the van was barely visible beyond a hundred meters. A van moved just ahead of the one in which Tyce rode, and one followed close behind.

The Maglan chief was true to his word. There was greatly increased security. There would be no more surprises, no more having his van cut off, no more machine-gun fire. At least, not without profound return fire.

He had heard about the strange orbs of light that appeared frequently in the skies of the capitals around the world. This was the first time he had witnessed them himself. They were dim lights in the sky—disk-shaped. Some pulsed more brightly, then dimmed again.

All in the van with him—most agents of the Maglan Embassy—ducked to see beyond the vehicle's roof to get a better view of the orbs. All conjectured what they might be, but they reached no consensus.

Something from the darkest regions of Tyce's cognition drew faint memories...of a time in his past, when such orbs traversed the skies. Or was it all just imagination?

The orbs had grown in numbers reported across the world. Many scientist-related analyses offered that the lights were a strange effect from the nuclear explosion that destroyed Damascus. Israel was blamed for what might have been done to the ecosystem because of the attack on the world's oldest inhabited city.

It certainly wasn't inhabited now. More than six hundred thousand had instantly lost their lives. Many had been Russians—military and diplomats who had been, the Israelis believed, colluding with the Syrian dictatorship and Islamic forces to plot an attack on Israel.

Part of the European Union meetings were to process all that had happened and try to bring peace to avert further unleashing of even more horrific nuclear weapons.

But others of the scientific community believed the orbs of light to be alien in nature—extraterrestrial traffic meant to somehow look into the dangerous activities those of planet earth had descended to.

Could they be an invasion from other worlds? was the question on broadcasts around the globe.

At this point, they seemed to stay confined to high orbits. It was impossible, according to reports Tyce had gathered, to determine whether they were solid, or gaseous, or some other form. He forced his thoughts from the orbs to his job ahead.

The meetings at the EU headquarters building ahead were to probe the issues of *peace and safety*. Israel and the tense situations of the Middle East were primary on the agenda. Israel, as always, was expected to bow to the will of the other hundreds of nations and absorb blame for bringing the world to the brink of thermonuclear annihilation.

Israel had, at its highest levels of governmental strata, held firm. If forced to do so, they would defend their territorial integrity with the Samson Option. This was, in effect, the same as the threat wrapped up in the old Cold War threat—the acronym MAD (Mutually Assured Destruction).

If threatened, whether by traditional enemies the Arab Islamists, or by any other nation or league of nations, the threat would be met with the unleashing of Israel's entire nuclear arsenal. And that arsenal was now known by all the world's diplomatic and governmental entities. The Jewish state had many more nuclear weapons than previously known. If attacked, and the Samson Option was called upon, the damage Israel's IDF could do would be unacceptable to any attackers.

He wondered just where this movement within the body of Europeans and others would take him. His deepest precognition gave assurances that the SEER implantation, or supernatural input, would, at the right moment, thrust him into exactly the right place at the right time, with the right interaction.

Beyond that inner assurance, he hadn't a clue about what to do next. But still, the drive within his passion for finding truth, understanding his whole purpose in all of it, was irresistible.

"Mr. Greyson?"

A young woman approached him from behind, moving between several of the milling delegation to finally offer her hand.

"Yes," he said, taking the slender hand and looking into the girl's smiling, pretty face.

"Greta Gothenberg," she said. "May I speak with you for a moment?"

"Let's move away from this loudness," he said, his mind running in many directions. There should be few among these who should know his name, much less seek him out. He settled on the thought that it was likely the result of the paperwork he had filled out at the French police headquarters after the shooting.

"Mr. Greyson, I am so pleased to meet you, at last," the woman said, her English without accent. "Your journalistic reputation is fascinating. I'm glad I have this opportunity to speak with you."

"Miss…Goteberg?"

"Gothenberg—Greta Gothenberg. Please, just call me Greta," she said.

"Greta it is. Call me Tyce."

"Great, Tyce."

"How may I help you, Greta?"

She hesitated, her expression continuing to be transfixed on his face, an admiring look in her eyes.

"Oh—" She broke the expression and fumbled a bit to

form her explanation. "I'm here on behalf of the Swedish delegation. I was reading through the list of journalists attending the Peace and Security Forum; I saw your name and wanted to meet you."

"Oh? To what do I owe the honor?"

"I've read at university about your investigations. In fact, in a paper for my master's thesis, I used some material from your work on investigations of the paranormal things you were involved in."

"Oh?"

"Well, it is my honor to get to meet you in person," the girl said touching his arm and smiling brightly. "But I must tell you that seeing you today isn't merely happenstance."

"It's not?"

"No. I've been sent to ask you to join a small group that represents sort of an inner circle of those who are helping shape publicity for this effort."

"Why me?"

"Actually, I saw that you were here, as I said. I explained my admiration for your work in journalism and some of the things you've done in the realm of the paranormal. They—that is, the chairman of the group, directed me to invite you to join us in helping shape the press coverage."

Tyce studied the pretty face for a moment before answering. He thought he detected in her expression something just beyond what was suggested.

"Again, I'm honored," he said. "But I have an assignment. I'm not allowed to moonlight," he said.

"Moonlight?"

He could see that her youth and non-American background called for explanation. "It's taking on extra work while taking pay full-time from an employer. You, know, working at night after your day job."

"Oh, yes. I see."

"Well, it would be a non-paying matter," she said. "It will be sort of like acting as a listener to the groupthink and adding any suggestions. Plus, you would get to meet some of the central shapers of the governing council's policies."

"Well, then, I accept your invitation on that basis, Greta. At least we will see how it goes after a couple of meetings."

"Wonderful! I will tell our chairman that you accept our request…at least for a meeting or two."

When he watched her move away into the crowd, one of the Maglan agents stepped close to speak loudly enough to be heard above the chatter around them.

"Our orders are to not let you be out of our protective circle at all times. This thing with the group she mentions sounds like it wouldn't allow us to be a part of it."

"Yeah…That will be a problem, I guess," Tyce said, wondering how the agent knew details of the conversation he had just had with the girl. He let the question in his mind go. "But this could be something that will greatly enhance my work for Maglan…for Israel. Tell you what, I'll clear it with Chief Kant."

IT WAS ALL TOO CONVENIENT. He mulled the thought while listening to the speaker who waxed eloquent on the need for peace and security now that the first nuclear weapon since Nagasaki had been unleashed in anger. "Peace and safety" was the hue and cry from every quarter. The times shared with Randolph Faust rang plainly in his memory now. For some reason, the exact words echoed in his mind now: "For when they shall say, Peace and safety; then sudden destruction cometh upon them, as travail upon a woman with child; and they shall not escape."

The gigantic screen behind the speaker pulsed with replays of the nuclear explosion that had destroyed Syria in a single burst from a medium-size thermonuclear bomb attached to the tip of an Israeli medium-range missile.

"And the bombs that now threaten civilization," the booming voice, spoken originally in German and translated into English through the earbud in Tyce' ear, was saying, "are a thousand times more destructive. If we do not take this opportunity to stop this build toward thermonuclear war, we are destined as a specie to suffer total annihilation. We must, without so much as a pause to consider the matter, grasp this moment to work with all our collective might to achieve peace and safety for our world."

Tyce again heard Randy's words within his many other thoughts: "For when they shall say, Peace and safety; then sudden destruction cometh upon them, as travail upon a woman with child; and they shall not escape."

It was just too convenient. The thought kept returning. There was more, much more, to the young woman's invitation. He knew it at gut level.

At the same time, there was another voice—one that wasn't Randolph Faust's—whispering to his innermost being. It was telling him that it was the right thing to do —pursue the matter, wherever it would lead. There was much more to the opportunity offered than met the eye, and he would find out what was involved.

"Mr. Greyson."

The male voice slightly behind him drew his attention from the screen and the speaker and from his inner-cerebral meanderings.

"Yes," he said, seeing, finally, the man who stood bending to say just above a whisper, "We were hoping you would join us. I believe Miss Gothenberg mentioned that we request that you join us."

"Yes, she did. Now? Do you want me to join you now?"

"Yes, sir. We will begin within the next fifteen minutes. Shall we give you time to prepare?"

"Yes, please. I have to make arrangements…"

"Very well," the man said. "Miss Gothenberg will come to escort you when you are ready."

"Okay…fifteen minutes," Tyce said. "I'll be ready then."

As if on cue, the big Israeli agent was next at his side.

"What was that about?" he asked.

"They want me to join them…in fifteen minutes. We will just have to do this without first checking with Chief Kant, okay?"

"Very well. Put this where it's hidden," the agent said, handing Tyce a device the size of a pencil eraser.

"If there's trouble of any sort, squeeze this device. We will know exactly where you are and that you need our help. Understood?"

"Understood," Tyce said, feeling like James Bond must have felt upon being handed such a device by MI6.

"We will be just seconds away, Mr. Greyson."

"I'll count on it. But most likely it won't be necessary."

Right on time, Greta Gothenberg touched his

shoulder and said in his ear, "Did I give you enough time, Tyce?"

"Yep. I'm ready," he said, retrieving his attaché case and weaving his way through the seated audience members, following her. With the spacious chamber outside the main lecture hall now without much traffic, she looked back over her shoulder while proceeding toward the stable of elevators.

"I know this is sooner than we had talked about, but the meeting was hastily arranged, and it promises to offer some things I believe you will find most interesting. It would be a shame to waste an opportunity to acquaint you with our group and the plans for accomplishing some important work on behalf of the peace and security forum."

Tyce said nothing, having to hurry to keep up with the woman, who held the sliding door open while he trailed her into the elevator.

"One reason we wanted you in on this meeting is that perhaps the key individual to the peace and security forum will be meeting with us. You will find him fascinating, I believe."

"Oh? Who is he?"

"He is not someone you would likely know. He prefers to keep an extremely low profile at this point," she said, looking at the lighted numbers while the elevator ascended.

"At this point?"

Tyce's words seemed to cause Greta a momentary loss of concentration before she recovered her train of thought.

"It will all be announced at some point soon," she said. "You will understand when the time comes. It will be quite..."

The elevator stopped and the doors slid apart before she finished her thought.

Tyce heard a rumbling of voices in conversation from down the broad hallway. Within seconds, Greta stopped in front of a set of double doors, one of which she opened and stood aside, allowing Tyce entrance before she, too, stepped through the doorway.

Some looked in their direction—mostly men in business suits and a scattering of business-attired women. Most paid no attention as he and Greta Gothenberg side-stepped between the people to move toward the front of the room and a small podium that faced chairs in which they would shortly all be seated.

When the meeting was called to order by a short, balding man who obviously held a leadership position, the crowd dispersed and took their seats facing the man.

"As you know, this meeting has been rather quickly convened," he said in accented English. Tyce thought it was of a Slavic nature, but couldn't tell for certain.

"We had to do so because of the one person central to all of this forum wanted to meet with us. We are greatly honored that he is with us."

Tyce, seated beside Greta, looked around when he heard the excited noises made by the group. There was expression of anticipation on all faces, it was easy to see.

"Here is our much-cherished guest, now," the man said, looking to a door to his right that opened, a man in a dark business suit standing in the doorway, seeming to be saying something of a last-minute sort to another man accompanying him. The man took something from the one who was the object of introduction, then receded into the other room.

Tyce couldn't make out the man's face while he

strode athletically toward the podium and the balding man who offered his right hand.

He stood a foot taller than the group's chairman, turning after the handshake to face the audience that stood and applauded. Finally, his features became discernable under the single spotlight that beamed from the high ceiling. Tyce's body jerked almost involuntarily at the revelation. The man's face! It was him! The man he had seen in the visions over and over.

The skin of the face beneath the hair that appeared lighter in color under the intensely bright light from above looked to be of a lighter hue, too. The star-shaped blemish above the left eyebrow stood out against the skin less distinctly than in the visions. But it was him— without the beard. It was the man who had haunted his life, the man the Kibbutz *oh-LAHM hah* Council wanted him to find.

He remembered times of past eeriness during the strange paranormal episodes. The young man who stood, taking in the applause, the adoration, moved within those memories, thoughts he fought to bring to the surface now. A time long ago, memories of a world that wasn't real, that nonetheless was as if an alternate reality. The time on Patmos and afterward. The beast that arose from the Aegean while in the grip of the serpent's bite...

"I give you Klaus von Lucis..."

The group's chairman motioned for the taller man to move to the podium as he stepped aside. Again, the group applauded vigorously before settling back into their seats.

When von Lucis spoke, the voice was strong, but calming. There was no sense of urgency in his tone, considering such important things as this conference apparently was set up to address.

Tyce's thoughts kept running through his attempts to remember those strange times that seemed now so long ago. The time after Patmos. The connection to this individual who had for so long occupied his attempts to get through the sleepless nights. The man who always seemed to pass right through him while he stood observing the scene that obviously was the Last Supper as painted by Rembrandt—the scene portrayed in the Bible.

"You are at the heart of our mission," the man said, scanning the many who sat in rapt attention.

"The power of the airwaves, of cyberspace, satellite, and all other forms of communicating to the world is at your fingertips. The need to seize this moment that destiny has given confronts now. The moment cannot, must not be postponed for any reason. You must grasp the gravity of your mission and perform using the great abilities with which you have been blessed."

The glazed eyes and frozen expressions of those lost in the grip of the man's flatteries of themselves struck Tyce while he glanced around the room. His own impression was that he had heard it all somewhere before, at some time. It was all tied somehow to the time from Patmos those years ago, the years that now seemed to meld with the present, to all coalesce and portend ominous things for the future.

"Our pathway to peace is through shaping the minds, attitudes, and actions of those we must control with the embrace of peace."

Still the words were issued calmly, with no sense of urgency. The audience scarcely moved, drinking in the man's every syllable, Tyce thought, his own inner voice calling to him to bring forward past times that would help him make sense of the unfolding present.

The young man introduced as Klaus von Lucis spoke eloquently, was calmly mesmerizing with his words. But the age of the man and the name was unimportant, Tyce thought, sensing that behind the dark eyes, the man had understanding that transcended time. The name could be different in any era…in any generation.

"Peace is what we must pursue, what we must promise, what we must process, and what we must possess. Peace is my all-consuming passion for this faltering world. It must be yours also. We will bring peace from chaos. From this moment forward, let us grasp this as our divine imperative. This is my commission to you here at this chosen moment."

The audience was silent while von Lucis concluded and turned to walk away from the podium. They then stood and erupted in effusive praise and applause for the man who had held them within his entrancing power of persuasion. But he was no longer in the chamber, having walked out of sight through the same door as he had entered.

With the gathering still mumbling their inspired approval of the message, Greta touched Tyce's arm, getting his attention.

"Well, Tyce. What is your opinion? Didn't you think Mr. von Lucis is an amazing person?"

"Yes. He is certainly a mesmerizing speaker," Tyce said.

"He is so comforting, don't you think? And so inspirational?"

"Yes, he is," Tyce agreed.

"Do you think you could be part of our effort to get

out this promise of peace to a world that needs peace at this time?"

"Well, I'll see what can be done…"

"Mr. Greyson," the man who had first summoned him to the meeting said, interrupting his conversation with Greta. "Can you meet with us for a short time?"

"What about?"

"Mr. Von Lucis wants to speak with you. He has requested that I ask you to join him."

A flood of questions gushed at once through Tyce's mind. It was as if all of the visions of his long history of such troubled other worldliness were emerging to the surface of his reality. It was a moment of realization he couldn't resist.

"Yes. I suppose I can meet for a few minutes," he said, astonished at his own disinterested tone in response. It was a response that was far from the sense of profound apprehension he in fact felt carom within his convoluting emotions.

"Perhaps I shall see you again soon," Greta said, Tyce thought, just a bit seductively.

"Yes. That would be nice," he said, smiling in her direction while beginning to follow the man who led the way through the crowded room toward the door exited earlier by Klaus von Lucis.

When he entered the area beyond the large conference room, Tyce felt his senses come to heightened alertness. The emotional ascent was not a normal response to an excitement caused by anticipation. He believed it to be something produced by the SEER. Yes. It had to do with the SEER planted in the Manchurian candidate.

His guide led Tyce through other doorways and small walkways, coming to a stop, finally, in front of a door at the end of a narrow hallway. The man knocked on the door and it opened, revealing a much larger area filled with large screens and technological paraphernalia.

"Mr. von Lucis will be with you momentarily," a man wearing a white lab coat said. "Please be seated," he said, gesturing toward chairs arranged in positions facing the large screens.

"Come, please," a man said from a door that had opened on a wall to the left.

Both Tyce and the man who had been his guide arose and walked to the one who had beckoned them.

Klaus von Lucis nodded to the two men standing on either side of Tyce. "You may go," he said, prompting them to leave the room and close the door behind them.

"Tyce," von Lucis said, reaching to take Tyce's hand and shake it. "It is good of you to accept my request."

Looking into the dark eyes once again elicited within Tyce's thoughts a sense of something beyond explanation. It was the SEER again, he thought. It had to be the SEER...

"I appreciate the invitation to meet you," was all he could think to say. The thought ran through his SEER-influenced cognitive process that this was the very person the Kibbutz *oh-LAHM hah* Council sent him to find. The man had instead found him.

"Your...particular talents in journalism...precede you. There are no others other with your...preternatural background."

Tyce spoke only after assessing von Lucis' words for several seconds.

"Well, Mr. von Lucis, that's one word I haven't heard used in describing my rather strange history."

Klaus von Lucis smiled broadly, a muted laugh leading into, "Ahh...then you may add that to your resume. Just attribute the designation to me."

"I'll do that," Tyce continued the banter.

The smile dissolved to a serious expression. Von Lucis touched Tyce's elbow and urged him toward a chair. They were both seated, and von Lucis studied Tyce for a few seconds, while crossing one leg over the other, his arms resting on the chair arms.

"You are here to represent Israel's interests," he said. The tone was one of declaration as much as questioning.

"Yes. To report on the proceedings," Tyce said, himself studying the man who was looking intently at him.

"And there are...deeper matters involved in your... search." Von Lucis let the word "search" linger in a way that indicated he knew the facts, not that he questioned what the facts were. "The assignment has...complex dimensions," he said.

Tyce's eyes were drawn to the man's facial blemish, where the star seemed to hold his attention transfixed. He had seen this man for months. He had to force his thoughts back to the conversation when von Lucis spoke.

"Israel and its future well-being are at stake as no other time."

The prolonged silence caused Tyce to feel he had to say something.

"That seems to be the consensus," he said, looking into the dark orbs—the eyes that seemed to penetrate into the very nucleus of his conscience.

"The consensus of the Kibbutz *oh-LAHM hah* Council?"

The question stunned Tyce. The man knew he was sent by the council. But how much? Did he know every-thing? The thoughts formed, then dissipated more quickly than the time it took to come to conclusions.

"Tyce, I am in need of your...unusual talents. The world is at a critical point. If the peace is lost, so, too, is mankind itself. Bringing peace is the imperative—my reason for my...and your...being at this place, at this time, to fulfill our roles."

The words from this man who had haunted his night visions seemed to swirl and blend with his own SEER-enhanced paranormality. There was no answer he could give at this moment. There were no words...nor did Klaus von Lucis solicit them.

"Report to the Kibbutz *oh-LAHM hah* Council that you have found the one whom they seek," he said.

CHAPTER 13

"I've never seen you like this. You are very pale."

Essie helped guide her husband to the sofa near the center of the Israeli Embassy suite.

"What has happened?" She felt his forehead while she looked into his eyes. "You are clammy. Do you have chest pains?"

"No, no, Ess. I'm okay. Just a bit weak," he said, sinking into the sofa cushions.

"I must know, right at this moment," Essie said, her accent becoming more pronounced because of her distress. "This very minute," she said.

"I believe it's the SEER, Essie. The device they implanted. It does something to the... It ratchets up the emotions...the adrenalin levels or something."

"We must call a doctor," she said, starting toward her phone several steps away.

"No... I'm feeling better now. I'll be okay," Tyce said, holding the cold, wet washcloth she had given him to his forehead.

"The meeting with the man was mind-bending, Ess. I

don't know how else to put it. He is the man that I see in the visions. His name is Klaus von Lucis."

"And you met him?"

"More than met him. He wants me to be part of his... his movement to save the world. A peace movement. He is at the center of...or the head of...I don't know. He is at the center of the EU Peace Forum or whatever they're calling it. He knows all about my history of the trances, visions, and all the rest. He says he can use my abilities in his efforts to form world peace."

"And this is what's disturbing you like this?"

"Ess, he knows about the Kibbutz *oh-LAHM hah* Council and their sending me to find him. He told me to tell them I had found the one they seek."

"He is saying that he is the Mashiach?" Essie's question expressed genuine shock.

"Yeah. It surprises you. Just imagine how it will surprise those who, like me, have seen the guy in dozens of the visions."

"Why is it making you react this way?"

"I don't know, but it all just doesn't ring true. He has knowledge nobody else could have, it seems. But the disappearances and all that's happening... Randy's words keep coming back to me. I have to figure it all out."

"And what are you going to do? Are you going to the council and tell them? Are you going to join this man in his seeking peace and things?"

"No. Joining this European Union forum is one thing I'm sure about. Joining it would be taking part in something that's evil at its core."

He sat up, leaning forward a bit on the sofa, continuing to hold the compress against his aching forehead.

"But I've got to go along...for now, at least. I have to at least make this guy who has haunted me for so long think I'm working with him. I've got to see where it leads. If things involve Israel…surviving…then I have to go along for now."

"And this will be dangerous. If he is evil, if they of the EU are evil in this Peace Forum thing, then you will be in danger. You must go to Papa with this, Tyce. Abba will be able to help, will keep you safe."

THE MAN, if he could know about all the past paranormal activity, he could also know things going on now. Tyce's thoughts rampaged through his mind while the technicians set up communications between Brussels and Tel Aviv.

This wasn't a matter of the natural unfolding of activities. The man was…what? It was more than just a sense spawned by the weird circumstances. The guy at the very least possessed out-of-the-ordinary powers. Klaus con Lucis was, Tyce thought, in the deepest reaches of his own strangeness, a man with extrasensory powers. No. the man was *supernatural.* He was someone to be genuinely feared.

Remembrances flooded back into his brain while he sat awaiting time to talk securely with Kant. It was the whole thing with the EU and the peace rants being made. Randolph Faust's voice kept echoing. "When they shall say peace and safety, then sudden destruction comes upon them as travail on a woman in labor; and they shall not escape."

The thoughts kept coming about Faust telling him about the coming disappearance of millions of people around the world. This would be the start of the era of horror Randy called the "Tribulation."

No. It wasn't the Rapture that would start God's wrath, His final judgments falling. That was the signing of the "covenant with the many" that the "prince that shall come" will sign or confirm. That is the action that will cause God to unleash His judgment and wrath.

The whole matter, he remembered now, revolved around the peace process. Israel agreeing to make a "covenant" and an "agreement with death and hell." That was what would initiate God's final dealing with Israel, His chosen nation and people.

The thought was at the same time frightening and thrilling. To his reporter's mind, to be part of one of the most profound prophecies ever would be…would be beyond any journalist's wildest imagination. And here he was. Right smack dab in the middle of such a building story!

But, like his wife had expressed, it would also be dangerous beyond imagination, as well.

"Sir, we have Chief Kant on the TransCom."

The operative accompanied Tyce to a booth where he had him sit, then provided earphones. He adjusted everything and manipulated buttons on a console to make the connection between Tyce and the Maglan chief complete.

Tyce's final thought before he heard Kant's voice was that the man who had supernatural powers as did Klaus von Lucis might also know of what was about to be said when he and his father-in-law spoke.

"Tyce?"

"Yes, sir. It's me."

"How is my Essie?"

"She is fine, Morticai. She says hello and wants to talk with you at first opportunity."

The answer seemed to satisfy Kant, who obviously

then was ready to get to Israel's business.

"Tyce, I understand you met with Klaus von Lucis personally."

"Yes. We had a meeting after I was invited to be part of the EU peace forum's communications arm."

"And? What was the meeting about?"

"It was a complete surprise. Von Lucis himself is the one who made the invitation. He asked questions about my history of the paranormal."

"And why did he call you in to talk?"

"Well, that's a strange thing. He knew all about the Kibbutz *oh-LAHM hah* Council sending me. He said to let them know that I had found the one whom they seek."

The Maglan chief was stunned by the revelation. It took him enough time to recover that Tyce had to speak.

"You there?"

"I'm here...I'm just trying to process this. What do you think it means?"

"I believe he is saying he is Israel's Mashiach—your Messiah."

Again there was silence on the line, before Kant finally said, "And, what do you think about that prospect?"

"Morticai, the guy is... He has something that is, I don't know how else to put it, he has something that's just not natural about him."

"Not natural?"

"Something beyond the natural," Tyce said. "Something paranormal... supernatural, even."

Again no response from Kant's end.

"What am I to do, Morticai? He has offered me a job."

"A job? What sort of job?"

"I don' know. He just said that he wants me to join in

his effort to achieve world peace. He didn't go beyond that. He quickly left, and we didn't talk beyond that." The Maglan chief again took time to assess the information. Finally, he said, "Tyce, I need you...Israel needs you to pursue this...job that von Lucis says he is offering. We must know where it is leading. Will you agree to do this?"

"I'm in so far now I couldn't back out if I wanted to. My 'want to' *wants to*," he said lightly. "The old reporter madness in me."

"Israel will be grateful. I'll be grateful. But, Tyce, don't tell Essie that we have put you on this assignment."

RANDOLPH FAUST'S words again traversed Tyce's thoughts. They were the words when his old friend had been so near death, when he was trying to stay conscious while lying in the hospital bed.

"I've been told to inform you...to instruct you," he had said, his consciousness fading before he said again, "Israel...Israel is searching...is looking for its Messiah. It is nearing the time of...the great delusion."

Finally, Faust had said before collapsing into unconsciousness, "You are to...pursue truth about that which seeks to bring about the evil one, Tyce."

The TV screens in the Israeli Embassy's World Monitoring System had at their centers at this moment, while Tyce sat watching, the image of Klaus von Lucis and alternately that of Freidrich Gunderson. The WNN broadcaster, recently given the job of top anchor with the introduction of the World News Network, was interviewing the young European about the disappearance of millions around the world.

Randolph Faust's words echoing within his head faded as Tyce concentrated to hear von Lucis' answer: "I can promise that all will be explained in due course."

The absolute assurance with which he said it left no doubt that he, in fact, knew for certain what it was all about. Klaus von Lucis had just indicated that he would give full explanation about the vanishing phenomenon at some future moment. That was the inference Tyce drew from his words.

"The details of what has happened perhaps will not be so extraordinary as is thought at this time," he said. The answer seemed to satisfy Gunderson, who moved to direct the interview toward the European Council's efforts at producing world peace.

"What is the key, do you believe, to pulling the world back from the threat of world war? The EU Council seems to have given us all a sense of…of believing that peace is…that the chance of real peace is very possible, even likely."

Von Lucis gesticulated with a raised hand and an extended index finger. "You have just hit on the main ingredient of any effort to bring a people together, Frei-drich. They must first be made to believe that the object of their desire, if the desire is strong enough, will bring a coalescence, a spiritual togetherness that will produce the object of their desire. We must convince those who are citizens of one world that they can achieve any goal —even world peace—if they do so within an orderly, planned blueprint."

Klaus von Lucis shifted slightly in the chair and crossed one leg over the other while smoothing the material on his suit pants.

"And, I will just give a hint, here. Such a…crisis…as this vanishing phenomenon is thought to be, is an ingredient within a blueprint that can be used to give coalescing impetus to an orderly construction."

The previously recorded interview cut away, and Tyce stood to meet Essie, who walked quickly to his side. She handed him a sheath of papers in a leather folder.

"Here are the papers you asked me to bring. Will you be meeting with von Lucis today?"

"No. I haven't heard any more from him, or the proposed things of our last conversation. I'm carrying on, on behalf of the council."

"Will you eventually be called on? Will he follow through, do you think?"

"I have no idea, Ess. It's all just too weird. It's like being sucked into some sort of gigantic vacuum."

"I don't like the sound of all this," she said, causing Tyce to be sorry he hadn't guarded his own thoughts better when talking with her about developments.

He touched her and leaned to kiss her cheek. "It'll be okay, sweetheart. It will all be okay."

Keeping things from her made him feel like he was cheating on her. But her father was right in the matter of his being drawn deeply into…whatever was drawing him. Essie was better left out of it. Her knowledge could bring her danger.

She was a brilliant woman. She was the Maglan chief's daughter. She sensed truth was being withheld. He could see it in her eyes. And…he knew she could see in his.

THERE WAS much buzz in the EU headquarters building main chamber when he arrived. Talk was of a proposal to completely reshape all nations within NATO.

The ramifications of the disappearance had disrupted the most powerful nation ever to exist. The United States is irreparable, was the assessment of all among the EU and most other of the NATO members. The heads of the American government who remained in positions of authority had, in effect, acquiesced to the wishes of all members of the Western alliance.

The appeal was for America to agree to surrender control of its government to a newly formed European government super-assembly. World economy, so intricately tied to the American dollar, was in a free fall. The collapse was all but complete. All assets—military, technological, and other—it was agreed, would merge to form the super assembly.

The absorption of the nuclear arsenal of the United States would make the new Western order a powerful entity that would assure peace and security.

Learning of the almost overnight arrangement was stunning. Tyce sat within the chamber, listening to the translation of the messaging coming from those who had made the comprehensive diplomatic moves and deals to bring about the changes.

Only it was not just overnight in the making, he learned, but had been in process since mere days following the phenomenon that removed so many people in the blink of an eye.

While the man with a British accent spoke, Tyce removed the translation device from his ear, wanting to hear without it blocking the volume of the chamber's large speakers.

As he did so, his senses began darkening. He struggled to understand what was happening, while all noises within the large chamber decreased, until he heard only the slight thumping in his ears that was the beating of his own heart.

His next sensation was of movement. He couldn't tell if it was his legs moving him through the people that surrounded him, or if he was floated by some strange conveyance above the audience. He next moved through walls and corridors and into far reaches of the building. Finally, the effortless glide, over which he had no control, came to an end, and he stood in a room with a number of men. No one acknowledged they knew he stood among them.

He recognized them as the same men in business attire as the ten he had been among before during that earlier, preternatural moment—the same men who had paid homage to Klaus von Lucis.

This time, there was some sort of controversy among them. Most of the men pointed fingers at three among their number. He watched as it became more obvious that the anger was escalating to more than mere finger-pointing. A door opened, and several uniformed men rushed into the room. They clubbed the three with metal riot-control rods, causing them to submit to being hand-cuffed. The uniformed men hustled the three from the room through the same doorway.

Now the remaining seven calmed and faced yet another door. Within a minute or so, a tall figure strode into the room. The men instantly bowed on their knees before him. The man who had entered was Klaus von Lucis.

"I GUESS it was the SEER's influence. It was another episode—one like when I first sought out the group that met with Klaus von Lucis."

Tyce spoke into the secure system to Morticai Kant in Tel Aviv.

"And what was the gist of their conversation...after the beatings and the removal of the three men?"

"I didn't hear anything. There are no sounds during these episodes. Am I supposed to hear something as well as see things?"

"What do you suppose this was about?" Kant's question ignored the one posed by his son-in-law. "These men. Do you recognize any of them? Do you know who they are?"

"No, sir. But I presume they have some sort of authority...are some sort of council, or something."

"Well, they are there within the European Union complex. They are obviously part of the proceedings. Perhaps you might soon identify them," the Maglan chief said.

"What are your thoughts?" Tyce said. "What do you think should be my next move?"

"Just continue to attend the main lecture chamber speeches for now. This Klaus von Lucis—he will make the next move in your direction, Tyce. I feel relatively certain that you are part of his plan, whatsoever that plan includes."

Tyce's sleep was restless, and he got up from bed to keep from disturbing Essie, who was sleeping soundly.

He looked through the refrigerator in the suite's kitchen, retrieving a small bottle of water. He downed prescription pills and chased them with several swallows of the water, hoping they would provide the needed sleep.

He would be up early, having some work to do on his laptop before heading back to EU headquarters. For now, he would sit in the big chair and watch any news he could find. The embassy was equipped with translation technology, so newscasts would be in English.

One thing sure, he thought, looking through the attaché case in his lap while going through several pages of information. With the world in complete chaos, there would be more than enough news to watch while he waited for the sleeping pills to do their job.

He pushed the power button on the remote. Instantaneously, a video replay of Klaus von Lucis, flanked by a number of men, appeared on the screen. Tyce's attention was drawn, not to von Lucis's image, but to the men immediately behind him. He recognized them as some of the men of his SEER-produced viewing. There were seven of them. They were the same men!

He pushed the volume button to hear von Lucis' words spoken the evening at some point after the day's proceedings at the EU Peace Forum. He spoke in French, but the TV translation technology changed the audio into English.

"We are pleased to announce the joining of our Earth Economic Council by the president of the United States, the prime minister of Great Britain, and the prime minister of Canada," von Lucis began.

He explained that three who formerly were part of the council had resigned, having run into difficulties with convincing their respective governing bodies to be a part of the new forum to restore economic stability.

But Tyce knew better. He had watched the three being convinced to resign...

CHAPTER 14

"**M**r. Von Lucis requests that you join him for lunch, Tyce."

Greta Gothenberg's voice when he answered his phone surprised him. He hadn't given her his number.

"Greta?"

"Yes. Mr. von Lucis is on a tight timeline and cannot schedule a specific meeting time. But he would like to speak with you over lunch, if possible."

"Yes, that should be good for me," he said, thinking that several days had passed since talking with von Lucis, and that he was surprised. He thought that the interaction was put on hold—or even dismissed by the European leader.

The SEER…could the implant technology be playing tricks on his mind?

Was the scene he had witnessed…the one he had told the Maglan chief about…the seven men subduing the three…be only a brain glitch as a result of the SEER's strange effect on his brain function?

Every movement through daily life he now questioned. The times were surreal, even at the height of his waking hours, like at this moment, talking with the young woman who first had guided him toward becoming involved with von Lucis.

"Very good, Tyce," she said. Then I will tell him you will meet him at twelve o'clock. I will meet you in the lobby, near the main elevators, at a few minutes before noon and will take you to him."

ESSIE LOOKED in through the bathroom door and her eyes met those of her husband in the bathroom mirror.

"Rabbi Amir Lubeka—head of the *oh-LAHM hah* Council—must talk with you," she said.

"Tell them I'll be there just as soon as I'm dressed. About twenty minutes."

He entered the embassy's communications center seventeen minutes later, an embassy technician bidding him to be seated in front of a console against a wall.

"Tyce," the familiar voice of Lubeka greeted. "There has arisen a most troubling matter."

"Oh?"

"Yansika Kocah has received visitation from Hashem's messenger. He has been told that the time of Mashiach's deliverance of Israel is at hand."

"What does it mean? What's troubling about your Mashiach's deliverance of Israel?"

The rabbi explained, anxiety in his voice. "Yansika has been told by Hashem's messenger that Israel's defense is not enough to ward off the attacks we will soon receive from our enemies. We must make haste to locate our Mashiach."

"What will that accomplish?" Tyce asked when the rabbi stopped his explanation.

"Mashiach will have the answers to our dilemma. Our entire council has consulted. We must have your help as soon as possible to avoid this…evil that is about to be done to our people."

Tyce didn't say anything in response, and Lubeka spoke again, his words becoming even more panicked.

"The American government has cut off all communications with our prime minister. We have lost the United States' protection. Yansika says Hashem's messenger told him the only remedy is to enlist the Mashiach's intervention."

Again there was silence on the line, and Lubeka continued. "You have found the person that most among the council have seen in the visions—the person with the star-shaped mark—have you not?"

"Well…yes, I have found the man they believe to be the Mashiach…"

Lubeka assessed Tyce's hesitance.

"You do not think this is the one who is Israel's Mashiach?"

"There are things about him, rabbi…things that make me question."

"It is not for you to determine the validity of our Mashiach. We are of Israel's highest ecclesiastical order…even more elevated than the Sanhedrin."

The rabbi's increased tone of irritation caused Tyce to remain silent. Lubeka then spoke more calmly.

"Tyce, I do not mean to be abusive. But this is of the most crucial implication imaginable. Israel's very existence depends upon bringing our Mashiach into His proper prophetic position. Do you understand?"

"Yes. I understand. You want me to continue to consider this...person with the mark...as your Messiah."

"He almost certainly is so. All indicators—the dreams, the visions, and now Yansika Kocah's direct communication from Hashem's messenger—these are sure signs that the man is Israel's Mashiach."

"Well, Rabbi Lubeka, you can tell your council that I am having lunch with your...Mashiach at exactly noon Brussels' time."

GRETA GOTHENBERG SMILED and waved when she saw Tyce approaching where she stood near the main lobby elevators. She reached to touch his arm and pull him gently toward the elevators by the sleeve of his suitcoat.

"Can you believe the way things are moving?" she said. "It seems we can barely catch our breath, before another earth shaking bit of progress comes into view."

Tyce smiled, seeing the enthusiasm of her youth. "Do you know something I don't?"

"What do you mean?"

"Well, nuclear war is a possibility, the world's economy is in a state of collapse, people are literally starving by the millions, earth's climate, they tell us, is on the brink of making life inhabitable..."

"Oh, no! All is coming under control, Tyce. This Peace and Security Forum is just quickly bringing all things into compliance. Klaus is just fantastic, don't you think? He is directing everything into cooperation...into compliance. It is wonderful! Cannot you see this happening?"

He didn't have to answer, needing to step into the

open door of the elevator after standing aside to allow passengers to disembark.

"This is quite an achievement, to have lunch with probably the most important person in all the world at the moment. And he has chosen you."

"Oh? Won't it be a group luncheon?"

"Oh, no…you will be dining alone with him!" she said, gripping his arm.

"Well, I suppose I should feel extremely honored," he said lightly chuckling at Greta's effusiveness.

"Oh, you should! You should!"

"Greta, what is your part in Mr. von Lucis' group?"

"Oh, I'm just assigned by my university in Sweden to serve as a…what do you Americans call them…as a *gopher*."

"Oh, you're a *gofer…a go-for,*" he said.

"Yes. That is my job. But it is one for which I would not trade," she said, bringing a smile of amused entertainment over her usage of Americanized English.

Klaus von Lucis stood to take his hand when Tyce walked into the private dining room. He winked in Greta's direction with a thumbs-up gesture.

"I am pleased that you have agreed to join me, Tyce," von Lucis said, bidding Tyce to be seated with a wave of a hand toward one of the luxuriously stuffed dining room chairs across a small table from where von Lucis took his seat.

"I've taken the liberty of ordering for you, Tyce. I hope what I have chosen will meet with your approval."

Tyce considered how the European's ordering of the meal didn't seem to be off-putting. It was as if it was his inherent right, as if he were born to act in such a royal way.

The cuisine was everything von Lucis promised and more, as waiters began bringing dish after dish. Finally, Tyce's host wiped his mouth with a plush cloth napkin and crumpled it to the side of the table.

"Now," von Lucis said, Tyce, sensing that he was about to be sold something of value. "Perhaps you have thought that our last conversation had drifted from my attention," he said.

"No…I just was unclear where the…conversation might be going. What my involvement in your thoughts…your plans…might be."

"I assure the conversation has not come to an end, but has just begun, Tyce. And you have a most important part in the plan."

The European' tone was one of authoritative certainty. His eyes seemed to penetrate into Tyce's own with pull that couldn't be resisted.

Von Lucis sipped from his coffee cup, looking to see the journalist's expression.

"I'm flattered," Tyce said, finally.

"Your preternatural, paranormality have piqued our interest, have made our PSF coalition know that we must call upon you to be part of our blueprint for restoring Earth."

"Restoring Earth…that's quite an assignment. I'm not sure I'm up to that level of…of contribution," Tyce said.

"None are, as you say, *up to contributing,* in the individual sense. But *collectively…*our blueprint will save this planet."

The European's countenance became one that Tyce thought took on an aura that projected prophetic foreknowledge.

"There are numerous aspects to the difficulties we

face, Tyce. But the economic collapses, the social and cultural chaos, the climate disasters we face are the very least of these things. If we cannot secure peace and security in solving the nuclear threat, all other exigencies do not matter. This is why I…we…have asked you to be part of the PSF."

Tyce could think of nothing to say but, "Again, I'm honored." Then the question surfaced again almost voluntarily. "What is my part? What do you expect me to do?"

An expression of understanding the journalist's question briefly crossed von Lucis' face. "And that is the purpose of our lunch today," he said, his gaze into Tyce's eyes becoming more intense.

"Israel, in a word, is our purpose at this moment."

"Israel? How can I help? I'm not part of the Israeli government."

"Not directly…I understand this to be true. But your wife…Essie is daughter of perhaps the most powerful man in Israel at present."

Tyce said nothing, studying the European's face, which continued to project the aura of foreknowledge.

"I told you before…report to the Kibbutz *oh-LAHM hah* Council that you have found the one whom they seek."

Still Tyce said nothing, stunned into silence.

"Have you done so, Tyce?"

"No. I did tell them I would be having this lunch with you today."

"And, why would our time together today interest them?"

Tyce sensed at that moment an ominous presence, a dark ambience, a strangely oppressive atmosphere surrounding himself and this man who had just declared himself Israel's Messiah.

Why was this…man of mystery…asking him the question? What was he trying to elicit? His intuition almost automatically produced a response.

"I believe you know the answer, Mr. von Lucis. Why are you questioning me?"

He watched as the European smiled tightly while straightening, then leaning back in the chair. The look was one of knowing his dining partner's thoughts before they were expressed verbally.

"The point is, Israel is the center of our…discussion. And there are forces that are intent on destroying this most important human nation-state…in the eyes of their Hashem. The question to you is, do you want to help the…Almighty…preserve Israel at its most critical juncture in its history?"

"Seems to me that Israel's Hashem has managed to preserve His chosen without my help, Mr. von Lucis."

"Then you don't wish to be part of our effort?" von Lucis' words were issued, Tyce thought, without any sense of being accusatory. Again, he thought the man's tone and demeanor were those of already knowing the answer his partner in the conversation might give.

"Oh. I don't want to offend the Almighty," Tyce said lightly. "And if I can be a part of defending Israel…I will. Now, is there an immediate threat? Can you share details?"

"The primary threats Israel faces are from the north, the north of Jerusalem. Specifically, from Russia and its coalition—Iran, Turkey, some of the Islamic states, some of Africa and what is left of Syria."

"These are about to attack?"

"We know that the attack will come, I'll say it that

way. It is inevitable. It will be overwhelming. Israel will unleash its nuclear force—"

"The Samson Option," Tyce said.

"Yes. And it is formidable at this point. So they could greatly damage the invading force. But Israel would… will…lose in the final analysis."

"And, how can I help avoid this…this destruction?"

"We are talking about the possible destruction of our planet. The entire world can be caught up in a nuclear catastrophe if Israel and these mad men unleash their arsenals. The climate that nurtures mankind would be so affected as to mean the possible end of life on the planet."

"And this is where the PSF comes in?"

"Yes, that is our purpose—our *primary* purpose at this point. We must prevent nuclear conflict. Israel and this northern coalition represent the number-one threat to world peace and security."

"And what is my part in this effort to stop this unleashing of nuclear war?"

"This is why I am sent at this time. To end mankind's plunge into nuclear holocaust. I am here to see that Israel is preserved. Do you understand?"

"You are Israel's…Mashiach?"

"You have said," Klaus von Lucis said.

"Again, what would you have me do?" Tyce said, the dark ambience he sensed of the moment growing more oppressive.

"The northern alliance devoted to the destruction of Hashem's chosen people are so driven by…by evil influence…that they will risk great damage and destruction to themselves to forever get rid of Israel. But, if this force from the north of Jerusalem knows the world is against it, the leaders will not attack. They will know that the

Western alliance and much of the rest of the world will utterly destroy them."

"And can you? Can you defeat those who threaten Israel?"

The European silently looked at Tyce before his expression softened a bit. "I am letting you in on some things that must be kept between us. The American government has placed in our hands the entirety of its nuclear arsenal. It's the same with all nuclear nations in the Western alliance. The PSF now has such an overwhelming thermonuclear force that even Russian and Chinese forces combined could not hope to survive engaging with our military.

"Plus, there is orbiting weaponry that the Americans developed secretly. These make any defense against their deployment impossible."

"And, again, what's my part in all this? I'm a journalist. I have no training or ability in international...relations, or whatever."

"No, Tyce. But you have direct relations with Israel's top IDF people. And more than that with the Jewish religious leadership. These can be most helpful in averting nuclear war."

"How?"

"Tell them their Mashiach is here. You have found this one sent to bring peace and safety to this world."

"What am I to tell them beyond that? That won't dissuade or influence opinion among the government, the military, or the religious council."

"You can be the first to unveil my plan that will bring Hashem's blessings and peace. Peace to the Jewish state...peace to this world."

"Okay. What is this...plan... all about?"

"I will guarantee Heaven's protection of Israel. We

will provide the umbrella of the Peace and Security Forum. Any attack even intimated by any power on earth, including the Islamic states, will face nuclear annihilation."

"So, Israel will receive this protection if…what?"

"We must take away the nuclear threat…the chance of the ignition point for nuclear warfare that Israel represents."

"So you want me to pass this along to the Israelis? And tell them what?"

"Tell them that I will guarantee Heaven's protection through the PSF nuclear defense umbrella if they agree to hand over all of their nuclear arsenal to the Peace and Safety Forum."

"What makes you believe they will be willing to—"

Von Lucis interrupted the question while it formed in Tyce's mouth.

"Because the American big-brother protection for Israel is no more. That now belongs to us. I am the one sent to protect Israel…to save the world…to bring peace and safety. You must begin the process by telling them that you have found their Mashiach."

THE VISIONS HAD NOT RETURNED since he had personally now met the man who was central to them. Klaus von Lucis was that man, and he was now reality, not made of the illusory stuff of dreams and visions.

But the reality was more troubling; it disrupted his sleep and was constantly at the center of his thoughts. Such was the case now, while he and Essie fastened their seatbelts in preparation for taking off from the private runway for leaders who visited the European Union.

Her father had told Essie that he wanted them back in Israel. The nation was being threatened by Russian leadership. If Israel continued to make plans to supply all of Europe and even some Mediterranean nations with gas from their huge, undersea reserves, Russia would take drastic steps.

Oil and gas were the commodities that kept the Russian nation afloat, and they held Europe hostage to their export of petroleum and gas. This had been the case since America's presidential administration had regulated their own energy production to the point they no longer supplied the US or other nations' needs. Russia had practically the sole supplier franchise. Israel cutting into the Russian oil and gas business would prove catastrophic to their economy.

Essie spoke to be heard above the whine of the jet engines while the G-650 revved to begin its taxi toward a runway in the distance.

"I still don't understand why Morticai called us home. Weren't you supposed to complete the assignment given you by the *oh-LAHM hah* Council?"

"It was Morticai who agreed to the council's request to send me on their behalf. So, I guess it is his call when to bring us home if he wishes."

"So, do you think Klaus von Lucis is the man you see in the visions? Could he be Israel's Mashiach?"

"He claims to be. And he is certainly a strange one, one who seems to have Israel's interest on his mind."

"And there is a message from him that he wishes to convey to my father?"

"Yes. But I'll have to let Morticai agree to fill you in, Ess. It's a need-to-know issue…"

"I have clearance," Essie said with irritation in her declaration.

"Yes, but I don't have clearance to tell you. That will have to come from your father," Tyce said.

Momentarily, the Gulfstream lifted from the center of the runway and set course toward Israel.

THE IDF WAS SEEMINGLY in every direction he looked. Tyce questioned the Maglan driver who picked them up at the base just outside Tel Aviv.

"What's going on? I know Israel's military movements are often on alert, but I've never seen this level of presence."

"I'm not exactly sure," the driver said while he steered the van toward Maglan's most secretive operations center. "All I heard was that because we struck the Buscher Mountains, they expect an attack in retaliation."

"From the Iranians?"

"No...from the Russians."

"Maybe that's why Papa called us back," Essie said.

"No. I don't think so. If he were expecting the Russians to attack, he wouldn't be calling *you* home," Tyce said. "Not his little girl…"

"But all of this somehow is tied up with the things going on in Brussels, the Peace and Security Forum, don't you think?"

"In this crazy world, especially since the vanishing, there's no telling what's tied up with what. The problems are worldwide."

The skies had darkened since the landing, and while they traveled, the now-familiar orbs of light began appearing. They were more prevalent here, Tyce thought, than in Europe. They also seemed less frenetic, more controlled, in their cruises against the dark backdrop.

"Do you think they are some sort of extraterrestrial things?" Essie ducked to look out the window at the moving lights.

"I don't know. Maybe your dad can give us more on what they're all about."

"Don't you have an idea, a thought, on them?"

"You wouldn't like what I had to say about what I think," Tyce said.

"Well, you know that just is going to keep me asking you until you tell me," she said, poking him in the ribs with a sharp fingernailed finger.

"I believe they're signs," Tyce said.

"Signs? Signs of what?"

"That these are the end of days," he said.

THE IDF SERGEANT stopped to put a metal key-card into the heavy metal gate, causing it to swing open. He drove through, the gate closing behind.

A hundred yards farther, a uniformed Israeli soldier stepped in front of the approaching vehicle, holding the weapon at arm's length to indicate a command to stop. He walked to the driver's side, the driver handed him an ID, and they were waved through.

The driver maneuvered the vehicle through several twists and turns, coming, finally, to a large, metal structure. The driver said some words in Hebrew into a hand-held device, and the metal plate lifted, allowing the vehicle through the opening.

"I've never been to MagOps," Tyce said. "Have you?"

"No. It is the most secure of all IDF facilities," Essie

said. "Morticai never brought the family here. It is reserved for the most of Israel's most crucial defensive matters. That's all I've ever been told about this facility."

"We descend beginning here," the sergeant said, steering the vehicle down a steep incline that corkscrewed downward until they reached a level fifty feet below the surface.

"Now is the real descent," he said, raising the device and pushing a button.

Two huge doors slid apart, allowing him to drive the vehicle into a massive elevator. With the manipulation of a few other buttons, the doors slid shut and the conveyance descended quickly for fifteen seconds to the next level.

"We are at 150 feet here," the driver said. "Almost there."

"This is spooky," Essie said, surveying their dark surroundings.

"Surely not for a Maglan girl," Tyce teased while she moved as close to him as possible.

After driving for a minute through a tunnel, the driver stopped the vehicle in front of a large gate of iron bars. Beyond the gate were armed soldiers doing various jobs among a computer center filled with lights of every color, some statically blinking, others doing so sequentially in gestalt fashion, giving the impression of forward movement.

"We have arrived," the sergeant said. Momentarily, the bars lifted and a soldier stepped through the opening.

"Hello, Mrs. Greyson," the man said, then added, "sir," nodding in Tyce's direction.

"I've come to accompany you to the inner core of MagOps," he said. "Please follow me."

When they reached the innermost core of the complex, a man in a lab coat greeted Essie.

"Hello, my dear," he said.

"Dr. Levi!" Essie said, reaching for a hug.

"This is the man who taught me calculus," Essie said, turning to Tyce.

"Dr. Levi, this is my husband, Tyce Greyson," she said, leading the scientist's hand to that of her husband.

"Your Abba is looking forward to having you back in Israel," Levi said after the greeting. "Let us move a little farther into the complex."

Morticai Kant's face lit up when he saw his daughter.

"My baby is finally here," he said, hugging and kissing Essie, who returned the affection.

"And it's so good to see you, too, Tyce," the Maglan chief said, vigorously shaking his son-in-law's hand.

"This complex is…quite the layout," Tyce said, letting his eyes sweep the room before they locked on Kant's steely blue eyes. "It is likely the safest area in all the world from nuclear detonations," he said. "And that is why we are here…and why I wanted you and my daughter here at this time."

"That's what all the frenzy up there is about?" Tyce said.

"The IDF taking out Iran's nuclear weapons factory in the Buscher Mountains has the Russians on edge. Whether they are determined to attack is, according to Maglan reconnaissance, a matter to be seriously considered. We take no chances in Israel, as you know. We cannot afford to take anything for granted."

"Israel's defense, sir, is something I'm supposed to discuss with you…with the IDF people at the top," Tyce said, wondering over his own brashness in cutting right to the point in delivering the message assigned him by Klaus von Lucis.

"Oh? A message from Mr. von Lucis?" Kant's question was not one that portrayed surprise, Tyce thought.

"You know about our…lunch meeting?"

"I know you met with him, of course. But not the details. But he does nothing without a reason. He chose to dine with you for obvious reasons. Your Israeli contacts were obviously foremost in his mind in choosing you, Tyce. It's just a matter of inductive reasoning on my part."

As the Sherlock Holmes of Israel's most secretive of services, the inductive reasoning by this man shouldn't surprise, was his thought. But he didn't verbalize the thought.

"We must get to this bit of thinking from Mr. von Lucis as top priority," Kant said, pulling Essie to his side and hugging her again while planting a kiss on her cheek. "My daughter, will you indulge us while we possibly save Israel and the world?"

Essie looked sternly at her father, then broke into a laugh. "No. Morticai, you go right ahead and save Israel and the world. But I will expect something extra in the paycheck, as my husband will be who will help you do the saving."

"Now, what is the message from Mr. Lucis?" the Maglan chief asked his son-in-law ten minutes later.

Tyce pulled a large envelope from his attaché case. "Here is what he asked me to give you.

Kant unsealed the envelope, removed the several pages, then read quickly. He looked up finally and spoke. "So he requires that Israel give up our arsenal of nuclear weaponry. He promises guaranteed protection against anyone attacking us. And he wants our arsenal to go into his possession. That is the gist," Kant said, as if to himself.

Tyce said nothing, studying the chief's face, seeing in his countenance a mask of non-emotion.

"He says the majority of nations by a vast percentage believe Israel to be the holdup to world peace. We represent the greatest likelihood of lighting off all-out nuclear war. By acquiescing to this…plan by the Peace and Safety Forum, we will win favor in the eyes of the world of nation-states."

Although Kant's voice didn't show emotion, nor did his expression, Tyce noticed that the knuckles on both fists were white with rage.

"So we win favor, while committing national suicide," Kant said.

IT HAD BEEN two full days since Kant had received the envelope he had delivered to the Maglan chief and, Tyce thought, taken the proposal and discussed it with the prime minister and key people in the Knesset. Tyce had heard nothing back. All relayed to him while he and Essie hunkered down in the MagOps bunker was the Maglan chief's instructions to meet with the Kibbutz *oh-LAHM hah* Council. They were awaiting word about his quest to locate the person at the center of the dream-visions they had experienced.

When Tyce entered the chamber, the scent of sweet, unfamiliar smells made him know he had reached the innermost part of the council's worship chamber.

There were no signs of anyone while he looked around the heavily draped, darkened room. Only scant light from candles placed around the walls illuminated the darkness.

Finally, a drape separated and a robed figure walked to greet him.

"Mr. Greyson. I am Rabbi Jerham Levitosh. I will take you to our council. We are much in anticipation of your report," he said, slowly leading the way through the curtain's opening.

The group, all in attire like that worn by his escort, watched in silence while Amir Lubeka arose to take his arm and lead him to the front of the seated council.

"There have been many visions since we last spoke, Tyce," Lubeka said. "It seems that Hashem is active at this time. We are moving into the time of the Mashiach and prophesied things are being observed."

All eyes were on Tyce while the rabbi led him to stand in front of the gathered holy men.

"Now, please. Tell us of your findings in Brussels. We understand your time spent there was most productive…and interesting."

"If you call having everyone around you murdered by machine-gun fire, yes, it was exciting—just to be the only one left alive."

"*Praise Hashem!*" the entire assembly chanted in unison.

"Hashem has his protective hand over you. We are thankful," Lubeka said, urging Tyce toward a large, plush chair at the front of the group.

"We will hear of your investigation, then, Tyce. Did you find the object of the visions…this man we believe to be our Mashiach?"

"Yes. I found him."

The group made a collective groan, turning to each other to express their excitement.

"And did you find him to be…to have the characteristics of…the Mashiach?"

"He is a very strange person," Tyce said. "He has what I perceive to be…supernatural qualities…abilities."

"Yes?" Lubeka said, obviously wanting him to get on with the report, Tyce mused.

"He said for me to tell you…to say to you…that I have found the one whom you seek."

Again there was noise from those gathered, their faces reflecting excitement as they looked to Tyce in anticipation.

"I will say, however—" Tyce started haltingly, knowing Lubeka wouldn't like what he had to say. "However, there are things about this man, Klaus von Lucis, that I can't explain. I just have questions about his true interest in your nation."

There was a rumble among the members, and Amir Lubeka stood to turn and hold out his hands for calm. "Please, let us hear him out. He is our guest and has done much to help us in searching out our Mashiach."

The rabbi turned to Tyce. "We, of course, want to hear your opinion, Tyce. However, let us first hear about this…Klaus von Lucis."

It was a milder response from Lubeka than he expected, and he told them all he knew about the man that so many of them, including himself, had seen time and time again in the dream-visions.

"He has risen to the top leadership of the Peace and Safety Forum, and at an age of no more than thirty or so. He is a remarkable person, one who has, I don't know how to describe it, paranormal…supernatural…ability."

He could see that the rabbis were hungry for every word.

"Von Lucis has asked me to pass along to your

government…certain proposals. Proposals that would, it seem, weaken Israel's defense system to a dangerous point. But he has at his fingertips an all-powerful military now, since the vanishing and the changes, particularly in the US, Israel's powerful ally to this point. Von Lucis will guarantee, through this awesome power, Israel's protection from all its enemies. But first you—that is, your government—must accept his PSF blueprint…that is, the plan of the Peace and Safety Forum in its entirety."

"Have you mentioned this matter to anyone in our Jewish leadership, in the Sanhedrin or others?"

"No…just to Israel's government representatives and this council. These are the only people von Lucis asked me to talk to about these proposals. And the Israeli Maglan head, whom you know is my father-in-law, said I could divulge to you only the things I've given here today."

Tyce looked around the chamber, seeing the rabbis whisper to each other to converse about what they had heard.

The rabbi turned to Tyce, his countenance frozen in a serious expression.

"Now, Tyce. Have you more to say to us?" Amir Lubeka said, standing and holding out his hands again for quiet among the chatting group of Jewish clergy.

"Yes. I want to give my opinion of these things, if I may."

"Very well," Lubeka said, then turned to the council members.

"This is only Mr. Greyson's opinion, remember. It is our council that must determine whether to pursue our Mashiach, that is, accept this man, Klaus von Lucis as Israel's prophesied divine representative of Hashem and

King David. Please give your opinion," he said and was seated.

"As I was saying at the beginning," Tyce began, "and as I expressed to Rabbi Lubeka in our call when I was in Brussels, there are things... Something about this man smacks of something. I don't know how else to say it... something sinister. I urge you, this council, to consider the matter deeply. To pray to your...Hashem...before embracing von Lucis as your Messiah."

CHAPTER 15

A mir Lubeka sat at the small desk in his study, his right hand in a fist over his mouth, his eyes shut in deep prayer. Hashem was implored to give guidance. Lubeka said nothing, but he ruminated troubling these matters.

Tyce Greyson's words of caution kept pounding against the foremost of his thinking. *"I'm not sure about von Lucis...there's something about him...something sinister..."*

Lubeka's concentration was suddenly disrupted, the study beginning to fill with smoke. An acrid smell that singed his nostrils and began a burning in his eyes caused him to stand and begin searching the room in a panic.

What was the source of the smoke? He had to find the fire. He had to save his home, to save his wife as she slept in the adjacent room.

The smoke grew thicker, and he stumbled through the room, bumping into furniture, knocking over free-standing shelves with worship icons and other items. He finally found the doorknob and turned it.

He stepped forward, his right foot meeting nothing of substance. His forward momentum was already committed. He couldn't grab the door facing in time. He fell headlong into the black nothingness, descending—ever descending.

This was to be his end? Was this the end of everything? Was he falling into Hell?

Somehow, the thoughts were not panicked, not terrified, while he fell face down, not tumbling.

Was there no bottom? Was the descent to be forever? A journey into inner space rather than into outer space?

In the next instant, he found himself upright, standing before a massive door of what looked to be solid iron. It began to open. From within the blackness billowed dark clouds of smoke. The stench was of rotten, decaying, human corpses.

He had smelled it before, administering to troops as they lay dying among the lifeless bodies of their fellow soldiers. It was the stench of corruption that could come only from remains that were in the late stages of decomposition.

Suddenly from the billows of blackness emerged a huge beast. It had a head like that of a hyena, but the body of a massive, nondescript beast, unlike any he had seen. It growled and roared, its enormous mouth displaying rows of dagger-like canines and powerful jaws from which dripped drool and foam, the stink of which was overwhelming.

Where was he? What was he doing here? Was he...in Hell? Was this the beast...Cerberus, the dog of Hell, according to mythology?

The beast strained to get to him. But it was restrained, Lubeka could now see. A collar was around its neck, attached to a thick iron chain that disappeared into the blackness behind the beast.

Then, in an instant, the beast was gone. It disappeared and, again, billowing clouds of thick, acrid smoke with the stench of corpses belched from the place beyond the huge iron doors.

Then, from the corruption emerged something...a humanlike figure. Was it Satan? Lucifer himself, come to usher Amir Lubeka into Hell's vortex?

It was...a man. The man stood staring at him. It was the man, the man of the council's search...of Tyce Greyson's report.

The man stood staring at him. There was a star-shaped image above his left eyebrow. The man was Klaus von Lucis...

TYCE WANTED to be out of the nightmare in which he was locked. But there was no egress, no ejecting from the heavy, black, rolling clouds that blinded him to all else.

He must awaken...he must.

But he could not. Instead, he was drawn more deeply into the darkness, until he stood behind the figure of a man, who faced a doorway to the abyss. He just knew it was the abyss. He instinctively knew.

The man stood frozen in place, looking into the boiling blackness.

He shouted as loudly as he could, trying to get the man's attention, trying to convince him not to enter the doorway...the doorway to the abyss that could be none other than the opening to Hades...Hell.

The man slowly turned his head to look over his shoulder. He was familiar. The face of Amir Lubeka.

The rabbi turned until he recognized the man shouting. The expression was paralyzed in a look of astonishment.

"Tyce Greyson?" the rabbi said with no emotion in his words, just an indication of recognizing who had called to him.

A sudden wind began to blow, and the black, stifling smoke, or fog, or whatever it was began to dissipate. The wind blew harder and harder until all things that surrounded him became clear. He was standing in the living room portion of the underground bunker.

He sat down in the recliner nearest him, his head reeling.

It had been like no dream in his remembrance. The man was there... It was Amir Lubeka, the head of Kibbutz oh-LAHM hah Council.

While he rubbed his temples, trying to clear his head, his phone chimed. It was 2 in the morning. Who would call at this hour? he thought, wanting only to sit and assess the dream that was like none other.

"Hello," he said, answering after five rings.

"Tyce," Amir Lubeka said, with panic in his voice. "We must talk."

AN HOUR AND A HALF LATER, Tyce walked into the doorway through the unlocked side door of the synagogue.

The head-fog had not yet cleared at the early hour, and he jerked with surprise when Lubeka grabbed his forearm and pulled him to himself, continuing to hold to his arm as they walked farther into the vestibule.

"I must tell you of my...my vision," Lubeka said as

they walked. "You were part of it… You called to me as I stood before… I think it was the gateway to Hell, itself," he continued, turning to face Tyce finally.

His eyes were wide, his fright obvious. "It was real, as real as anything I have experienced," he said.

Tyce felt his own emotions flood in a gush of realization. The dream wasn't a dream. It was something else.

"Amir, I was there. I called to you. You turned and questioned if it was me. Then a wind began to blow—"

"Yes, yes! That was what happened! What does it mean?"

Both stood staring at each other, stunned into silence, each searching their surroundings for explanation. Finally, Tyce said, "What did you stare at? You were looking into that huge doorway."

"At first, the…the hound of Hell came forward from the smoke. It was…terrible. Its jaws gnashed, as if it wanted to eat me where I stood, unable to move."

"I saw no…hound," Tyce said.

"No, no…the hound then was pulled back, or it retreated into the abyss. And from the smoke, the disgusting clouds boiling in the abyss, came…came the figure of a man. He stared at me. It was Klaus von Lucis."

"Von Lucis?"

"Yes. It was him. The scar was there, on his face. He just stared at me but said nothing. Then I heard you calling, and I seemed to be able to move again. The wind began blowing, and I was back in my home."

Again, both stood, dumbfounded by their mutual experience.

"What does it mean, Tyce?" The rabbi looked at him with an expression of confusion and terror.

"I think your Hashem is telling us something, Amir."

"I believe you are right. I believe Hashem is validating your findings in Brussels."

∾

THE MAGLAN CHIEF was excited like Tyce hadn't seen before. He slammed a book onto his desk, all but shouting into the phone.

"This is something that should not be done, Mikan! It cannot be done!"

Tyce watched his father-in-law's face go from normal to a red hue.

"I thought when I briefed Nokoli on this European's proposal that he would reject it out of hand. Never did I think he would accept it as a matter to include in Israel's defense. Never!"

Tyce understood little to none of the rant, as it was in Hebrew. He turned to Essie, who translated in a whisper, cutting her eyes to her ranting father as she spoke. After translating, she said, "Of all my years, I have never heard Papa so angry."

"What is he talking about? What did the prime minister do?"

"Apparently, the information you gave Papa to pass on to him, the prime minister took it to the Knesset defense committee, who then took a hurried vote to approve of Israel's acceptance of meeting with von Lucis and the Peace and Safety Forum to discuss accepting von Lucis' offer to guarantee Israel's future security."

"Then I understand his anger. It seems a foolish thing to do," Tyce said, watching Kant continue to slam things from a shelf onto his desktop while he screamed into the receiver.

He had, several days before, told Kant about the

vision he shared with Amir Lubeka—that it was, Lubeka declared, a message of warning directly from Israel's Hashem. The Maglan chief had refused Tyce's offer to explain to the prime minister or to anyone else in the government about the vision and von Lucis' appearance…the meaning it portended.

Kant wanted to pass along the information to the Israeli prime minister himself, providing the sheath of papers Tyce had given him to the PM to share with key government officials. He would give them to the prime minister as a matter of briefing him, never thinking things offered by the PSF would be voted upon and approved by the Israeli government.

But now it was a done deal. The government of Israel would meet in talks with the people in Brussels. The thought of Israel ever giving up its own defensive arsenal to any other entity was unthinkable.

"Yes. I insist on having a hearing before the Knesset Defense Committee," Kant said into the receiver angrily. "Nopoli, I can think of no more foolish thing to do than trust Israel's security to the European cabal."

His anger seemed to cool a bit, while Tyce and his daughter looked on.

"Yes. That is right. We must live and die by the Samson Option. That is exactly my insistence," the Maglan chief said, more as a punctuation of agreement to the Israeli prime minister's question than to his own frustration.

"Then you will arrange the meeting between myself and the KDC? That will be satisfactory," he said and hesitatingly placed the phone on its cradle while he looked down in concentration. Then he turned to Tyce and Essie.

"Did you hear all that?"

"Yes, Papa," his daughter said soothingly. "Your side, anyway."

"It is unbelievable," Kant said in English. "We have fought from our country's rebirth in 1948, and even before, to fend off enemies, to keep Israel as part of God's land grant to us. Now this European, a thirty-year-old upstart from the inept European Union convinces our prime minister and government in just a simple communiqué to forget the history of the hate for us by the world. They agree to von Lucis' proposal."

"Why, Abba? Why would they do such a thing?"

"You want to know why they betrayed all of us?"

Neither Essie nor Tyce said anything, knowing the answer was on the way.

"Because of the religionists...the people who are supposed to have a direct line to Hashem. They have influence upon all members of the Knesset, that even I, the head of Mossad's most inner-security apparatus, didn't know."

"What do you mean? How is that so?" Essie's question caused her father's eyes to narrow and his jaw to clench as he answered.

"Because von Lucis promised a temple on Moriah."

"A temple?"

"He, personally...this thirty-year-old upstart...says he personally promises they can have their temple, if they sign on to the Peace and Safety Forum's blueprint, as he calls it."

"What kind of blueprint?"

Kant went back to unloading books from a shelf before stopping to turn and address his daughter's question.

"Israel must give up all nuclear weaponry, and all laser-defensive instrumentalities. In other words, we will be completely defenseless. This…European…says he guarantees to defend Israel with the over-arching shield of the newly forming global order. We must give him our nuclear and all other arsenals of significance."

"And there is no way to stop this?" Essie said.

"No. The Knesset is totally in on it. The rabbis and all the religious entities are all lunatics over this Temple Mount reconstruction. They have it already constructed, you know? I have seen it. It is warehoused at the center of Jerusalem—all that is needed is to take it over there in several major parts and construct it within a day or so."

"And the Islamics, what is von Lucis going to do about their hatred?"

Tyce's question caused Kant to again stop unloading the bookshelf. "I can't tell you, Tyce. This is so new to even us within Maglan. I just don't know."

"I suspect it will involve a heavy presence of the so-called world order they claim to be producing."

Morticai Kant looked at Tyce, his jaw jutting, his anger again rising. "You are exactly right. They have always wanted to control Jerusalem. Now they will have the right…in their own eyes…to do the unthinkable to all who truly love Israel…who love Jerusalem."

MORTICAI KANT'S temper had cooled the next morning before he left for the meeting with the Kibbutz *oh-LAHM hah* Council. Tyce remembered now Kant's words while he was being driven toward the council's facility.

"Somehow the prime minister equates our position to that of America. The US has become so weakened that they can't provide our security. With the administration that was in charge at the time of the…the vanishing…

there was no help from the Americans. And just because America has given all such weaponry to this European consortium doesn't equate to our needing to get rid of our arsenals."

Everything was in total chaos, as was obvious by what he was seeing while the van drove past beggars holding signs in Hebrew.

"It's pitiful," the IDF driver said. "All the children just...just gone." There was a muffled moment of emotion in the big driver's voice.

"It's this way everywhere," Tyce said. "I don't have any little kids in my life, but I have family in the states, cousins and the like, who lost little ones. They were four and eight, I think."

"Do you think this...economic collapse all over the world...is going to be resolved?"

Tyce didn't answer, and the man continued. "This European guy. Do you think he has the answers? Everybody I talk with thinks so."

"We will just have to wait and see, I suppose. Do... did...you have children?"

The driver managed to gather the resolve not to answer with emotion in his voice, so he spoke more boldly. "Yes, my wife and I had three...ages three, five and nine."

There was silence in the van until they pulled into the compound.

Rabbi Yansika Kocah met Tyce at the main door in front of the building, taking his offered hand. Rather than shaking it, Kocah pulled him along while he talked.

"We are all excited to hear what you have to tell us, Tyce. Amir has filled us in on your mutual dream. Hashem is at work, and we are all wondering what will be next."

"So am I," Tyce said, following the rabbi through several corridors and deep into the building.

"You know what all of us are believing, do you not?"

"No. Who…who is thinking what?"

"The Kibbutz *oh-LAHM hah* Council, all of the Sanhedrin. Every true believer within Judaism. All are excited at what will happen next in God's program for Israel."

"And what do you and everybody think?"

"That Elijah will appear soon. That is the prophecy most on our minds at this time."

"Well, I've heard nothing of…Elijah…and a prophecy."

"Oh, yes. He will return in these end of days, the prophecies tell us."

Momentarily, they stepped into the main chamber of the complex. The members of the council greeted him with smiles and with an energy he hadn't seen before in the group.

"Welcome, Tyce," Rabbi Levitosh said, smiling, while holding his arm and leading him to the front of the chairs that faced the platform and small podium.

"We are all anxious to hear what you have for us," the rabbi said in heavily accented English. "We will know what Hashem has to say through you."

"Well…I hope that Hashem and I don't disappoint you," Tyce said flippantly, seeing a brief laugh from Levitosh that made him know the statement meant to be a joke didn't seem to offend the rabbi.

Shortly he was joined on the platform by Amir Lubeka, who gave him a brief hug of greeting. "We have much to say to them, do we not, my friend?"

Tyce said nothing, but smiled, looking at the assembled group of rabbis while they were seated. Lubeka introduced him using English, his demeanor becoming serious when the introduction was completed.

"Hashem is with us of the *oh-LAHM hah* Council. We have been given truth…truth that others of Judaism in Israel do not have. As you have heard, Tyce and myself have been visited by the same Heaven-sent vision. We shall, together, determine what this vision means and what we must do with the knowledge we have been given."

Lubeka and Tyce filled the members of the council in on all that had happened in their night spent looking into the abyss, and what and who had emerged.

Where there had before been jubilation that they had found their Mashiach, there now was at the same time trepidation and excited optimism that Hashem would soon make all things clear. His protection of Israel was assured. The promises made to Abraham, Isaac, and Jacob were unalterable. Israel would survive. Israel would be the apex nation of all nations. Jews would be God's chosen people in the coming Kingdom!

Tyce, seeing the resolve and the anticipation on each of the faces, determined to listen to the inner voice that now spoke to him. It was the voice of the friend he missed every day of this strange time since the disappearing. It was the voice of Randolph Faust.

The voice said, "The Bible, God's Holy Word, has the answers, Tyce. Get into God's Word, the Bible."

THERE WAS much to take from the *oh-LAHM hah* Council meeting, more than he could easily grasp at the moment. He felt the urge to get into the Bible he had long owned but not much looked into that lay just to the right of the laptop.

He studied it for several seconds, hearing again in his mind's ear Randolph Faust's words. *Get into God's Word, the Bible. The Bible has answers.*

How to approach his search for…the search for what? He opened the laptop cover and booted up the machine, hearing the chime when it was ready.

He opened the default search engine. After a minute of thinking, he entered the terms of his research: "Scripture about Elijah's reappearance at the end of days."

He read the results:

Malachi 4:5–6 foretells Elijah's return: Behold, I will send you Elijah the prophet before the coming of the great and dreadful day of the Lord. And he will turn the hearts of the fathers to the children, and the hearts of the children to their fathers.

He looked further into the research findings. He found it interesting that a modern theologian with the last name "Jeremiah" expounded upon the verse.

The False Prophet's Counterfeit Ministry

The False Prophet described in Revelation 13:11–18 will deceive people into believing he is Elijah by counterfeiting Elijah's miracle. Verse 13 says, "[The False Prophet] performs great signs, so that he even makes fire come down from heaven on the earth in the sight of men." Anyone familiar with Malachi's prophecy, particularly Jews, will immediately draw a connection to Elijah when they see the False Prophet's supernatural fire. However, he will receive his power from Satan rather than God."

Tyce looked up from the monitor, remembering looking at Rabbi Amir Lubeka's back while the rabbi stood before what was, by both of their reckoning, the gate to the Abyss. Lubeka had said the European von Lucis had appeared in the black smoke…

Now he read of how the coming reemergence of the prophet Ezekiel would involve satanic deception. The false person would receive power from Satan.

He read further.

This points to an important truth: Miraculous signs are not necessarily from God. That is why 1 John 4:1 tells us, "Beloved, do not believe every spirit, but test the spirits, whether they are of God; because many false prophets have gone out into the world."

Elijah's miracle caused people to worship Almighty God, but the False Prophet's signs will cause people to worship the Antichrist.

The information was as if it were prepared just for him in this moment of his need to understand…everything surrounding his life, the disappearance phenomenon, his being brought into Israel and the Maglan chief's orbit, being personally given information of the Peace and Safety Forum by the very one the vision seemed to point to as being from Hell itself—all began the process of congealing within his thought process.

He looked again at the screen for the enlightenment he now felt compelled to voraciously devour.

The False Prophet will not be Elijah reincarnated, but Elijah will return according to Malachi's prophecy. Revelation 11 describes two witnesses who will preach to the world after the Rapture. After the Church is taken away, God will raise up 144,000 new believers and appoint the two witnesses to preach the Gospel and God's judgment to everyone who is left to hear it. Through these witnesses, God will continue to provide opportunities for people to place their faith in Him right up until the end of the world.

Most scholars believe one of the two witnesses will be Elijah. Consider these similarities:

- The witnesses will ascend to heaven while they are alive (2 Kings 2:11; Revelation 11:12).
- The witnesses will prevent rain from falling (1 Kings 17:1; Revelation 11:6).
- The witnesses will employ fire in their ministry (2 Kings 1:10; Revelation 11:5).
- The witnesses will minister for three years and six months, which mirrors the length of Elijah's drought (1 Kings 17:1; Revelation 11:3).

The theologian's words concluded.

From beginning to end, the Bible tells the story of God's love for humanity. It weaves threads throughout the annals of history that testify to His unchanging nature, His unfailing love, His unfathomable grace, and His unescapable judgment. Elijah's ministry is one of these threads. The same God who rained down fire on Mount Carmel will ignite the ministry of His two end-times

witnesses as they offer a final olive branch to the world
before its King returns in judgment.

Tyce sat back and stared at the screen that provided
the only light disrupting the darkness. The writer
mentioned the Rapture. He remembered Randolph
Faust's words about the prophesied event that Faust said
would be "the next great intervention into mankind's
history."

Certainly, the worldwide vanishing of people made it
the most colossal intervention into mankind's history.

He reread the words:

> The False Prophet will not be Elijah reincarnated, but
> Elijah will return according to Malachi's prophecy.
> Revelation 11 describes two witnesses who will preach
> to the world after the Rapture. After the Church is
> taken away, God will raise up 144,000 new believers
> and appoint the two witnesses to preach the Gospel and
> God's judgment to everyone who is left to hear it.
> Through these witnesses, God will continue to provide
> opportunities for people to place their faith in Him
> right up until the end of the world.

Tyce looked again at the scripture referenced: Revelation chapter 11. He picked up the Bible next to the
laptop, switched on the small lamp, and quickly flipped
through the book, finding the last book of the New
Testament. Soon he found the chapter he wanted. He
read until he came to the third verse.

> *11:3 And I will give power unto my two witnesses, and they
> shall prophesy a thousand two hundred and threescore days,
> clothed in sackcloth. 11:4 These are the two olive trees, and*

*the two candlesticks standing before the God of the earth. 11:5
And if any man will hurt them, fire proceedeth out of their
mouth, and devoureth their enemies: and if any man will hurt
them, he must in this manner be killed. 11:6 These have
power to shut heaven, that it rain not in the days of their
prophecy: and have power over waters to turn them to blood,
and to smite the earth with all plagues, as often as they will.
11:7 And when they shall have finished their testimony, the
beast that ascendeth out of the bottomless pit shall make war
against them, and shall overcome them, and kill them. 11:8
And their dead bodies shall lie in the street of the great city,
which spiritually is called Sodom and Egypt, where also our
Lord was crucified. 11:9 And they of the people and kindreds
and tongues and nations shall see their dead bodies three days
and an half, and shall not suffer their dead bodies to be put in
graves. 11:10 And they that dwell upon the earth shall rejoice
over them, and make merry, and shall send gifts one to
another; because these two prophets tormented them that
dwelt on the earth. 11:11 And after three days and an half the
Spirit of life from God entered into them, and they stood upon
their feet; and great fear fell upon them which saw them.
11:12 And they heard a great voice from heaven saying unto
them, Come up hither. And they ascended up to heaven in a
cloud; and their enemies beheld them.*

The revelation stunned him momentarily, and he
looked back to the words that electrified his already
stimulated attention.

*And when they shall have finished their testimony, the beast
that ascendeth out of the bottomless pit shall make war
against them, and shall overcome them, and kill them.*

"The beast that ascendeth out of the bottomless pit"!

CHAPTER 16

E verything moved in speeded-up motion, it seemed. Despite Morticai Kant's pleas before the Knesset—before the prime minister and all others who held in their hands the ability to determine Israel's fate— the moment had come.

The group of leaders gathered around an ornately carved conference table of highly polished mahogany. They had come from the Middle East, Europe, and Israel to do the unthinkable. They would now ink their signatures on the covenant of peace designed by those within the Peace and Safety Forum.

Although it was to be a peace that was guaranteed by the world's most powerful military, because of the nations all surrendering their nuclear arsenals and even their powerful conventional weaponry to the PSF, the expressions on the faces of all concerned were at best stoic and at worse glum.

"The prime minister of Israel will now please sign the Peace and Safety covenant."

The announcing voice rang throughout the world over satellite, while Israel's prime minister leaned over the table and signed his name.

"Now the Islamic Alliance will please sign," the voice said, prompting an Arab in a dark business suit to sign, while burnoose-clothed Arabs looked on from behind.

"Finally, Mr. von Lucis will please sign the Peace and Safety Covenant on behalf of the Western Alliance."

Klaus von Lucis, sitting at the table, signed the document that was slid in front of him. He signed with several fountain pens, which were then given to each of the signatories.

A boom microphone swung from the ceiling until it was several inches in front of von Lucis' face. Cameras directly across from where he sat, framed the European while he spoke.

"The covenant of peace, forever ending the centuries of war and bloodshed of the peoples of the Middle East and the rest of the world is now confirmed. Our children, our families, all who want only to live in peace and safety can now rest assured: Today you have the assurance of the deity that looks upon these proceedings from on high."

With that, von Lucis stood and began shaking hands with the signatories, all of whom now broke into smiles, backslaps, and handshakes. Arabs embraced Israelis, and all paid homage with their smiles toward the young European who had brought them together.

Tyce Greyson watched from the Maglan underground bunker along with Morticai Kant, Essie, and a cadre of Israeli Maglan personnel.

"Well, that does it," Kant said in English. "The prime

minister will have my resignation tomorrow upon his return."

"Are you really going to resign, Papa?" Essie said. "What will the country do if you are no longer looking after us?" She wiped away streaming tears with her finger and was handed a tissue by an Israeli soldier standing to her left.

"There is nothing I can do, daughter. The deed is done. Israel is now in the hands of this Klaus von Lucis. He has stripped us of all ability to defend against enemies who are blood-vowed to destroy us. Now they can do so. There is no resistance on our part."

"But he has promised to defend with the over-whelming power they now possess."

"To trust anyone to Israel's defense is pure madness," Kant said, his face pale and more serious than Essie had ever seen her father's countenance.

"Is there no place…no place within the IDF you can serve?"

"No, sweetheart. The IDF is no more. Mr. von Lucis, this…*genius*…as they deem him, is now Israel's defense force."

LATER IN THE evening following the signing of the peace agreement, the broadcast was set to begin that many of the elite geopoliticians of the world had awaited.

From the TV speakers of the Maglan bunker media room, the voice of the network anchor announced that the US networks were joining in a live broadcast from Brussels. Essie followed Tyce to the sofa, from which they watched hundreds of men and women mill about in the huge chamber of the PSF headquarters building.

At first, the camera swept the delegates, then drew back to frame the entire chamber. Far away, a colorfully attired figure walked slowly toward the lectern on the vast podium. The camera zoomed in on the figure until only he filled the television screen.

A man in religious robes of white, red, gold, and purple, with medallions shaped like crosses and unfamiliar symbols, suspended against his breast by gold chains. A tall, gleaming headdress sat atop his head, while he moved to the ornate lectern and held aloft a scepter, which glinted in the beams of brilliant light radiating from the ceiling.

As if the raising of the scepter was a signal, the people stood and applauded, while the television cameras captured their ecstatic expressions from many angles. The religious man's face and diadem filled the screen in a ghost image over the mass of people. Still, cameras flashed and strobe-like lights illuminated the ecclesiastical figure and the men and women of the audience while the applause increased, along with shouts of approving exultation.

"Is that the pope?" Essie said, not taking her eyes from the scene.

"It's him," Tyce said, remembering Randolph Faust's once derogatory words for this pope who, Randy said, perverted the scriptures.

Still, the religious man stood receiving the accolades, the scepter held aloft in his right hand, holding the other hand above his head in a symbolic gesture of humble acceptance and gratitude.

"His Holiness looks to be enjoying his first public appearance in quite awhile, despite his advanced age," the anchor said from the DC studio while the applause continued.

"There is gathered in that great hall probably the largest, most diverse cross section of the world's nationalities ever assembled anywhere at any time. Even the United Nations has never seen anything like it. From just about every known country, representatives have come, at the request of this new pope. Every religion, including Christianity, Buddhism, Muslim, Hinduism, and the many sects and denominations within those great religions, as well as many reclusive, little-known cults, have come at the request of His Holiness."

The announcer was silent for twenty seconds, letting the video and the noise of the adoring throng within the great hall of the PSF put across to the viewer the exultation of this historic moment. Finally, the crowd began to quiet.

"We don't know what language His Holiness will use, or whether he will speak more than one language; he is a master of many. Whichever he chooses, those in attendance at Brussels, and we here, will have the benefit of instantaneous translation, thanks to the recent breakthroughs in computer-language vocoder technology, which can almost exactly duplicate the speaker's own voice tone after translating the meanings of his words."

"Greetings!" the holy man said in mildly accented English, smiling when the mass of people before him responded with a tumultuous, synchronized shout. "It is past time that we come together as one!" Again, a single shout of response. "Now, let us begin anew!"

The people were on their feet before the pontiff could finish his sentence. A sustained, frenzied show of acceptance. The screen in the bunker was imaging the Brussels' camerawork that combined a series of quick-cuts, dissolves, and super-over impositions, which captured the spirit of oneness raging within the chamber. The man drew his hands into a palms-together position, holding the scepter erect between them, and he bowed toward the representatives while maintaining the prayerful pose. The exuberance was infectious, drawing one into its excitement. The talk of oneness, of the brotherhood of man, of beginning anew. All deceptions of the most insidious kind, promising a bright future—all problems solved—perfection.

Maybe this religious man really did believe, but Tyce knew the price for the proffered paradise. He had experienced, through visions and dreams, the evil of the utopian bill collectors. And the knowledge of their painful tactics made it easy to churn reality of the evil back to the surface while the eager, accepting faces beamed glowingly toward the pontiff, who now stood with his hands clasped before his bowed face.

Tyce watched the faces, those bright faces, effulgent in the television lights while the cameras panned up and down the aisles. They differed in expressions from all the faces he had seen since that day the Mossad agent's face vanished from the seat beside him. Absent were the fear, the apprehensions. As if they knew something other faces of the world did not know. And somehow, in an instant of fleeting foreknowledge, Tyce, too, knew what those at Brussels held secreted away behind their glowing, jubilant facades. This religious man who stood before them had the map that would, they thought, lead them out of the greatest world crisis ever. He was about to introduce them to the system, the person, who had the answers.

"How could the pope be mixed up in government that would be cruel to people? They wouldn't have selected a man who wasn't concerned about people, about human rights. He couldn't be a part of a dictatorship, could he?"

But Randy Faust's words flooded back. This pope wasn't what other popes had been.

Still, he wanted to believe otherwise. Wanted to believe that the pope desired peace and security for the world above all else.

Tyce's confusion was no less than that of Essie, who was a Jew. Even she understood that popes were regarded as the world's great champions of social justice, constantly putting forward the principle that man is responsible for taking care of man, and that the individual's rights must not suffer at the hands of any collective will. That society must serve the individual, not the other way around. Yet this man had apparently thrown his lot in with those who spit on that principle.

"Maybe he decided the globalists' ideas are the lesser of evils. That what they're offering is better than the chaos we have now," Tyce said, thinking that the real answer was that this pope had been fooled by the promise that, once things were under control, a more humane rule could be instituted. One that served rather than oppressed. His Holiness had not experienced the real character of the globalist assassins.

"We have come to a most crucial time in man's history," the holy man said when the noise quieted. "A most terrible time. And yet, a most opportune time. For we hold in our hands the ability to destruct our world in a moment of nuclear insanity, or to destroy it through years of slow deterioration. At the same time, we have the capability to build heaven on earth. Does it not make better sense, human, common sense, to choose the course of life, rather than make the choice of extinction for the human race?"

Again, the great hall at Brussels erupted in deafening applause and shouts of agreement, while the video presented the faces of the hundreds of world represen-tatives.

"There is, I am convinced with all my heart, one sent from God to lead us upon that sensible path that will take us into the prophesied millennium. And, this servant, I am equally convinced, has been given 'The Plan' drawn directly by God's hand. A plan as divinely appointed as the Ten Commandments and all the great truths God has given mankind throughout the ages. Give your ears and your hearts to this, God's servant."

The Pope put his palms together and addressed his deity, face raised toward the ceiling.

"Oh great Father, the Light of the universe. Grant your Son the power to lead in this hour of trouble. Grant, too, the understanding of us all and give us the will to accept what thou hast for us through Thy divine hand upon this your chosen one, whom you have borne into this world to lead the way into Thy eternal king-dom. In the name of the Father, the Son, and the Holy Spirit. Amen."

The prayer concluded, the pontiff waited for the audience to settle, his robed arms stretched forward, his white hands gripping the edges of the lectern's top.

"My friends, my children…God's man for this critical hour!"

Spotlights near the stage swung their beams from the pontiff and crisscrossed, their large circles of light congruently fixing on a human figure approaching the lectern from the darkened area behind the platform. A striking masculine form in a dark suit, whose quick, graceful stride was of youth. He smoothed the suitcoat near the hips while he walked, reaching then to take the hand of the pope, who met him enthusiastically.

There seemed an unnatural stillness in the chamber

while the men held hands briefly in the circle of light, then broke their grasp. The holy man issued the younger toward the lectern with a gesture of his right hand. The camera zoomed in for a close-up, and, as Tyce expected, the young man was Klaus von Lucis, a somber expression on his handsome face, the star-shaped mark prominent above the left eyebrow.

The pope was smiling broadly and saying something the microphones could not pick up. The audience responded at first with a few scattered handclaps, then, more sure of what their response should be, released their feelings in a frenzy of cheering and applause.

Von Lucis stood behind the lectern, acknowledging with generous, though controlled, smiles and slight nods of his head to his right, to his left, and to those directly in front of the stage. He began in the familiar, slightly accented baritone that charismatically commanded the attention of all whose ears the now famous voice fell upon.

"We have indeed reached, as His Holiness said, 'a terrible moment in man's history.' Yet it is a moment of magnificent opportunity—a time which, I assure, will never again be ours. For, in the words once spoken by a great leader, 'Man holds in his mortal hands the power to abolish all forms of human poverty, and all forms of human life.' And, as John Kennedy also said, 'Asking His blessings, and His help, but knowing that here on earth, God's work must truly be our own.'

"That is the message I bring to you, my friends of the global community. This is the hope that rests within our own God-given capabilities. To be...to really be...or not to be." Von Lucis held an index finger aloft and paused, looking about the vast chamber at the many faces held in the grip of his words.

"Ahhh...that is truly the question of our precarious time, my brothers and sisters of the world-family. What shall it be? The joining of hands and hearts and minds to eradicate poverty, disease, crime, hunger, natural catastrophes, and war? Or will we begin again to take the same path mankind has taken for so long? That of self-serving nationalism? Thus, all of the scourges that such a course brings with it, ending in nuclear holocaust. And, as His Holiness said, 'extinction as a species'—the end of the greatest drama God has allowed mankind to act out. Only we can write the next chapter. Only we can begin writing the most glorious chapter of all!"

No wavering on the part of this man who would be savior, who inspired certainty that he could deliver what the pope promised—leadership out of the calamitous mess in which the world found itself. That inspiration showed in reflected belief from the faces at Brussels. Von Lucis was in the process of activating the germ of noble aspiration, which all people who were sane harbored dormant in their core beings. The young European was able, Tyce knew now, to cause those coming under his influence to ignite others in a chain reaction that would ultimately link all together in the promised global familyhood. But, it would be a linkage in the form of manacles, because in order for that global design to succeed, stumbling blocks had to be removed—of which Tyce Greyson was one.

"My fellow passengers on spaceship earth, is it not time we put aside the prejudices and biases separating the family of man one from the other... a separation which would soon bring us to that Armageddon so long predicted by the myopic doomsayers? Instead, should we not concentrate on the things common to all? The good, productive things...the human things which are the inherent right of every citizen of our world community to enjoy?

"Make no mistake: if we do not take action beginning here, beginning now—and there is no one else to take action for us—we will be forever lost. The ultimatum is this: Build a great and glorious world in which there are none of the plagues humanity has endured since the moment man stood erect and began recording human events, or else disintegrate in the future fireballs of our own creative folly and be consumed in the blackness of nuclear winter. There is no turning back. The Great Universal Mind, who issues the ultimatum, has also provided the technology and intellectual capability through which man can solve his potentially fatal dilemmas.

"Do not worry for now about what has happened... about why millions have vanished. Be assured that the great giver of all knowledge will put into each and every mind, individually, the acceptance of what has happened, as each becomes able to comprehend. I will say, for now, only that for some who are gone from our midst, it is a great evolutionary reward, while for others it is, sadly, punishment for false teaching of things about the Father of all. Most crucially, we must understand that although this phenomenon seems a tragedy, it is in fact God's gift to His creation, offering a new beginning, a purified pathway to a higher evolutionary order."

The speaker's piercing eyes engendered the feeling that they were x-raying one's brain, that those black, intelligent orbs were invading, unveiling the soul. Von Lucis stood with almost arrogant posture, surveying the silent, intensely attentive representatives, then turned his eyes again to the camera encased within its mobile, mechanized scaffolding just above the center aisle.

"I must tell you also, although the end result of the course the Great Universal Mind has prescribed will be glorious beyond imagination, that course will require many sacrifices from everyone. Those who refuse to live within lawful boundaries must be dealt with and shall be treated as not worthy of our love, of God's love. Let us begin by understanding this precept, yet…with the prayer in our hearts that there will be none among us who will be so unloving and so foolish as to test our resolve as we begin our march into the glorious New Age of, ultimately, perfection."

A gigantic reflective screen descended from the ceiling at mid-stage while von Lucis spoke. Its expanse covered the blackness that previously had framed the European and the lectern. Projected light streamed from above and behind the audience, lighting the screen with a graphic presentation that highlighted what von Lucis was saying.

The Plan

"The blueprint for perfecting mankind in a less sudden and less dramatic way than the disappearance phenomena…the great leap into perfection in which our now ascended brothers and sisters participated… 'The Plan' to make God's creation what he intended…I now give the world…INterface!"

The screen above and behind the young European reflected the word: "INterface."

"INterface…the joining together of human to human…linking, through our self-created miracles, each to the other…Oneness!"

The screen above the platform was alive with brilliant visual effects. Von Lucis' eyes seemed ablaze while the lights and colors burst, disturbing the general darkness of the chamber.

INterface

"And INterface, the period of learning to live together as true children of God's Universal Family. The final evolutional period that will lead each to the godhood locked within the inner-self. INterface...to consist of the Six Ways.

"1. Terrorism and crime will dissolve into exemplary citizenship through joint effort and innovative discipline.

"2. Poverty and economic chaos will be eliminated by working together to share abundance equally through computer disbursal ingenuity.

"3. Hunger, like poverty, will be forever done away with through distribution of the wealth left by those who were taken in the great dissolution and evolutionary leap, plus, through sharing of the plenty. No more will there be third-world nations.

"4. Ecological disaster caused by floods, earthquakes, wind, and fire, can and shall ultimately be overcome through human determination and divine help within our technologies.

"5. Disease and pandemics will be eradicated through intensive, concerted efforts of the world medical community.

"6. Peace shall replace war as man learns to give rather than only to take.

"This is the Six-Ways design I give to you, my fellow citizens of the world."

With the six points outlined in huge letters upon the screen, Klaus von Lucis gestured with a motion of his right hand toward the projected image, then turned to again grip the lectern and address his global audience.

"Every nation, every people, is represented in this chamber. I appeal to each representative, on behalf of your people. Join in this effort...I implore you in the name of God. Endorse and embrace this gift of love, this gift of life and a future free from the threat of nuclear annihilation and all other of the horrible scourges outlined. It is mankind's last chance. Your only chance, my friends...my brothers and sisters." The graphic changed while von Lucis paused; he spoke again, his tone now grave, yet inspirational, while his appeal rose to authoritative finality.

"Join with me. Together let us create the world God meant for you to have.

"Six Ways to Law!

"Six Ways to Order!

"Six Ways to Peace!

"Six! Six! Six!"

Tyce sensed what he knew those at Brussels must be feeling, what everyone who heard the dynamic young European's words must be feeling at this moment. A coursing of excitement, causing eruptions of goose-bumps. He, like they, wanted to believe, accept, what von Lucis was saying, so desperate was the plight of every human being who prayed for something to give them hope. But even now, with the good will gushing from the many representatives in the Brussels chamber, he knew better. Knew at the most primitive gut level that the price von Lucis was asking for Utopia was too great—more than anyone should have to pay. Klaus von Lucis walked toward the blackness, the screen having ascended into the ceiling, and paused to shake the hand of the pope before departing the platform. A noise, inde-cipherable at first but becoming clearer, the volume increasing. A chant by the representatives, who were on their feet now and clapping hands while they gave the incantation in English.

"Six ways to law! Six ways to order! Six ways to peace! Six! Six! Six!"

The audio and video from the television set in front of Tyce and Essie was that emanating from Brussels. The image remained for several seconds, before the anchor again took control in the Washington, DC, studio, his image superimposed through chromakey over the scene at Brussels.

"A most stirring and profound message," the newsman said, turning from watching a monitor to face the camera. "It would seem that the billions of people, represented by these national and religious leaders in attendance at the Peace and Safety Forum headquarters, will not have to pressure their leaderships into going along with this magnificent plan put forward by Mr. von Lucis. I have never in my years of journalism seen such complete agreement or enthusiasm by such a diverse group of government officials as we are now witnessing. It seems also that Mr. von Lucis has inadvertently created what might become the battle cry for "The Plan" he tells us comes directly from God. As you can hear in the background, they are chanting, 'Six ways to law! Six ways to order! Six ways to peace!' and they cap off the appeal with the words, 'Six, six, six.' Klaus von Lucis' message comes as a welcome harbinger of hope at a time when we all need, above all else, hope."

Tyce saw on his wife's face the expression that asked if the journalist's words, if von Lucis' plan, could be a true effort at solving the world's great problems. It was the same question he fleetingly asked himself.

No! It could not! More than that, it was a lie—a wicked lie of the cruelest sort. A deception that dangled in front of a chaotic, terrified world hope for a solution, while the deceivers were even now tightening their deadly coil around their billions of victims. How appropriate, he considered while looking at the screen that displayed the almost gleeful expression on the anchor's face—that he, Tyce Greyson, should compare the PSF group to a snake coiling around its victim, something he had experienced on Patmos. Man was first deceived and enslaved by a serpent, according to the Bible. Yes, Randy Faust would have appreciated the analogy.

"To the message given by the pontiff, and by Klaus von Lucis, I, on behalf of my fellow journalists throughout the world, say, 'Amen.' We will do our parts to disseminate that word of promise offered by the Six Ways Plan.

"INterface should become a part of our daily lives now. The Six Ways to Peace, our motto. One gets the feeling that we are indeed marching into a new age, which will see the end of these six great scourges of man —crime, poverty, hunger, ecological disaster, disease, and finally, war. Most of all, peace will replace war."

The broadcaster looked to be in deep concentration, his tone was reasoning. "And the simple elegance of one part of 'The Plan' at which Mr. von Lucis allowed us a brief look—that all wealth left behind by those gone in the dissolution will be distributed to the least of our brothers and sisters—demonstrates 'The Plan's' brilliance. It is a beautiful picture. A biblical picture, really, of the commandment to 'love thy neighbor as thyself.' Let us make that principle a part of our daily lives. 'Do unto others, as we would have them do unto us.' Only give even more…always more than we receive."

"It's all happening too fast for me," Essie said, jarring Tyce from his thoughts of what they had witnessed. "But it's just like you said. It all seemed so fantastic when you first told me about what was happening."

"When people are panicked and desperate, it's easy to get them to accept a rope," Tyce replied. "Even one that has a noose on its end. They're beginning to get hungry. They'll grab on to anything to keep from going under. This thing has been in the works for a long time. It took more than a day to construct that blueprint, that's for sure. If this so-called dissolution hadn't happened, they would've manufactured something, some crisis, in order to get what they wanted. I'm not sure whether they manufactured the disappearance. I don't know how they could've...but it came with perfect timing, didn't it?"

"The whole thing is crazy," Essie said.

"More than crazy. And there's more to it than a magician's trickery, more than merely sleight-of-hand. It's as if they really didn't have control over what happened, but were fully prepared to take advantage of the situation when it did happen. I know it doesn't make sense, but they are taking full advantage of the disappearance... and it's fulfilling prophecies of the end of days."

TYCE'S research had intensified during the months. Bible prophecy was all-consuming his ever-waking moment. The words of Randolph Faust returned to his mind time after time as he searched the pages.

Now the words "covenant made with death and hell" were front and center while he tried to remember Faust telling him about Israel's fate.

"Israel will make the mistake of depending upon another to protect them," he remembered his friend telling him. "Israel will make a peace agreement with the prince that shall come. It will be what God's prophetic words called 'a covenant made with death and hell,'" the old man had said.

This would result in the worst time in all of human history, Faust had told him. Israel would accept this man who would be the prince that shall come, but they would still reject Jesus Christ, their true Messiah, their rightful King.

He remembered now Faust's exact words: "Jesus Himself said there would come a worst time than any time up to that moment the covenant with death and hell would be made, or ever will be thereafter."

He had to find that exact scripture…but what to put in the search? Finally, he typed in "Scripture for Jesus saying worst time ever for Israel."

The search was a success. It came up with chapter and verse:

> *Matthew 24:21 For then shall be great tribulation, such as was not since the beginning of the world to this time, no, nor ever shall be.*

Randolph Faust had said that when the "prince that shall come" confirms the covenant, that terrible time would invoke God's wrath and judgment.

Tyce again tried to remember the scripture reference about the "prince that shall come." He couldn't, so he typed in the search box and came up with another good result:

> *Daniel 9:26-27—9:26 And after threescore and two weeks shall Messiah be cut off, but not for himself: and the people of the prince that shall come shall destroy the city and the sanctuary; and the end thereof shall be with a flood, and unto the end of the war desolations are determined. 9:27 And he shall*

> *confirm the covenant with many for one week: and in the*
> *midst of the week he shall cause the sacrifice and the oblation*
> *to cease, and for the overspreading of abominations he shall*
> *make it desolate, even until the consummation, and that*
> *determined shall be poured upon the desolate.*

Randolph Faust had told him, he now remembered in part. The signing of this covenant or peace treaty between Israel and her enemies would result in the greatest time of horror in all of mankind's history. This period of great trouble would be known as "the Tribulation," Randy had said. It would conclude only in the battle of Armageddon and the Second Coming of Jesus Christ.

RABBI AMIR LUBEKA was ashen-faced when he came from the newly formed Sanhedrin *gerousia*, the council of elders. He moved in a state of stunned disbelief through the Kibbutz *oh-LAHM hah* Council facility. When he reached the innermost chamber, the council members noted their group head's state and moved to surround him, touching the sleeves of his robes and bidding him to sit.

"What is the cause of this distress?" Yansika Kocah asked in Hebrew while he patted Lubeka's arm, looking into his eyes, from which flowed a tear stream. "What did the *gerousia* say to you?"

Lubeka looked up into Kocah's concerned eyes. "They are disbanding the council, Yansika."

"Disbanding? Disbanding the *oh-LAHM hah*?"

"Yes," Lubeka said, nodding. "They say we are no longer needed, that the Peace and Safety Forum has edicted that as part of the covenant their new council will henceforth work closely with the Ecumenical Collective…as they are calling it."

There was silence in the chamber while the members looked on and listened.

"The gerousia is embracing von Lucis as the Mashiach. He has given permission for them to begin the Temple construction. It should be completed, they are saying, within one week. There will be full Temple function within the month, they are saying."

Lubeka's words brought mumbled expressions of wonder over what was divulged.

"We no longer have any say in matters involving the holy mount or worship protocols. There is a leader within this…this Ecumenical Collective. He is a rabbi, but he is unknown to me. His name is Rabbi Elias Koahn."

The rabbis looked at each other, shaking their heads negatively and indicating they had not heard the name.

"This leader of the Ecumenical Council is pointing to von Lucis as the holy one from Hashem. All of the gerousia believe him to be so sent from Hashem," Lubeka said, "but he is not so sent. He is from the Abyss, as I have told you."

"What are we to do?" Yansika Kocah's question was the one on the minds of all of the council.

IT HAD BEEN MORE than a year since Klaus von Lucis was made head of the New Roman Order—the name given the collective Western-world regime by von Lucis himself shortly after the signing of the covenant of peace. The complete breakdown of law and order and collapse of the world economy followed quickly on the heels of the massive disappearances.

Von Lucis created a computer-satellite regime that brought about the cashless system of economic controls toward which the world of global finance had been gravitating. All buying and selling, further, was done through computer-chip implants within human flesh.

Many people, particularly those who joined the increasing ranks of hundreds of thousands, then millions of believers within reviving Christianity during the post-disappearance world now questioned von Lucis as being God-sent. These viewed the NRO Electronic Funds Transfer computer system as the evil system prophesied by John in the biblical book of Revelation.

Tyce studied the prophecy now, while sitting before the computer screen. His eyes devoured the words he had just pulled up for the tenth time over the past week.

13:16 And he causeth all, both small and great, rich and poor, free and bond, to receive a mark in their right hand, or in their foreheads: 13:17 And that no man might buy or sell, save he that had the mark, or the name of the beast, or the number of his name. 13:18 Here is wisdom. Let him that hath understanding count the number of the beast: for it is the number of a man; and his number is Six hundred threescore and six.

Tyce read again the prophecy that many believed to be the very economic system the NRO now worked to advance. A system that, while seeming to bring economic order after the catastrophic collapse, nonetheless put the individual under economic slavery.

With the system came scrutiny of the most draconian, surveillance sort.

Every transaction was watched by computers, information reported to and recorded by NRO intelligence operatives. Thus, von Lucis and his regime could monitor every transaction and make laws, rules, and regulations to achieve the state's desired ends. At the same time, most every person was tracked by satellite, having been implanted just beneath the skin with computer chipping.

He concentrated while reading the prophecy, thinking on how the regime could control the masses through this system that looked to be the one prophesied by John —the same John whose cave on Patmos started Tyce, himself, on the journey that had brought him to this moment of realization. He was living out the final days of the years leading to Christ's return.

Yet, although von Lucis and his ruthless surveillance state police could control the masses, they couldn't stop the many preachers from within the Jewish community as they, having been converted to Christianity, now brought thousands daily to acceptance of the gospel of Christ across the world.

The converts were increasingly becoming problematic to the regime. They were therefore the target of the Ecumenical Collective. Rabbi Elias Koahn, the clerical head of the religious amalgamation, had put out warrants for the arrest of the thousands of Jewish evangelists who were converted to Christianity. Not one had been arrested. The frustration by Koahn and his ecclesiastical police force had become ever more paranoid and enraged. The result was the New Roman Order attacking groups of believers. These were now either underground, were languishing in prison, or were dead.

Tyce felt overwhelmed by the things he knew were of world-shattering importance—of heavenly importance beyond that which he could hope to fathom. Randolph Faust…if only Randy were here to guide. If only someone were here to help him understand the things involved.

The desire to know the truth of what was happening burned at his innermost being, his very soul. His self-assured, journalist bravado vanished, disappeared, as surely as had all those millions…all the children…

"Dear God," he heard himself saying for the first time since he could remember. "Please help me understand…"

Tyce felt strange sensation while his eyes tightly closed in prayer. His body felt as if it was tumbling. A familiar, inner-being, slowly turning motion through blackness ended with a soft touch-down on sand he recognized, remembered from past times he thought forgotten. It was a seashore—one on which he once had stood.

He looked through expectant senses at the vast seascape in front of him. A calm, not turbulent sea as in those other times. The wind blew in his face, but it was a gentle, not violent, wind, while he scanned the water's horizon.

The sea beast. It would appear at any moment like on the shores of Patmos. The leviathan, its ten horns, and seven heads, with fangs gnashing.

"Tyce Greyson." The voice abruptly snapped his attention back to the shore where he stood. It was a familiar voice from a past he couldn't sufficiently recall.

"You shall encounter a multitudinous meeting of Israel's House, overshadowed by a strange being, Tyce Greyson."

His eyes met those of holy men like in other times… in other visions.

"It is Eli, and Moshi," one of the men said. He was

strangely comforted by the recognition, despite his astonishment.

Tyce started to speak, but the words of the one who introduced himself as Eli preempted. The two men stepped forward, as if gliding on a cushion of air, he thought, his senses of alertness heightened when contact with their fingertips was felt upon his arms.

"You shall follow the directive, Tyce Greyson. You shall be led into the pathway lighted by divine directive."

He was moved to speak to the two men in robes of antiquity. But he was unable to do so. These were as familiar as friends…from somewhere within his most cherished memories.

"You are not here without purpose, Tyce. You will soon be shown the divine directive."

Although his ability to speak was somehow locked in a tightness that was almost painful, his hearing and sense of understanding seemed heightened.

"We are men of the Word of God about whom you have read," Eli said. "What has been will be again. We have met in past visions. We will again meet as future things come to pass. Blessed be His Holy Name."

"There are twelve thousand of each tribe of the house of Israel," Moshi said. "These are for bringing Light to the darkening world of evil."

Eli said, "You will have visitation by these anointed. Trust and obey. Your mission is set by Heaven's directive."

As the one called Eli spoke, both figures standing just feet away from him dissolved before his astonished eyes.

"Tyce!"

Essie's voice and her pushing his shoulder caused his trance to break. Still he was unable to speak.

"Tyce! What is wrong?"

His wife's words finally broke the trance and he looked at her, his eyelids blinking, his recovering vision bringing her face into focus.

"It was two...holy men from the past...from my past. They were sent to tell me that I will receive instructions..."

"What holy men? What instructions?" Essie said, still seeing in his eyes a look that made her know he was not fully back to reality.

"Eli and Moshi. Two men I somehow knew many years ago, when I had the visions following the snake bite in that Patmos cave."

"And they are the same...this Eli and Moshi?"

Tyce looked into Essie's eyes, an expression of disbelief on his face, and his intonation expressing the same.

"I prayed. I prayed that I would have understanding of what is happening. It's all going so fast, Essie."

She said nothing, waiting for further explanation, while examining his features with concern.

"I prayed and almost instantly Eli and Moshi appeared. They just...were suddenly there in the room. They said they were sent from Heaven...from God."

"And they were men you knew in the past?"

"Yes. After the snake bit me, I had a series of visions, like I told you. It was all a world that wasn't reality, but seemed as if it was. Maybe it was more real than this world."

"And Eli and Moshi helped direct you through that dream or vision world?"

"Yes. And here they are now again in my life. They said I would receive directives from Jewish preachers... there are thousands of them, they said."

"What kind of directives?"

"Of what to do next, I guess. To help me negotiate all this madness."

"These…preachers. Where will you meet with them?"

"I don't know, Ess. Maybe they will just appear like these old guys appeared."

"They are Jews?"

"Yes. They are Jewish men, they said. They are of the house of Israel, they said."

"And this all is in Bible prophecy?"

"Yes. This preacher named Jeremiah who wrote articles I found in my research wrote that two witnesses will appear at the time of Tribulation—the last seven years before Christ's Second Advent. He wrote that there will be Jewish evangelists at that time…twelve thousand altogether. A thousand from each of the twelve tribes of Israel."

"Then who these men were talking about might be those men…those preachers?"

"Yes, that's what I believe they were telling me."

"But you mention the Second Advent of Jesus. The Jewish priests don't believe in Him. They consider him to be an imposter," Essie said.

"But these will be converted to belief in Jesus, is what I remember Randy telling me. They will be fervent evangelists for preaching the gospel message."

But how will you meet them? How—"

"I'll just trust that I will somehow be introduced to them, Ess. Eli said it was my mission and heavenly directive. That these men are anointed to deliver Heaven's message. Is there any doubt that will happen, after what I've…what we have…experienced?"

≈

MORTICAI KANT WAS RESTLESS. It had been a year since he resigned from Maglan. And the Mossad's most secretive organization was defunct at any rate, so he had stopped mourning the loss. His concern now was brought to the point of near-rage, seeing the activities on the large TV screen.

"The Russians are deliberately showing what they plan," he said, cursing at the screen and shaking his fist. "They are angry because Israel has guaranteed to deliver to Europe and parts of Asia petroleum and natural gas through the Mediterranean conduits. This robs Russia and its allies of economic means. They had an exclusive when the Americans stopped all their drilling and fracking because of the lunatics' demands to go green. Now Israel is to provide the gas and oil and the Russians no longer have that leverage."

"Do you think they are serious about doing something militarily?" Essie's question raised her father's temper a degree hotter.

"What do you think, daughter?" He paced while he alternately glanced at her, then at Tyce, who sat facing the screen. "The Knesset has given away our nuclear deterrence. We have no defense."

"But the new European government...they guarantee the peace...Israel's protection," Essie said. "Theirs is the most powerful military in the world."

"They are not talking of protecting Israel. There has not been even a whimper from the New Roman Order." Kant let the words "New Roman Order" linger and roll off his tongue in disgust.

Tyce sat upright on the sofa, seeing the scroll along the bottom of the screen both in Hebrew and in English. "Look, Morticai. There might just be that whimper you were mentioning."

They watched the scroll. It read: "The Defense coalition of the NRO along with the North American NRO geoquadrant and the Saudi Kingdom NRO geoquadrant issued today a diplomatic note of protest. The communiqué stated: "We must know the Russian coalition purpose in gathering of forces across the region above Israel."

"Well, there is indeed the whimper," Kant said, gritting his teeth and throwing his hands in the air. "I don't believe the NRO betrayers will lift a finger to defend Israel. They have wanted this to happen to this nation all along…since our founding in 1948!"

MORTICAI KANT HAD LEFT the room the day before in a state that even his beloved Essie couldn't assuage.

"You are going to have to calm, Abba," she had said. "Your blood pressure is not good. You must not get so upset."

Her father had said nothing while he walked from the room. He spent the next hours trying to reason with Israel's prime minister and the head of the IDF, which he knew was no longer the authority in control of Israel's defense.

That was supposed to be the responsibility now of the New Roman Order military wing. But it was obvious, from the diplomatic note of protest, that their response to the threat north of Jerusalem would be weak at best.

Tyce sipped from a cup of tea that Essie had made for him, then left him alone with his thoughts to study things bothering him, causing him, he surmised, to be almost as anxious as his father-in-law.

But Kant's anxiety was of a physical nature; his own was spiritual. His was anxiety over what Bible prophecy next had in store for the world...for Israel, for himself, and for Essie.

He just knew it. He could sense it at the very core of his troubled being. Bible prophecy was now moving forward at a rate his own observations couldn't control or keep up with.

America, despite its infrastructure still maintaining some semblance of being a technical superpower, was anything but. The dollar had collapsed, as had the economy. Food shortages in the North American continent weren't as critically affected as other nations of the world. But the shortages were becoming more problematic by the hour, and riots, especially in the large cities, had turned civilization into every man...or woman...for themselves.

Despite the New Roman Order and their superstar Klaus von Lucis' best efforts, the computer system of buying and selling had not yet come to the point of beginning to resolve the massive food shortages and the financial crises facing humanity. The word was that the most draconian measures imaginable would be implemented in order to reestablish commerce and all other forms of human interaction—a draconian regime of economic control that to violate the orders of the NRO's fiscal mandates would result in execution.

Rumor had it that to instill fear and compliance, the method of such execution would involve beheading. Guillotines were being produced to carry out the executions when necessary.

There had always been rumors of such dire things, Tyce thought, while finishing the tea and setting the empty cup on the table beside the laptop.

But this time he had no doubt that such rumors were about to turn into reality.

Eli and Moshi again came into his troubled cogitations. What did they say? That he would be shown things…he would be visited by…the men of prophecy. The 144,000 chosen to evangelize the world.

The senses-darkening ambience began the familiar recognition that something of otherworldly significance was about to occur. He turned to face the room while sitting in the swivel chair where he was working with the laptop. There stood before him two men, young men. They wore what looked to be immaculately white jumpsuits, their waists wrapped with broad, golden sashes.

"Don't be afraid," one of the men said, a broad smile across his face. "We are flesh and blood, like you, Tyce."

Tyce was on his feet facing them. "Who are you?"

"You know who we are, Tyce," the other man said.

There was silence for several seconds while the men faced each other.

Tyce said, "You are of the 144,000. The men who will preach the gospel of Christ to the world. The ones Eli and Moshi told me would—"

"We are the very ones," one of the men said, interrupting Tyce's analysis. "We have come to tell you of the coming attack from the north. The attack from Israel's enemies."

"Then there will be an attack from this Russian coalition…"

"Yes. It is foretold. The prophet Ezekiel has said."

"When? When will the attack come?"

"You will be witness, Tyce. You will be given full view of the fulfillment."

"When? When will this happen?"

"Read the prophecy. Study what God's Word says,"

one said, ignoring his question. "You are to know the details through God's Word, through the words given Ezekiel to pronounce."

Tyce said nothing but stared at the young men who smiled a knowing smile that he was chosen for this visit by the God they served. One of them then said, "You will find the prophecy in the book of Ezekiel. In the chapter of 38. That is where to begin. We have been directed to tell you to tell Amir Lubeka and the Kibbutz *oh-LAHM hah* Council. Do not tarry. The attack is imminent."

"What?" Tyce asked. "Why am I to tell them?"

"Tell them that the prophecy of Ezekiel about the Gog-Magog attack is on the cusp of taking place. These are steeped in the Holy Writings. They will know. But first, study the prophecy to understand. Do not tarry, Tyce Greyson."

Like Eli and Moshi before them, the men dissolved and vanished before his astonished gaze.

Ten minutes later, he came to the object of his search. He read the prophet's words:

38:1 And the word of the LORD came unto me, saying, 38:2 Son of man, set thy face against Gog, the land of Magog, the chief prince of Meshech and Tubal, and prophesy against him, 38:3 And say, Thus saith the Lord GOD; Behold I am against thee, O Gog, the chief prince of Meshech and Tubal: 38:4 And I will turn thee back, and put hooks into thy jaws, and I will bring thee forth, and all thine army, horses and horsemen, all of them clothed with all sorts of armor, even a great company with bucklers and shields, all of them handling swords: 38:5 Persia, Ethiopia, and Libya with them; all of them with shield and helmet: 38:6 Gomer, and all his bands; the house of Togarmah of the north quarters, and all his bands: and many people with thee. 38:7 Be thou prepared, and prepare for thyself, thou, and all thy company that are assembled unto thee, and be thou a guard unto them.

38:8 After many days thou shalt be visited: in the latter years thou shalt come into the land that is brought back from the sword, and is gathered out of many people, against the mountains of Israel, which have been always waste: but it is brought forth out of the nations, and they shall dwell safely all of them. 38:9 Thou shalt ascend and come like a storm, thou shalt be like a cloud to cover the land, thou, and all thy bands, and many people with thee.

He read all the prophet had to say, all of chapter 38 and chapter 39. The account was harrowing, but at the same time thrilling—if one wasn't on the side of Gog.

He read again the foretelling of the force that even now was poised above Israel, prepared to strike according to the two young men…and to God's prophetic Word.

38:18 And it shall come to pass at the same time when Gog shall come against the land of Israel, saith the Lord GOD, that my fury shall come up in my face. 38:19 For in my jealousy and in the fire of my wrath have I spoken, Surely in that day there shall be a great shaking in the land of Israel; 38:20 So that the fishes of the sea, and the fowls of the heaven, and the beasts of the field, and all creeping things that creep upon the earth, and all the men that are upon the face of the earth, shall shake at my presence, and the mountains shall be thrown down, and the steep places shall fall, and every wall shall fall to the ground. 38:21 And I will call for a sword against him throughout all my mountains, saith the Lord GOD: every man's sword shall be against his brother. 38:22 And I will plead against him with pestilence and with blood; and I will rain upon him, and upon his bands, and upon the many people that are with him, an overflowing rain, and great hailstones, fire, and brimstone. 38:23 Thus will I magnify myself, and sanctify myself; and I will be known in the eyes of many nations, and they shall know that I am the LORD.

CHAPTER 17

Sirens near and far sounded constantly in all of Israel, particularly in Tel Aviv, while they rode into the Kibbutz *oh-LAHM hah* Council facility.

"What are you to tell the council?" Morticai Kant said.

"I don't have a clue," Tyce said. "I guess I'll just wing it."

"You will know what to say," Essie said. "If you are to be visited by these emissaries of Hashem, don't you think you will be given what to say?"

"We'll see," Tyce said, not having prepared for the hastily arranged visit to the rabbis.

Amir Lubeka and several of the robed men welcomed them when the door opened. When all had settled in the central chamber, Lubeka invited Tyce to speak.

"This is about victory, not defeat," he heard himself saying. "Israel will not fall victim to this evil." He looked at the men, who knew him to be one possessed of supernatural influence at the very least. Therefore, whatever he said had to be taken seriously.

"You, of all people in Israel, know of Ezekiel's prophecy, about the Gog-Magog attack. I can't improve on your knowledge of what the prophecy says. However, I can tell you that the assault by Russia, Turkey, Iran, and others...many of them of the Islamic nations...will attack any minute. The prophecy is going to have its fulfillment any minute."

The rabbis seemed to go into a prayerful pose, their eyes closed while they hummed a monotone chant. Tyce looked to Lubeka, who said, "They are invoking Hashem's blessings and watch care over Israel."

"My message to you, I believe, is to tell you that it is God, Himself, who will defend the chosen people."

Tyce's words created among the chanting rabbis an increase in volume and quickened pace.

"You of all people know the prophesied outcome of this time and place in Israel's history. In all of mankind's history...the victory will be Heaven's."

Having delivered what he knew to be the message he was sent to deliver, Tyce walked to Essie's side, who embraced him and moved close against his side.

FROM JUST OUTSIDE the Maglan compound, they watched the clouds grow darker by the minute. The sky seemed to roll in gigantic, sideways tornadoes that twisted and boiled. Yet all seemed eerily quiet without lightning or thunder that followed.

"Is this the beginning of the...the prophecy's fulfillment, Tyce?"

Essie's question drew his attention from his own thoughts that this indeed might be the time. If so, he thought of what the two emissaries from the 144,000 religious young, Jewish men meant. What did they mean that he would be given a view of the fulfillment of the prophecy?

He remembered their exact words. "You will be witness, Tyce Greyson. You will be given full view of the fulfillment."

Still, the skies darkened. Essie moved as close as possible to Tyce, holding to him tightly, while together they looked at the black, rolling clouds of what surely must be the beginning of God's judgment.

As the wind began to blow against them, its chill wrapping them, they sensed being in a vortex of darkness swirling from the clouds surrounding them. Just as suddenly as the vortex seemed to lift them, their feet settled on hard ground and the almost-total darkness dissipated.

They stood high on a promontory, huddled together, their eyes taking in a vast plain far below.

"I've been here before," Essie said, her fear tempered by her astonishment. "It is Mount Carmel. Papa took us here once as teenagers. That valley…it's the place where Armageddon is said to take place. It's the plains of Esdraelon."

The skies continued to boil, growing ever more violent, seemingly not far above them.

"What does this mean?" Essie's question didn't sound fearful, her emotions still caught in the moment of astonishment.

"Looks like you're going to join me in one of my vision things, kiddo. Let's just enjoy the show. There is about to be one, I suspect."

The clouds rolled and boiled even more intensively, and the words started replaying in Tyce's mind while he glanced upward to see the lightning that began to fracture their violence. The conversation with the two men in the white clothing with the golden sashes, the men from the 144,000 sent to evangelize Israel and the world.

"We have come to tell you of the coming attack from the north. The attack from Israel's enemies."

"Then there will be an attack from this Russian coalition..."

"Yes. It is foretold. The prophet Ezekiel has said."

"When? When will the attack come?"

"You will be witness, Tyce Greyson. You will be given full view of the fulfillment."

"When? When will this happen?"

"Read the prophecy. Study what God's Word says," one of them said, ignoring his question. *"You are to know the details through God's Word, through the words given Ezekiel to pronounce."*

The words replayed as they had in the room at the time. They faded as the scripture he then researched came up—words Randy Faust had read him:

And it shall come to pass at the same time when Gog shall come against the land of Israel, saith the Lord GOD, that my fury shall come up in my face. For in my jealousy and in the fire of my wrath have I spoken, Surely in that day there shall be a great shaking in the land of Israel.

And I will call for a sword against him throughout all my mountains, saith the Lord GOD: every man's sword shall be against his brother. And I will plead against him with pestilence and with blood; and I will rain upon him, and upon his bands, and upon the many people that are with him, an overflowing rain, and great hailstones, fire, and brimstone. Thus will I magnify myself, and sanctify myself; and I will be known in the eyes of many nations, and they shall know that I am the LORD.

Tyce and Essie heard it then. Thunder, not from the clouds above, but of mechanized military forces moving in the distance. The sound grew in volume until they could see the assaulting force spread across the entire triangle of the Megiddo valley.

"They are coming to attack us," Essie said, clutching to Tyce more tightly.

"This is what Ezekiel prophesied, Ess. It's the fulfillment we are watching."

"And what is to happen?" she said, trying to hold back tears of fear.

"They lose, Essie. If the Bible is true, they lose in the most devastating way imaginable."

The valley looked from their elevated position as if a wave of boiling dust was sweeping across the vast expanse. This must have been the vantage from which Napoleon Bonaparte had once observed, saying that this valley was the greatest place for battle in the world.

The thought crossed his mind while, not horses, as Napoleon would have envisioned, but tanks and troop carriers by the thousands moved at top speed across the plain.

"What…will happen, according to the prophecy?"

"Just watch and see. Israel's God has it all under control. Just keep watching."

Above and behind the tanks and rolling battle armaments came hundreds of helicopters. Tyce recognized them as the type that carried missiles of devastating capabilities.

He knew without reservation that they were about to see what no one in modern history could have ever witnessed.

When the leading edge of the force passed them from their observation point, a massive lightning strike split

256

the now entirely blackened clouds. Rain suddenly deluged in massive waves onto the scene below.

Tyce held his wife close while they watched the rain pour in a flood on the forces below. While the rain continued to look like a tremendous waterfall, at first huge hailstones could be seen, making the almost solid sheet of water become blackened with their profusion.

Already the forces had stopped or were moving erratically upon the great plain.

The gush of water from the burst-asunder clouds continued while there begin to fall from the entire length and breadth of the clouds over the valley huge, red-hot fireballs. They landed everywhere there was invading army's war machinery.

All movement now was stopped. There didn't appear to be a single vehicle or troop carrier in which there was any life whatsoever.

They could do nothing but stare. Nothing could be spoken at this moment of truth. Tyce remembered seeing Yul Brynner portray Pharoah in the movie *The Ten Commandments,* and he remembered Pharaoh's words about Israel's leader, Moses, after he watched his forces drown after pursuing the Jews through the parted Red Sea: "His God…is God."

"AND YOU WITNESSED it from Mount Carmel?"

Morticai Kant's words were issued in a tone of disbelief.

"Yes, Abba. We were…taken there by some strange, cloud-like wind. We were just suddenly standing there."

"It was spectacular beyond description, Morticai. If only you could have been there to see Israel's enemies completely destroyed, except for maybe a few stragglers. They headed back the other way—toward Syria."

"And there were no weapons. It was weather related?"

"There were only God's weapons, Papa," Essie said. "Rain fell like it was being poured out of a gigantic vessel. Hail and spheres of flaming fire fell and covered all of the enemies' tanks and people."

"And you, Tyce, do you believe this to be supernatural?"

"No, not *just* supernatural, Morticai. It was God who did it."

"That's not what the talking heads of the New Roman Order are saying. No more than a half hour after the decimation of the Russian coalition's military, the NRO has claimed that it was Klaus von Lucis and secret weapons he used that did the devastation."

"Von Lucis?" Tyce said.

"Yes. And he, himself, gave an explanation that it was all part of his promise to protect Israel."

"Secret weapons? Were they some kind of weaponry that could turn rain off and on and somehow bring the hail and fire from somewhere…almost as if it just formed right in the clouds and fell specifically on all the targets below?"

"Well, Tyce, he didn't say how he did it. I took it that von Lucis wanted to make us believe he had supernatural abilities of some sort."

"And people are falling for these lies?" Essie said.

"Actually, there are many who believe it to be the Almighty who saved us, not Klaus von Lucis and his New Roman Order magic," Kant said.

"That can't make such an egomaniac as von Lucis very happy, having people disbelieve his claims to have god-like power," Tyce said.

"He has begun rounding up those who don't go along with every nuanced bit of the NRO demands. He is especially going after those who are converting to belief in Jesus Christ under all these strange preachers who claim to be Jews."

"What is he doing to them?"

"We heard about the guillotines that were being produced, daughter. Well, they have been rolled out and are now being used to behead all who are contrarian to the NRO and von Lucis and his proclamations."

Tyce stiffened from his position on the sofa next to his wife. Kant's words struck him as if he had been poked by an invisible finger. He stood and walked across the room to retrieve the Bible next to the laptop. He returned and sat again.

"What are you looking for?"

"Something Randy and I talked about a long time ago. It was after my visions following the snake bite on Patmos."

Tyce continued to thumb through the old Bible's pages, finally coming to the area of his search.

"Here it is. I remembered it was in the twentieth chapter of Revelation."

He scanned the words until his eyes fell on the object of his search. "Here we are," he said, and begin reading Revelation 20:4:

And I saw thrones, and they sat upon them, and judgment was given unto them: and I saw the souls of them that were beheaded for the witness of Jesus, and for the word of God, and which had not worshipped the beast, neither his image, neither had received his mark upon their foreheads, or in their hands.

"So, this von Lucis, he is your Antichrist?" Kant's words were spoken with a tone of incredulity.

"Well, I would say things are beginning to add up," Tyce said. "Don't you think?"

"Explain to me. I don't see how this Jesus you and others have always talked about has any relevance to today. We have always been taught, and it just makes sense. Israel's Mashiach will make Israel the most powerful nation on earth. He won't just be meek and agree to be nailed to some post," Kant said.

When Tyce didn't say anything, Kant continued.

"If there's no Christ, then there is no Antichrist. Mashiach, when He comes, will fulfill the promises of the scrolls."

"Many in Israel are saying now that von Lucis is the Christ…the Messiah of Israel, Papa. Do you believe him to be our Mashiach?"

Kant remained silent, looking to his daughter, then to his son-in-law.

"This is greatly troubling to me," he said, finally. "Our people are more and more embracing this imposter from the New Roman Order. If the *true* Mashiach is to save Israel, he had better hurry. Or else there will be no Israel to save, if this regime is allowed to complete its mission from Satan."

RABBI AMIR LUBEKA was on the phone, his voice high-pitched with panic.

"You were right in all your foretellings, Tyce. This man is, as we saw together, from the eternal abyss."

"We shouldn't be talking on the phone, Amir," Tyce said. "They are everywhere with their surveillance."

"Perhaps you are right, but we must have direction for our congregants. They are terrified. They do not wish to be participant in the things the Sanhedrin hierarchy are directing all within Judaism to join. Demanding that we join with this amalgamation...this Ecumenical Collective and this man of the devil, Elias Koahn."

"Why are they afraid? I haven't heard any direct threats—so far, at least."

"Members are getting threatening calls. They are receiving looks, as if the entire population of Jerusalem, or Tel Aviv, or wherever, know them personally, and are threatening with their stares."

"All within your...congregants are against this Elias Koahn's pointing to von Lucis as the Mashiach?"

"Yes. He is a false prophet...a false leader sent to deceive us. All of our following are aware of this false rabbi and von Lucis are about," Lubeka said, pausing then for Tyce's response.

"How many of these...followers...do you have?"

"Perhaps thirty thousand. It is hard to say. No census has been taken since the disappearing took place. Everything fell apart within Judaism when it happened. It seems that our congregants maintain holy precepts of Torah, while most follow the ways of this...this hybrid of Jewish law."

"What about these new converts to Christianity? These thousands of strange Jews who now preach everywhere—throughout the entire world, as a matter of fact? What is your thinking on these factors as part of all that's taking place?"

"This, too, is troubling. There is a concerted effort to weaken our ranks. These men in white garb...we view them as part of the NRO evil trying to tear apart our belief in Yahweh. They are not of Hashem, but of Satan."

Tyce knew in that moment that although those of the Kibbutz *oh-LAHM hah* Council understood the evil they faced, they didn't accept the truth as he had come to understand it. The white-clad young men were indeed from the heavenly realm. They were not the equivalent of the New World Order and Elias Koahn's Ecumenical Collective.

"What would you have me do, Amir? What can I do to help?"

"You are close to the most…knowledgeable man in all of Israel, when it comes to…secretive matters."

When the rabbi hesitated, Tyce said, "Yes? And what do you want from me, from my father-in-law?"

"We want you to find a hiding place for us. There is coming a great purge. There have always been great purges from tyrants against those of Judaism, Tyce. Hitler, Stalin, ideology—makes no difference. The hatred is from the devil, from Satan himself. He directs the tyrants to purge us who are of Hashem."

"Morticai Kant is no longer in power, or near the power that controls Israel, Amir. You know that."

"Yes. But he has forgotten more than any of those in power have ever known."

"What do you mean?"

"I mean that Mr. Kant knows of places underground and other sites that have been built by those who are now dead and gone. They are abandoned. We need to have shelter in such as these."

"Thirty thousand of you…or more?"

"There are such places…and Morticai Kant knows of them. He can give us shelter."

"Even if he could do this, how would you survive for long just hiding out?"

"Have you read your scriptures?"

"Well, yes."

"What do you think the miracles are all about? God provided for Elijah. He provided for David in slaying Goliath, he had his angel slay many thousands as they lay sleeping awaiting to overrun our cities. Do you not believe Hashem can feed us while we shelter?"

"Well, why don't you have shelter from Hashem already?"

"Because the need, as a matter of life and death for us, has just come to the surface. He will provide, and He will use a human agent to see to it," the rabbi said.

"And that's my father-in-law."

"Yes," Amir Lubeka said, his tone brightening. "And that makes you the second human agent in helping Hashem…in helping us."

Within a few hours, Tyce sat watching the screen of the advanced technology the Israeli government still allowed the former Maglan chief to have in the home they also continued to provide.

Tyce and Essie had moved into the spacious residence at the demand of Essie's father. He wanted her close by—to protect her from the hard times he knew were about to befall the world. Kant would use all within his power and ability to assure that Essie was safe for as long as possible.

The screen on the large monitor was alive with scenes from around the world. Much of North America had been destroyed, especially along the East Coast, when strange explosions burst and flames consumed everything. It all happened, the broadcasters claimed, when Klaus von

Lucis' secret weapons had destroyed the advancing Russian coalition. Fires and bursts from huge explosions also had made impacts on the coasts of European nations.

Many cities across the world were in turmoil, and black-uniformed NRO civil constables pounded on people in the streets. They clubbed those who resisted their orders. And, in some cases, they shot them with machine pistols.

The streets in many scenes were covered in blotches of blood that pooled where the NRO riot controllers had shot whoever would not comply with demands for order.

Tyce turned up the volume when the image of a familiar anchor appeared on screen. "And the most dangerous of all to law and order are the neo Christians whom the NRO is determined to eliminate."

The screen changed to the image of an NRO government official speaking. "If you are one of these terrorists who insists on pushing your evil religious mantra, you will soon taste the bite of the NRO guillotine."

The scene changed again. It was Rabbi Elias Koahn, who looked into the camera as he spoke. "You must repent of this false and dangerous lie from the pit of Hell. You must reject this myth that one who many believe to be God Himself can save the soul by His sacrifice many centuries ago."

The scene on a street in France showed converts being put on platforms of "Mobile Decap Units," as they were dubbed. The mechanized guillotines whirred from within the large vans, the victims were placed on their knees, heads locked within metal stocks, and the blade descended, slicing off the heads of all who would not repent of their belief in Jesus Christ.

The male anchor again appeared on the screen, a

grim look on his now familiar-to-the-whole-world countenance. The technology translated his words, spoken in French, into perfect English.

"The formula is simple to avoid this fate. The New Roman Order does not take pleasure in dealing in this way with its enemies. Neither does President Klaus von Lucis wish to deal harshly with NRO citizenry.

"But if repentance isn't forthcoming, the guillotine must do its purging work, eliminating all who put out dangerously false, anti-god lies."

Tyce turned off the volume, scenes of the sickening blood purges continuing to be shown from around the world.

While he watched, he sensed a familiar ambience surrounding him. The screen before him and all else faded, and a voice called from somewhere within the darkness.

"Tyce. It is Eli and Moshi. We have a word from on high."

Tyce felt at the same time unable to move, his entire body seeming to be frozen in the chair, and at ease, sensing comfort from the presence of the robed figures.

"What is the word?" was all he could manage in reply.

"Rabbi Amir Lubeka and the Kibbutz *oh-LAHM hah* Council are essential to carrying out Jehovah's plan to bring in His Holy Kingdom. You must do as the rabbi asks."

"Exactly what? What do you want of me?"

"You will know what to do as you proceed," the one called Moshi said. "Just begin your mission by doing what the rabbi asks. Do not be afraid. We will be near at all times. The Lord will direct."

He suddenly was again sitting before the monitor, the bloody scenes continuing to move across the screen.

CHAPTER 18

"Whatever happened that day the Russians were destroyed has caused a degeneration of the ecology," Morticai Kant said, entering the room and glancing at both Tyce and Essie while choosing a chair.

"The food shortages are horrific. The regime has determined to take their commerce dictatorship to a new level of dystopia."

They said nothing, awaiting his heated explanation.

"They now are demanding that in order to control an equitable distribution of diminishing food reserves, we must agree to be implanted with a chip. This is all somehow tied to the central computers in Brussels, as I take it.

"If a person refuses, they are likely to feel the guillotine's blade, according to the latest threat."

"Abba, Tyce has had a visit by the two who call themselves Eli and Moshi," Essie said, interrupting her father's NRO update. "And there's more."

"Oh? Well. Let us have it," Kant said, turning to his son-in-law.

"They just appeared out of a mist while I was at work on the laptop. They wanted to validate Rabbi Lubeka's conversation."

"Yes? And what did that involve?"

"Lubeka and the council asked me to talk with you… about using your knowledge of all of Israel's defense structure…to find them a place of safety from a purge he says he knows is coming against them."

"Against the *oh-LAHM hah* Council?"

"Actually, against their entire branch of Judaism. Thirty thousand of them."

"Thirty thousand?! And just how am I to do this? Supposing I could hide even the twenty or so among them…"

"And that's where the visit from Eli and Moshi comes in, I guess. They said for me to do whatever Rabbi Lubeka says. So I'm telling you, just like Lubeka requested."

"Well, this…Eli and Moshi…didn't tell *me* this. Why not so?"

"I don't know, Morticai. I don't know anything about much of all this. I know it all involves prophecy, and that I'm in the middle of it for some reason. But I can't tell you why they haven't directly come to you."

"I believe it's because you are some sort of channel Eli and Moshi are directed by Hashem to use in delivering his messages, as he used Elijah and others in delivering messages," Essie said.

"With the things going on in the streets," Tyce said, "…the NRO shooting people on the spot…decapitating people without trials…I'm not so sure Rabbi Lubeka isn't right. They might be next."

"This Rabbi Elias Koahn is more and more von Lucis' right hand," Kant said. "He is declaring that all who don't go along with everything he and von Lucis command to be against Hashem. They are attacking these who are converted by those who wear the white uniforms. Maybe these are the ones they will continue to pursue, and not the followers of the *oh-LAHM hah* Council."

"Somehow, I don't think so. Eli and Moshi wouldn't have appeared to me…and said that I must do what Lubeka says if the council's followers were not in danger."

"All this supernatural insertion. I just can't bring myself to…embrace it," Kant said, standing and gritting his teeth while scowling and gesticulating with his fists in frustration.

"But you have to admit, Papa," Essie said, "things going on are not natural. It is a time, perhaps, to put away traditional thinking."

"A good example," Tyce put in, "is the disappearances of millions. Just that alone should make us know these are times that are—"

"Yes, yes!" Kant said, interrupting him. "I'm aware. It is just difficult for one so steeped in rationale in order to assess and take care of problems to grasp this strangeness," Kant said.

There was silence between them for a time, before Tyce spoke.

"This is of God, Morticai. I have no doubt. The only chance we have to assess and take care of the problems involved…as you put it…is to trust in Heaven's directives. And we know that, for some reason, I've been chosen to be the conduit to channel God's messages, as Ess said."

IF THIS WAS ALL HEAVEN-DIRECTED, and Tyce was in the middle of it, it made sense to think that this book would tell the fate of God's chosen nation. That was what Randy had called Israel; that's what he had heard it called for years.

God's chosen people. Surely God will take care of His chosen people. The thoughts went quickly through his brain while he typed into the search engine: "Scripture for where God's chosen people are hidden during Tribulation."

He looked at the screen, seeing the reference, which he quickly looked up in the old Bible next to his laptop.

Revelation 12:

> *12:1 And there appeared a great wonder in heaven; a woman clothed with the sun, and the moon under her feet, and upon her head a crown of twelve stars: 12:2 And she being with child cried, travailing in birth, and pained to be delivered. 12:3 And there appeared another wonder in heaven; and behold a great red dragon, having seven heads and ten horns, and seven crowns upon his heads. 12:4 And his tail drew the third part of the stars of heaven, and did cast them to the earth: and the dragon stood before the woman which was ready to be delivered, for to devour her child as soon as it was born. 12:5 And she brought forth a man child, who was to rule all nations with a rod of iron: and her child was caught up unto God, and to his throne. 12:6 And the woman fled into the wilderness, where she hath a place prepared of God, that they should feed her there a thousand two hundred and three-score days.*

Tyce pushed back from the computer desk, swiveled in the desk chair, and stood. He paced, still reading the Bible he held in his hands. He was not a Bible scholar. He tried to be, but couldn't understand. Still, he knew there was something in these verses that told the end of these things that faced him…as well as Israel and the world. He again did the thing he had rarely done. He prayed to Heaven for help in understanding the scripture before him. If God wanted him involved in all this, then surely He would provide understanding.

If help in understanding was to come, there would be another visitation…one by the two men in robes. But no such dark ambience was beginning to encapsulate him. Neither the two men, nor the men in the white jump-suits and golden sashes, were anywhere in sight.

From somewhere in the deep recesses of his brain there came a sound, raising the hair on his neck. It was not an audible voice, but one that pulsed within his inner senses. It spoke to him as surely, even more surely, than an audible voice.

It began by saying, "I AM."

The voice went on to explain the scripture in the book he held in front of him. It said that this was of the Lord sending his Son in the flesh into the world to offer grace for the salvation of fallen mankind. That this was God's plan from the beginning.

Satan, Lucifer the fallen one, and one-third of the angelic forces rebelled. They were expelled from Heaven.

The Man-Child, God's Son, was born of a woman of Israel, so Israel was the *woman* mentioned in the scripture.

Satan and his hordes pursued the woman to destroy her. God's child was caught up into Heaven after the crucifixion, burial, and resurrection. Israel will flee into the desert at the end of the era of Jacob's trouble to a place of safety prepared by God Himself.

The explanation was simple and complete in Tyce's mind. He could but bow his head.

"Thanks, Lord," he said in barely a whisper. But within his spirit that now soared, he was shouting, "Yes!"

TYCE'S SLEEP WAS TROUBLED. He had come down from the high he had felt upon getting understanding of the scripture. But now he stared into the darkness while he lay beside his soundly sleeping wife.

How long would they be able to remain safe? So many were now being brutalized by the regime. The New Roman Order was becoming as dangerous for Christian converts as for Christians of the times of ancient Rome in the days of Nero.

How long before they came to take all who didn't go along with Klaus von Lucis and Rabbi Elias Koahn? How could he protect Essie? When they came for him and Essie, how could he react defensively? Or would it just be suicide by NRO police, or whatever force would be sent?

Morticai Kant's ring of protection would only last as long as the NRO's attention was diverted by the many people who still resisted. As long as attention was on those poor people, the more prominent, like Kant, former director of Maglan, could, maybe, be kept from being brought within von Lucis' deadly crosshairs.

He would talk with Morticai tomorrow. He would tell him of the scripture interpretation about Israel's prophetic fate. He would tell him all about…

Suddenly his senses were being pulled into an envelope of swirling thoughts that momentarily had moved him through walls and into a room with white-smocked men and women.

It was obviously a laboratory setting of some sort. He stood in their midst, yet they didn't appear to see him. No. They hadn't a clue he was among them.

A group of a half-dozen people walked in the room and took seats in front of a woman who stood facing them. She held a laser pointer.

The woman's language was not English, and Tyce couldn't determine its ethnic origin. However, he heard in perfectly spoken English.

The large monitor on the wall behind the woman, too, displayed a language Tyce couldn't determine, but as he watched, the words became ones he could understand in some inexplicable way.

"As all of you are aware, the extracts derived from the discoveries involving the Euphrates artifact have at last successfully been combined with microchip for achieving universal implantation." The woman moved the red dot of the laser pointer to describe to the room of scientists the details of the achievement.

"To this point, of course," she continued, "the implanted chips have been tested on but a moderate number. We now can begin implantation with total confidence. The chipping of all within NRO universe will now have their biology integrated with that of the Euphrates artifact. The process will begin within the month. The resurrection must first take place—the manifestation of the power for which we have awaited so long."

The men and women in the lab coats mumbled their elated approval of the woman's words, ones issued with gleeful excitement.

Tyce, who reckoned what the woman had said to be

good news to the group, then again felt his senses being tugged from their midst.

The emotion wasn't fear-engendered, nor was it even of wonder. His thoughts seemed to be of remembered times of his past. His movement seemed to bring solace rather than trepidation as his memories flooded back, and he stood in another time, but in a somehow familiar place, and with Essie by his side.

He stood with Randolph Faust while the memory unfolded precisely as that earlier time.

Harnak al Mufi, smiling broadly, thrust his hand out to take that of Faust. The men embraced, and Faust turned to introduce Tyce Greyson.

"Ah, yes. I have met Mr. Greyson," the Egyptian said, taking Tyce's offered hand.

"And, it is so good to see you once more, Essie," he said, hugging her warmly.

"Mr. Greyson and I met while at the institute in Bethesda," al Mufi said, turning to lead the three new arrivals deeper into the building.

"This laboratory is not unlike the previous you visited," he said, addressing the journalist. "However, on this occasion, you will find we can be much more forthcoming regarding the Euphrates artifact and the project."

"I hope that means I'll get to see what's in the sarcophagus," Tyce said.

"Absolutely. We will see all momentarily," the Egyptian said, standing to one side to allow the three to pass through the large door. He walked to a table near one wall of the semi-darkened room, pressed a button on a table, and spoke into an intercom microphone. "Please—may we have some assistance in LC66?"

He pushed another button and the wall slid apart, revealing a large room even darker than the one before.

"We must keep the lighting as subdued as possible, as you know, Dr. Faust. To prevent deterioration is always of the essence."

"How have the contents held up?" Faust said, while they approached the huge, golden sarcophagus sitting atop a three-foot-high platform of what looked to be made of solid concrete.

"We have not seen any apparent deterioration."

"Is this thing made of solid gold?" Tyce asked, amazed at the size and polished brilliance of the massive burial chamber.

"It is gold overlaid upon a composite structure of wood, indigenous asphalt, and other material. We are not certain of its precise makeup," al Mufi said.

"It's beautiful in its own way," Essie said, moving closer to see the ornate engraving along the edge of the top nearest them.

"Yes. There was much care involved by the ancients in preparing this chamber," al Mufi said, bidding with his hand for the three lab-coated men who had just entered the room to step forward. Two of the men moved to each end of the sarcophagus and the third stood at the center. They lifted together, having to strain to move the lid until it rested against the back wall.

A dark-gray covering lay across the open vault, and the Egyptian moved in to remove it from right to left.

"Behold Gilgamesh!"

Al Mufi's exclamation seemed appropriately spoken as the contents were unveiled. Only Essie's slight gasp of amazement broke the silent astonishment of the three who were for the first time seeing the figure lying face-up in the sarcophagus.

The mummy was a smudged gray color in its overall appearance. Occasional dark- greenish tints of

274

various gradations covered the surface. The head, considerably more than twice the size of a man's, bore distinctive facial characteristics, the large, slightly curved nose ending at a sharp point just above the definitive mouth formed by the tightly pressed-together lips.

The thick, swept-back hair was clearly discernable, despite the substance covering its surface. The hair streamed over part of the upper-left ear. The giant looked as if he were merely asleep.

Tyce thought how he had never seen such a mummy. Its state of near-perfect preservation most likely could be credited to the substance used rather than use of bandages like on mummies of Egypt.

"How long does the being measure?" Randolph Faust asked, moving close to the figure's head and looking it over carefully.

"Just over four meters," al Mufi said.

"More than twelve feet?"

Tyce stepped beside Faust, looking into the vault and following the legs to the end, where the mummified feet looked to be more than twice the length of ordinary human male feet.

"The substance covering the mummy—how thick is it?"

"About three centimeters, no more," al Mufi said in answer to Faust's question.

"You mean there are no bandages? There's a substance of some sort."

"It is a substance found from ancient times," al Mufi said. "The best way it can be described is that it is an asphalt-like material."

"It's the slime of the plain of Shinar referred to in Genesis chapter 11, Tyce," Randolph Faust said, bending near the gigantic corpse's face. "It's the substance that was used to build the ziggurat—the Tower of Babel."

Harnak al Mufi's facial expression took on a look of concentration while he thought how best to explain. "You are familiar with DNA?" he said to Tyce.

"Yes, basically," Tyce said. "They are able to get precise genetic identification on rapists and do IDs on bodies through DNA testing."

"Forensics are now moving at fantastic speed," the Egyptian scientist said, nodding agreement. "Until this moment in time, we thought there was no living or dead being with any DNA that could be found that could not be identified and thoroughly defined."

His face twisted into a frown of consternation. "But, with our large friend, here, it is a stopping point."

"What do you mean?" Tyce said, when al Mufi paused longer than his curiosity could stand.

"It means that we cannot identify this particular DNA," al Mufi said. "There is none to which to compare it. The genetic material taken from this being is not purely human."

"What do you mean 'purely'?"

"Part of the DNA is human, but the other we cannot identify. It is totally new to us."

"What does all that mean?" Essie's question caused the Egyptian to turn to face her, his face again in a frowning expression of concentration.

"Although we have only begun to explore, this…finding…does seem to give some credence to the contention of some within the scientific community that humanity was somehow placed here by extraterrestrials. Although, like I said, we have only begun to investigate."

The remembered time of looking at the giant in the sarcophagus and the explanations by the Egyptian gave way to another scene as it replayed vividly in Tyce's senses.

All-encompassing blackness and cold had engulfed him, he remembered. Tyce Greyson, this time, was ready for whatever came. It was another trip to the land of vision the otherworldly powers assigned him to go to whenever they chose. He didn't know where he had just been, or where it was leading, just that he was here, now, and the darkness would, he knew, soon burst into light and into scenes he was to see and hear.

A pinpoint of light, as always, first pierced the center of the blackness and seemed to shoot directly into his consciousness. The scene before him then burst into totality, filled with a number of lab-coated men surrounding a large computer monitor screen, upon which all eyes were locked.

"Dr. Gravelan," one of the men to the left side of the screen pointed to something in the information displayed. "See, here. This is what must be comprehended if the serum is to stabilize, thus attain transferability from the material taken from the subject to the human DNA for the results we must obtain."

"Very well," a short, balding man standing directly in front of the screen said.

Tyce's eyes widened while looking upon the scene before him. A dark, shadow-like figure in the shape of a man emerged from the scientist who had first spoken. The being entered the scientist who had answered, taking on the man's shape, then disappeared.

Moments later, the scientist whom the shadow figure had just possessed spoke, while continuing to study the screen.

"Yes, I see now; it is all very clear. Unless there is a complete restructuring at the subatomic level, nothing changes. But, here and here," the scientist touched the screen with an index finger, "we restructure, and the transferability is achieved."

Another of the men, after studying the screen for several moments, spoke. "When will the human subjects be prepared for the injections?"

"Each must be individually genetically made compatible, their genetics reengineered according to the precise directive for each. The slightest variance from the exact model tailored for their DNA profile will cause mutation that will prove calamitous. Probably death would be inevitable within hours," the scientist who hosted the shadow figure said.

"And they agree to that risk?" the questioner continued.

"How could they not? This is an offer of ultimate opportunity. It presents possibilities that those who seek the power and authority of leadership have always coveted."

"And, what of the individuality factor—the soul that is the individual? There is an inalterable effect, I understand," the questioning scientist said.

"This is a matter each fully understands and accepts," the scientist whose body the shadow being had entered said. "To assume the responsibility, they will be called upon to carry out, they will have to attain…extradimensional…abilities."

"What is the timeline for the total conversion? When will the transformation be complete?" another of the scientists asked.

"We must proceed judiciously," the scientist directly in front of the screen said. "The time factor for complete conversion is not clear at this point. There has not been any similar attempt. However, the conversion should be complete within a maximum of two months, I should think."

"Then, the procedure will progress much more rapidly, once we have established parameters and protocols within our methodologies, and so forth," he added. The scientist who seemed to be in charge concluded, "It will then be possible to initiate entire populations within, say, a matter of weeks."

He spoke, then, while running his fingers over the controls as the screen changed accordingly. He said, as if to himself, "All will then be in place for the one chosen to be Earthlord."

Tyce's senses began changing while the scene before him suddenly filled with many people in an immense science laboratory, all wearing the familiar white smocks. Dark, shadowy figures, like the one that had entered the scientist, intermingled with the humans. He gawked, astonished at seeing the smoke-like beings enter and exit their human hosts, while the people in the lab coats went about various duties within the laboratory.

His surroundings faded quickly to total blackness, before the now-familiar, brilliant point of light burst from somewhere in the center of the ambient vision in which he stood.

When his environment changed from quickly growing brighter surroundings to a scene he could see clearly, it became obvious that the same, small scientist who was the leader of the group—the one the shadow being had entered—stood, speaking to a small group of men dressed in business attire. The rumpled scientist spoke in good, but broken, English, while the others sat in rapt attention to his every word.

"So, this is the essence of our work, thanks to your

beneficence and largesse. Now, I will be pleased to answer any questions."

Immediately, a man Tyce recognized as the German who had helped inculcate him during his initial introduction to the being in the sarcophagus stood from his chair and blurted his question. "So, you have determined that the giant being is offspring of extraterrestrial visitors to earth at some point, probably at the time of the first settlers in Mesopotamia?" he asked.

"Yes," the scientist answered. "We have proven our postulate in that regard beyond any doubt, I think. The studies prove the creature is from the human element and another element not of this sphere."

The German continued, "So, what are the next experiments to be done on the mummy? Are there any commercial applications to be extracted from this creature's...contributions to science, do you anticipate?"

"Our—that is, the scientific community chosen by the Brussels Commission to investigate—our conclusions satisfy that earth was once visited, and that many of the wonders of the world at that time were directly built, or directed in being constructed, by these...visitors."

The German pressed, "and, these were—that is, the offspring—were giants?"

"They were giants, in many cases, both physically and intellectually. We have concluded, for example, that the Great Pyramid of Giza was constructed by such giant entities, perhaps even by the visitors who themselves sired those like the one who lies in the golden sarcophagus—"

"Yes, yes," the questioner interrupted. "All of the scientific findings on behalf of history is understood and are duly noted as quite fascinating, even amazing. But, we have investors who expect much more than to fatten history books or scientific journals."

There were rumblings of muffled laughter, with the British man Tyce recognized from days earlier saying, "hear, hear," with amused agreement in his voice.

"We are aware of the financial exigencies that hold sway over this project," the scientist said, nonplused in his retort to the German. "We have concluded that, for at least a number of months, it will be wise to proceed slowly in trying to find the application that might be made to the improvement to the human genome—to the gene pool—so that great physical and intellectual advantage can be developed."

"You mean, so you can find ways to create growth hormones, or whatever?" an American among the group of men stood and asked.

"Well, 'hormones' perhaps is not the correct term, but yes…we believe we can substantially improve the human biological future with the work we are doing."

"Then, the improvement of the human race is the whole, the entire, purpose involved, here," the American followed up.

"That is accurate. That is the primary thrust of the effort. What could there be beyond that? This is why we were asked to proceed. Naturally, there should follow great financial benefits from improving one's children, in helping to create a healthier, heartier breed of people…greater longevity, and so forth, I should think."

Tyce watched the agreement on the seated men's faces—faces whose features began to dissolve as his senses again gathered the reality of his own surroundings.

Again in the present, Tyce reached to his right in the

darkness. He felt Essie there, turned away to face the direction opposite her husband.

The vision was real, he thought. *It was no dream.*

It was just as it happened those years earlier, only a few years earlier. And Tyce again felt the tug against his senses into those years. There was no way to stop the moving-away from this time and place.

When he saw the small gathering of lab-coated men near the center of the room, his premonition came to life. The short man who turned to give a quick, tight smile and offer his hand, upon Harnak al Mufi's intro-duction, was the man he felt as if he had already met. It was the scientist he'd seen in the vision, the one the shadow being had possessed.

"Dr. Rudolf Gravelan, Mr. Tyce Greyson," al Mufi said with a smile, while the men reached for each other's right hands.

"Mr. Greyson is writing the articles introducing the world to the fabulous find and the marvelous things going on here at Antiquities," the Egyptian said with a bright tone.

"I am pleased to meet you, Mr. Greyson," the scientist said, then looked past him to Essie. "And, you must be Essie, Morticai's daughter," he added, smiling broadly and taking Essie's hand, holding it lightly, and patting the top of her hand with the tips of his fingers.

"Nice to meet you, Dr. Gravelan," she said, a quick smile crossing her lips.

After several other introductions, Gravelan lightly gripped Tyce's elbow and pulled him aside.

"Our interview was scheduled for this morning, Mr. Greyson, I realize. Something has developed that requires that I leave for Europe as soon as possible, however. I am sorry that I must ask that you speak to several of our other scientists on the project, if you don't mind terribly."

Gravelan had poked one of Tyce's pet peeves in its most sensitive places—an interviewee trying to weasel out of a promised interview—and something within his combative spirit caused him to blurt the words.

"I'm terribly disappointed, of course, Dr. Gravelan. I had specifically wanted to ask you about the Earthlord. I'm most interested—fascinated, really—with your serum, the DNA combination of the two distinct species, and the results you anticipate with regard to the infusion of the first two volunteer subjects. I understand you expect the result to be complete within two months."

Tyce watched for the scientist's reaction. Gravelan stiffened and stood more erect, almost reaching Tyce's own height. He heard a guttural groan that seemed to come from somewhere within the man's throat. Gravelan's eyes widened, then resumed a normal look that turned into a transfixed stare at Tyce.

Tyce had no idea why he had blurted the information that he knew Gravelan wouldn't expect him to know. It came from an unconscious thought about the scene he had witnessed. But, there it was, and the scientist was visibly shaken by its bluntness.

Gravelan spoke after several seconds of obvious reflection on the journalist's unexpected remarks. "Perhaps I can delay my departure for a time longer," the still somewhat flustered scientist said, almost whispering the words. He looked around them sheepishly, as if to learn whether others had heard the exchange. "Let us move to another room so as to conduct the interview in a quieter setting," he said, again lightly gripping Tyce's elbow and moving with him toward a door several feet away.

Tyce winked at Essie just before he and Gravelan

entered the small room just off the large laboratory. He would give the reluctant scientist with a dark side a grilling worthy of the esoteric information he harbored.

"Your series of articles for this project, as I understand, consists of informing the world of our findings," the scientist said, after they were seated across a small table from each other.

"Yes," Tyce said. "That's my understanding, too. However, I sense there are two, distinct projects going on in this lab." He was getting right to the point he knew troubled Gravelan.

"And what would those be?" the scientist said, coyly.

"What I thought would be the *only* information collected from the project—that is the *main* information —was that this big guy in the sarcophagus is a combination of human DNA and that from some alien civilization—of extraterrestrial origin."

"Yes, that is our finding. And what other…information…do you believe is forthcoming?"

"Oh, do you plan to announce the other?"

"What, other, Mr. Greyson?" Gravelan's countenance had metamorphosed. His skin had changed from a reddish, hypertensive hue to pallor, as if most of the blood had been drained from his face. The demeanor had shifted from almost nervous to calm that bordered on drowsiness. The voice, too, was different. It was deeper, more measured—almost sinister in quality.

"What I mentioned a few minutes ago," Tyce said, reaching into the briefcase he carried to retrieve the microcassette recorder. "I'm particularly interested in the serum you want to produce for, apparently, injecting the entire world with, eventually."

"Where did you get any such information?" Gravelan's words came with a tone of incredulity.

"I'm sorry, Dr. Gravelan, but I'm the reporter, not the interviewee. Suffice it to say that I know such an outcome is sought through the experimentation on this giant being."

"And...what else have you heard that might be part of our little project?" Now the scientist's tone was mocking.

"That the injections somehow will change the very soul of the individual. That someone—or something—called Earthlord will come from this genetic manipulation."

Gravelan's expression changed from amusement to somberness. His voice became as hard as his look.

"If you write that, Mr. Greyson, you will make our entire work here the laughingstock of all of the scientific community. It will greatly damage the wonderful work our people have in fact accomplished. And, it will do your journalistic integrity no good to write such things and be later proven wrong."

"Then you are denying that what I have just laid out has any truth?"

"I am denying it completely—emphatically," Gravelan said with a quick nod of his head, while glaring at Tyce.

Tyce started to say more, to tell about the shadow beings he had seen entering and exiting Gravelan and the others during the vision. He thought better of it, and instead thumbed the small recorder and spoke into it.

"Dr. Rudolf Gravelan flatly denies that any other outcomes are being worked toward than that of proving the giant man-creature in the sarcophagus from the Euphrates Riverbed is the genetic offspring of two distinctive species—one human, the other, apparently, extraterrestrial."

When he had finished, Tyce looked back at Gravelan with resolve as tough as that exhibited by the scientist's demeanor. "I hope I've accurately reflected your answer to the allegations about the possible secondary purpose of the project, Dr. Gravelan. I wouldn't take any pleasure in uncovering secrets that lead to malfeasance of any sort."

The scientist paused purposefully before responding.

"Do not worry, Mr. Greyson. I personally guarantee that you will not report—that is, not find—such allegation to be true or such *malfeasance* to be the case."

Tyce sat up in the bed, the remembrance suddenly ending. Essie turned to see him sitting up, her sleep-affected senses causing her to reach to him.

"What is wrong?" she said, holding to his arm while half-sitting to see his face in the darkness. She turned to turn on the lamp that sat on the nightstand.

"You remember that time in the lab with Randy, and that little Egyptian guy who explained about the Gilgamesh mummy?"

"Yes. Who could forget?"

"The dream… It wasn't a dream… It was very real… A vision, I guess."

"A vision of that thing in the sarcophagus?"

"Yes. That and the whole time there. That Dr. Gravelan I interviewed. The whole thing about their group of scientists…and those other guys, the ones representing international businesses and governments."

"Yes. What was it about?"

"You remember…. They were experimenting, taking living tissue or DNA from the thing they said was Gilgamesh, but Randy believed to be Nimrod, the dictator at the time of the building of the Tower of Babel."

"Yes, I remember they were combining some DNA from extraterrestrials…from the giant in the sarcophagus...with human DNA. They were going to produce something they could give through injections into people."

"Not bad memory for a sleepy-head," Tyce said.

"They said it would make mankind much improved, didn't they?"

"Yes. But the real motive, this Gravelan guy said back when I saw those black, cloud-like things going in and out of the scientists, was to produce something called the Earthlord."

"Yes. I remember you telling it all to Randolph."

"Gravelan wanted...the group of scientists wanted to...develop a serum from this combination that would somehow be injected into all of humanity. This would make them compliant, and there's the scariest part. The injection would change the DNA from human to something not human."

"And what do you think? Why were you given this vision?"

"I recall it being mentioned that this injection of the serum would alter not only physical genetics, but would change the very soul of the person injected."

Both reflected for a moment before Essie spoke.

"And this Earthlord. What do you think that means?"

"The way I remember is that the scientists were to turn some person into a super-human man as world leader."

The thought ran through both of their minds at the same time. Essie is the one who voiced it: "Klaus Von Lucis? Do you think—?"

Tyce interrupted her. "There's certainly something strange to his sudden rise to power," he said.

CHAPTER 19

T he words kept pouring over his hotly brewing cauldron of thoughts while Tyce looked at the screen.

"Anyone who receives Antichrist's mark can't be redeemed. They will be lost forever and doomed to Hell for eternity."

The words were those of Randolph Faust during that time seemingly now so long ago. Tyce had to find the place in scripture where that warning was given. He researched until he found it in the book of Revelation.

14:9 And the third angel followed them, saying with a loud voice, If any man worship the beast and his image, and receive his mark in his forehead, or in his hand, 14:10 The same shall drink of the wine of the wrath of God, which is poured out without mixture into the cup of his indignation; and he shall be tormented with fire and brimstone in the presence of the holy angels, and in the presence of the Lamb: 14:11 And the smoke of their torment ascendeth up for ever

and ever: and they have no rest day nor night, who worship
the beast and his image, and whosoever receiveth the mark of
his name.

Tyce again found the place in scripture he knew
related to the declaration of doom he had just read.

13:16 And he causeth all, both small and great, rich and poor,
free and bond, to receive a mark in their right hand, or in
their foreheads: 13:17 And that no man might buy or sell,
save he that had the mark, or the name of the beast, or the
number of his name. 13:18 Here is wisdom. Let him that hath
understanding count the number of the beast: for it is the
number of a man; and his number is Six hundred threescore
and six.

These words made it clear. Anyone who took the
"mark" would be forever doomed. They would spend all
of eternity in Hell, being tormented day and night.

He examined the prophecy—the warning—more
closely. Those who take the mark would somehow "worship" the "beast"—also the beast's "image" in some way.

The thought leaped to his understanding. The word
"Earthlord." The word, or the part of the word, "lord,"
indicated a worship of some sort. There would be a
worship…a religious system.

The *Earth*…of course. The understanding began
unfolding as surely as if he read it in a news briefing. The
people of Planet Earth had long been subjected to the
proclamation that climate change was the number-one
enemy of humanity and of Mother Earth. Man was
destroying his mother planet—–the Earth—and it was
man who must *save Mother Earth.*

It all fit. The *Earthlord...* He would bring that *salvation* to the Earth, which was dying because of carbon dioxide and all of the greenhouse evil. Anyone who didn't worship the Earthlord and the religion he brought to save Mother Earth deserved death and destruction.

The scripture about dealing with those who resisted the religion, he remembered now—again from the Revelation. He looked it up and read:

> *13:11 And I beheld another beast coming up out of the earth; and he had two horns like a lamb, and he spake as a dragon. 13:12 And he exerciseth all the power of the first beast before him, and causeth the earth and them which dwell therein to worship the first beast, whose deadly wound was healed. 13:13 And he doeth great wonders, so that he maketh fire come down from heaven on the earth in the sight of men, 13:14 And deceiveth them that dwell on the earth by the means of those miracles which he had power to do in the sight of the beast; saying to them that dwell on the earth, that they should make an image to the beast, which had the wound by a sword, and did live. 13:15 And he had power to give life unto the image of the beast, that the image of the beast should both speak, and cause that as many as would not worship the image of the beast should be killed.*

THE LEVEL of Tyce's excitement wasn't something Kant and his daughter were used to seeing. His words all but exploded from him when he hurried through the door to Kant's study.

"It's all clear," Tyce said. "You've got to hear this!"

Kant and Essie almost together asked what was wrong.

"Von Lucis is the one the Bible says is the beast! He is Antichrist!"

He had explained all the conclusions he had reached about Klaus van Lucis and Rabbi Koahn. Now, three days later, he was determined to watch carefully every move of the man most all of Israel proclaimed as Messiah.

Von Lucis had promised, and had delivered, Israel's right to rebuild the Temple atop Mount Moriah. All of the Temple rituals and sacrifices were once again being carried out each day.

He claimed Jerusalem as his new headquarters, having left offices in Brussels.

Rabbi Koahn had declared him to be Israel's promised Mashiach, their deliverer from bondage and their king who would establish their God's kingdom, with Israel the head of all nations.

Most of Israel's population had grasped on to the rabbi's words of affirmation that von Lucis was the promised Messiah.

Tyce watched now, seeing on the large screen in Kant's great room the rabbi and thousands of Israelis surrounding Klaus von Lucis while he walked among them. The crowd seemed to part a bit, and Tyce saw that someone was leading a white horse toward their center.

Soon he realized the purpose. Von Lucis, having abandoned the stretch limousine a hundred meters on the very city limits of Jerusalem, now mounted and sat proudly on the gleaming white stallion.

The crowd followed him while he rode the steed toward the interior of Jerusalem.

Their hands were in the air. They were chanting and singing in mantra fashion while the horse and its rider, the object of the people's praise, looked straight ahead, acknowledging neither the throngs nor their songs of worship.

"The great man is reveling in his time in the spotlight," Kant said.

"So you believe him to be this...this *beast*?"

"Look at them, Morticai. He's claiming to be their Mashiach. Do you believe him to be your...*Messiah*?"

The Maglan chief stood beside Tyce while he sat watching proceedings. "I have watched his regime come to power by means of the devil. I have watched as they beat to death people on the streets. This is not how I perceive the Torah to describe Israel's prophesied warrior-king."

He sat in the chair beside his son-in-law. "You have studied this...prophecy from your New Testament. What does it tell you?"

"I've gone over some of it with you. The prophecy— well, the many prophesies—include the development of the economic system of marks and numbers. All will be forced to take the number and mark of...the regime's choosing."

"And it's all part of this Earthlord project...using the serum they've developed from the mummy of Gilgamesh, or Nimrod?"

"This has been at the center of my otherworldly experiences over these years," Tyce said. "I've just now connected it all. Or, at least I just now have *begun* to connect it all. Memories of all these disjointed experiences...these supernatural-type experiences...are now flooding back for some reason. This man, von Lucis...he is the *first beast* of Revelation 13. And Rabbi Elias Koahn is, I believe, the *second beast* of that prophecy."

"If not the Mashiach, he certainly is enjoying playing the part," Kant said.

The cameras all focused on the man who sat atop the horse, surrounded by worshipful, chanting and singing throngs, while the beast walked in prancing-fashion farther into Jerusalem.

"My one question for you, Tyce, is, if this is prophecy from your New Testament in process of fulfillment, what does it mean for my nation? What is to be Israel's part in all of this?"

The Maglan chief was still on Israel's guard, Tyce mused. And it was something he admired in his father-in-law. Morticai Kant was ready to put aside all else, including his holding the Christian New Testament as not being applicable to Israel, neither to the people nor to the country.

"In brief, I don't know," Tyce admitted. "I've not made a thorough study. Randy Faust gave me ideas, and some of those come to memory, but actually knowing what the Bible's prophets of the New Testament predict, I'll have to study."

"Maybe Eli and Moshi will intervene to inform," Kant said. His tone was not one of mocking, but of genuine hope.

Essie smiled, seeing her father's expression as he offered his thought.

"Abba, now do you begin to understand my husband's work for Israel?" she said.

"I suppose there is no need for Maglan, or for the IDF, if Hashem Himself is going to fight the battle," Morticai said with a smile that proved to his daughter that he was now relieved of the anxiety he had suffered over the past days. The great Maglan chief was now a believer in a power higher than any in Israel, or within the New Roman Order.

～

THE ORBS WERE BRIGHTER NOW, seemed larger, and moved about with more apparent purpose, Tyce noticed while driving along the street toward the Jerusalem Kibbutz *oh-LAHM hah* Council compound. The dark skies seemed darker, too. The sun had rarely appeared since the day the peace agreement was signed by von Lucis and the signatories of Israel and he Arab contingency.

Although Tel Aviv and most of the nation Israel had been free of the weather phenomena daily raking much of the Mediterranean world, the clouds boiled as if they could release a torrent at any moment.

The Western world, too, had been hit by unprecedented winds of the tornadoes and hurricanes. And earthquakes were shaking the world in magnitudes the seismologists proclaimed were record-breaking.

Volcanoes and calderas had exploded, especially in North America, and the skies were filled with unbreathable atmospheres. The bread baskets of the world were affected by the ash and caustic emissions to the point that crop destruction and food-production loss caused starvation on a massive scale—not only in the usual places of Africa and the Far East, but also in Europe, as well as North and South America.

The fallout from the destruction of Russia and its coalition during its attack on Israel, when those forces were totally destroyed—by the God of Heaven, Tyce believed—continued to circle the globe. Whether nuclear or not, the things spewed from the explosions that occurred simultaneously on the nations' coastlines continued to pollute and cause tremendous health issues.

The curses and viruses that had several pandemics inundating the globe simultaneously were still kept for some reasons from Israeli territory. Again, Tyce considered that it was all from Heaven. Randolph Faust had forewarned that God's judgment and wrath hung over the world like Damocles' Sword.

Tyce considered the things going on and remembered the words he recently read in his study of this time that was almost certainly, in his mind, the Tribulation. He recalled the words attributed to Jesus, in the Olivet Discourse recorded in the book of Matthew.

24:21 For then shall be great tribulation, such as was not since the beginning of the world to this time, no, nor ever shall be.

The orbs had not descended to more than five thousand feet above the surface of earth, the scientists were reporting to the news outlets. They had not contributed to the pollutants or to other problems, like interferences with electric grids and other things that man had made and were now failing on a sporadic basis.

The only interference that had been proven was the overt action by one of the orbs over North Korea. Observers and satellite detection showed that the North Korean dictator had ordered a missile launch and subsequent launches. The singular orb hovered above the weapons facilities and caused ignition failures.

This was, in the mind of Tyce Greyson, the Tribulation. No doubt about it. But if the Tribulation, it was obvious that it was a controlled time...controlled by Heaven's forces? He didn't know for sure. But he took a certain comfort in the thought that God might be the one in complete control, while the council's facility came into view.

When Tyce arrived, he was met, as usual, by Amir Lubeka and a number of the council's rabbis. Lubeka looked up, and his countenance was one of fear as he observed the orb that pulsed brightly, seeming no more than a mile above in the blackened sky.

Lubeka quickly grabbed Tyce's arm and accompanied him inside, following the other few council members deeper into the building. He spoke once they arrived among the enclave and all were seated.

"Tyce Greyson has come to again be among us," Lubeka said. "He has words from on high about Israel's future. Like some of you, his dreams and visions continue."

Lubeka turned toward Tyce. "You have been intensively studying these things of the prophetic word from Hashem. Please share with us of *oh-LAHM hah* what you have been permitted to tell."

Tyce looked out at the gathering. Each rabbi sat in rapt attention, anxiety etched into each face. What was he to tell them? They didn't accept the Bible's authority —at any rate not that of the Christian Bible. Yet he was here and supposed to deliver a message. Not the message they wanted, but the message his innermost being told him he was to deliver.

"You…we…all agree that this man who is even now in Jerusalem, meeting with the ecclesiastical hierarchy of the Sanhedrin, is not the Mashiach you at first believed him to be?"

Heads nodded "yes" while he scanned the members for their responses.

"All of the Sanhedrin believe him. They say he has done great miracles," one of the council's rabbis said.

"Rabbi Elias Koahn preaches that von Lucis will soon take David's throne on Moriah," another said.

"What do you have for us Mr. Greyson? Your dreams and visions are known throughout Israel," Lubeka said. "Let us hear. Your words, we believe, are from on high."

Tyce knew the things he said would not be acceptable to Jews steeped in their law. But he was here, and this was his commission. He would tell them what the Christian Bible said about this man who claimed to represent Heaven's answers to humanity's dilemmas.

"What I have to tell you is something that comes from this book." He held up Randolph Faust's old Bible.

"This man you and I know to be *not* Israel's Mashiach...your Messiah...but the son of perdition. He is, your Amir Lubeka and I have seen, from the lower regions of earth...the Abyss."

The rabbis listened intently while Tyce walked back and forth in front of them, trying to think of how best to frame his explanation. "This man is, I believe, somehow, one who has returned from the regions of the dead. From the nether regions...from the Abyss."

He saw the rabbis becoming restless, their looks at each other questioning the possibility of what he was telling them.

"I have never believed in people returning from the dead, in reincarnation, of somehow coming back into this life," Tyce continued. "But it seems this might be an exception. I believe that somehow, this must be the return of Judas Iscariot."

One of the council stood.

"Judas Iscariot? That is a person who has scant place in our theology. You call this person a *being*. What is meant by this?"

"I don't know what I mean by using the term. Von

Lucis seems to have some sort of…supernatural ability. And I'll just say that you invited me to give my findings. That's what I believe the Higher Power…Hashem… wants of me. So my findings, my senses at every level, tell me that von Lucis is the one this book," Tyce held the Bible in the air, "says is the *beast* in Revelation chapter 13.

"I believe von Lucis will supposedly die of a head wound, maybe very soon. I believe he will be, somehow, resurrected—or will seem to be resurrected."

The rabbis mumbled their surprise at the prediction.

Amir Lubeka stood and turned to face his fellow rabbis. "Let us hear him out. Then we will wait as time unfolds to see if this prediction…based upon Tyce's study and commission on high, as he put it, comes to pass."

TYCE HAD TOLD the council members about his past experiences with those scientists and others who worked with the laboratory experiments involving the giant in the sarcophagus. He described how they found the giant mummy to be that of Gilgamesh or Nimrod of the time of the Tower of Babel—that the DNA they had extracted from that being was found to still be alive, as if it couldn't die.

He told them how the scientists planned to create a serum, combining the DNA from the creature with human DNA. They would create some being they called *Earthlord.* This, he believed, was possibly the person they were watching come on the scene as the head of the New Roman Order.

The rabbis had been respectful of his explanations,

but their skepticism remained intact. Still, Lubeka instructed his fellow members to watch patiently as time unfolded to see if Tyce's predictions, based upon the Christian Bible, came to pass.

Morticai Kant, he told them, would do what he could to advise on moving to a hiding place in advance of any purge against them. At the moment, von Lucis and the NRO regime seemed to be championing the Jews. Worship on the Temple Mount in the newly constructed Temple was going as planned. There seemed no genocidal rampage planned against the Jewish race.

But the appearance of things was not as it seemed. The NRO Enforcers were rounding up dissidents, and without trials, were either incarcerating them in large fortifications just outside the city or executing those they wanted to execute on the spot as they wished. Mostly those killed were those who wouldn't recant their conversion to Christianity.

The two men in robes who preached and convinced these to convert were posted on all of NRO media as the most wanted by the authorities. They were criminals the regime was determined to catch and eliminate.

Tyce now knew that the ones he knew as Eli and Moshi were, themselves, prophesied to do the work of preaching, just as the 144,000 Jewish men in the white garments. All who accepted their message of the gospel of Christ were subject to incarceration and death. The two men in robes were supernaturally protected from harm, as were the 144,000. But those of Judaism were, for the most part, not accosted by the regime. As a matter of fact, they were allowed to go and come as they wished to the Temple Mount, to take part in Temple rituals, sacrifices, and worship.

Tyce watched while Klaus von Lucis walked up the

Temple Mount, surrounded immediately by Jewish priests and by others encompassing him in the larger crowd. There was a constant chant from the Jewish population, "Six! Six! Six!"

The broadcast was a taped recording of von Lucis' first visit to the Temple since worship had begun weeks before. The leader, who had guaranteed the Jews right to build on Moriah, then delivered on that promise made in the peace covenant, walked into the Temple's huge double doors of gold plate.

The crowds outside continued the chant, "Six! Six! Six!"

The next scene was of the Temple entourage walking outside again at a later time.

The voice of the broadcast anchor was saying, "President von Lucis met with the priests for the dedication of the Temple. His riding into Jerusalem on the white steed set the stage for what has become a new era of peace and safety for the whole world. Words of this new era of world peace were spoken by chief priest of the new Temple, Elias Koahn, who, himself, welcomed just now President von Lucis to this time of dedication."

The camera zoomed in on Koahn, who stood before several microphones.

"Planet Earth is entering the era of the Six-Way Plan given Israel's Mashiach to deliver. This Temple visit represents Hashem instituting his blueprint for saving all of mankind, through the Jews who remain true to the teachings of Law. It is Hashem's guarantee of peace and safety through Heaven's law and order, administered by Heaven's own son, who stands before you today."

Tyce watched the recording of the proceedings as, following Rabbi Koahn's remarks, the party of ritually robed priests surrounding Koahn and von Lucis turned and reentered the Temple to complete ceremonies within its ornately carved walls of cedar and inlaid gold and silver.

"So he is claiming to be the Mashiach?" Essie's question pulled Tyce from his own thoughts involving a similar conclusion.

"I presume so. Sounds like the rabbi has designated him Heaven's emissary at the very least," Tyce said.

"His New Roman Order—It certainly isn't my concept of what Heaven must be like," Essie said, coming to stand beside her husband.

"Or mine. Quite opposite of Heaven—totally in the other direction," Tyce said. "But look at the people...the Jewish masses. They believe he is sent by their Hashem... that he is their Messiah."

"WE HAVE BEEN WARNED by the Chief Rabbinate Temple Council," Rabbi Yansika Kocah said, after being issued into Morticai Kant's home along with Rabbi Amir Lubeka. "Our efforts to warn the Sanhedrin and all other Jews that this man is an imposter will meet with severe actions by the New Roman Order."

"We have used all means within our power to forewarn that this man, von Lucis, is not from Hashem, but from the Abyss," Lubeka said.

"And how is your message being received...by the general Jewish population?" Kant said.

"The people at large...the Jews...are accepting that he is their long-awaited Mashiach. When we try to give them truth, they call us liars, infidels, and worse. They tell the Enforcer authorities that we are inciting them to insurrection against the regime," Kocah said. "Several of our number were beaten, and several were taken in by the Enforcers."

"And what about the Temple council, the Sanhedrin and the others?" Kant said.

"They believe this man to be the Mashiach. Some are hesitant to totally believe, however. Those who are hesitant have read the prophecy that indicates deception will come in the last day," Kocah said.

"But it is the anger of the Rabbinate Temple Council that is most troubling," Lubeka said.

"These tell that we of Kibbutz *oh-LAHM hah* Council are directly opposing the New Roman Order's Six Ways to Peace blueprint for saving Planet Earth," Lubeka said.

Tyce leaned forward from the sofa across from the rabbis. "When do you think they might move against you?"

"Those within the Temple council who don't accept that von Lucis is Mashiach tell us there are plans within the council's innermost membership who are working with the regime to begin rounding us up to be put in the compounds outside Jerusalem," Kocah said.

"Thirty thousand! There is no place to hide thirty thousand people," Kant said. "Well, there is, but it would be crowded, and I'm not sure it could be arranged."

"Where? Where is this place?"

"Petra."

"Yes, that is a city carved in stone," Kocah said. "And what problem is there about this place?"

"The Jordanian government, for one thing," Kant said. "And I can't imagine the logistics of such a thing. At the same time, I'm not sure the Jordanian government would…or even could…keep von Lucis' NRO forces from assaulting Petra."

Tyce began thumbing through the old Bible again. "Here is a reference about Israel I was studying, from Revelation. It's Revelation 12:14:

"And to the woman were given two wings of a great eagle, that she might fly into the wilderness, into her place, where she is nourished for a time, and times, and half a time, from the face of the serpent."

The rabbis were silent.

"Wings of an eagle?" Kant said. "Could be a reference to aircraft, but that's not possible in that area…not to transport by C-117 or any other plane, for that matter."

"Here's from some more research I've done," Tyce said. "I printed it for this meeting." He picked up a folder and took out a number of sheets of paper.

"This is from a guy…name's Ray Brubaker, written many years ago. He says:

"Personally, we believe that the reference here to 'two wings of a great eagle' is a reference to the way God is going to bring the remnant into this secret hiding place. Although no plane, unless it were a helicopter, could land in Petra, there is enough evidence in scripture to see where God could pick up the remnant as he did Elijah and transport them marvelously and miraculously to the place He has prepared for them.

"In the 68th Psalm we read: 'Sing unto God, sing praises to his name; extol him that rideth upon the heavens, by his name JAH, and rejoice before him.'

"Then, after describing the Lord as riding upon the heavens, mention is made of His chariots. We read: 'The

303

chariots of God are twenty thousand, even thousands of
angels are among them.'

"What are the chariots? Are they similar to the chariots of fire that came for Elijah? Could they be
conveyances to bring the remnant of Israel to their
hiding place who are seen coming on 'two wings of a
great eagle?'"

Both Lubeka and Koahn sat forward. They recognized the references. Their expressions were almost
effusive when they spoke.

"That is the answer!" Koahn said, glancing at his
fellow rabbi next to him.

"Yes! It will be a supernatural transport by Hashem
when the time comes," Lubeka agreed. "You need not do
further arrangements, Morticai. Our Hashem will
deliver us to this…Petra in the Jordanian desert, or to
wheresoever He deems the proper place for our people."

THE RABBIS' words, issued with such excitement, and
even more with a faith that impressed, still rang and
echoed within his mind's ears while he continued to
study the prophecy. Tyce pored over the document on
the laptop.

So, it is our belief based upon the Word of God that
somehow God will pick up the remnant of Israel wherever they may be and miraculously transports those
seeking to escape the cruelty of the antichrist's despo-
tism in demanding the world's worship. He will bring
those who cannot flee by foot to this place prepared in
the wilderness which many believe to be Petra.

It is said that Dr. W. E. Blackstone and George T. B. Davis have placed Bibles in sealed containers in some of the rocks and crannies of Petra. Whether this is true, and whether they are still there, we do not know. If they find such Bibles we're sure the book in the New Testament they will want to read is the book of Hebrews.

Here is where we believe Isaiah refers to when he says, "Come, my people, enter thou into thy chambers and shut thy doors about thee: hide thyself as it were for a moment, until the indignation be over past. For, behold the Lord cometh out of his place to punish the inhabitants of the earth for their iniquity; the earth also shall disclose her blood, and shall no more cover her slain." What a picture!

Petra may very well be the hiding place referred to by Isaiah in the day when the armies of earth gather in plains near Petra for the battle of Armageddon.

Tyce looked up from his intensive study of the information on the screen. The rabbis had somehow grasped the things this writer had written decades earlier. The things written somehow seemed to plug into their understanding, and it seemed to answer their questions.

Hashem would deliver them to the place of safety. They believed what the New Testament said, and this was even more amazing. These men of Judaism knew... they just knew that their people would be delivered by God.

But why should it seem so out of the question to him...to Tyce Greyson? He had sat beside the driver... the Mossad agent...when he disappeared.

He, Tyce, shouldn't find it strange to believe the scripture about these thirty thousand Jews being lifted by the God of Heaven and deposited in a safe place wherever He wished. He had parted the Red Sea; why not lift thousands of Jews to safety in some miraculous way?

Tyce's attention again went to the screen. He *must* know more...about this tremendous matter of God rescuing His people.

The screen began to grow darker, as did Tyce's senses. The all-too-familiar blackening all around him told his reeling brain he was about to have a visitation.

"Tyce Greyson," he heard spoken from somewhere behind his chair. He swiveled to see where the voice had come from. He heard it again, echoing, and becoming more clear from within the almost total darkness in the room.

"Tyce Greyson...it is Eli and Moshi," the voice said, while there appeared, like so many times before, a bright pinpoint of light that grew until it became a diffused ball of light that dissipated the blackness, out of which stepped the two robed figures.

"We are men of the word of God about whom you have read," Eli said. "What has been will be again. We have met in past visions. We will again meet as future things come to pass. Blessed be His Holy Name."

The exact words as given when they last met echoed in Tyce's brain, although neither man spoke. They stood, looking intensely into his eyes.

The one called Eli said, "Your commission from on high is in process. Soon will come the necessity to implement Israel's flight into the wilderness. Watch for the fall from the heavenlies."

"Fall from the heavenlies? What does it mean?" he said, standing dumbfounded before the two men.

"You will know. You will understand," Moshi said." The time draws near. Many will worship to their doom at the fall from the heavenlies. The people of the Lord will know when the time is at hand."

Again, the two men seemed to be moved by a cushion of air back into the diffused ball of light, then the luminescence shrank into the pinpoint of brilliant light and disappeared.

CHAPTER 20

Colonel Geromme Rafke was one of Morticai
Kant's men who wouldn't leave the former
Maglan chief's side when Maglan was ordered disbanded
by the Israeli Knesset. He drove his former boss, Essie,
and Tyce along the Jerusalem street in the semi darkness
that was perpetually like a late evening in the Holy City.

But it was midday, and it was one of the rare times
when they had ventured into the streets. The NRO
Enforcer units were everywhere, and the black-
uniformed officers frequently stopped vehicles to ask for
their papers before allowing them to proceed.

It was the same over most all of the Western world.
Word was that it was much worse in the Far East, as
China had now, without opposition, taken Taiwan,
Japan, South Korea, and the Far Eastern nations. These
were all under China's rule, and the people were brutalized beyond even the Christians who were now seen
being herded into large vans by the Enforcer thugs.

Tyce scanned the immediate foreground as they traveled slowly in the van. He saw it then, a large throng of

people, standing, facing two figures. The two were gesticulating, thrusting their arms upward.

The people were settled, scarcely moving, taking in every word being said.

The two! They were Eli and Moshi. They were preaching!

While they watched the men preach to the large crowd, a black Enforcer vehicle cut them off at an intersection, blocking all traffic flow.

Next, they watched as other Enforcer vehicles drove behind the crowd, and uniformed men jumped out and began dispersing the gathering in front of Eli and Moshi.

Several of the uniformed men carried backpacks with large tubes extending into pipe-like instruments.

They looked to be flame-throwers, and when only Eli and Moshi faced the uniformed men, the NRO police lit their flame-throwers. They were about to assault Eli and Moshi with the weapons.

"No!" Tyce screamed. He started to try to open the van's door, but it was locked.

Essie held onto his arm.

"It's them, Essie. It's Eli and Moshi!"

"We can do nothing," Kant said from the front seat beside his adjutant.

In the next instant, the flames shot out only several feet, then the instruments seemed to fail. The NRO policemen couldn't reignite them.

Suddenly, the area became a gigantic ball of flame that had fallen from somewhere above. The brightness from the blaze was painful to the eyes, and the van's occupants had to look away.

When the flame died and it was again semi dark, they looked at the scene.

Eli and Moshi were no longer there. The flaming corpses of a dozen NRO Enforcers burned in the street.

TYCE'S brain was still reeling from the scene they had witnessed—the attempted murder of Eli and Moshi. The balls of fire suddenly seeming to fall from above as out of nothing...the flaming corpses of the would be murderers...the NRO Enforcers sent to murder the two robed men who preached to the throng.

He remembered the last visit from Eli and Moshi while he worked at the computer. He recalled their words: "Your Commission from on high is in process. Soon will come the necessity to implement Israel's flight into the wilderness. Watch for the fall from the heavenlies."

"Fall from the heavenlies? What does it mean?" he had said.

"You will know. You will understand," Moshi had said. "The time draws near. Many will worship to their doom at the fall from the heavenlies. The people of the Lord will know when the time is at hand."

Tyce stood and walked to a table nearby, partially filled the mug he held with coffee from the carafe.

Were the falling balls of fire from somewhere above the "falling from the heavenlies" Eli and Moshi were talking about? Certainly it was a dramatic display from the Almighty. All of the Enforcers were left burning in the street. Eli and Moshi were nowhere to be found. It was as if they had been removed completely out of harm's way.

His thoughts made sense, but something in the back of his mind made him remember something...something about these two men who would preach during this very time.

The answer to what had just happened was in the Bible. It was in the last book of Revelation. He sat back down at his laptop and typed in "Scripture telling of two witnesses during Tribulation." The screen immediately displayed, "The two witnesses of the prophetic era called Tribulation by some is Revelation 11:3–13."

Tyce found the passage, then read silently:

11:3 And I will give power unto my two witnesses, and they shall prophesy a thousand two hundred and threescore days, clothed in sackcloth. 11:4 These are the two olive trees, and the two candlesticks standing before the God of the earth. 11:5 And if any man will hurt them, fire proceedeth out of their mouth, and devoureth their enemies: and if any man will hurt them, he must in this manner be killed. 11:6 These have power to shut heaven, that it rain not in the days of their prophecy: and have power over waters to turn them to blood, and to smite the earth with all plagues, as often as they will. 11:7 And when they shall have finished their testimony, the beast that ascendeth out of the bottomless pit shall make war against them, and shall overcome them, and kill them. 11:8 And their dead bodies shall lie in the street of the great city, which spiritually is called Sodom and Egypt, where also our Lord was crucified. 11:9 And they of the people and kindreds and tongues and nations shall see their dead bodies three days and an half, and shall not suffer their dead bodies to be put in graves. 11:10 And they that dwell upon the earth shall rejoice over them, and make merry, and shall send gifts one to another; because these two prophets tormented them that dwelt on the earth. 11:11 And after three days and an half the Spirit of life from God entered into them, and they stood upon their feet; and great fear fell upon them which saw them.

> *11:12 And they heard a great voice from heaven saying unto them, Come up hither. And they ascended up to heaven in a cloud; and their enemies beheld them. 11:13 And the same hour was there a great earthquake, and the tenth part of the city fell, and in the earthquake were slain of men seven thousand: and the remnant were affrighted, and gave glory to the God of heaven.*

Tyce sat back in the chair, awestruck that he was given such knowledge—personal knowledge given him by Providence. These two *witnesses*—Eli and Moshi. Why was he given such knowledge? What was the purpose?

The thought came, they—Eli and Moshi—told him it was a commission, a mission, given to tell the Jewish leaders, the ecclesiastical men of Judaism, things of his visions.

And now he was living through times foretold in the book of Revelation—the book John the apostle and prophet was given on Patmos...where all of this first began for him.

Was this the "fall from the heavenlies" Eli and Moshi had told him about?

"Your Commission from on high is in process. Soon will come the necessity to implement Israel's flight into the wilderness. Watch for the fall from the heavenlies."

Whatever was the truth of the things they had told him, he was witnessing prophecy unfold. These men he had been given the privilege to know personally had a tremendous role yet to play. Apparently, so did he.

"Do you think all of this you've been part of is because of that SEER technology they used on you?"

Essie's question was one Tyce had mulled many times over the past three years.

"It must be part of it. But if it involves the SEER, it must be something allowed...or brought about by... Providence," he said, holding her hand as they walked in her father's garden.

"Yes. This could not happen without the permission of Hashem," Essie said.

They looked at the sky, which was growing darker by the day. A number of light orbs moved about high above.

"Those lights, are they from Heaven or from...somewhere else?" Essie wondered out loud.

"They are far away," Tyce said, "and it is as dark at midday as if heavy clouds covered the sky. Yet these orbs stand out against the blackness, so the darkness couldn't be clouds. The lights go and come from great distance to near. It is like it's dimensional, rather than physical."

"Dimensional? Yes, that must be it," Essie said in a lighter tone. "Some say they are from other planets."

"I don't know about that...but they aren't from here. Maybe we'll know soon."

"It's been so long since...since they all vanished. There's so much taking place that is terrible...so many people suffering. Why aren't we suffering so terribly as others?"

"I can't answer that either, Ess. We are in Israel...in Jerusalem. Randy said that Jerusalem is God's touchstone to humanity. Maybe that's why."

"The *oh-LAHM hah* Council...they haven't been harmed as they feared. What do you think will happen to them? There is much hatred for them and those who follow them."

"Amir and the rabbis all have faith that God will remove them to safety when they are in danger," Tyce said. "God is about the only power that could help them now. They are prisoners within their compound for the most part. There's no place else to go."

"Then how are the others, the ones who follow— more than thirty thousand…how do they worship? How do they hear words of Hashem from the council?"

"Satellite. The regime hasn't destroyed the satellite communications. Surely they've tried to disrupt the transmissions, but they haven't been able to."

"What do you think will next happen? What will von Lucis do?"

"Everything is building, I can sense it, Tyce said, gesturing toward the erratically moving light orbs. "Even those light things up there are in increased frenzy. Something is about to break."

RABBI ELIAS KOAHN watched the huge crowd of Israelis and others as they cheered and applauded the appearance of Klaus von Lucis when he emerged from the Church of the Holy Sepulchre. The throng chanted the familiar mantra as it had been chanted since the confirming of the peace covenant between Israel and many surrounding nations three and one-half years earlier.

"Six! Six! Six!"

Koahn turned to the NRO president and held out a robed arm and hand flourish as if presenting von Lucis to his adoring crowd.

The cameras zoomed in on the tall, youthful von Lucis when he paused to apparently enjoy the adulation.

Something in Tyce's senses made him stiffen to attention when he saw the European's face in close-up, the star-shaped mark above the left eyebrow standing out clearly.

"What's wrong, Tyce?"

Essie's words didn't dissuade his gaze from being affixed upon the TV image emanating from just outside the traditional crucifixion site.

"President von Lucis seems to be enjoying his moment, having just visited the crucifixion site of Christianity's martyred founder, Jesus of Nazareth who, tradition says, was executed by the ancient Romans on this site, now known as the Church of the Holy Sepulchre."

The announcer spoke while the European stood observing the crowd, gesticulating with a quick wave of his right hand in acknowledgment of the chant, "*Six! Six! Six!*"

Suddenly, a black spot appeared in the center of the star-shaped image just above the European's left eyebrow. The man's head seemed to lift with the impact, his hair flying upward.

Von Lucis' face was instantly gone from the screen, and the TV cameras seemed to be in utter confusion while the cameramen tried to make sense of what had happened.

Screams arose from the crowd, and von Lucis' security detail quickly gathered around the fallen leader, while some scanned the surroundings to see who had fired the shot.

Other people of leadership were hustled back inside the Church of the Holy Sepulchre, while the gathering of perhaps one thousand fell to the ground or ran for shelter.

"Something has happened," the broadcast voice was saying. "It seems the president was struck. They are attending to him."

～

BOTH MORTICAI KANT and his daughter stood over Tyce while he thumbed through Randolph Faust's Bible.

"You say you think you know what this is about—that it has to do with prophecy?" Kant said.

"Yes, it is unbelievable," Tyce said. "We have just witnessed it. I've read it several times, and it never stuck." He found the passage he was after.

"Yes. Here it is, in Revelation chapter 13:

"13:1 And I stood upon the sand of the sea, and saw a beast rise up out of the sea, having seven heads and ten horns, and upon his horns ten crowns, and upon his heads the name of blasphemy. 13:2 And the beast which I saw was like unto a leopard, and his feet were as the feet of a bear, and his mouth as the mouth of a lion: and the dragon gave him his power, and his seat, and great authority. 13:3 And I saw one of his heads as it were wounded to death; and his deadly wound was healed: and all the world wondered after the beast."

"And von Lucis is the beast," Kant said after several seconds of considering the prophecy.

"It is symbolic, somehow, of the various systems of human government, finally headed by one man, which the prophecy calls the beast. Morticai, it describes the same beast I saw in the vision after the snake bit me."

"And this...deadly wound?" Essie said. "This is what we just witnessed?"

"I think so. Yes, Ess, I would say it is the very deadly wound John prophesied here."

"What did it say?" she said. "That the deadly wound would be healed? What does it mean, do you think?"

"I guess, if it's fulfilled prophecy, we will soon find

out," Kant said. "That was definitely a head shot. I've seen many of them. The man is dead," he said.

The door opened, and Geromme Rafke stepped into the room. "Chief Kant, one of the rabbis wants to speak with you," he said, causing Kant to leave with his adjutant.

Minutes later, he returned, a grim expression on his face.

"That was Lubeka. The council says they have been told that is time to move to their place of safety," Kant said. "He says he was awakened from sleep to see the two men, Eli and Moshi, in the room. They said that the council and all followers would go to the place of safety."

"Where, did they say?" Tyce said.

"They don't know. No one knows. The men just said they would be moved before three days have passed."

THE NATION and much of the Western world were in mourning. Klaus von Lucis' body lay in state at the Brussels' NRO headquarters building, renamed from the EU headquarters. Long lines of people walked past the ornate, gold-colored casket, while NRO military guards surrounded the slain leader.

"Well, he still looks deceased," Morticai Kant said, watching proceedings with his daughter and son-in-law.

Two days had passed since the assassination in Jerusalem. The assassin had not been caught, and Kant was perplexed.

"How can it happen in such an open forum and the shooter not be quickly found? There were hundreds of NRO people as far back in the crowd as could be imagined. It makes no sense that the assassin has gone without capture."

"Almost seems like it's an inside job...planned and executed by those within NRO ranks," Tyce said, his journalistic suspicions aroused.

"Indeed. Almost like it's an assassination that is a ruse of some sort."

"What do you mean, Abba? He was obviously killed," Essie said. "What do you mean by ruse?"

"We have talked, Tyce and myself. He points out something in the prophecy. It is something to think about, considering that we are dealing with what are obviously operatives of the devil," Kant said.

Essie looked at her husband. "And what have you found that makes my die-hard Maglan chief father believe things from the Christian Bible?"

"It's in the wording of the scripture. The prophecy says this."

He read from the Bible while she looked closely at the words from over his shoulder.

I saw one of his heads as it were wounded to death; and his deadly wound was healed.

"Yes? So, what have you found?"

"The words 'as it were' seem to have the meaning of 'as *though*' it was a deadly wound. It seems to indicate that it wasn't really a deadly wound, but it is made to *seem* as if there was a deadly head wound."

"It could all be a phony assassination," Kant said. "Knowing with whom we are dealing, the possibility exists."

"And why would they do that?" Essie said.

"The reason might be found in the words of the

prophecy about worship of the beast," Tyce said. "The prophecy says that, following the healing from the deadly head wound, 'all the world wondered after the beast.'"

"So the *ruse* might be that there is a false healing so it will fool the masses?"

"The prophecy says the whole world will wonder after the beast. I guess that means most people will fall for this...this false resurrection, or however it all plays out."

"What about these two, strange men...Eli and Moshi...who are being hunted?" Essie said. "They are not just being hunted because they preach against the regime, they are blamed for the droughts and the rivers being bloody, the earthquakes, and the insect infestations and all the rest taking place around the world. Only Israel seems to not be affected. They are in the prophecies. What will their part be in all this?"

Tyce reached for the Bible again. He knew exactly where to look now and thumbed through until he found the spot. "It is here in Revelation. I've studied this carefully." He ran his finger down the page. "Revelation, chapter 11."

Essie again looked over his shoulder while he pointed to the passage and began reading aloud.

> *"These have power to shut heaven, that it rain not in the days of their prophecy: and have power over waters to turn them to blood, and to smite the earth with all plagues, as often as they will. 11:7 And when they shall have finished their testimony, the beast that ascendeth out of the bottomless pit shall make war against them, and shall overcome them, and kill them. 11:8 And their dead bodies shall lie in the street of the great city, which spiritually is called Sodom and Egypt,*

where also our Lord was crucified. 11:9 And they of the people and kindreds and tongues and nations shall see their dead bodies three days and an half, and shall not suffer their dead bodies to be put in graves. 11:10 And they that dwell upon the earth shall rejoice over them, and make merry, and shall send gifts one to another; because these two prophets tormented them that dwelt on the earth. 11:11 And after three days and an half the Spirit of life from God entered into them, and they stood upon their feet; and great fear fell upon them which saw them. 11:12 And they heard a great voice from heaven saying unto them, Come up hither. And they ascended up to heaven in a cloud; and their enemies beheld them.'"

Both were silent, considering the words of the two men of prophecy that were so powerfully a part of their lives.

"One thing for sure," Tyce said, then. "There's no doubt that we are in the middle of the wrap-up of things. One way or the other, Christ's return must be very near."

BRUSSELS' NRO headquarters was alive with people milling about, while the large, golden coffin rested atop a black-velvet-draped catafalque. Network cameras caught the proceedings from every angle, while the lights in the huge chamber were darkened by rheostat until only the spotlights from high above shone on Klaus von Lucis' casket and the immediate surroundings.

"We don't know exactly what the ceremony is about," the network anchor said. "But it was all apparently hastily arranged. The leaders of the various governments of the world are here. So the ceremony must have been planned for some time, giving the dignitaries time to arrange travel schedules."

While the broadcaster talked, a procession of figures, clothed in many different types of religious garb, moved in slow, deliberate steps toward the casket containing the slain NRO president. Von Lucis' face was brightly lit from one particular spotlight beaming from near the ceiling. The skin seemed to glow, the bullet wound that had erupted within the blemish above his eye having been taken care of by the mortuary cosmetologists.

"It is our understanding that the procession now entering the chamber here at NRO headquarters are holy leaders of the various world religions. Leaders who have all come together at the behest of the Catholic pope under the Ecumenical Collective. The procession, as you can see, is led by Rabbi Elias Koahn, a most remarkable holy man, as we have seen over recent months."

The men, in their colorful robes and chains, glittered beneath the bright spotlights as they spread and surrounded the coffin that sat several feet off the floor on the catafalque.

"Rabbi Koahn is thought to possess abilities to perform miracles. We have witnessed his healing sick, paralyzed, and blind people. He has caused a transport truck of many tons to levitate, freeing people trapped beneath it in an accident."

Tyce sat forward, seeing Koahn move to stand before the coffin only a foot from von Lucis' face.

Koahn looked toward the ceiling, the floodlight stream causing his face flesh to shimmer while the television cameras framed him in a close-up head-and-shoulders shot.

He closed his eyes and lifted his arms to full length toward the ceiling. The camera pulled back to capture the gesture. His mouth moved, but the words were not made audible by the broadcast engineers. When his arms came down, he moved in and bent slightly to bring his face near that of Klaus von Lucis.

Koahn stretched his arms over the casket, just above the corpse. The camera moved in for a close-up of von Lucis' face.

"We don't know what the ceremony is about. We've not been told," the TV anchor was saying while Koahn, it was obvious, was saying something over the corpse.

"I know what it's about," Tyce said, while he, Essie, and her father looked on.

"This is fulfillment," he said, not taking his eyes off the proceedings.

It looked for a second as if the corpse's face was darkening because of Koahn's robed arms blocking the spotlights streaming from above.

Then the flesh lightened again, and the flesh seemed to twitch and puff, as if hit by an electric shock.

"Can we be watching—?" The broadcaster seemed unable to speak his thoughts. "Yes! The face…the president's face is moving, is reacting to something!"

Tyce and the others watched while von Lucis' eyelids started fluttering slightly, then they slowly opened, while Koahn continued to stand with arms outstretched over his face.

"Ladies and gentlemen, we are witnessing something that hasn't been done, except in reports from the past… reports of resurrections that are thought to be myth… fantasy…fiction."

"He's moving!" Essie said, while watching the screen, her eyes wide in disbelief.

"He's moving, alright," Tyce said. "And now the real troubles begin."

The TV cameras trained on Klaus von Lucis' face. The flesh had a glow that the faces of the holy men near him didn't have.

The thousand-plus people in the chamber were on their feet, eyes glazed with emotional fervor. They shouted in unison after several tries.

"Six ways to law! Six ways to order! Six ways to peace! Six! Six! Six!"

CHAPTER 21

"Von Lucis is in Jerusalem," Tyce said, informing his father-in-law, who had just entered the study where Tyce sat watching the large screen while working at his laptop.

"He hasn't been seen since the...resurrection," Kant said caustically. "What do you think all this is about...his coming to Jerusalem?"

"Tyce has been studying the prophecies, Papa," Essie said, looking from behind her husband at the laptop screen. "We believe he knows what is going on."

"Oh? And what have you found?" Kant said.

"I believe he will be headed for the Temple," Tyce said.

"On Moriah?"

"Yes. I believe we are about to see prophetic fulfillment as dramatic as what we just witnessed...maybe even more."

All along the route across Jerusalem, the crowds lined

324

the sides of the streets, while von Lucis' motorcade moved slowly toward the Temple Mount. The cries and cheers were the same at every place along the procession. The crowds chanted in unison, "Six ways to law! Six ways to order! Six ways to peace! Six! Six! Six!"

When the motorcade arrived at the base of the Temple Mount, the von Lucis entourage surrounded him while he walked within their midst toward the Temple that stood now near where the Muslim Dome of the Rock once sat.

Tyce heard it then. There was no mistaking the voice or the words it uttered: "Tyce Greyson. Tell those with you to remove. You have things to witness on behalf of Hashem."

The words stunned him for a brief moment. But they were from the voice of Eli, and they were irresistible.

"Essie, Morticai, you need to leave the room. I'm being summoned."

"Summoned?" Essie said, not understanding.

"Yes…it's the voice of Eli. You both must leave the room for now."

"But, I don't understand…"

Essie's father gently took her arm, seeing Tyce's face taking on a strange look Kant had never seen in his son-in-law.

"Come, child. Let us go for now. Tyce will be okay."

The moment the door closed behind them, Tyce's surroundings darkened. The familiar ball of diffused light grew from a brilliant point in the blackness.

"Come with us, Tyce Greyson," Eli's voice said from within the luminescence. "The time of Jacob's trouble is at hand."

Tyce stood within the Temple instantly, the darkness

around him dissipating. Several robed figures passed by him but didn't indicate they noticed him.

They were speaking in Hebrew, but he somehow understood them. "He is resurrected lord, praise be to he who sits in the heavens," he understood one rabbi to say.

The Temple seemed aglow with light, from a source he couldn't locate. The direction the group of rabbis headed harbored a brighter light source, and they soon walked through a door into that inner chamber.

The next instant, Tyce had passed through a wall and stood watching the proceedings. He saw then the man, Klaus von Lucis, sitting high on a large throne, his hands draped over each of the broad, ornately carved arms.

Von Lucis was covered in a purple and gold robe. He looked down on everyone in the assembly. All in the inner chamber had heads bowed, their hands clasped together in prayerful poses.

Tyce then saw Rabbi Elias Koahn walk from somewhere behind the raised platform and throne to face the bowed rabbis.

"Time has come," he said in Hebrew. "Time to worship god's son, his only son…Israel's Mashiach. He is now Earthlord…the one who offers salvation to all."

Koahn turned to look upward at von Lucis, who looked with an expression of harshness toward the bowed rabbis below.

Tyce noticed that the bullet hole looked to be still in the center of the star-shaped image on von Lucis' forehead. His left eye below the star drooped a bit, and the eye seemed to gleam within the eyelid, giving the impression that anger resided within in some way.

When he spoke, von Lucis moved his head, almost mechanically, from left to right, then from right to left, as if looking above the rabbis who knelt before him.

His voice echoed in reverb fashion, as if he spoke into a microphone that fed through an echo chamber.

"This day, I declare that all must worship their Earthlord. I am god come to earth to bring six ways to law, six ways to order, six ways to peace. No one comes to my father, the great one in the heavenlies, but through me. Accept your Earthlord and there is redemption. Reject Earthlord and there is only death."

Tyce noticed that some of the rabbis looked upward at von Lucis, stunned looks on their faces. Then, many of the Jewish rabbis straightened and hurried out of the chamber.

Elias Koahn stood looking out over the rabbis who remained.

"Those among you who fled are apostate. They will be dealt with, I assure."

From the top of the throne pedestal, von Lucis said, "They do not accept Earthlord or the Six Ways to Peace blueprint brought through Earthlord to this planet. I order that all who do not believe be brought into subjection. They must submit or face consequence of death."

Elias Koahn spoke to the rabbis. "You who remain and are faithful are given the mission by the resurrected Earthlord, who is now indwelt by his father, to tell the word first in Jerusalem, then to the world that the people of earth must submit to Earthlord and the great father's heavenly edict. Either submit or face the consequence of death. Now, go and tell all you have seen and heard."

TYCE INSTANTLY WAS BACK in the study of Morticai's home. He was disoriented by the experience, and he almost fell, his senses affected, making his legs nearly weakened to the point he had to hold to the back of the desk chair.

"Tyce, are you okay?" Essie held to his arm, then embraced him. "You weren't here when we checked. Where...how did you—?"

"I was in the Temple," he said, interrupting Essie's question. "Eli and Moshi must have somehow sent me there. I was in the Temple. I watched Klaus von Lucis. He sat on a throne, dressed in purple and gold, a robe of some sort. Elias Koahn proclaimed him to be Earthlord."

"Are you okay? You don't look well," Kant said, having just walked in the study.

"Morticai, I've seen the culmination of all these... these dreams and visions I've ever experienced."

"I heard...this rabbi...Elias Koahn...has declared von Lucis to be Earthlord?"

"Yes, and he seems different, like he is mechanically controlled in some way. He moves almost robotically. He has said that all who won't submit to his father in the heavenlies, who Koahn says indwells Earthlord, will face consequence of death."

"And did the rabbis go along? What were their reactions?"

"The majority of them, who were before the declaration that von Lucis was Earthlord...in effect was God... and had been in prayerful poses, looked stunned. They seemed...some...to gasp in disbelief. They hurried from the chamber. A few stayed. Koahn called the ones who left apostate. The others he commanded to spread the word about Earthlord and the Six Ways to Peace ultimatum."

"And about this...ultimatum. What do you think it means...in terms of your Bible's prophetic prognosis?"

Tyce sat in the desk chair and retrieved the old Bible

from near the laptop. "It's in Revelation. I've seen it a number of times," he said, quickly finding the last book of the New Testament. "Here it is. It's Revelation, again it's chapter 13, like so much of this about the beast."

He began reading aloud:

"13:15 And he had power to give life unto the image of the beast, that the image of the beast should both speak, and cause that as many as would not worship the image of the beast should be killed. 13:16 And he causeth all, both small and great, rich and poor, free and bond, to receive a mark in their right hand, or in their foreheads: 13:17 And that no man might buy or sell, save he that had the mark, or the name of the beast, or the number of his name. 13:18 Here is wisdom. Let him that hath understanding count the number of the beast: for it is the number of a man; and his number is Six hundred threescore and six."

After a few seconds of reflection on the words, Morticai Kant said, "This one who gives this…beast… power and so forth, I take it this refers to Elias Koahn?"

"Yes. He must be the *first beast* of this chapter," Tyce said.

"He is saying that all must accept this system mentioned here—apparently the Six Ways to Peace Plan —or be killed," Essie said.

"Yes," Tyce said. "It says that people must have a mark or number in their right hand or forehead in order to buy and sell. I remember reading somewhere that those who refuse will be executed by beheading. We are seeing this already. The NRO Enforcers and their Decap units are doing this now."

"And the rabbis, why were they so…astonished?" Essie said.

Her father said, "He declared himself to be Hashem, daughter. Even I, a heathen, know that the Jews and the Law will never accept that a mere man is God, not even if the Mashiach Himself declares it to be so. I believe that finally these of Sanhedrin—many, anyway—see that von Lucis is an imposter, not their Mashiach."

"And what does this mean, Tyce?" Essie said, turning to her husband.

The thought struck, and he said, "It's something Eli said just before I was in the Temple. He said that time of Jacob's trouble is at hand."

He turned to the back of the Bible now, to the concordance, then whispered to himself, "Jeremiah 30, verse 7…"

He began turning to the back of the Bible, to the concordance, then whispered to himself, "Jeremiah…I remember Dr. Faust telling me all this was in the book of Jeremiah… Yes, in Jeremiah, chapter 30 verse 7…"

"What is that?" Essie asked.

Tyce ran his finger down the alphabet of terms and found the reference. He then turned to the book and verse. "Here it is. Jeremiah chapter 30. I want to look at verse 7, but I'll have to get the context."

He began reading aloud:

"30:3 For, lo, the days come, saith the LORD, that I will bring again the captivity of my people Israel and Judah, saith the LORD: and I will cause them to return to the land that I gave to their fathers, and they shall possess it.

"30:4 And these are the words that the LORD spake concerning Israel and concerning Judah. 30:5 For thus saith the LORD; We have heard a voice of trembling, of fear, and not of peace. 30:6 Ask ye now, and see whether a man doth travail with child? wherefore do I see every man with his

hands on his loins, as a woman in travail, and all faces are turned into paleness? 30:7 Alas! for that day is great, so that none is like it: it is even the time of Jacob's trouble; but he shall be saved out of it."

After several moments of dissecting the prophecy silently, Kant said, "It sounds ominous. Israel will face unprecedent evil against her. If it's the worst time ever, and we haven't already experienced it in Hitler's ovens, then Jacob is in for trouble, indeed."

"But, Abba, the prophecy says that Jacob will be saved out of that trouble," Essie said.

"I guess we shall see," her father said.

THE EARTHLORD'S image projected from every television and computer screen in Israel and across the world. Von Lucis' voice boomed through speakers throughout every media venue. His message was the same.

"To worship me is to worship God. To choose to worship me or not to worship is the difference between war and peace, between life and death. I, your Earthlord, am the I Am."

"The great trouble of Jeremiah has begun," Morticai Kant said, watching the video of the black-uniformed NRO Enforcers clubbing men and women as they dragged victims from shops and into NRO vans. Some Decap units were shown executing people on the spot. The black vehicles with the mechanized guillotines were now everywhere, and some video was from Europe, where Jewish people were being rounded up. Like in Jerusalem and Tel Aviv and other places, there were on-the-spot executions or people being clubbed, then dragged into the vans.

"They will be coming for us, Papa," Essie said, fear trembling her voice. "We must go."

"There are plans," he said. "There are tunnels that the Mossad long ago prepared for defense of Jerusalem. We will be removed by helicopters at the end of the tunnels. I will put the escape protocol into action."

When the former Maglan chief left the study, Tyce put his arm around his wife. "We will be okay, sweetheart. Heaven's forces have been with me since Patmos. We will yet witness things that no journalist on earth has witnessed."

Essie laughed at her husband's typically journalistic mind coming to the forefront of his thinking, even during the direst crisis.

"Why are you laughing?"

"You…the reporter to the very end."

"Well, it is a terrific story, you have to admit. Don't know when I'll have a chance to write it, but I certainly have the material."

"All is prepared," Kant said, quickly striding into the room. "Geromme has everything lined up for our escape. Come. We must move quickly."

Less than five minutes later, they rode in a Humvee driven by Rafke. Several other Humvees followed.

"Abba, do you think we can do this? Can we get by these NRO police? They are everywhere you look."

"We will make it to the tunnels soon," Kant said. "If we can get by this section of the city, we will be clear."

They drove through streets that became increasingly filled with people and vehicles and came to a halt when the traffic ahead stopped.

"There is a roadblock ahead, chief. Do you wish

me to take a side street?" The Maglan colonel scanned from side to side to see if there was an escape route.

"Let us just move ahead with traffic," Kant said. "To cut out of line would cause them to pursue," Kant said.

Within minutes, they were at a standstill, and they saw a group of the NRO Enforcers checking each vehicle ahead.

"They will discover us," Essie said, holding to her husband.

"It will be okay," Tyce said, hugging her. But his own thoughts involved the *fight or flight* scenario.

Kant heard a semi-automatic pistol mechanism pulled back and released. He looked at his adjutant's hands. They held a black Glock.

"Let's not be hasty, Geromme. We are outnumbered at the moment, despite our equalizers, like that one you hold."

Rafke reached down and slid the firearm just under the seat for quick retrieval if needed. Soon the Enforcer unit reached the Humvee.

"What is your business?" the man said sternly.

"Step aside, lieutenant," another black-uniformed officer said, stepping to look into the vehicle.

"We must inquire as to what is your purpose for travel," the man said, more pleasantly than the man he replaced.

"I am Israeli government liaison, assigned by NRO to control Israeli compliance," Kant said. He handed the man several pages. After looking them over, the officer handed them back, and, with a brief smile, said, "Thank you, General Kant. We will have the traffic cleared momentarily."

They watched while the Enforcers jerked people

from their vehicles, clubbing them and shoving them into vans.

The NRO police then drove the commandeered vehicles away on the untraveled left side of where the Humvees sat.

"What do you think, Geromme?" Kant looked at his colonel.

"I think they aren't finished with us, sir," he said. "Firefight might be our only option."

"Always ready for battle," Kant said, patting his adjutant's right shoulder. "You might be right. If it comes to that, we will be ready, eh, colonel?"

"Yes, sir," Rafke said, watching the roadway ahead being cleared.

When the last vehicle, directly in front of them, was cleared, its occupants brutally removed and taken away in a police van, the same officer came to Kant's side of the Humvee.

"General, please follow the police vehicle coming now. It will lead you to a place for making traveling more freely possible."

A large military vehicle pulled in front of them and began moving slowly ahead.

"Do I follow?" Rafke said grimly.

"For now," Kant said.

They were waved through several roadblocks, the other Humvees following their lead. They came to the stopping point and followed the police vehicle into an alley of sorts. When all vehicles were through the road that went between two large buildings, they followed the Enforcers to a parking lot.

A dozen or more uniformed NRO troops met them. Each had automatic rifles.

Geromme Rafke leaned forward, feeling for the Glock.

"Not yet, Colonel," Tyce said from the rear seat. "Something tells me we should wait."

Rafke straightened and rolled down the window when the NRO trooper came to his side of the Humvee.

"We have been ordered to ask that you come into the center for processing," the man said in broken English. "Weapons will be left in the vehicle," he said.

"What processing?" Kant said from across Geromme Rafke.

"All government officials within Israel must comply with the new directive," the man said.

Soon all were out of the vehicles and moved into the building. They were herded into a room, where a guard, his AR-15 weapon held at parade rest, eyed the fifteen people he had been charged with guarding.

Ten minutes passed while they stood talking among themselves. Essie clung to her husband, while her father's legendary Maglan confidence strengthened his former IDF operatives' courage.

When the door opened, a tall NRO officer stepped through the doorway.

"Chief Morticai Kant?"

"I am he," Kant said, stepping from among the others.

"Will you please come with me? Also, Mr. Tyce Greyson," the man said, looking at the paper he held. "Will you please accompany me?"

"Take care of her," Tyce said to Geromme Rafke, nudging his wife toward the big Maglan operative.

Rafke nodded assurance he would, and both men left the room, following the one who had summoned them.

"General Kant," the man said after leading them into

a chamber with large screens, all active with scenes of things going on in the cities of the world.

"This set-up isn't what it appears to be," he said while Essie and Rafke were ushered into the room. Essie quickly went to Tyce's side.

Kant's eyebrows raised, and Tyce smiled.

"Why are you smiling, Mr. Greyson?" the man said, looking into Tyce's eyes.

"You are one of the 144,000, are you not?"

The man's countenance changed to one of friendly acknowledgment. "The Lord has given you this insight," the man said, reaching to squeeze Tyce's forearm.

Kant was perplexed, looking at his son-in-law for explanation.

"It is prophecy fulfilling, Morticai," Tyce said. "He is one of the 144,000 Jewish men chosen to…" Tyce looked at the man in the NRO Enforcer uniform. "Tell him. What is your name?"

"Yurom," the young man said.

"Yurom, you tell them," Tyce said.

"Each of us of the 144,000 are to preach the gospel of the Lord Jesus Christ into the world," Yurom said. He smiled even broader, looking at the former Maglan chief. "Yes. I'm a Jew…like you, Morticai. Like you, Essie, and like you, Geromme Rafke."

"How do you know us?" Essie said. "We haven't been introduced."

"We are guided by the Spirit of our Father," he said. "We are twelve thousand from each of Israel's tribes, as the prophecy says. I am from the tribe of Benjamin."

When the others seemed unable to say anything in response, Yurom said, "Morticai, you have no belief, either in the Christian Messiah, or in the Mashiach as believed to be the savior of Israel?"

"Religion isn't the operative protocol for Mossad," Kant said.

"And you, Essie?" The young man turned to her, a quizzically friendly expression crossing his face.

"I believe as Tyce," she said, nodding toward her husband, pressing against his side.

"And you, Tyce?" Yurom looked into Tyce's eyes, his own eyes seeming to spark with understanding that Tyce didn't have.

"Frankly, Yurom, I know my mission here, according to Eli and Moshi, and to one of your number who visited me. But, I thought I had become...a believer in Jesus Christ back before the...the disappearing. I understood, through my friend who was a Bible expert, that if you believed in Christ for salvation you would go in the...the Rapture. Yet, here I am in what has to be the middle of the time of Tribulation...the time that will be the worst in history, according to Jesus, Himself. I have been wondering why, although I haven't had time to try to get understanding."

"You are in this time...now entering the Great Tribulation...the time of Jacob's trouble, because it is indeed your mission from on high. You have been at the center of those who will be the remnant."

Yurom cocked his head slightly, his countenance taking on a strange glow while he looked at Tyce. "This is most profound, Tyce Greyson. You have been privileged to carry out the great purpose that fulfills the final destiny of all of God's chosen people. This strangeness will be made clear to you when these things preordained are accomplished.

"Come, I will show the things taking place even now," Yurom said, then, leading the way into an adjoining room.

When the four followed him, they entered a gigantic chamber. Enormous screens ringed the rounded room. Each monitor displayed scenes of things currently taking place.

"The beast is at work, as you see," Yurom said. "It is the time of Jacob's trouble."

The screens displayed Jewish people being shot or beaten. They were being murdered not just by the uniformed Enforcers, but by their own neighbors who were non-Jews.

Many were being beheaded by the Muslims, who were encouraged to kill them.

One of the huge screens now projected the image of the inner Temple. Klaus von Lucis sat atop the throne platform. He moved, like before, mechanically, almost as if manipulated by a puppet master. Elias Koahn stood below, looking up at von Lucis.

"Behold the beasts," Yurom said. "The one all of Israel thought to be Mashiach now exhibits truth of his perdition. He is the Antichrist, not the Christ!"

Von Lucis began to speak, and his voice echoed throughout the chamber and the entire world. Every nation and people understood through artificial intelligence technologies.

"The Jew is the bane of mankind! These spawns of wickedness must be eradicated! Murder them! Kill them! All Jews must die, beginning now."

"All are now being injected and imprinted with the beast's 666 mark, as you see," Yurom said, gesturing toward another of the gigantic screens.

They watched while something was injected, and at the same time a laser-like beam inserted the indelible "Earthlord" imprint beneath the skin in the submissive person's forehead or right hand.

"These are forever lost, who accept the beast's mark and injection. Their very souls are made unredeemable. Their flesh and souls are mixed with that of the essence of Nephilim...of the one called Nimrod."

Lines of people were eagerly awaiting their turns to get the injections that von Lucis demanded they take. This, the regime, promised, would allow them to buy food and transact life in a sustainable way. Anyone refusing the mark was suspected to be in concert with the Jews in opposing New Roman Order law.

"Christians are being slaughtered, too," Yurom said, waving his hand and causing the screen to change to a scene of many taken and forced upon the Decap Units' platforms of death. Each time the shimmering, blood-stained blade descended, a head dropped into a metallic basket and another Christian believer was martyred for the cause of the True Christ.

"And, here are those you will recognize," the young man said, waving his hand yet again, causing the largest of the screens to change. It was a scene of many thousands running somewhere in the desert.

"These are the people, the followers of the Kibbutz *oh-LAHM hah* Council. They are fleeing the beast's rampage against the Jews."

"How can they ever escape?" Essie said, watching the obviously terrified people by the thousands running for their lives.

"Remember Moses. Remember Israel in the Exodus," Yurom said. "The God of Israel never sleeps or slumbers."

Some of the fleeing Jews fell and had to be helped up by others, the women falling farther and farther behind the men, particularly the younger men of Israel.

Momentarily, the screen displayed helicopters in the

distance. Any second they would catch up with the throng. All eyes were on the many thousand and the fate that would befall them within seconds.

"Behold the Lord's mighty hand!"

The screen suddenly became blindingly bright. Tyce's eyes widened in amazement when he saw the brilliantly white and yellow-gold creature, the wings covering the entirety of the view the screen presented. The brilliant creature...the magnificence...the face of fierce countenance! He knew instantly what...who he was seeing.

And when the light dissipated, the desert was bare; only the dust of the desert floor arose and finally settled.

The helicopters flew over where the people had been running.

"What happened?" Essie said. "Did the helicopters do something to them?"

Tyce pulled his wife close to his side, wrapping his arm around her shoulder.

"No. The helicopters didn't do anything to them...*Michael* did it *for* them," he said, looking to Yurom, who looked back knowingly, their minds somehow co-mingling in the moment of supernatural comprehension.

TIME HAD INEXPLICABLY MOVED AHEAD as they stood within the strange chamber. A day later, Yurom again directed them to observe the things the enormous screens projected.

"Behold Heaven's witnesses," he said, and, with a wave of his hand caused the scene to appear that all recognized as a street near the Temple Mount.

Two robed figures stood near each other, on a broad

sidewalk by a building. They stood facing a gathering mob of people. They were surrounded by the mob with the building wall at their backs.

The live video zoomed in on the men.

"Eli and Moshi!" Tyce's words identifying the men made all look at Yurom for explanation.

"Watch, but do not be fearful for these witnesses of Christ's gospel. Jacob's trouble now begins. These must perish for the moment. Their judgments are complete. Their twelve hundred and sixty days are accomplished."

The crowd, which had grown to number several hundred, suddenly began moving, splitting to make a pathway for three black-uniformed men carrying automatic weapons. They trained the rifles on the two and unleashed several bursts, the bullets finding their mark, killing them instantly.

Essie, against Tyce's arm, looked away, hiding her face behind her husband.

The mob cheered the deaths, slapping each other in congratulatory displays of joy. Audio from a news network studio joined the video feed.

"These unholy minions have, as Rabbi Elias Koahn has been saying, caused much evil to befall the world. They have escaped all attempts to capture them. NRO Enforcement has thus ordered them shot on sight.

"No criminal on earth more deserves their punishment. The people, as you see by their celebration, agree."

Time again somehow slipped forward without recognition of its movement. Now the screen displayed the crumpled bodies in the street where they lay after falling in death.

"The cameras have been on the witnesses for three days," Yurom said, bringing the four into the advanced time.

The network anchor said, "These dead bodies are being displayed throughout the entire earth by satellite. There have been celebrations around the globe, thanking the Earthlord for bringing them to justice."

The video changed to show the inner sanctum of the Temple. All within the chamber were on their knees, bowed before von Lucis, who stared without expression from his elevated position on the throne.

Rabbi Koahn spoke to the television satellite audience that spanned the globe. He stood in front of the Earthlord throne. While he did, the screens of the worldwide audiences presented the images of the two men who had been murdered lying where they had fallen.

"The great disappearance was accomplished in order that the children…all of them…even in the wombs…will be in a place of safety. They will remain until the Earthlord makes all things right so that the ascended masters…the…extraterrestrials, whose light orbs even now are observing from their heights, will descend as flaming spheres to the planet's surface.

"All others who seemingly vanished will remain with the children for inculcation into the new age of peace safety, and prosperity."

Koahn saw movement on the large screen behind the bowed people of the Ecumenical Collective that stopped his explanation of the disappearance phenomenon.

The dead bodies began to move, then stood.

A cavernous voice was heard to say, *"Come up here!"*

Tyce, standing with the others watching the scene, said, "*Yes!*"

"Tyce, what is happening?" Essie said, watching the men rise into the air from where they had been left to decompose so the whole world could see and celebrate.

"Just watch," he said. "Remember, Ess what I read to

you about the two witnesses of the Revelation." He looked to Yurom. "Will we feel it?"

Yurom, who stood looking with a relaxed expression at him, then at Essie, said, "Only slightly, perhaps."

"Feel what?" she said, fear still in her voice, while she saw the men disappear somewhere far above, as the camera followed the ascent of Eli and Moshi, now raised from death.

The floor beneath them, even in their surreal setting, did begin to tremble slightly, while Yurom continued to remain calm.

The screen displayed the scene of the crowds that had been observing the corpses. They were screaming while they tried to run but fell to the ground. The building against which the NRO Enforcer had gunned down Eli and Moshi shook, cracked, then crumbled into a heap, its brick tonnage spilling into the street and crushing many. The concrete and earth then broke apart, and the earth parted, swallowing the carnage.

Elias Koahn stood speechless still, the Temple beginning to shake mightily. Those bowed before him and their Earthlord were also trying to stand—to run, to find safety from falling debris.

"Their twelve hundred sixty days are up," Tyce said, looking at Yurom, who only smiled.

CHAPTER 22

A cavernous voice resounded throughout the chamber.

"For then shall be great tribulation, such as was not since the beginning of the world to this time, no, nor ever shall be!"

"And now we will stand afar off and watch Jesus' prophecy given on the mountain called Olivet come to pass."

The four, standing in the strange chamber and having witnessed Eli and Moshi go upward and out of sight, upon hearing Yurom's declaration, were suddenly swept into a wind that blurred all sensibility. They next were somewhere upon a promontory. They overlooked the city of Jerusalem, but the view at the same time presented vistas of many other places of the world.

New York, Los Angeles, London, Rome, and all the large cities of the Western world—all in chaos from earthquakes—pulsed in and out of view from their exceedingly high vantage.

The skies above also pulsed with bright flashes that

seemed like lightning. But it wasn't lightning Tyce could see. The entire skyscape from horizon to horizon was exploding with tremendous bursts of light that seemed to crash into each other.

The brightness that was blinding to the eye then seemed to diminish or change in order to witness the cause of the spectacular display in the heavens.

Tyce saw them in exquisite detail, the brilliantly shining warriors doing battle. Their fiery swords swung and clashed, some strokes cutting through supernatural flesh and sinew.

The gaping cuts by the swords, swung by creatures with wings that could be a thousand miles from tip to tip, spurted what looked to be white-hot slag from a steel mill processing smelter. The wounds gaped, spewed their supernatural liquid-like eruption, and just as quickly the wounds looked to be healed.

The battle went on for…how long? Tyce couldn't determine. Time and all sense of self-awareness was lost to the stupendous show of war making in the heavens.

"Do you know what you are privileged to witness?" Yurom's question drew the attention of his four astonished companions to himself, his countenance and tone exulting with excitement.

"Behold the Voice of Heaven!"

Upon his declaration, the words thundered as the beings battled above the scenes of the cities below.

> *"And there was war in heaven: Michael and his angels fought against the dragon; and the dragon fought and his angels, And prevailed not; neither was their place found any more in heaven. And the great dragon was cast out, that old serpent, called the Devil, and Satan, which deceiveth the whole world: he was cast out into the earth, and his angels were cast out*

with him. And I heard a loud voice saying in heaven, Now is come salvation, and strength, and the kingdom of our God, and the power of his Christ: for the accuser of our brethren is cast down, which accused them before our God day and night. And they overcame him by the blood of the Lamb, and by the word of their testimony; and they loved not their lives unto the death. Therefore rejoice, ye heavens, and ye that dwell in them. Woe to the inhabiters of the earth and of the sea! for the devil is come down unto you, having great wrath, because he knoweth that he hath but a short time."

The skies above again grew brighter than the eyes could bear, and when they could again look, they watched the vast expanse of sky with fiery red orbs that streamed downward toward the many cities they somehow could see at once with their supernatural perspective.

Momentarily, the scene they viewed changed again, becoming that of Klaus von Lucis standing just behind Rabbi Elias Koahn, who spoke. "The Earthlord speaks! Hear the words of earth's salvation."

Von Lucis lifted his arms heavenward while the fiery orbs grew larger and larger as they descended. "These have come to rescue earth from the terminal condition it suffers," he said. "These, the world finally knows, are brothers from galaxies, from universes beyond which man can never reach.

"They have observed for eons until man has brought Planet Earth to terminal crisis. And now they are here to do my bidding...to bring all under my plan of Six Ways to Law, Six Ways to Order, Six Ways to Peace."

While von Lucis spoke, the sky immediately above became filled with disks, whose bright, spinning outer rings pulsed with light that at first obscured the actual skin of the craft. Each then became more discernible as flying saucer-like disks when the light grew less bright, then dimmed and completely extinguished when the disks sat on the earth just outside Jerusalem.

The four in the presence of Yurom watched in stunned amazement as the same scenes played out throughout the cities of the world. The saucers alighted on earth and the lights extinguished, while the vast multitudes stood gawking.

"These Galactic Brothers will interact with all of humanity to create peace on earth as it is in Heaven," von Lucis said, while the ships' bottoms opened and round, metallic contrivances descended to the ground. The large, tubular devices, when they contacted the earth, split apart, and tall beings in golden uniforms began exiting the shafts.

All cities presented identical scenes, the disks landing, the shafts descending from the craft, and the tall human-like beings exiting the tubular devices and walking toward the astonished peoples of the world.

In Jerusalem, one of the beings, the first to emerge following the landing, approached von Lucis.

While Tyce and the others looked on in unspoken astonishment, the tall being turned into a creature that Tyce had seen many times before. The thing was dark and smoke-like in appearance. It was human-shaped, but without any distinctive features.

The thing that had metamorphosed from a being of distinction into a dark creature he saw enter and exit the scientists in the laboratories where they talked of producing the thing called Earthlord, walked to von Lucis and stepped into his body.

EPILOGUE

"Okay, Tyce. The session is over and our work here is done for the moment."

The psychiatrist's voice began the process of unscrambling Tyce's thoughts, while he struggled to sit on the side of the couch.

"How long—?" He couldn't complete the question.

"You were under for about an hour," Mandell said, helping him to sit straight on the couch. "Your mind will clear momentarily."

"Where am I?"

Victor Mandell reached to check Tyce's eyes by pulling down the eyelids. He shined the penlight into them.

"Are you feeling okay, Tyce?"

"Where's Essie? And her father? And Morticai's adjutant?"

Mandell smiled, but with a concerned look on his face. "They are not here," he said.

"But…I was just with them."

"Not for the past hour or so, you weren't."

Tyce sat with the palms of his hands holding himself on the doctor's couch. He looked around, trying to make sense of things.

"Maybe you'd better recline for a minute or two longer," Mandell said, again looking deeply into his patient's eyes.

"No, I feel fine. But there's something, doc. There's something that isn't right about all this."

"The SEER can sometimes produce rather…strange effects. Perhaps—"

"No," Tyce interrupted. "I was there, in Jerusalem. I was with them, and with Yurom."

"Yurom?"

"Yeah. One of the one hundred forty-four thousa—"

He stopped himself, realizing the psychiatrist had no idea who or what he was talking about.

"Doctor, I just went through…"

Again he stopped himself. This was not something to discuss with this psychiatrist…at least not yet. Maybe he needed such help, but not just yet.

TYCE OPENED the door to the government vehicle and looked at the driver behind the wheel. His eyes widened with recognition when the driver looked over at him.

"Hi, Mr. Greyson. How are you doing?"

Barely able to respond, Tyce said, "You're Theodore Gesin."

"Yes, sir. Did they tell you I would be driving you?"

"You are a Messianic Jew," Tyce said.

The driver's expression became one of confusion. "Yes…yes, sir. I am a Messianic Jew. Who told you that?"

"Theodore…you wouldn't believe me if I told you

how I know your name is Theodore Gesin. Or how I know you are Messianic."

Before Tyce could begin to explain, his phone chimed and Essie was on the line.

"Tyce! Randy is anxious to talk with you. He wants to tell you something important," she said.

He could but sit stunned, his eyes searching nothingness. "Randy?" he said, before recovering his sensibility.

"Did he say what?"

"No, he wouldn't tell me, but whatever it is, he is excited."

"Well, if I get there, I'll call him…"

"What do you mean *if* you get here?" she said.

"Oh nothing, sweetheart. Never mind. *When* I get there," he said with a subdued laugh.

With the driver busy negotiating the increasingly heavy traffic, Tyce kept details of the reason he knew about Theodore Gesin to himself, not wanting to divert the driver's attention. When they arrived at the perimeter of the Maglan headquarters, Tyce was greeted by his wife, who took his hand and turned to quickly move into the building. Tyce waved to Gesin, who nodded and gave a goodbye with a chopping salute of the hand.

While they moved deeper into the building, Essie explained excitedly in her Israeli-accented English.

Tyce's head was still reeling in fog-coagulating thoughts. "Slow down, Ess," he said.

She did, saying finally, "Papa and Dr. Faust have been speaking for the past several hours. They are talking about something. I'm not certain what about, but it is important."

Walking into the innermost room of the Maglan complex, the screens around the walls were alive with the main power centers of the geopolitical world. The several men at work within the chamber looked up only briefly to greet Essie and her husband.

"Where is Morticai?" she asked one of the operatives, who nodded toward the closed door of the Maglan chief's office.

She went to the door and knocked several times, then opened it in and peeked in.

Her father, a phone receiver to his ear, stretched his right arm toward her and summoned her to come in with an index finger. He then turned to continue his conversation

He looked up and his expression brightened when he saw his son-in-law. Kant spoke forcefully into the phone receiver. "I'm telling you, Mr. Prime Minister, this will never do. Entering any sort of agreement with the Europeans will be disastrous for Israel."

He then listened while he heard what must have been a countervailing argument from the other end of the call.

When he next spoke, his voice sounded to be trembling. He was obviously trying to control his anger.

"I tell you, this European cannot decide our defensive posture. You cannot allow, the Knesset cannot allow, this to go forward."

The rest of the conversation was spoken in Hebrew. Tyce turned to Essie. She watched her father, his face turning red. Now he was shouting into the receiver.

Her eyes were wide, her mouth open with the fingertips of her right hand against her lips in an expression of amazement. "He is telling the prime minister...well, I won't say what he is telling him. He is very angry," she said, her voice displaying disbelief in what she was hearing.

Finally, the anger calmed and Kant dropped the

receiver gently onto its cradle. He looked straight ahead, as if into nothingness, obviously in thoughts of the now-concluded conversation.

"Abba," Essie said. "Are you okay?"

He seemed to snap out of his transfixion on some distant place and turned to Essie and Tyce. "Yes. All is well," he said, approaching them.

"How was the session with Mandell?" Kant gestured for them to be seated when he spoke.

"I…I can't begin to tell you, sir," Tyce said, the emotional crush of all that still gushed through his thoughts overwhelming him.

"Oh," Kant said, standing to grab Tyce's shoulder while he seemed to fall to the left.

"Tyce!" Essie, just realizing something was wrong, stood and tried to hold him upright.

"Papa, get some help!" she said, trying to hold her husband up and at the same time lift his chin to see his eyes. They were glazed, and her panic increased. "Quickly, Papa!"

More than ten minutes later, Tyce sat straight in the chair. A Maglan secretary handed him a glass filled with ice and water.

"You didn't tell me you felt bad," his wife said, taking the glass from him when he finished drinking.

"It's just so astonishing," he said, looking at her and at Kant. "Much of what I've been through I just can't unlock from my mind, I guess," he said, knowing he wasn't making much sense.

"It's okay, Tyce," Kant said. "Just say it when you can."

The door opened, and one of the operatives said, "Chief, your call from Mr. Faust is ready."

"We will be there momentarily," Kant said, looking

then to his son-in-law's eyes. "Tyce, are you up for talking with Randolph Faust?"

Tyce's face brightened. "Randy is on the phone?"

"Yes, there is something most profound he has to say."

Essie and her father helped Tyce to his feet. His legs were steady, so they walked him into the adjoining chamber.

The features of Randolph Faust were large on the big screen, while they sat in chairs facing the console and monitors in the walls.

"Tyce! It's so good to see you," the old man said. He looked much better than Tyce had last seen him, he thought. Then the thought traversed his thoughts. *He was dead and now is alive!*

"Randy…" Tyce's voice cracked with emotion, and he caught himself, recovering. "I can't tell you what it's like to see you and looking so healthy."

"Tyce, I have things to report. You just won't believe it." There was excitement in Randy's voice.

"The visions you have…the vision of the Last Supper scene…Jesus and the disciples having the meal in the Upper Room. I am seeing the same visions. I am seeing the same things you describe."

"What are you seeing?" Tyce said.

"The man…it has to be Judas Iscariot. He takes the sop when Jesus hands it to him. He then listens as the Lord whispers into his ear. He then slips from beneath the table and walks from the room. I'm standing there, like you describe, and he passes as if right through me."

Tyce listened, his heart beginning to pound at the old man's words.

"His face is there. I can't miss it. That star-shaped blemish…above the left eye. It's there…"

Tyce was speechless. What did it mean? Before he could manage to express a thought, Kant spoke.

"Randy, tell him what has happened. Tell him what we've seen just this morning, while Tyce was in the SEER session with Robert Mandell."

"Tyce, the EU headquarters building in Brussels… there is a meeting going on that I believe is of profound prophetic significance."

"Prophetic significance?" is all Tyce could manage to say.

"And this is what the prime minister and I were screaming at each other about, Tyce," the Maglan chief said. "While you were with Mandell, all of this broke loose. It is something we can't let happen. Israel will not survive if it goes forward."

Kant realized his diatribe and calmed. "I'm sorry, Randy," he said. "Please tell the rest."

"Tyce…this man you described, with the star-shaped impression above his left eye. This man, a very young man…he is being thrust forward by the elitist, globalist leadership. They are saying his plan will bring peace and safety…the very thing that God's Word, in Second Thessalonians chapter 5 warns against…"

"And our Israeli diplomats say they intend to agree to this plan," Kant's impassioned words interrupted Faust's description. "It involves the dismantling of all nuclear stockpiles except for those of the United States and the European Union. Our people are trying to give away our only option…the Samson Option…as deterrence."

Faust piped up again, "Tyce, this young man…he looks like he could be Antichrist."

Tyce's senses again flooded with all he had been through. The reality was inexpressible and caused him to remain silent. When there was no response from Tyce, Faust said, "His name is—"

"I know his name," Tyce Greyson interrupted. "It is Klaus von Lucis."

AUTHOR'S NOTE

The following commentary, "End-times Timeline," is "fact" not "fiction," as the novel above. However, the fiction, like this commentary, is based on God's Word—the Bible.

This article was written quite a number of years ago. The truth within has not changed, because God does not change. Jesus Christ is the same yesterday, today, and forever.

Christ calls all to Himself for salvation. He is the only Way, Truth, and Life. No person comes to the Heavenly Father, except through the Son Jesus Christ (John 14:6).

Here is the way to come to Jesus Christ for salvation of your eternal soul. If you reject Him, your soul is doomed for all eternity. If you accept Christ, as given in the scripture below, you will instantaneously upon death, or the Rapture, be in the holy presence of Heaven and will enjoy life that only gets more wonderful forever.

That if thou shalt confess with thy mouth the Lord Jesus, and shalt believe in thine heart that God hath raised him from the dead, thou shalt be saved. For with the heart man believeth unto righteousness; and with the mouth confession is made unto salvation (Romans 10:9–10).

END-TIMES TIMELINE

This generation stands upon the precipice of the wrap-up of human history. We can say this upon a platform of certainty. Our end-time stage is built upon a solid structure of knowledge. It provides strength of understanding from which no other generation of human beings could have spoken.

The prophet Daniel predicted precisely this time on God's prophetic timeline, I am convinced: "But thou, O Daniel, shut up the words, and seal the book, even to the time of the end: many shall run to and fro, and knowledge shall be increased" (Daniel 12:4).

THE BOOK OPENED

Those who studied Bible prophecy throughout the decades since the close of the second century did so in the dark, from the point of history not shedding much illumination on how God's prophetic Word would unfold. The angel had told Daniel the prophet that this would be the case—that the book (the understanding of end things) would remain closed until the time of the very end was reached.

Bible prophecy was then put on the back burner, for the most part, as far as any endeavors into understanding end-times matters was concerned. The Catholic Church in its various manifestations, then the Reformation church derivatives of Martin Luther and the others, drifted far from the early church fathers' devotion to studying the part of the scriptures that dealt with prophecy yet future. It was, in my view, intellectual and spiritual laziness, as much as luciferin influence, that caused this callous disregard for prophecy to infect the Body of Christ.

Some would say that this must have been the way God wanted it. He must have desired for believers to not have understanding, so doused the light of understanding during this long period—longer even than the four hundred-plus year drought of prophetic activity just prior to Christ's First Advent. That's one way of looking at the dearth of prophetic enlightenment during the around two thousand years since Christ's resurrection. However, I believe the words of the angel to Daniel telling the old prophet to "shut up the book" were more akin to the Bible telling of Abraham, David, and Solomon having multiple wives, and even concubines. God reported these things, but He did not cause them to happen. Nor did God approve of these goings-on. The Lord used reports of these sins to show His children down through the ages the folly, even deadly consequences, of disobeying their Heavenly Father. The lessons of these sinful activities of even the greatest of the Bible heroes is that we are fallen, and without staying close to the Creator, our Father, we, too, can and will slip into egregious activities that push us away from God's loving, directing hand.

This disobedience, He is telling us, causes severe repercussions and ramifications. There is no better example than what has happened since Abraham and Sarah decided to get ahead of God's will when Sarah sent her handmaid, Hagar, to her husband to produce an heir. And this is where that disobedience and prophecy, yet future, converge and merge. The whole world faces the consequences of that sin today in the hate-filled conflict between Arabs and Jews that is gushing humanity toward man's final conflagration—Armageddon. So, the angel's instruction to Daniel to "close up the book" (of under-standing end-times things) was God reporting, in my view, the deliberate intellectual and spiritual slothfulness—even callous disregard—that would clutch the minds of even God's best Bible students until the very end of days. God was reporting this dearth of His people being able to ascertain end-time matters. God did not cause the book of understanding to be closed so they wouldn't comprehend.

The vital, glorious thing to see is that now that book has, it is overwhelmingly obvious, been opened, and each and every hour seems to bring increased understanding. Knowledge is indeed increasing, and at an exponential rate!

TIMELINE ISSUES AND EVENTS

Signals that we are in the end times are so ubiquitous, and at the same time proliferating at such a profound pace, that it is sometimes difficult even for those of us who watch diligently to fully gather all that is occurring. But Jesus, right after giving those signals that would be prevalent leading up to His Second Coming, concluded, as reported in the book of Mark: "And what I say unto you I say unto all, Watch" (Mark 13:37).

It is therefore incumbent upon us, "all Christians," to discern the signs of the times. We will look at them, trying to put them in the order given us by Jesus and the prophets as they foretold these end-times things. Those who consider such things calculate that about 27 percent of God's Word is given to prophecy. Roughly half of that has been fulfilled. Therefore, about 14 percent of Bible prophecy is yet to be fulfilled. Careful study of the historical record validates Bible prophets as 100 percent accurate, in considering prophecies already fulfilled. We can, through application of human rationale, therefore, think the rest of prophecy will likely be fulfilled. Christians should trust, without reservation, that their Lord, the Word (John 1:1–2), will accomplish fulfillment of the remaining prophecies.

Those who read this article following the disappearance of millions of people, the Rapture of all believers in Jesus Christ, are urged to examine the history of these matters. Those who read this post-Rapture will have considerable, and quite recent, history to look to and consider whether God's Word is true, about end-times matters.

As this is written, the world stands on God's prophetic timeline facing the apocalyptic storm in the distance while it approaches. If you are reading this following the Rapture, you are likely actually in the early stages of that prophesied storm of evil, the last seven years of human history that lead to the Second Coming of Jesus Christ to Planet Earth.

There are no prophecies yet to be fulfilled before the Rapture of Christ's Church. That is not to say prophecies yet future will NOT be fulfilled before the Rapture, just that none are given that MUST BE fulfilled before that stunning event.

I will not address here all of the many geophysical and even societal and cultural "perilous times" signals all around us in this generation. We will look at specific major events scheduled to unfold. However, it is unavoidable to think of the birth-pang like convulsions of earthquakes, record hurricanes, and the upheavals of violence that seems to fill the whole earth, while thinking on the following.

ISRAEL: PROPHECY FULFILLED

Many of us who carefully study these matters believe that Israel once again being a nation in its ancient home-land, and with its ancient language, Hebrew, is a fulfill-ment of prophecy. I don't see how it can be otherwise. Israel has to be back in the land for the final prophecies to roll out as foretold. That nation is at the very heart of end-times things to come. The most profound prophecy in that regard is the fact that the Messiah—the returning Lord of Lords and King of Kings—will set His throne atop Zion once He returns. That will be a topographi-cally changed Mt. Moriah, with Christ's Millennial Temple set high above the city of Jerusalem.

But, before that happens, Israel will have to endure the time of "Jacob's trouble" (Jeremiah 30:7). It will be the worst time ever in history for that people, according to Jesus, Himself. As a matter of fact, His prophecy indi-cates the same degree of horror for the whole world at that time. He said: "For then shall be great tribulation, such as was not since the beginning of the world to this time, no, nor ever shall be" (Matthew 24:21). Zechariah the prophet foretold there would be an Israel and a Jerusalem during that period. God spoke the following through His prophet: "And in that day will I make Jerusalem a burdensome stone for all people: all that burden themselves with it shall be cut in pieces, though all the people of the earth be gathered together against it" (Zechariah 12:3).

Israel today is already the center of attention, and of much scorn from its neighbors and the rest of the world. As I often say when interviewed, no matter which way the news microphones and cameras turn to capture other stories, they always swing right back to Israel, Jerusalem, and the surrounding areas. That is because that region offers the greatest threat to spark thermonuclear conflagration. The Bible foretells that it WILL host the most horrific conflict of human history —Armageddon!

END-TIMES ORDER OF THINGS TO COME

With that framework—that Israel is back in the land, which is surely a fulfilling of prophecy—let us look at where things unfold from here on God's end-times timeline.

Rapture—While the storm clouds of apocalypse gather and approach, Christians attuned to God's whole Word should watch, according to the Lord Jesus Christ. They should be aware of the elements of that approaching storm of Tribulation. Things of society, cultures, in every endeavor of life, will, at the same time, seem to be business as usual. Times will be like the days of Noah and Lot at the moment of His next intervention into the affairs of humanity, according to Jesus. Read Luke 17:26–30. It will be a catastrophic intervention.

Jesus will step out on the clouds of glory and shout, "Come up here!" (Revelation 4:1–2). All Christians—those who accept Christ's blood atonement for salvation (born-again believers) will instantly be with Jesus above the earth. Read 1 Corinthians 15:51–55 and 1 Thessalonians 4:13–18. Millions of people (those raptured) will vanish, disappearing from the planet before the astonished eyes of those left behind. Those who have gone to be with the Lord will be taken back to Heaven, where He has prepared a place of eternal dwelling for them (John 14:1–3). The Bema Judgment (to give rewards for service to the Lord while on earth) will take place. Crowns will be handed out to God's family. The Marriage Supper of the Lamb will occur (Christ's Bride made ready for the wedding), then the Wedding Feast (Revelation 19:9). Things on Planet Earth will be gearing up for the great end-time storm. God, the Holy Spirit, according to 2 Thessalonians, chapter 2, will remove as Restrainer during the times following the Rapture.

World Leader Comes Forth—The nations of earth will be in chaos. The turmoil will cause severe ramifications while governments seek to restore civil order and regain governmental and economic equilibrium. Profound shifts of power will likely take place, with the EU becoming the new superpower, absorbing America's power and authority, the US having lost the most people in key places, thus having suffered the most loss of control. According to prophecy, one man will step forward to proffer a plan to quell the fears of war in the Middle East (Daniel 9:27). This prophecy correlates to Revelation 6:2, with the rider on the white horse riding forth.

Peace Covenant Confirmed—The great world leader will arrive just in time to look to be the shining

365

knight on the white horse. He will have the answer to the looming all-out war in the Middle East. He will be able to sell a seven-year peace plan that is already available, apparently. Israel will agree to the covenant, as will her enemies, and, in effect, the whole world will accept the European leader's masterful sales pitch. But Israel's acceptance will fly in the face of God. This "covenant made with death and Hell," as it is called in Isaiah, chapter 28, will cause God's judgmental wrath to begin to fall.

Attack upon Israel—The Gog-Magog attack prophesied by Ezekiel is one that is controversial, so far as to where it will fit into the end-times timeline is concerned. Some have the event just before or in conjunction with the Rapture, while others believe it will happen right after the Rapture or nearer the midpoint of the seven-year Tribulation period. Russia is destined to present some of the most fearsome trials and tribulations for Israel. Gog, "chief prince of Rosh," is the leader of Russia described in Ezekiel 38 and 39. In ancient language, "Gog" means "leader." "Rosh" is the ancient name for the land of Russia. In the last days, Russia will be the leading nation of the Gog-Magog coalition that will make a move against Israel and be defeated by a supernatural act of God. Persia (Iran) comes right along beside Russia, in prophetic parlance. According to Ezekiel 38:5, Iran will aid Russia in attacking Israel before or during the tribulation. Even now, Iran acts as a destabilizing force in the world.

144,000 Evangelists—The Lord will not allow the dark, satanic realm to go unchallenged. God will seal (protect from Satan and his minions) 144,000 Jewish men with the gospel message of Jesus Christ, the only way to salvation, redemption, and reconciliation to God, the Father. Read Revelation 7:3–8. These will proclaim the gospel message throughout the world. Millions upon millions of people will hear the message and become Christians of the Tribulation period.

Two Old Testament-Type Prophets Preach—Two Jewish men during this period will preach the gospel and point the finger of judgment if repentance isn't forthcoming. No one knows for sure who these men will be, but there seems good evidence that at least one of them will be Elijah, the Old Testament prophet whom God took up from earth in a fiery whirlwind. The satanic governmental regime will seek to kill these men but will not be able to do so until God allows. Anyone who tries to kill them will, in like manner, be killed, according to the prophetic Word. Finally, the regime will be able to kill them. Their dead bodies will lie in the streets of Jerusalem for three days, then they will be resurrected to life, and will lift into the sky before the astonished eyes of their murderers and the whole world.

Antichrist Revealed—The great world leader, who confirmed the seven-year peace covenant, convincing Israel and its enemies to rely on him and his regime to keep the peace, will be struck with a deadly head wound. But he will resurrect, supposedly, from death. He will, following this, in what I believe will be a false resurrection (possibly following the defeat of the Gog-Magog forces), suddenly walk into the Jewish temple atop Mt. Moriah at Jerusalem and declare himself to be God. He will demand worship from all of the world's inhabitants. Read 2 Thessalonians 2 and Revelation 13. He is then revealed as Antichrist, the son of perdition, the man of sin. He will cause all to accept his mark or be cut out of the economic system—all buying and selling. He will order all killed, who will not worship him. The chief method of death dealing will be beheading. His partner in the satanic duo will point all worship to the beast— Antichrist. The False Prophet will be Antichrist's John the Baptist figure.

Jews Flee—Jesus forewarned the Jews who will occupy Jerusalem at the time of Antichrist's revelation to flee to the mountains. Read Matthew 24 and Revelation 12. This era, the midpoint of the seven-year Tribulation, will begin the time of Jacob's trouble (Jeremiah 30:7)—a time Jesus says will be the worst in all of history (Matthew 24:21). Antichrist will begin the greatest geno-cide ever to be visited upon the planet.

Antichrist Institutes Regime—Antichrist's regime will cause all to worship the "beast," the Revelation 13 term for "Antichrist." He will apparently set up some sort of idol, before which all must bow. This will likely be done by the image of himself being telecast in some way to all the world. Read Revelation 13. His regime will consist of ten kingdoms, whose newly crowned kings (political leaders of the region) will give all of their authority and power to Antichrist. We might be seeing the formative months and years of the formation of this ten-kingdom development with the various trading blocs beginning to form. The European Union seems to be the prototype for those that will follow. The North American Union (NAU) that seems to be underway in development, bringing America, Canada, and Mexico together in an economic trading bloc, appears to be one such kingdom in the making. Antichrist will bring together one world government, one world economy, and one world religion, to some extent—for a brief time, at least. This is a Babylonian-type system that will all but enslave the entire world.

Babylon System of Religion, Economy, Govern-

ment Rules—The Babylonian system will actually be an extension of the revived Roman Empire. This was prophesied in Daniel, chapters 2, 7, 9, and 11, as well as in Revelation, chapter 13. Ancient Babylon's and the ancient Roman Empire's influence upon this end-time regime of Hell on earth are described in Revelation, chapters 17 and 18. God will completely destroy the chief city of the end-time Babylon in one hour, the Bible prophesies in Revelation, chapter 18.

Kings of East Threaten, Then Move—China, today, is a growing economic and military behemoth. It exerts hegemony over its neighbors of the Orient. The Bible predicts a day during the Tribulation when the "kings of the east" will march across the dried-up Euphrates River to do battle at Armageddon. This juggernaut will consist of two hundred million troops, all, prophecy seems to indicate, demon-possessed, while they cross the area of the Euphrates. Read Revelation, chapters 9 and 16.

All Meet at Armageddon—The kings of the east march toward a rendezvous with all other nations of the world. God says this about this meeting: "For, behold, in those days, and in that time, when I shall bring again the captivity of Judah and Jerusalem, I will also gather all nations, and will bring them down into the valley of Jehoshaphat, and will plead with them there for my people and for my heritage Israel, whom they have scattered among the nations, and parted my land" (Joel 3:10–2). Also read Revelation 16:16 and 19:17–18.

Christ Returns—Just as the battle is becoming so violent that it threatens the end of all people and animals on earth, the black clouds of apocalypse unroll like a scroll, and brilliant light from Heaven's core breaks through, revealing the King of Kings and His armies and myriad angelic hosts. "And I saw heaven opened and behold a white horse; and he that sat upon him was called Faithful and True, and in righteousness he doth judge and make war. His eyes were as a flame of fire, and on his head were many crowns; and he had a name written, that no man knew, but he himself. And he was clothed with a vesture dipped in blood: and his name is called The Word of God. And the armies which were in heaven followed him upon white horses, clothed in fine linen, white and clean. And out of his mouth goeth a sharp sword, that with it he should smite the nations: and he shall rule them with a rod of iron: and he treadeth the winepress of the fierceness and wrath of Almighty God" (Revelation 19:11–15).

Christ Judges Nations—The conquering Creator of all things will establish His earthly throne atop Mt. Moriah, which will be supernaturally reconfigured from topographical renovations made for the Millennium. All the nations of the world will come before the Lord Jesus Christ. Read about the Sheep-Goats Judgment in Matthew 25. Those who have made it alive through the Tribulation will either be believers or unbelievers. Believers will be ushered into Christ's thousand-year reign on earth, while unbelievers will be cast into everlasting darkness, the scripture prophesies.

Christ Sets up Millennial Kingdom—The millennial reign of Christ will begin, a time during which the False Prophet and the beast (Antichrist), the first to be thrown into the Lake of Fire, will begin to serve their eternal sentences. Satan will be confined in the bottomless pit, and there will be none of his minions to torment and tempt the millennial earth-dwellers. It will be a time much like those of Eden, with the earth restored to its pristine beauty. Read Revelation 20:10. After the thousand years, the devil will be released from the pit for a short time. He will lead millions of those who have been born during the Millennium in an assault on Christ at Jerusalem. God will send down fire and consume them all. Satan will be cast into the Lake of Fire. The lost dead will be resurrected (their eternal bodies joined to their souls), and all will stand before the Great White Throne of Christ to be judged. All will be cast into the Lake of Fire for eternity. Read Revelation 20:10–15. God, Jesus Christ, will remake the heavens and the earth in preparation for everlasting, ever-growing ecstasy in God's presence. Read Revelation 20:16–22: 16.

IF YOU LIKE THIS, YOU MAY ALSO ENJOY: THE FINAL REMNANT

BY TERRY JAMES AND HEATHER RENAE

After the disappearance of nearly half the world's population, Caden Johnson is convinced God totally sucks. In fact, He can take His holiness and shove off. The world is crawling with mutant animals and invisible monsters—who all enjoy human being with a side of fries. And what is God doing? Watching it burn.

But when Caden hears his little sister might be alive—and stuck on the other side of the world—he decides things are *going* to change. Dragging his brother along, and armed with nothing but a baseball bat, he sets off to keep what's left of his family alive.

In a gang he hardly trusts, and enemies at every turn, Caden must face the Cosmic Bully he's learned to hate all his life… Or die trying.

A unique blend of genres, The Final Remnant is teen fantasy and apocalyptic Christian fiction at its best.

AVAILABLE NOVEMBER 2022

ABOUT TERRY JAMES

Terry James is author, general editor, and co-author of numerous books on Bible prophecy, hundreds of thousands of which have been sold worldwide. James is a frequent lecturer on the study of end time phenomena, and interviews often with national and international media on topics involving world issues and events as they might relate to Bible prophecy.

He has appeared in major documentaries and media forums, in all media formats, in America, Europe, and Asia.

He appeared in the History Channel series, The Nostradamus Effect.

He is an active member of the PreTrib Research Center Study Group, a prophecy research think-tank founded by Dr. Tim LaHaye, the co-author of the multi-million selling "Left Behind" series of novels. He is a regular participant in the annual Tulsa mid-America prophecy conference, where he speaks, and holds a Question and Answer series of sessions on current world events as they might relate to Bible prophecy.

Terry James has been blind since 1993 due to a degenerative retinal disease (retinitis pigmentosa). He uses the Jobs Accessible Word System (JAWS) –which is voice synthesis—to write and conduct business over the Internet.

His former profession was in public relations, advertising, marketing, and publicity and promotion.

He received his education from Arkansas Polytechnic Institute, Memphis Academy of Arts, and University of Arkansas at Little Rock.

He served in both corporate and government positions for 25 years, before becoming a full-time writer.

James also served in the United States Air Force from October 1966 through October 1970.) He served at Randolph AFB, Texas, in the T-38 section, a mission dedicated to training pilots in high-performance jet fighter-trainers.

Terry James and his wife, Margaret, live near Little Rock, Arkansas.

Made in the USA
Las Vegas, NV
12 December 2023

82611771R00225